Deal with the Devil

CATHY WILLIAMS
MICHELLE CONDER
JENNIFER HAYWARD

First Published in Great Britain 2017
By Mills & Boon, an imprint of HarperCollins*Publishers*
1 London Bridge Street, London, SE1 9GF

DEAL WITH THE DEVIL © 2017 Harlequin Books S. A.

Secrets Of A Ruthless Tycoon, *The Most Expensive Lie Of All* and *The Magnate's Manifesto* were first published in Great Britain by Harlequin (UK) Limited.

Secrets Of A Ruthless Tycoon © 2014 Cathy Williams
The Most Expensive Lie Of All © 2014 Michelle Conder
The Magnate's Manifesto © 2014 Jennifer Drogell

ISBN: 978-0-263-92962-1

05-0517

Our policy is to use papers that are natural, renewable and recyclable products and made from wood grown in sustainable forests.The logging and manufacturing processes conform to the legal environmental regulations of the country of origin.

Printed and bound in Spain
by CPI, Barcelona

SECRETS OF A RUTHLESS TYCOON

BY
CATHY WILLIAMS

Cathy Williams is originally from Trinidad, but has lived in England for a number of years. She currently has a house in Warwickshire, which she shares with her husband Richard, her three daughters, Charlotte, Olivia and Emma, and their pet cat, Salem. She adores writing romantic fiction and would love one of her girls to become a writer—although at the moment she is happy enough if they do their homework and agree not to bicker with one another!

CHAPTER ONE

IN THE DIMINISHING light, Leo Spencer was beginning to question his decision to make this trip. He looked up briefly from the report blinking at him on his laptop and frowned at the sprawling acres of countryside reaching out on either side to distant horizons which had now been swallowed up by the gathering dusk.

It was on the tip of his tongue to tell his driver to put his foot down, but what would be the point? How much speed would Harry be able to pick up on these winding, unlit country roads, still hazardous from the recent bout of snow which was only now beginning to melt? The last thing he needed was to end up in a ditch somewhere. The last car they had passed had been several miles back. God only knew where the nearest town was.

He concluded that February was, possibly, the very worst month in which to have undertaken this trip to the outer reaches of Ireland. He had failed to foresee the length of time it would take to get to his destination and he now cursed the contorted reasoning that had made him reject the option of flying there on the company plane.

The flight to Dublin had been straightforward enough but, the minute he had met his driver outside the airport, the trip had evolved into a nightmare of traffic, diversions and, as they'd appeared to leave all traces of civilisation behind, a network of bleak, perilous roads made all the more threatening by the constant threat of snow. It hung in the air like a death shroud, biding its time for just the right unsuspecting mug to come along.

Giving up on all hope of getting anything useful done, Leo snapped shut his laptop and stared at the gloomy scenery.

The rolling hills were dark contours rising ominously up from flat fields in which lurked a honeycomb network of lakes, meandering streams and rivers, none of which was visible at this time of the late afternoon. Leo was accustomed to the almost constant artificial light of London. He had never had much time for the joys of the countryside and his indifference to it was rapidly being cemented with each passing mile.

But this was a trip that had to be undertaken.

When he reflected on the narrative of his life, he knew that it was an essential journey. The death of his mother eight months previously—following so shortly after his father's own unexpected demise from a heart attack whilst, of all things, he had been playing golf with his friends—had left him with no excuses for avoidance. He had to find out where he really came from, who his real birth parents were. He would never have disrespected his adoptive parents when they were alive by searching out his birth family but the time had come.

He closed his eyes and the image of his own life flickered in front of him like an old-fashioned movie reel: adopted at birth by a successful and wealthy couple in their late thirties who had been unable to have children of their own; brought up with all the advantages a solid, middle-class background had to offer; private school and holidays abroad. A brilliant academic career followed by a stint at an investment bank which had been the springboard for a meteoric rise through the financial world until, at the ripe old age of thirty-two, he now had more money than he could ever hope to spend in a lifetime and the freedom to use it in the more creative arena of acquisitions.

He seemed to possess the golden touch. None of his acquisitions to date had failed. Additionally, he had been bequeathed a sizeable fortune by his parents. All told, the only grey area in a life that had been blessed with success was the murky blur of his true heritage. Like a pernicious weed, it had never been completely uprooted. Curiosity had always been there, hovering on the edges of his consciousness, and he knew that it would always be there unless he took active measures to put it to rest once and for all.

Not given to introspection of any sort, there were moments when he suspected that it had left a far-reaching legacy, despite all the advantages his wonderful adoptive parents had given him. His relationships with women had all been short-lived. He enjoyed a varied love life with some of the most beautiful and eligible women on the London scene, yet the thought of committing to any of them had always left him cold. He always used the excuse of being the kind of man whose commitment to work left little fertile ground on which a successful relationship could flourish. But there lurked the nagging suspicion that the notion of his own feckless parents dumping him on whatever passing strangers they could had fostered a deep-seated mistrust of any form of permanence, despite the sterling example his adoptive parents had set for him.

He had known for several years where he could locate his mother. He had no idea if his natural father was still on the scene—quite possibly not. The whereabouts of his mother was information that had sat, untouched, in his locked office drawer until now.

He had taken a week off work, informing his secretary

that he would be contactable at all times by email or on his mobile phone. He would find his mother, make his own judgements and he would leave, putting to rest the curiosity that had plagued him over the years. He had a good idea of what he would find but it would be useful having his suspicions confirmed. He wasn't looking for answers or touching reconciliations. He was looking for closure.

And, naturally, he had no intention of letting her know his identity. He was sinfully rich and there was nothing like money to engender all the wrong responses. There was no way he intended to have some irresponsible deadbeat who had given him up for adoption holding out a begging bowl and suddenly claiming parental love—not to mention whatever half- siblings he had who would feel free to board the gravy train.

His mouth curled derisively at the mere thought of it.

'Any chance we could actually get this car into fifth gear?' he asked Harry, who caught his eye in the rear-view mirror and raised his eyebrows.

'Aren't you appreciating the wonderful scenery, sir?'

'You've been with me for eight years, Harry. Have I ever given any indication that I like the countryside?' Harry, strangely, was the only one in whom Leo had confided. They shared an uncommonly strong bond. Leo would have trusted his driver with his life. He certainly trusted him with thoughts he never would have shared with another living soul.

'There's always a first, sir,' Harry suggested calmly. 'And, no, there is no way I can drive any faster. Not on these roads. And have you noticed the sky?'

'In passing.'

'Snow's on the way, sir.'

'And I'm hoping that it will delay its arrival until I'm through…doing what I have to do.' From where he was sitting, it was hard to see where the sky met the open land. It was all just a black, formless density around them. Aside from the sound of the powerful engine of the car, the silence was so complete that, with eyes closed, anyone could be forgiven for thinking that they were suffering sensory deprivation.

'The weather is seldom obedient, sir. Even for a man like yourself who is accustomed to having his orders obeyed.'

Leo grinned. 'You talk too much, Harry.'

'So my better half often tells me, sir. Are you certain you don't require my services when we reach Ballybay?'

'Quite certain. You can get a cab driver to deliver the car back to London and the company plane will return you to your better half. I've alerted my secretary to have it on standby; she'll text you where. Make sure you tell my people to have it ready and waiting for when I need to return to London. I have no intention of repeating this journey by car any time soon.'

'Of course, sir.'

Leo flipped back open the laptop and consigned all wayward thoughts of what he would find when he finally arrived to the furthermost outer reaches of his mind. Losing yourself in pointless speculation was a waste of time.

It was two hours by the time he was informed that they were in Ballybay. Either he had missed the main part of the town or else there was nothing much to it. He could just about make out the vast stillness of a lake and then a scattering of houses and shops nestling amidst the hills and dales.

'Is this it?' he asked Harry, who tut-tutted in response.

'Were you expecting Oxford Street, sir?'

'I was expecting a little more by way of life. Is there even a hotel?' He frowned and thought that allowing a week off work might have been over- estimating the time he would need. A couple of days at most should see him conclude his business.

'There's a pub, sir.'

Leo followed his driver's pointing finger and made out an ancient pub that optimistically boasted 'vacancies'. He wondered what the passing tourist trade could possibly be in a town that time appeared to have forgotten.

'Drop me off here, Harry, and you can head off.' He was travelling light: one holdall, suitably battered, into which he now stuffed his slim laptop.

Already, he was making comparisons between what appeared to be this tiny town of splendid isolation and the completely different backdrop to life with his adoptive parents. The busy Surrey village in which he had been brought up buzzed with a veritable treasure trove of trendy gastropubs and designer shops. The landscape was confined and neatly manicured. The commuter links to London were excellent and that was reflected in the high-end property market. Gated mansions were hidden from prying eyes by long drives. On Saturdays, the high street was bursting with expensive people who lived in the expensive houses and drove the expensive cars.

He stepped out of the Range Rover to a gusty wind and freezing cold.

The ancient pub looked decidedly more inviting given the temperatures outside and he strode towards it without hesitation.

Inside the pub, Brianna Sullivan was nursing an incipient headache. Even in the depths of winter, Friday nights brought in the crowds and, whilst she was grateful for their patronage, she yearned for peace and quiet. Both seemed about as elusive as finding gold dust in the kitchen sink. She had inherited this pub from her father nearly six years ago and there were no allowances made for time out. There was just her, and it was her livelihood. Choice didn't feature heavily on the menu.

'Tell Pat he can come and get his own drinks at the bar,' she hissed to Shannon. 'We're busy enough here without you carrying trays of drinks over to him because he broke his leg six months ago. He's perfectly capable of getting them himself, or else he can send that brother of his over to get them.' At one end of the bar, Aidan and two of his friends were beginning to sing a rousing love song to grab her attention.

'I'll have to chuck you out for unruly behaviour,' she snapped at Aidan as she slid refills for them along the counter.

'You know you love me, darling.'

Brianna shot him an exasperated look and told him that he either settled his tab in full, right here and right now, or else that was the last pint he was going to get.

She needed more people behind the bar but what on earth would she do with them on the week days, when the place was less rowdy and busy? How could she justify the expenditure? And yet, she barely had enough time to function properly. Between the bookkeeping, the stock taking, the ordering and the actual standing behind the bar every night, time —the one thing she didn't have—was galloping past. She was twenty-seven years old and in the blink of an eye she would be thirty, then forty, then fifty, and still doing the things she was doing now, still struggling to kick back. She was young but, hell, she felt old a lot of the time.

Aidan continued to try his banter on her but she blocked him out. Now that she had begun feeling sorry for herself, she was barely aware of what was going on around her.

Surely her years at university had not equipped her to spend the rest of her life running this pub? She loved her friends and the tight-knit community but surely she was entitled to just have some *fun*? Six months of fun was all she had had when she had finished university, then it had been back here to help look after her father who had managed to drink himself into a premature grave.

Not a day went by when she didn't miss him. For twelve years after her mother had died it had been just the two of them, and she missed his easy laughter, his support, his corny jokes. She wondered how he would feel if he knew that she was still here, at the pub. He had always wanted her to fly away and develop a career in art, but then little had he known that he would not be around to make that possible.

She only became aware that something was different when, still absorbed in her own thoughts, it dawned on her that the bar had grown silent.

In the act of pulling a pint, she raised her eyes and there, framed in the doorway, was one of the most startlingly beautiful men she had ever seen in her life. Tall, wind-swept dark hair raked back from a face that was shamefully good-looking. He didn't seem in the slightest taken aback by the fact that all eyes were on him as he looked around, his midnight-black eyes finally coming to rest on her.

Brianna felt her cheeks burn at the casual inspection, then she returned to what she was doing and so did everyone else. The noise levels once again rose and the jokes resumed; old Connor did his usual and began singing lustily and drunkenly until he was laughed down.

She ignored the stranger, yet was all too aware of his presence, and not at all surprised that when she next glanced up it was to find him standing right in front of her.

'The sign outside says that there are vacancies.' Leo practically had to shout to make himself heard above the noise. The entire town seemed to have congregated in this small pub. Most of the green leather stools assembled along the bar were filled, as were the tables. Behind the bar, two girls were trying hard to keep up with the demands—a small, busty brunette and the one in front of whom he was now standing. A tall, slender girl with copper-coloured hair which she had swept up into a rough pony tail and, as she looked at him, the clearest, greenest eyes he had ever seen.

'Why do you want to know?' Brianna asked.

His voice matched the rest of him. It was deep and lazy and induced an annoying, fluttery feeling in the pit of her stomach. 'Why do you think? I need to rent a room and I take it this is the only place in the village that rents rooms…?'

'Is it not good enough for you?'

'Where's the owner?'

'You're looking at her.'

He did, much more thoroughly this time. Bare of any make-up, her skin was satin-smooth and creamy white. There was not a freckle in sight, despite the vibrant colour of her hair. She was wearing a pair of faded jeans and a long-sleeved jumper but neither detracted from her looks.

'Right. I need a room.'

'I will show you up to one just as soon as I get a free moment. In the meantime, would you like something to drink?' What on earth was this man doing here? He certainly wasn't from around these parts, nor did he know anyone around here. She would know. It was a tiny community; they all knew each other in some way, shape or form.

'What I'd like is a hot shower and a good night's sleep.'

'Both will have to wait, Mr…?'

'My name is Leo and, if you give me a key and point me in the right direction, I'll make my own way upstairs. And, by the way, is there anywhere to eat around here?'

Not only was the man a stranger but he was an obnoxious one. Brianna could feel her hackles rising. Memories of another good-looking, well-spoken stranger rose unbidden to the foreground. As learning curves went, she had been taught well what sort of men to avoid.

'You'll have to go into Monaghan for that,' she informed him shortly. 'I can fix you a sandwich but—'

'Yes—but I'll have to wait because you're too busy behind the bar. Forget the food. If you need a deposit, tell me how much and then you can give me the key.'

Brianna shot him an impatient glance and called over to Aidan. 'Take the reins,' she told him. 'And no free drinks. I've got to show this man to a room. I'll be back down in five minutes, and if I find out that you've helped yourself to so much as a thimble of free beer I'll ban you for a week.'

'Love you too, Brianna.'

'How long would you be wanting the room for?' was the first thing she asked him as soon as they were out of the bar area and heading upstairs. She was very much aware of him following her and she could feel the hairs on the back of her neck rising. Had she lived so long in this place that the mere sight of a halfway decent guy was enough to bring her out in a cold sweat?

'A few days.' She was as graceful as a dancer and he was tempted to ask why a girl with her looks was running a pub in the middle of nowhere. Certainly not for the stress-free existence. She looked hassled and he could understand that if it was as busy every night of the week.

'And might I ask what brings you to this lovely part of Ireland?' She pushed open the door to one of the four rooms she rented out and stood back, allowing him to brush past her.

Leo took his time looking around him. It was small but clean. He would have to be sharp-witted when it came to avoiding the beams but it would do. He turned round to her and began removing his coat which he tossed onto the high-backed wooden chair by the dressing table.

Brianna took a step back. The room was small and he seemed to over-power it with his presence. She was treated to a full view of his muscular body now he was without his coat: black jeans, a black jumper and the sort of olive-brown complexion that told her that, somewhere along the line, there was a strain of exotic blood running through him.

'You can ask,' Leo agreed. Billionaire searching for his long-lost, feckless parent wasn't going to cut it. One hint of that and it would be round the grapevine faster than he could pay her the deposit on the room; of that he was convinced. Checking his mother out was going to be an incognito exercise and he certainly wasn't going to be ambushed by a pub owner with a loose tongue, however pretty she was.

'But you're not going to tell me. Fair enough.' She shrugged. 'If you want breakfast, it's served between seven and eight. I run this place single-handed so I don't have a great deal of time to wait on guests.'

'Such a warm welcome.'

Brianna flushed and belatedly remembered that he was a paying guest and not another of the lads downstairs to whom she was allowed to give as good as she got. 'I apol-ogise if I seem rude, Mr...'

'Leo.'

'But I'm rushed off my feet at the moment and not in the best of moods. The bathroom is through there...' She pointed in the direction of a white-washed door. 'And there are tea- and coffee-making facilities.' She backed towards the door, although she was finding it hard to tear her eyes away from his face.

If he brought to mind unhappy memories of Daniel Fluke, then it could be said that he was a decidedly more threatening version: bigger, better looking and without the readily charming patter, and that in itself somehow felt more dangerous. And she still had no idea what he was doing in this part of the world.

'If you could settle the deposit on the room...' She cleared her throat and watched in silence as he extracted a wad of notes from his wallet and handed her the required amount.

'And tell me, what is there to do here?' he asked, shoving his hands in his pockets and tilting his head to one side. 'I guess you must know everything...and everyone?'

'You've picked a poor time of year for sightseeing, Mr... eh...Leo. I'm afraid walking might be a little challenging, especially as snow is predicted, and you can forget about the fishing.'

'Perhaps I'll just explore the town,' he murmured. Truly amazing eyes, he thought. Eyelashes long and dark and in striking contrast to the paleness of her skin. 'I hope I'm not making you nervous... Sorry, you didn't tell me your name, although I gather it's Brianna...?'

'We don't get very many strangers in this part of town, certainly not in the depths of winter.'

'And now you're renting a room to one and you don't know what he does or why he's here in the first place. Understandable if you feel a little edgy...' He shot her a crooked smile and waited for it to take effect; waited to see her loosen up, smile back in return, look him up and down covertly; waited for the impact he knew he had on women to register. Nothing. She frowned and looked at him coolly, clearly assessing him.

'That's right.' Brianna folded her arms and leaned against the doorframe.

'I…' He realised that he hadn't banked on this. He actually hadn't expected the place to be so small. Whilst he had acknowledged that he couldn't just show up on his mother's doorstep and do his character assessment on the spot, he was now realising that the other option of extracting information from random drinkers at some faceless, characterless bar close to where the woman lived was quite likely also out of the question.

'Yes?' Brianna continued to look at him. She might be grateful for the money—it wasn't as though people were falling over themselves to rent a room in the depths of winter—but on the other hand she *was* a single woman, here on her own, and what if he turned out to be a homicidal maniac?

Granted it was unlikely that a homicidal maniac would announce his intentions because she happened to ask, but if he seemed too shifty, just too untrustworthy, then she would send him on his way, money or not.

'I'm not proud of this.' Leo glanced around him. His gaze settled on an exquisite watercolour painting above the bed and moved to the row of books neatly stacked on the shelf just alongside it. 'But I jacked in a perfectly good job a fortnight ago.'

'A perfectly good job doing what?' Brianna knew that she was giving him the third degree; that he was under no obligation to explain himself to her; that she could lose trade should he choose to spread the word that the landlady at the Angler's Catch was the sort who gave her customers a hard time. She also knew that there was a fair to middling chance that Aidan had already had a couple of free whiskies at her expense, and that Shannon would be running around like a headless chicken trying to fill orders, but her feet refused to budge. She was riveted by the sight of his dark, handsome face, glued to the spot by that lazy, mesmerising drawl.

'Working at one of those big, soulless companies…' Which was not, strictly speaking, a complete lie, although it had to be said that his company was less soulless than most. 'Decided that I would try my luck at something else. I've always wanted to…write, so I'm in the process of taking a little time out to try my hand at it; see where that takes me…' He strolled towards the window and peered out. 'I thought a good place to start would be Ireland. It's noted for its inspiring scenery, isn't it? Thought I would get a flavour of the country…the bits most people don't see; thought I would set my book here…'

He glanced over his shoulder to her before resuming his thoughtful contemplation of the very little he could actually see in the almost complete, abysmal darkness outside. 'The weather has knocked my progress off a little, hence—' he raised his shoulders in a rueful, elegant shrug '—here I am.'

A budding author? Surely not. He certainly didn't *look* like one, yet why on earth would he lie? The fact that he had held down a conventional job no doubt accounted for that hint of *sophistication* she was getting; something intangible that emanated from him, an air of unspoken authority that she found difficult to quite define but…

Brianna felt herself thaw. 'It gets a little quieter towards the end of the evening,' she offered. 'If you haven't fallen asleep, I can make you something to eat.'

'That's very kind of you,' Leo murmured. The passing guilt he had felt at having to concoct a lie was rationalised, justified and consigned to oblivion. He had responded creatively to an unexpected development.

Getting her onside could also work in his favour. Publicans knew everything about everyone and were seldom averse to a bit of healthy gossip. Doubtless he would be able to extract some background information on his mother and, when he had that information, he would pay her a visit in the guise of someone doing business in the area—maybe interviewing her for the fictitious book he had supposedly jacked his job in for. He would add whatever he learnt to whatever he saw and would get a complete picture of the woman who had abandoned him at birth. He would get his closure. The unfinished mosaic of his life would finally have all the pieces welded together.

'Right, then…' Brianna dithered awkwardly. 'Is there anything you need to know about…the room? How the television works? How you can get an outside line?'

'I think I can figure both out,' Leo responded dryly. 'You can get back to your rowdy crew in the bar.'

'They are, aren't they?' She laughed softly and hooked her thumbs into the pockets of her jeans.

Without warning, Leo felt a jolt of unexpected arousal at the sight. She was very slender. Her figure was almost boyish, not at all like the women he was routinely attracted to, whose assets were always far more prominent and much more aggressively advertised; beautiful, overtly sexy women who had no time for downplaying what they possessed.

He frowned at his body's unexpected lapse in self-control. 'You should employ more people to help you out,' he told her abruptly.

'Perhaps I should.' Just like that she felt the change in the atmosphere and she reminded herself that, writer or not, guys who were too sexy for their own good spelled trouble. She reminded herself of how easy it was to be taken in by what was on the outside, only to completely miss the ugly stuff that was buried underneath.

She coolly excused herself and returned to find that, just

as expected, Aidan was knocking back a glass of whisky which he hurriedly banged on the counter the second he spotted her approaching.

Shannon appeared to be on the verge of tears and, despite what Brianna had told her, was scuttling over with a tray of drinks to the group of high-spirited men at the corner table, most of whom they had gone to school with, which Brianna thought was no reason for them to think they could get waitress service. Old Connor, with several more drinks inside him, was once again attempting to be a crooner but could scarcely enunciate the words to the song he was trying to belt out.

It was the same old same old, and she felt every day of her twenty-seven years by the time they all began drifting off into an unwelcoming night. Twenty-seven years old and she felt like forty-seven. The snow which had thankfully disappeared for the past week had returned to pay them another visit, and outside the flakes were big and fat under the street lights.

Shannon was the last to leave and Brianna had to chivvy her along. For a young girl of nineteen, she had a highly developed mothering instinct and worried incessantly about her friend living above the pub on her own.

'Although at least there's a strapping man there with you tonight!' She laughed, wrapping her scarf around her neck and winking.

'From my experience of the opposite sex…' Brianna grinned back and shouted into the darkness with a wave '…they're the first to dive for cover if there's any chance of danger—and that includes the strapping ones!'

'Then you've just met the wrong men.'

She spun round to see Leo standing by the bar, arms folded, his dark eyes amused. He had showered and changed and was in a pair of jeans and a cream, thickly knitted jumper which did dramatic things for his colouring.

'You've come for your sandwich.' She tore her eyes away from him and quickly and efficiently began clearing the tables, getting the brunt of the work done before she had to get up at seven the following morning.

'I gathered that the crowd was beginning to disperse. The singing had stopped.' He began giving her a hand.

Clearing tables was a novel experience. When he happened to be in the country, he ate out. On the rare occasions when he chose to eat in, he ate food specially prepared for him by his housekeeper, who was also an excellent chef. She cooked for him, discreetly waited until he was finished and then cleared the table. Once a month, she cooked for both him and Harry and these meals were usually preplanned to coincide with a football game. They would eat, enjoy a couple of beers and watch the football. It was his most perfect down time.

He wondered when and how that small slice of normality, the normality of clearing a table, had vanished—but then was it so surprising? He ran multi-million-pound companies that stretched across the world. Normality, as most people understood it, was in scarce supply.

'You really don't have to help,' Brianna told him as she began to fetch the components for a sandwich. 'You're a paying guest.'

'With a curious mind. Tell me about the wannabe opera singer...'

He watched as she worked, making him a sandwich that could have fed four, tidying away the beer mugs and glasses into the industrial-sized dishwasher. He listened keenly as she chatted, awkwardly at first, but then fluently, about all the regulars—laughing at their idiosyncrasies; relating little anecdotes of angry wives showing up to drag their other halves back home when they had abused the freedom pass they had been given for a couple of hours.

'Terrific sandwich, by the way.' It had been. Surprisingly so, bearing in mind that the sandwiches he occasionally ate were usually ornate affairs with intricate fillings prepared by top chefs in expensive restaurants. He lifted the plate as she wiped clean the counter underneath. 'I'm guessing that you pretty much know everyone who lives around here…'

'You guess correctly.'

'One of the upsides of living in a small place?' He could think of nothing worse. He thoroughly enjoyed the anonymity of big-city life.

'It's nice knowing who your neighbours are. It's a small population here. 'Course, some of them have gone to live in other parts of Ireland, and a few really daring ones have moved to your part of the world, but on the whole, yes, we all know each other.'

She met his steady gaze and again felt that hectic bloom of colour invade her cheeks. 'Nearly everyone here tonight were regulars. They've been coming here since my dad owned the place.'

'And your dad is…?'

'Dead,' Brianna said shortly. 'Hence this is now my place.'

'I'm sorry. Tough work.'

'I can handle it.' She took his plate, stuck it into the sink then washed her hands.

'And, of course, you have all your friends around you for support… Siblings as well? What about your mother?'

'Why are you asking me all these questions?'

'Aren't we always curious about people we've never met and places we've never seen? As a…writer you could say that I'm more curious than most.' He stood up and began walking towards the door through which lay the stairs up to his bedroom. 'If you think I'm being too nosy then tell me.'

Brianna half-opened her mouth with a cool retort, something that would restore the balance between paying guest and landlady, but the temptation to chat to a new face, a new person, someone who didn't know her from time immemorial, was too persuasive.

A writer! How wonderful to meet someone on the same wavelength as her! What would it hurt to drop her guard for a couple of days and give him the benefit of the doubt? He might be good-looking but he wasn't Danny Fluke.

'You're not nosy.' She smiled tentatively. 'I just don't understand why you're interested. We're a pretty run-of-the-mill lot here; I can't imagine you would get anything useful for your book.' She couldn't quite make him out. He was in shadow, lounging indolently against the wall as he looked at her. She squashed the uneasy feeling that there was more to him than met the eye.

'People's stories interest me.' He pushed himself away from the wall and smiled. 'You'd be surprised what you can pick up; what you can find...useful.' There was something defiant yet vulnerable about her. It was an appealing mix and a refreshing change from the women he normally met.

'Tomorrow,' he said, 'Point me in the direction of what to do and you can relax. Tell me about the people who live here.'

'Don't be crazy. You're a guest. You're paying for your bed and board and, much as I'd love to swap the room for your labour, I just can't afford it.'

'And I wouldn't dream of asking.' He wondered how she would react if she knew that he could buy this pub a hundred times over and it would still only be loose change to him. He wondered what she would say if she knew that, in between the stories she had to tell, there would be that vital one he wanted to hear. 'No, you'd be helping me out, giving me one or two ideas. Plus you look as though you could use a day off…'

The thought of putting her feet up for a couple of hours dangled in front of her like the promise of a banquet to a starving man. 'I can work and chat at the same time,' she conceded. 'And it'll be nice to have someone lend a hand.'

CHAPTER TWO

BRIANNA WOKE AT six the following morning to furious snowfall. Outside, it was as still as a tomb. On days like this, her enjoyment of the peace and quiet was marred by the reality that she would have next to no customers, but then she thought of the stranger lying in the room down from hers on the middle floor. Leo. He hadn't baulked at the cost of the room and, the evening before, had insisted on paying her generously for an evening meal. Some of her lost income would be recovered.

And then…the unexpected, passing companionship of a fellow artiste. She knew most of the guys her age in the village and it had to be said that there wasn't a creative streak to be found among the pack of them.

She closed her eyes and luxuriated for a few stolen minutes, just thinking about him. When she thought about the way his dark eyes had followed her as she had tidied and chatted, wiped the bar counter and straightened the stools, she could feel the heat rush all through her body until it felt as though it was on fire.

She hadn't had a boyfriend in years.

The appearance of the stranger was a stark reminder of how her emotional life had ground to a standstill after her disastrous relationship with Daniel Fluke at university. All those years ago, she had fancied herself in love.

Daniel had been the complete package: gorgeous, with chestnut-brown hair, laughing blue eyes and an abundance of pure charm that had won him a lot of admirers. But he had only had eyes for her. They had been an item for nearly two years. He had met her father; had sat at the very bar downstairs, nursing a pint with him. He had been studying law and had possessed that peculiar surety of someone who has always known what road they intended to go down. His father was a retired judge, his mother a key barrister in London. They were all originally from Dublin, one of those families with textbook, aristocratic genealogy. They still kept a fabulous apartment in Dublin, but he had lived in London since he had been a child.

Looking back, Brianna could see that there had always been the unspoken assumption that she should consider herself lucky to have nabbed him, that a guy like him could have had any pretty girl on campus. At the time, though, she had walked around with her head in the clouds. She had actually thought that their relationship was built to last. Even now, years after the event, she could still taste the bitterness in her mouth when she remembered how it had all ended.

She had been swept off her feet on a post-graduation holiday in New Zealand, all expenses paid. She shuddered now when she thought back to the ease with which she had accepted his generosity. She had returned to Ireland only to discover that her father was seriously ill and, at that point, she had made the mistake of showing her hand. She had made the fatal error of assuming that Daniel would be right there by her side, supporting her through tough times.

'Of course,' he had told her, 'There's no way I can stay there with you. I have an internship due to start in London…'

She had understood. She had hoped for weekends. Her

father would recover, she had insisted, choosing to mis-read the very clear messages the doctors had been giving her about his prognosis. And, when he did, she would join him in London. There would be loads of opportunities for her in the city and they would easily be able to afford a place to rent. There would be no need to rush to buy... not until they were ready really to seal their relationship. Plus, it would be a wonderful time for her finally to meet his family: the brother he spoke so much about, who did clever things in banking, and his kid sister who was at a boarding school in Gloucester. And of course his parents, who never seemed to be in one place for very long.

She had stupidly made assumptions about a future that had never been on the cards. They had been at university together and, hell, it had been a lot of fun. She was by far the fittest girl there. But a future together...?

The look of embarrassed, dawning horror on his face had said it all but still, like the young fool she had been, she had clung on and asked for explanations. The more he had been forced to explain, the cooler his voice had become. They were worlds apart; how could she seriously have thought that they would end up *married*? Wasn't it enough that she had had an all-expenses-paid farewell holi-day? He was expected to marry a certain type of woman... that was just the way it was...she should just stop cling-ing and move on...

She'd moved on but still a part of her had remained rooted to that moment in time. Why else had she made no effort to get her love life back on track?

The stranger's unexpected arrival on the scene had opened Pandora's box in her head and, much as she wanted to slam the lid back down, she remained lying in bed for far longer than she should, just thinking.

It was after eight by the time she made it down to the

bar, belatedly remembering the strict times during which her guest could have his breakfast. As landladies went, she would definitely not be in the running for a five-star rating.

She came to a halt by the kitchen door when she discovered that Leo was already there, appearing to make himself at home. There was a cup of coffee in front of him, and his laptop, which he instantly closed the second he looked up and spied her hovering in the doorway, a bit like a guest on her own premises.

'I hope you don't mind me making myself at home,' Leo said, pushing his chair back and folding his hands behind his head to look at her. 'I'm an early riser and staying in bed wasn't a tempting thought.' He had been up since six, in fact, and had already accomplished a great deal of work, although less than he had anticipated, because for once he had found his mind wandering to the girl now dithering in front of him. Was it because he was so completely removed from his comfort zone that his brain was not functioning with the rigid discipline to which it was accustomed? Was that why he had fallen asleep thinking of those startling green eyes and had awakened less than five hours later with a painful erection?

He might be willing to exploit whatever she knew about his mother, if she knew anything at all, but he certainly wasn't interested in progressing beyond that.

'You've been working.' Brianna smiled hesitantly. His impact on all her senses seemed as powerful in the clear light of day as it had been the night before. She galvanised herself into action and began unloading the dishwasher, stacking all the glasses to be returned to the bar outside; fetching things from the fridge so that she could make him the breakfast which was included in the money he had paid her.

'I have. I find that I work best in the mornings.'

'Have you managed to get anything down? I guess it must be quite an ordeal trying to get your imagination to do what you want it to do. Can I ask you what your book is going to be about? Or would you rather keep that to yourself?'

'People and the way they interact.' Leo hastened to get away from a topic in which he had no intention of becoming mired. The last time he had written anything that required the sort of imagination she was talking about had been at secondary school. 'Do you usually get up this early?'

'Earlier.' She refilled his mug and began cracking eggs, only pausing when he told her to sit down and talk to him for a few minutes rather than rushing into making breakfast.

Brianna blushed and obeyed. Nerves threatened to overwhelm her. She sneaked a glance at him and all over again was rendered breathless by the sheer force of his good looks and peculiar magnetism. 'There's a lot to do when you run a pub.' She launched into hurried speech to fill the silence. 'And, like I said, I'm doing it all on my own, so I have no one to share the responsibility with.'

Leo, never one to indulge his curiosity when it came to women—and knowing very well that, whatever information he was interested in gathering, certainly had nothing to do with *her* so why waste time hearing her out?—was reluctantly intrigued. 'A curious life you chose for yourself,' he murmured.

'I didn't choose it. *It* chose *me*.'

'Explain.'

'Are you really interested?'

'I wouldn't ask if I wasn't,' Leo said with a shrug. He had wondered whether she was really as pretty as he had imagined her to be. Subdued lighting in a pub could do flattering things to an average woman. He was discovering that his first impressions had been spot on. In fact, they had failed to do her justice. She had an ethereal, angelic beauty about her that drew the eye and compelled him to keep on staring. His eyes drifted slightly down to her breasts, small buds causing just the tiniest indentations in her unflattering, masculine jumper, which he guessed had belonged at one point to her father.

'My dad died unexpectedly. Well, maybe there were signs before. I didn't see them. I was at university, not getting back home as often as I knew I should, and Dad was never one to make a fuss when it came to his health.' She was startled at the ease with which she confessed to the guilt that had haunted her ever since her father had died. She could feel the full brunt of Leo's attention on her and it was as flattering as it was unnerving, not at all what she was accustomed to.

'He left a lot of debts.' She cleared her throat and blinked back the urge to cry. 'I think things must have slipped as he became ill and he never told me. The bank manager was very understanding but I had to keep running the pub so that I could repay the debts. I couldn't sell it, even though I tried for a while. There's a good summer trade here. Lots of fantastic scenery. Fishing. Brilliant walks. But the trade is a little seasonal and, well, the economy isn't great. I guess you'd know. You probably have to keep a firm rein on your finances if you've packed your job in…'

Leo flushed darkly and skirted around that ingenuous observation. 'So you've been here ever since,' he murmured. 'And no partner around to share the burden?'

'No.' Brianna looked down quickly and then stood up. 'I should get going with my chores. It's snowing outside and it looks like it's going to get worse, which usually means that the pub loses business, but just in case any hardy souls show up I can't have it looking a mess.'

So, he thought, there *had* been a man and it had ended badly. He wondered who the guy was. Some losers only stuck by their women when the times were good. The second the winds of change began blowing, they ran for the hills. He felt an unexpected spurt of anger towards this mystery person who had consigned her to a life on her own of drudgery, running a pub to make ends meet and pay off bills. He reined back his unruly mind and reminded himself that his primary purpose wasn't as counsellor but as information gatherer.

'If you really meant it about helping—and I promise I won't take advantage of your kind offer— you could try and clear a path through the snow, just in case it stops; at least my customers would be able to get to the door. It doesn't look promising…' She moved to one of the windows and frowned at the strengthening blizzard. 'What do you intend to do if the weather doesn't let up?' She turned to face him.

'It'll let up. I can't afford to stay here for very long.'

'You could always incorporate a snow storm in your book.'

'It's a thought.' He moved to stand next to her and at once he breathed in the fragrant, flowery smell of her hair which was, again, tied back in a pony tail. His fingers itched to release it, just to see how long it was, how thick. He noticed how she edged away slightly from him. 'I'll go see what I can do about the snow. You'll have to show me where the equipment is.'

'The equipment consists of a shovel and some bags of sand for gritting.' She laughed, putting a little more distance between them, because just for a second there she had felt short of breath with him standing so close to her.

'You do this yourself whenever it snows?' he asked, once the shovel was in his hand and the door to the pub thrown open to the elements. He thought of his last girl-friend, a model who didn't possess a pair of wellies to her name, and would only have gone near snow if it happened to be falling on a ski slope in Val d'Isere.

'Only if it looks as though it would make a difference. There've been times when I've wasted two hours trying to clear a path, only to stand back and watch the snow cover it all up in two minutes. You can't go out in those… er…jeans; you'll be soaked through. I don't suppose you brought any, um, waterproof clothing with you?'

Leo burst out laughing. 'Believe it or not, I didn't pack for a snow storm. The jeans will have to do. If they get soaked, they'll dry in front of that open fire in the lounge area.'

He worked out. He was strong. And yet he found that battling with the elements was exercise of a completely different sort. This was not the sanitised comfort of his expensive gym, with perfectly oiled machinery that was supposed to test the body to its limits. This was raw na-ture and, by the time he looked at his handiwork, a mea-gre path already filling up with fast falling snow, an hour and a half had flown past.

He had no gloves. His hands were freezing. But hell, it was invigorating. In fact, he had completely forgotten the reason why he was in this Godforsaken village in the first place. His thoughts were purely and utterly focused on try-ing to outsmart and out-shovel the falling snow.

The landscape had turned completely white. The pub was set a distance from the main part of the village and was surrounded by open fields. Pausing to stand back, his arm resting heavily on the shovel which he had planted firmly in the ground, he felt that he was looking at infinity. It evoked the strangest sensation of peace and awe, quite different from the irritation he had felt the day before when he had stared moodily out of the window at the tedium of never-ending fields and cursed his decision to get there by car.

He stayed out another hour, determined not to be beaten, but in the end he admitted defeat and returned to the warmth of the pub, to find the fire blazing and the smell of food wafting from the kitchen.

'I fought the snow...' God, he felt like a caveman returning from a hard day out hunting. 'And the snow won. Don't bank on any customers today. Something smells good.'

'I don't normally do lunch for guests.'

'You'll be royally paid for your efforts.' He stifled a surge of irritation that the one thing most women would have given their eye teeth to do for him was something she clearly had done because she had had no choice. She was stuck with him. She could hardly expect him to starve because lunch wasn't included in the price of the room. 'You were going to fill me in on the people who live around here.' He reminded her coolly of the deal they had struck.

'It's not very exciting.' She looked at him and her heartbeat quickened. 'You're going to have to change. You're soaked through. If you give me your damp clothes, I can put them in front of the fire in the snug.'

'The snug?'

'My part of the house.' She leaned back against the kitchen counter, hands behind her. 'Self-contained quarters. Only small—two bedrooms, a little snug, a kitchen, bathroom and a study where Dad used to do all the accounts for the pub. It's where I grew up. I can remember loving it when the place was full and I could roam through the guest quarters bringing them cups of tea and coffee. It used to get a lot busier in the boom days.'

She certainly looked happy recounting those jolly times but, as far as Leo was concerned, it sounded like just the sort of restricted life that would have driven him crazy.

And yet, this could have been his fate—living in this tiny place where everyone knew everyone else. In fact, he wouldn't even have had the relative comforts of a village pub. He would probably have been dragged up in a hovel somewhere by the town junkie, because what other sort of loser gave away their own child? It was a sobering thought.

'I could rustle up some of Dad's old shirts for you. I kept quite a few for myself. I'll leave them outside your bedroom door and you can hand me the jeans so that I can launder them.'

She hadn't realised how lonely it was living above the pub on her own, making every single decision on her own, until she was rummaging through her wardrobe, picking out shirts and enjoying the thought of having someone to lend them to, someone sharing her space, even if it was only in the guise of a guest who had been temporarily blown off-path by inclement weather.

She warmed at the thought of him trying and failing to clear the path to the pub of snow. When she gently knocked on his bedroom door ten minutes later, she was carrying a bundle of flannel shirts and thermal long-sleeved vests. She would leave them outside the door, and indeed she was bending down to do just that when the door opened.

She looked sideways and blinked rapidly at the sight of bare ankles. Bare ankles and strong calves, with dark hair... Her eyes drifted further upwards to bare thighs... lean, muscular bare thighs. Her mouth went dry. She was still clutching the clothes to her chest, as if shielding herself from the visual invasion of his body on her senses. His *semi-clad* body.

'Are these for me?'

Brianna snapped out of her trance and stared at him wordlessly.

'The clothes?' Leo arched an amused eyebrow as he took in her bright-red face and parted lips. 'They'll come in very handy. Naturally, you can put them on the tab.'

He was wearing boxers and nothing else. Brianna's brain registered that as a belated postscript. Most of her brain was wrapped up with stunned, shocked appreciation of his body. Broad shoulders and powerful arms tapered down to a flat stomach and lean hips. He had had a quick shower, evidently, and one of the cheap, white hand towels was slung around his neck and hung over his shoulders. She felt faint.

'I thought I'd get rid of the shirt as well,' he said. 'If you wouldn't mind laundering the lot, I would be extremely grateful. I failed to make provisions for clearing snow.'

Brianna blinked, as gauche and confused as a teenager. She saw that he was dangling the laundry bag on one finger while looking at her with amusement.

Well of course he would be, she thought, bristling. Writer or not, he came from a big city and, yes, was ever so patronising about the *smallness* of their town. And here she was, playing into his hands, gaping as though she had never seen a naked man in her life before, as though he was the most interesting thing to have landed on her doorstep in a hundred years.

'Well, perhaps you should have,' she said tartly. 'Only a fool would travel to this part of the world in the depths of winter and *not* come prepared for heavy snow.' She snatched the laundry bag from him and thrust the armful of clothes at his chest in return.

'Come again?' *Had she just called him a fool?*

'I haven't got the time or the energy to launder your clothes every two seconds because you didn't anticipate bad weather. In February. Here.' Her eyes skirted nervously away from the aggressive width of his chest. 'And I suggest,' she continued tightly, 'That you cover up. If I don't have the time to launder your clothes, then I most certainly do not have the time to play nursemaid when you go down with flu!'

Leo was trying to think of the last time a woman had raised her voice in his presence. Or, come to think of it, said anything that was in any way inflammatory. It just didn't happen. He didn't know whether to be irritated, enraged or entertained.

'Message understood loud and clear.' He grinned and leaned against the doorframe. However serious the implications of this visit to the land that time forgot, he realised that he was enjoying himself. Right now, at this very moment, with this beautiful Irish girl standing in front of him, glaring and uncomfortable. 'Fortunately, I'm as healthy as a horse. Can't remember the last time I succumbed to flu. So you won't have to pull out your nurse's uniform and tend to me.' Interesting notion, though... His dark eyes drifted over her lazily. 'I'll be down shortly. And my thanks once again for the clothes.'

Brianna was still hot and flustered when, half an hour later, he sauntered down to the kitchen. One of the tables in the bar area had been neatly set for one. 'I hope you're not expecting me to have lunch on my own,' were his opening words, and she spun around from where she had been frowning into the pot of homemade soup.

Without giving her a chance to answer, he began searching for the crockery, giving a little grunt of satisfaction when he hit upon the right cupboard. 'Remember we were going to...talk? You were going to tell me all about the people who live here so that I can get some useful fodder for my book.' It seemed inconceivable that a budding author would simply up sticks and go on a rambling tour of Ireland in the hope of inspiration but, as excuses went, it had served its purpose, which was all that mattered. 'And then, I'll do whatever you want me to do. I'm a man of my word.'

'There won't be much to do,' Brianna admitted. 'The snow's not letting up. I've phoned Aidan and told him that the place will be closed until the weather improves.'

'Aidan?'

'One of my friends. He can be relied on to spread the word. Only my absolute regulars would even contemplate trudging out here in this weather.'

'So...is Aidan the old would-be opera singer?'

'Aidan is my age. We used to go to school together.' She dished him out some soup, added some bread and offered him a glass of wine, which he rejected in favour of water.

'And he's the guy who broke your heart? No. He wouldn't be. The guy who broke your heart has long since disappeared, hasn't he?'

Brianna stiffened. She reminded herself that she was not having a cosy chat with a friend over lunch. This was a guest in her pub, a stranger who was passing through, no more. Confiding details of her private life was beyond the pale, quite different from chatting about all the amusing things that happened in a village where nearly everyone knew everyone else. Her personal life was not going to be fodder for a short story on life in a quaint Irish village.

'I don't recall telling you anything about my heart being broken, and I don't think my private life is any of your business. I hope the soup is satisfactory.'

So that was a sore topic; there was no point in a follow-up. It was irrelevant to his business here. If he happened to be curious, then it was simply because he was in the unique situation of being pub-bound and snowed in with just her for company. In the absence of anyone else, it was only natural that she would spark an interest.

'Why don't you serve food? It would add a lot to the profits of a place like this. You'd be surprised how remote places can become packed if the food is good enough...' He doubted the place had seen any changes in a very long time. Again, not his concern, he thought. 'So, if you don't want to talk about yourself, then that's fair enough.'

'Why don't *you* talk about yourself? Are you married? Do you have children?'

'If I were married and had children, I wouldn't be doing what I'm doing.' Marriage? Children? He had never contemplated either. He pushed the empty soup bowl aside and sprawled on the chair, angling it so that he could stretch his legs out to one side. 'Tell me about the old guy who likes to sing.'

'What made you suddenly decide to pack in your job and write? It must have been a big deal, giving up steady work in favour of a gamble that might or might not pay off.'

Leo shrugged and told himself that, certainly in this instance, the ends would more than justify the means—and at any rate, there was no chance that she would discover his little lie. He would forever remain the enigmatic stranger who had passed through and collected a few amusing anecdotes on the way. She would be regaling her friends with this in a week's time.

'Sometimes life is all about taking chances,' he murmured softly.

Brianna hadn't taken a chance in such a long time that she had forgotten what it felt like. The last chance she had taken had been with Danny, and hadn't *that* backfired spectacularly in her face? She had settled into a groove and had firmly convinced herself that it suited her. 'Some people are braver than others when it comes to that sort of thing,' she found herself muttering under her breath.

Leading remark, Leo thought. He had vast experience of women dangling titbits of information about themselves, offering them to him in the hope of securing his interest, an attempt to reel him in through his curiosity. However, for once his cynicism was absent. This woman knew nothing about him. He did not represent a rich, eligible bachelor. He was a struggling writer with no job. He had a glimpse of what it must feel like to communicate with a woman without undercurrents of suspicion that, whatever they wanted, at least part of it had to do with his limitless bank balance. He might have been adopted into a life of extreme privilege, and that privilege might have been his spring board to the dizzying heights of his success, but with that privilege and with that success had come drawbacks—one of which was an inborn mistrust of women and their motivations.

Right now, he was just communicating with a very beautiful and undeniably sexy woman and, hell, she was clueless about him. He smiled, enjoying the rare sense of freedom.

'And you're not one of the brave ones?'

Brianna stood up to clear the table. She had no idea where this sudden urge to confide was coming from. Was she bonding with him because, underneath those disconcerting good looks, he was a fellow artist? Because, on some weird level, he *understood* her? Or was she just one of those sad women, too young to be living a life of relative solitude, willing to confide in anyone who showed an interest?

Her head was buzzing. She felt hot and bothered and, when he reached out and circled her wrist with his hand, she froze in shock. The feel of his warm fingers on her skin was electrifying. She hadn't had a response like this to a man in a very long time. It was a feeling of coming alive. She wanted to snatch her hand away from his and rub away where he had touched her… Yet she also wanted him to keep his fingers on her wrist; she wanted to prolong the warm, physical connection between them. She abruptly sat back down, because her legs felt like jelly, and he released her.

'It's hard to take chances when you have commitments,' she muttered unsteadily. She couldn't tear her eyes away from his face. She literally felt as though he held her spellbound. 'You're on your own. You probably had sufficient money saved to just take off and do your own thing. I'm only now beginning to see the light financially and, even so, I still couldn't just up and leave.' She was leaning forward in the chair, leaning towards him as though he was the source of her energy. 'I should get this place tidied up,' she said agitatedly.

'Why? I thought you said that the pub would be closed until further notice.'

'Yes, but…'

'You must get lonely here on your own.'

'Of course I'm not lonely! I have too many friends to count!'

'But I don't suppose you have a lot of time to actually go out with them…'

Hot colour invaded her cheeks. No time to go out with them; no time even to pursue her art as a hobby. She hated the picture he was painting of her life. She was being made to feel as though she had sleepwalked into an existence of living from one day to the next, with each day being exactly the same. She dragged herself back to reality, back to the fact that he was just a budding writer on the hunt for some interesting material for his book. He wasn't interested in *her*.

'Will I be the sad spinster in your book?' She laughed shakily and gathered herself together. 'I think you're better off with some of the more colourful characters who live here.' She managed to get to her feet, driven by a need to put some distance between them. How could she let this one passing stranger get to her with such breath-taking speed? Lots of guys had come on to her over the years. Some of them she had known for ever, others had been friends of friends of friends. She had laughed and joked with all of them but she had never, not once, felt like *this*. Felt as though the air was being sucked out of her lungs every time she took a peek…as though she was being injected with adrenaline every time she came too close.

She busied herself tidying, urging him to sit rather than help. Her flustered brain screeched to a halt when she imagined them standing side by side at the kitchen sink.

She launched into nervous conversation, chattering mindlessly about the last time a snow storm had hit the village, forcing herself to relax as she recounted stories of all the things that could happen to people who were snow bound for days on end, occasionally as long as a fortnight: the baby delivered by one panicked father, the rowdy rugby group who had been forced to spend two nights in the pub; the community spirit when they had all had to help each other out; the food that Seamus Riley had had to lift by rope into his bedroom because he hadn't been able to get past his front door.

Leo listened politely. He really ought to be paying a bit more attention, but he was captivated by the graceful movement of her tall, slender body as she moved from counter to counter, picking things up, putting things away, making sure not to look at him.

'In fact, we all do our bit when the weather turns really bad,' she was saying now as she turned briefly in his direction. 'I don't suppose you have much of that in London.'

'None,' Leo murmured absently. Her little breasts pointed against the jumper and he wondered whether she was wearing a bra; a sensible, white cotton bra. He never imagined the thought of a sensible, white cotton bra could be such an illicit turn-on.

He was so absorbed in the surprising disobedience of his imagination that he almost missed the name that briefly passed her lips and, when it registered, he stiffened and felt his pulses quicken.

'Sorry,' he grated, straightening. 'I missed that…particular anecdote.' He kept his voice as casual as possible but he was tense and vigilant as he waited for her to repeat what she had been saying, what he had stupidly missed because he had been too busy getting distracted, too busy missing the point of why he was stuck here in the first place.

'I was just telling you about what it's like here—we help each other out. I was telling you about my friend who lives in the village. Bridget McGuire…'

CHAPTER THREE

So HIS MOTHER wasn't the drunk or the junkie that he had anticipated, if his landlady was to be believed...

Leo flexed his muscles and wandered restlessly through the lounge where he had been sitting in front of his computer working for the past hour and a half.

Circumstance had forced him into a routine of sorts, as his optimistic plan of clearing off within a few days had faded into impossibility.

After three days, the snow was still falling steadily. It fluctuated between virtual white-out and gentle flakes that could lull you into thinking that it was all picture-postcard perfect. Until you opened the front door and clocked that the snow you'd cleared moments previously had already been replaced by a fresh fall.

He strolled towards the window and stared out at a pitch-black vista, illuminated only by the outside lights which Brianna kept on overnight.

It was not yet seven in the morning. He had never needed much sleep and here, more than ever, he couldn't afford to lie in. Not when he had to keep communicating with his office, sending emails, reviewing reports, without her knowing exactly what was going on. At precisely seven-thirty, he would shut his computer and head outside to see what he could do about beating back some of the snow so that it didn't completely bank up against the door.

It was, he had to admit to himself, a fairly unique take on winter sport. When he had mentioned that to Brianna the day before, she had burst out laughing and told him that he could try building himself a sledge and having fun outside, getting in touch with his inner child.

He made himself a cup of coffee and reined in the temptation to let his mind meander, which was what it seemed to want to do whenever he thought of her.

His mother was in hospital recovering from a mild heart attack.

'She should have been out last week,' Brianna had confided, 'But they've decided to keep her in because the weather's so horrendous and she has no one to take care of her.'

Where was the down-and-out junkie he had been anticipating? Of course, there was every chance that she *had* been a deadbeat, a down and out. It would be a past she would have wanted to keep to herself, especially with Brianna who, from the sounds of it, saw her as something of a surrogate mother. The woman hadn't lived her whole life in the village. Who knew what sort of person she had been once upon a time?

But certainly, the stories he had heard did not tally with his expectations.

And the bottom line was that his hands were tied at the moment. He had come to see for himself what his past held. He wasn't about to abandon that quest on the say-so of a girl he'd known for five minutes. On the other hand, he was now on indefinite leave. One week, he had told his secretary, but who was to say that this enforced stay would not last longer?

The snow showed no sign of abating. When it *did* abate,

there was still the question of engineering a meeting with his mother. She was in hospital and when she came out she would presumably be fairly weak. However, without anyone to act as full-time carer, at least for a while, what was the likelihood of her being released from hospital? He was now playing a waiting game.

And throughout all this, there was still the matter of his fictitious occupation. Surely Brianna would start asking him questions about this so-called book he was busily writing? Would he have to fabricate a plot?

In retrospect, out of all the occupations he could have picked, he concluded that he had managed to hit on the single worst one of them all. God knew, he hadn't read a book in years. His reading was strictly of the utilitarian variety: legal tomes, books on the movements of financial markets, detailed backgrounds to companies he was planning to take over.

The fairly straightforward agenda he had set out for himself was turning into something far more complex.

He turned round at the sound of her footsteps on the wooden floor.

And that, he thought, frowning, was an added complication. She was beginning to occupy far too much space in his head. Familiarity was not breeding contempt. He caught himself watching her, thinking about her, fantasising about her. His appreciation of her natural beauty was growing like an unrestrained weed, stifling the disciplined part of his brain that told him that he should not go there.

Not only was she ignorant of his real identity but whatever the hell had happened to her—whoever had broken her heart, the mystery guy she could not be persuaded to discuss—had left her vulnerable. On the surface, she was capable, feisty, strong-willed and stubbornly proud. But he sensed her vulnerability underneath and the rational part of him acknowledged that a vulnerable woman was a woman best left well alone.

But his libido was refusing to listen to reason and seemed to have developed a will of its own.

'You're working too hard.' She greeted him cheerfully. Having told him that she would not be doing his laundry, she had been doing his laundry. Today he was wearing the jeans she had washed the day before and one of her father's checked flannel shirts, the sleeves of which he had rolled to the elbows. In a few seconds, she took in the dark hair just visible where the top couple of buttons of the shirt were undone; the low-slung jeans that emphasised the leanness of his hips; the strong, muscular forearms.

Leo knew what he had been working on and it hadn't been the novel she imagined: legal technicalities that had to be sorted out with one small IT company he was in the process of buying; emails to the human resources department so that they reached a mutually agreeable deal with employees of yet another company he was acquiring. He had the grace to flush.

'Believe me, I've worked harder,' he said with utmost truth. She was in some baggy grey jogging bottoms, which made her look even slimmer than she was, and a baggy grey sweatshirt. For the first time, her hair wasn't tied back, but instead fell over her shoulders and down her back in a cascade of rich auburn.

'I guess maybe in that company of yours—'

'Company of mine?' Leo asked sharply and then realised that guilt had laced the question with unnecessary asperity when she smiled and explained that she was talking about whatever big firm he had worked for before quitting.

She had noticed that he never talked about the job he had done, and Brianna had made sure to steer clear of the subject. It was a big enough deal getting away from the rat race without being reminded of what you'd left behind, because the rat race from which he had escaped was the very same rat race that was now funding his exploits into the world of writing.

'You still haven't told me much about your book,' she said tentatively. 'I know I'm being horribly nosy, and I know how hard it is to let someone have a whiff of what you're working on before it's finished, but you must be very far in. You start work so early and I know you keep it up, off and on during the day. You never seem to lack inspiration.'

Leo considered what level of inspiration was needed to review due diligence on a company: none. 'You know how it goes,' he said vaguely. 'You can write two...er... chapters and then immediately delete them, although...' He considered the massive deal he had just signed off on. 'I must admit I've been reasonably productive. To change the subject, have you any books I could borrow? I had no idea I would be in one place for so long...'

When had his life become so blinkered? he wondered. Sure, he played; he enjoyed the company of beautiful women, but they were a secondary consideration to his work. The notion of any of them becoming a permanent fixture in his life had never crossed his mind. And, yes, he relaxed at the gym but, hell, he hadn't picked up a novel in years; hadn't been to a movie in years; rarely watched television for pleasure, aside from the occasional football match; went to the theatre occasionally, usually when it was an arranged company event, but even then he was always restless, always thinking of what needed to be done with his companies or clients or mergers or buyouts.

He impatiently swept aside the downward spiral of introspection and surfaced to find her telling him that there were books in her study.

'And there's something I want to show you,' she said hesitantly. She disappeared for a few minutes and in that time he strolled around the lounge, distractedly looking at the fire and wondering whether the log basket would have to be topped up. He wondered how much money she was losing with this enforced closure of the pub and then debated the pros and cons of asking her if he could have a look at her books.

'Okay...'

Leo turned around and walked slowly towards her. 'What do you have behind your back?'

Brianna took a deep breath and revealed one of the small paintings she had done a few months back, when she had managed to squeeze in some down-time during the summer. It was a painting of the lake and in the foreground an angler sat, back to the spectator, his head bent, his body leaning forward, as if listening for the sound of fish.

'I don't like showing my work to anyone either,' she confided as he took the picture from her and held it at a distance in his hands. 'So I fully understand why you don't want to talk about your book.'

'*You* painted this?'

'What do you think?'

'I think you're wasted running a pub here.' Leo was temporarily lost for words. Of course he had masterpieces in his house, as well as some very expensive investment art, but this was charming and unique enough to find a lucrative market of its own. 'Why don't you try selling them?'

'Oh, I could never produce enough.' She sighed regretfully. She moved to stand next to him so that they were both looking at the painting. When he rested it on the table, she didn't move, and suddenly her throat constricted as their eyes tangled and, for a few seconds, she found that she was holding her breath.

Leo sifted his fingers through her hair and the door slammed shut on all his good intentions not to let his wayward libido do the thinking for him. He just knew that he wanted this woman, more than he had ever wanted any woman in his life before, and for the hell of him he had no idea why. He had stopped trying to work that one out. He was not a man who was accustomed to holding out. Desire was always accompanied by possession. In fact, as he looked down at her flushed, upturned face, he marvelled that he had managed to restrain himself for so long because hadn't he known, almost from the very start, that she was attracted to him? Hadn't he seen it there in those hot, stolen looks and her nervous, jumpy reactions when he got fractionally too close to her?

He perched on the edge of the table and drew her closer to him.

Brianna released her breath in a long shudder. She was burning up where he touched her. Never in a million years would she have imagined that she could do this, that she could *feel* this way, feel so connected to a guy that she wanted him to touch her after only a few days. Showing him that painting, had he only known it, had been a measure of how much she trusted him. She felt *easy* in his company. Gone were the feelings of suspicion which had been there when she had first laid eyes on him, when she had wondered what such a dramatic looking stranger was doing in their midst, standing there at the door of the pub and looking around him with guarded coolness.

She had let down her defences, had thawed. Being cooped up had blurred the lines between paying guest and a guy who was as amusing as he was intelligent; as witty and dry as he was focused and disciplined. He might have worked in a company and done boring stuff but you would never guess that by the breadth of his conversation. He knew a great deal about art, about world affairs, and he had travelled extensively. He had vaguely told her that it was all in connection with his job, and really not very exciting at all because he did nothing but work when he got to his destination, but he could still captivate her with descriptions of the places he had been and the things he had seen there.

In short, he was nothing at all like any of the men she had ever met in her entire life, and that included Danny Fluke.

'What are you doing?' she asked weakly.

'I'm touching you. Do you want me to stop?'

'This is crazy.'

'This is taking a chance.'

'I don't even...know you.'

No, she certainly didn't. And yet, strangely, she knew more about him than any other woman did. Not that there was any point in getting tied down with semantics. 'What does that have to do with wanting someone?' His voice was a low murmur in her ear and, as he slid his hand underneath the jumper to caress her waist, she could feel all rational thought disappearing like dew in the summer sun.

So, she thought, fighting down the temptation to moan as his fingers continued to stroke her bare skin, he wasn't going to be sticking around. He was as nomadic as she was rooted to this place. But wasn't that what taking chances was all about?

She reached up and trembled as she linked her fingers behind his neck and pulled him down towards her.

His kiss was soft, exploratory. His tongue mingled against hers and was mind-blowingly erotic. He angled his long legs open and she edged her body between them so that now she was pushed up against him and could feel the hardness of his erection against her.

'You can still tell me to stop...' And, if she did, he didn't know what he would do. Have a sub-zero shower? Even then, he wasn't sure that it would be enough to cool him down. 'Taking a chance can sometimes be a dangerous indulgence...'

And yet there was a part of her that knew that *not* taking this chance would be a source of eternal regret. Besides, why on earth should she let one miserable experience that was now in the past determine her present?

'Maybe I want to live dangerously for once...'

His hand had crept further up her jumper and he unhooked her bra strap with practised ease.

Brianna's breath caught in her throat and she stilled as he inched his way towards one small breast. She quivered at the feel of his thumb rubbing over it. She wanted him so badly that she was shaking with desire.

Leo marvelled that something he knew they just shouldn't be doing could feel so damned *right*. Had he been going stir crazy here without even realising it? Was that why he had been so useless at disciplining his libido? The lie that had taken him so far, that had started life as just something he had been inspired to do because he had needed an excuse for being there in the first place, hung around his neck with the deadly weight of an albatross.

He shied away from the thought that she might find out, and then laughed at the possibility of that happening.

'I won't be around for much longer.' He felt compelled to warn her off involvement even though he knew that the safest route he could take if he really didn't want to court unwanted involvement would be to walk away. 'Sure you want to take a chance with someone who's just passing through?' He spoke against her mouth and he could feel her warm breath mingling with his.

Brianna feverishly thought of the last guy she had become involved with—the guy she had thought wasn't passing through, the guy she had thought she might end up spending the rest of her life with but who, in fact, had always known that he would be moving on. This time, there would be no illusions. A fling: it was something she had never done in her life before. Danny had been her first and only relationship.

'I'm not looking for permanence,' she whispered. 'I thought I had that once and it turned out to be the biggest mistake I ever made. Stop talking.'

'Happy to oblige,' Leo growled, his conscience relieved. 'I think I wanted this within hours of meeting you.' He circled her waist with his hands and then pushed the jumper up, taking the bra with it as well.

For a split second, Brianna was overwhelmed by shyness. She closed her eyes and arched back, every nerve and pore straining towards a closeness she hadn't felt in such a long time. When she felt the wetness of his mouth surround her nipple, she groaned and half-collapsed. Her hands coiled into his thick, dark hair as he continued sucking and teasing the stiffened peaks until she wanted to faint from the pleasure of it. When he drew back, she groaned in frustration and looked at him drowsily from under her lashes, her heartbeat quickening to a frantic beat as she watched him inspecting her breasts with the same considered thoroughness with which he had earlier inspected her painting.

'I want to see you,' Leo said roughly. He was surprised at the speed with which his body was reacting, racing towards release. His erection was uncomfortable against his jeans, bulging painfully. Yet he didn't want to rush this. He had to close his eyes briefly and breathe deeply so that he wouldn't be thrown off-balance by the sight of her bare breasts, small and crested with large, pink nipples that were still glistening from where he had sucked them.

In response, Brianna traced the contours of his shoulders, broad and powerful. It was driving her crazy just thinking about touching his chest, the bronzed, muscled chest that had sent her imagination into overdrive on that first day when he had stood half-naked in front of her, waiting for the shirts she had brought for him.

'I don't want to make love to you here...' He swung her off her feet as though she weighed nothing and carried her up the stairs towards his bedroom, and then, pausing briefly, up the further flight of stairs that led to her bedroom. He didn't dare look down at her soft, small breasts or he would deposit her on the stairs and take her right there. His urgency to have her lying underneath him was shocking. Not cool; definitely not his style.

He found her bedroom, barely taking time to look around him as he placed her on the bed and ordered her to stay put.

'Where do you think I'm going to go?' She laughed with nervous excitement and levered herself onto one elbow, watching with unconcealed fascination as he began to strip off. With each discarded item of clothing, her heart rate picked up speed until she had to close her eyes and take deep breaths.

Her response was so wonderfully, naturally open and unconcealed that Leo experienced a raw, primitive thrill that magnified his burning lust a thousand-fold.

He took his time removing the jeans because he was enjoying watching her watching him. Most of all he enjoyed her gasp as he stepped out of his boxers and moved towards her, his erection thick, heavy and impressively telling of just how aroused he was.

Brianna scrabbled to sit up, pulses racing, the blood pumping in her veins hot with desire.

She couldn't believe she was doing this, behaving in a way that was so out of character. She sighed and moaned as the mattress depressed under his weight; the feel of his hands tucking into the waistband of the jogging bottoms, sliding them down, signalled the final nail in her crumbling defences

'You're beautiful.' He straddled her and kissed her with intimate, exquisite thoroughness, tracing her mouth with his tongue, then trailing his lips against her neck so that she whimpered and tilted her head to prolong the kiss.

Every small noise she made, every tiny movement, bore witness to how much she was turned on and it gave him an unbelievable kick to know that she had allowed herself to be pulled along by an irresistible force even though it went against the grain.

Her skin was supple and smooth, her breasts perfect, dainty orbs that barely fitted his large hand.

He teased the tip of her nipple with his tongue and then submerged himself in the pleasure of suckling on it, loving the way she writhed under him; the way her fingers bit into his shoulder blades; the way she arched back, eyes closed, mouth parted, her whole body trembling.

He let his hand drift over her flat stomach to circle the indentation of her belly button with one finger while he continued to plunder her breasts, moving between them, sucking, liking the way he could draw them into his mouth. He was hungry for more but determined not to take things fast. He wanted to savour every second of tasting her body.

He parted her legs gently with his hand and eased the momentary tension he could feel as she stilled against him.

'Shh,' he whispered huskily, as though she had spoken. 'Relax.'

'It's…been a long time.' Brianna gave a half- stifled, nervous laugh. He raised his head and their eyes tangled, black clashing with apple-green.

'When you say *long*…'

'I haven't slept with anyone since… Well, it's been years…' She twisted away, embarrassed by the admission. Where had the time gone? It seemed as though one minute she had been nursing heartbreak, dealing with her father's death, caught up in a jumble of financial worries, her life thrown utterly off course, and the next minute she was here, still running the pub, though with the financial worries more or less behind her. She was hardly sinking but definitely not swimming and living a life that seemed far too responsible for someone her age.

Leo tilted her face to his, kissed her on the side of her mouth and banked down his momentary discomfort at thinking that he might be taking advantage of her.

Yet she was perfectly aware of the situation, perfectly aware that he wasn't going to be hanging around. Naturally, she was not in possession of the true facts regulating his departure, but weren't those just details? Looking at the bigger picture, she knew where she stood, that this was just a fling—not even that.

'I'll be gentle.'

'I guess you…you've had a lot of girlfriends?'

'I haven't espoused a life of celibacy.' He slipped his finger into the wet groove of her femininity and felt whatever further questions she wanted to ask become stifled under her heated response. She moved against his finger and groaned.

He could have played with her body all day, all night. Right now, he couldn't get enough of her and he moved downwards. She sucked in her breath sharply and he rested the palm of his hand flat on her stomach, then he nuzzled the soft hair covering the apex between her thighs. He breathed in the musky, honeyed scent of her and dipped his tongue to taste her. How did he know that this was something she was experiencing for the first time? And why was that such a turn on?

He teased the throbbing bud of her clitoris and, when she moaned and squirmed, he flattened his hands on her thighs so that her legs were spread wide open for his delectation.

Brianna had never known anything like this before. There wasn't a single part of her body that wasn't consumed with an overpowering craving. She wanted him to continue doing what he was doing, yet she wanted him in her, deep inside. She weakly tugged at his hair but was powerless to pull him up. When she looked down and saw his dark head between her legs, and his strong, bronzed hands against the paleness of her thighs, she almost passed out.

Could years of living in icy isolation have made her so vulnerable to his touch? Had her body been so deprived of human contact that it was now overwhelmed? It felt like it.

When he rose, she was so close to tipping over the edge that she had to squeeze her eyes shut and grit her teeth together to maintain self-control.

'Enjoying yourself?' Leo raised some hair from her flushed face to whisper in her ear. He rubbed his stiff erection against her belly and felt sensation lick through his body at frightening speed.

Brianna blushed and nodded, then raised herself up so that she could kiss him on the mouth, draw him down over her so that their bodies were pressed together, fused with slick perspiration. She reached down and took him in her hand and he angled himself slightly away to accommodate her. His breathing thickened as she continued to work her movements into a deep rhythm.

He was impressively big and she shivered with heady anticipation.

'A condom… Wait; in my wallet…'

Already he was groping in the pocket of his jeans for his wallet and fumbling to fetch a condom, his eyes still pinned to her flushed, reclining body. How on earth could he be thinking of *anything* at a time like this? She just couldn't wait for him to be inside her, filling her with his bigness.

'You're well prepared.' She sighed and thought that of course he would be; he was a man of the world after all.

She groaned and felt the slippery, cool sheath guarding his arousal; her hands impatiently guided him to her, longing for the moment when he would fill her completely. She flipped onto him and arched up, her hands on his broad chest, her small breasts tipping teasingly towards him. 'I know you're moving on and I like it that way.' Did she? Yes, she did! 'I *need* this.' She leaned forward, bottom sticking up provocatively, and covered her mouth with his. 'The last thing I would take a gamble on is with a pregnancy.'

'You wouldn't want to be stuck with a loser like me?' Leo grinned, because those words had never passed his lips before. 'A travelling writer hoping to make his fortune?' He curved his hands on her rear and inserted himself into her. He drove into her and Brianna felt a surge of splintering pleasure as he moved deep inside her. Her head was flung back and he could feel the ends of her long hair on his thighs, brushing against them.

'A guy could feel insulted.'

She was on her back before she knew it and he was rear-ing up over her, big, powerful and oh, so breathtakingly beautiful, one-hundred per cent alpha male.

She came with such intensity that she had to squeeze her eyes shut on the gathering tears. She knew her fingers were digging in to the small of his back and they dug harder as she felt him swell and reach his orgasm inside her.

God, nothing had ever felt *that* good. Years of celibacy, running the pub and coping with all the day-to-day worries had obviously had the effect of making her respond like a wanton to being touched. She had never been like that before. But then, she had been so much younger when she had met Danny. Had the years and the tough times released some sort of pent-up capacity for passion that she had never known about?

'So...' Leo drawled, rolling onto his side then pulling her to face him so that their naked bodies were front to front and still touching, almost as though neither of them wanted to break the physical contact. 'You were telling me all about how you were using me to get you out of a dry patch.' He inserted his thigh between her legs and felt her wetness slippery against his skin.

'I never said that,' Brianna murmured.

'You didn't have to. The word "need" gave it away.'

'Maybe you're right. It's been a slog for the past few years. Don't get me wrong, there have been times when I've enjoyed running this place. It's just not how I expected my life to turn out.'

'What had you expected?'

'I expected to be married with a couple of kids, pursuing the art career that never took off, as it happens.'

'Ah. And the couple of kids and the wedding ring would have been courtesy of the heartbreaker?'

'He dumped me.' It had haunted her, had been responsible for all the precautions she had taken to protect herself. Yet lying here, with his thigh doing wonderful things between her legs, stirring up all the excitement that had only just faded, she could barely remember Danny's face. He had stopped being a human being and had become just a vague, disturbing recollection of a past mistake. She couldn't care less what had become of him, so how on earth had he carried on having such an influence on her behaviour?

'I wasn't good enough,' she said, anger replacing the humiliation that usually accompanied this thought. 'We went out for ages; when I thought that we really were destined to be together, he broke it to me that I had just been a good time at university. Dad was ill and I had discovered that the guy I thought I was in love with had been using me all along for a bit of fun. At least *you've* been honest and up-front.'

'Honest and up-front?'

'You're moving on. You're not here to stay. No illusions. I like that.'

'Before you start putting me on a pedestal and getting out the feather brush to dust my halo, I should tell you that you know very little about me.'

'I know enough.'

'You have little to compare me with. I'm a pretty ruthless bastard, if you want the truth.'

Brianna laughed, a clear, tinkling sound of pure amusement. She sifted her fingers through his dark hair and curled up closer to him which kick-started a whole lot of very pleasurable sensations that had him hardening in record time.

He edged her back from him and looked at her, unsmiling. 'You've been hurt once. You've spent years buried here, working beyond the call of duty to keep the wolves from the door. You've had no boyfriends, no distractions to occupy your time. Hell, you haven't even been able to wring out an hour or two to do your painting. And then along I come. I'm not your knight in shining armour.'

'I never said that you were!' Brianna pulled back, hurt and confused at a sudden glimpse of ruthlessness she wouldn't have imagined possible.

'It's been my experience that what women say is often at variance to what they think. I won't be hanging around—and even if I lived next door to you, Brianna, I don't do long-term relationships.'

'What do you mean, you *don't do long-term relationships*?'

'Just what I say, so be warned. Don't make the mistake of investing anything in me. What we have is sexual attraction, pure and simple.' He softened and gentled his voice. 'We have something that works at this precise moment in time.'

But it was more than that. What about the conversations they had had; the moments of sharing generated by close proximity? Some sixth sense stopped her from pointing that out. She was finding it difficult to recognise the cool, dark eyes of this stranger looking at her.

'And stop treating me as though I'm a stupid kid,' she bit out tightly, disentangling herself from him. 'I was one of those once.' Her voice was equally cool. 'I don't intend to repeat the same mistake twice. And, if you think that I would ever let myself get emotionally wrapped up with someone who doesn't want to spend his life in one place, then you're crazy. I value security. When I fall for someone, it will be someone who wants to settle down and isn't scared of commitment. I'm thankful that you've been honest enough to tell me as it is, but you have nothing to fear. Your precious independence isn't at risk.'

'If that's the case, why are you pulling away from me?'

'I don't like your tone of voice.'

'Just so long as it's not what I say but how I'm saying it,' he murmured softly. He tugged her back towards him and Brianna placed her hand on his shoulder but it was a pathetically weak attempt to stave off the fierce urgings of her body.

As his hand swept erotically along her thigh, she shimmied back towards him, the coolness in his eyes forgotten, the jarring hardness of his voice consigned to oblivion.

They made love slowly, touching each other everywhere, absorbing each other's pleasurable groans. She tasted him with as much hunger as he tasted her. She just couldn't get enough of him—at her breasts, between her thighs, urging her to tell him what she wanted him to do and telling her in explicit detail what he wanted her to do to him.

Eventually, just as she was falling into a light, utterly contented doze, she heard the insistent buzz of her mobile phone next to the bed where she had left it charging. She was almost too sleepy to pick up but, when she did, she instantly sat up, drawing the covers around her.

Leo watched her, his keen antennae picking up her sudden tension, although from this end of the phone he could only hear monosyllabic replies to whatever was being said.

'Remember I told you about my friend? Bridget Mc Guire?' Brianna ended the call thoughtfully but remained holding the mobile, caressing it absently.

Leo was immediately on red-hot alert, although he kept his expression mildly interested and utterly expressionless. 'The name rings a bell...'

'They need to release her from hospital. There's been an accident on the motorway and they need all the beds they can get. So she's leaving tomorrow. The snow is predicted to stop. She's coming here...'

CHAPTER FOUR

'WHEN?' HE SLID out of the bed, strolled towards the window and stared down to a snowy, grey landscape. The sun had barely risen but, yes, the snow appeared to be lessening.

This was the reason he was here, pretending to be someone he wasn't. When he had first arrived, he had wondered how a meeting with his mother could possibly be engineered in a town where everyone seemed to know everyone else. Several lies down and his quarry would be delivered right to his doorstep. Didn't fate work in mysterious ways?

Brianna, sitting up, wondered what was going through his head.

'For the moment, they're going to transfer her to another ward and then, provided the snow doesn't get worse, they're going to bring her here tomorrow. You're making me nervous, standing by the window like that. What are you thinking? I have room here at the pub. It won't make any difference to you. You won't have to vacate your room—in fact, you probably won't even notice that she's here. I shall have her in the spare room next to my bedroom so that I can keep a constant eye on her, and of course I doubt she'll be able to climb up and down stairs.'

Leo smiled and pushed himself away from the window

ledge. When he tried to analyse what he felt about his birth mother, the most he could come up with was a scathing contempt which he realised he would have to attempt to conceal for what remained of his time here. Brianna might have painted a different picture, but years of preconceived notions were impossible to put to bed.

'So...' He slipped back under the covers and pulled her towards him. 'If we're going to have an unexpected visitor, then maybe you should start telling me the sort of person I can look forward to meeting and throw me a few more details...'

Brianna began plating their breakfast. Was it her imagination or was he abnormally interested in finding out about Bridget? He had returned to the bed earlier and she had thrown him a few sketchy details about her friend yet, off and on, he seemed to return to the subject. His questions were in no way pressing; in fact, he barely seemed to care about the answer.

A sudden thought occurred to her.

Was he really worried that their wonderful one-on-one time might be interrupted? He had made it perfectly clear that he was just passing through, and had given her a stern warning that she was not to make the mistake of investing in him, yet was he becoming possessive of her company without even realising it himself?

For reasons best known to himself, he was a commitment-phobe, but did he respond out of habit? Had he warned her off because distancing himself was an automatic response?

He might not want to admit it, but over the past few days they had got to know one another in a way she would never have thought possible. He worked while she busied herself with the accounts and the bookkeeping but, for a lot of the time, they had communicated. He had even looked at her ledgers, leading her to think that he might have been an accountant in a previous life. He had suggested ways to improve her finances. He had persuaded her to show him all the paintings she had ever done, which she kept in portfolios under the bed, and had urged her to design a website to showcase them. She had caught herself telling him so much more than she had ever told anyone in her life before, even her close friends. He made a very good listener.

His own life, he had confided, had been as uneventful as it came: middle class, middle of the road. Both of them were single children, both without parents. They laughed at the same things; they bickered over the remote control for the television in the little private lounge which was set aside for the guests, on those rare occasions she had some. With the pub closed, they had had lots of quality time during which to get to know one another.

So was he *scared* that the arrival of Bridget would signal the end of what they had?

With a sigh, she acknowledged that if the ambulance could make it up the lane to the pub to deliver their patient then her loyal customers could certainly make it as well. The pub would once again reopen and their time together would certainly be curtailed.

'I've been thinking,' she said slowly, handing him a plate of bacon, eggs and toast and sitting down. 'I might just keep the pub closed for a couple of weeks. Until the snow is well and truly over and the path outside the pub is completely safe.'

She told herself that this was something that made perfect sense. And why shouldn't she have a little break? The last break she had had was over summer when she had grabbed a long weekend to go to Dublin with her friends. At other times, while they'd been off having lovely warm holidays in sunny Spain or Portugal, she had always been holed up at the pub, unable to take the time off because she couldn't afford to lose the revenue.

So why shouldn't she have time off now? A couple of weeks wouldn't break the bank—at least, not completely. And she would make up for it later in the year. Leo had suggested a website to promote the pub and she would take him up on that. He had intimated that she could really take off with only minimal changes, a few things to bring the place up to date.

And, if she closed the pub for a couple of weeks, they would continue to have their quality time until he disappeared.

'It would be better for Bridget as well,' she hurried on, not wanting to analyse how much of this idea was down to her desire to keep him to herself for a little longer. 'She's going to need looking after, at least in the beginning, and it would give me the opportunity to really take care of her without having to worry about running the pub as well.'

'Makes sense, I suppose…'

'You won't be affected at all.'

'I know. You've already told me.'

'And I don't want you to think that your needs are going to be overlooked. I mean, what I'm trying to say is…'

Leo tilted his head to one side. She blushed very easily. Especially when you considered the hard life she had had and the financial worries she had faced. No one would ever be able to accuse her of not being a fighter.

'Is that you'll carry on making my breakfast for me? Fixing me sandwiches for lunch? Slaving over a recipe book for something to cook for dinner? Making sure my bed is…warm and that you're in it?'

'I'm not part of a package deal.' Brianna bristled, suddenly offended at the picture he painted of her. 'You haven't paid for me along with the breakfast, lunch and dinner.' She stood up and began clearing the dishes, only pausing when she felt his arms around her at the sink. When she looked straight ahead, she could see their dim reflection in the window pane, his head downbent, buried in her hair. He didn't like it when she tied it back so she had left it loose the past couple of days and now he wound one of the long, auburn strands around his finger.

His other hand reached underneath the sweater and she watched their hazy reflection, the movement of his hand caressing her breast, playing with her nipple, rubbing the pad of his thumb over it. Liquid pooled between her legs, dampening her underwear and making her squirm and shift in his embrace.

She could feel his hard arousal nudging her from behind and, when she half-closed her eyes, her imagination took flight, dwelling on the image of her touching him there, licking and sucking with his fingers tangled in her hair. She wanted to do the same now. She pictured him kneeling like a penitent at her feet, her body pressing against the wall in her bedroom, her legs parted as he tasted her.

He seemed to have the ability to make her stop thinking the second he laid a finger on her and he did it as easily as someone switching a tap off.

She watched, eyes smoky with desire, as he pushed the jumper up; now she could see the pale skin of her stomach and his much darker hands on her breasts, massaging them, teasing them, playing with her swollen, sensitive nipples.

She shuddered and angled her neck so that he could kiss her.

'I know you're not part of the package,' he murmured. 'And, just to set the record straight, I enjoy you a hell of a lot more than I enjoy the meals you prepare.'

'Are you implying that I'm a bad cook?' He had undone

the top button of her jeans and she wriggled as he did the same with the zip, easing the jeans down over her slim hips, exposing her pale pink briefs.

'You're a fantastic cook. One of the best.' He stood back slightly so that she could swivel to face him.

'You're a terrible liar.'

Leo flushed guiltily at this unwittingly inaccurate swipe, said in jest.

'Don't bank on that,' he murmured into her ear. 'You forget that I've already warned you that I'm a ruthless bastard.'

'If you really *were* a ruthless bastard, then you wouldn't have to warn me. I'd see all the giveaway signs.' She tip-toed and drew his head down so that she could kiss him. Her body was heating up, impatiently anticipating the moment when it could unite with his.

In the heat of passion, it was always him who thought about protection. So he was scrupulous when it came to taking no chances—that didn't mean that he wasn't becoming more attached to her, did it? The fact he didn't want an unwanted pregnancy any more than she did, didn't indicate that his nomadic lifestyle wasn't undergoing a subtle ground-change...

'Touch me,' he commanded roughly and he rested his hands on her hips and half-closed his eyes as she burrowed underneath his jumper, her hands feathering across his chest, pausing to do wonderful things to his nipples. He was breathing quickly, every sinew and muscle stretched to a point of yearning that made a nonsense of his legendary self-control.

He yanked his jumper off and heard her sigh with pleasure, a little, soft sigh that was uniquely hers. His eyes were still half-closed and he inhaled slightly to accommodate her fumbling fingers as they travelled downwards to un-button and unzip his jeans.

Outside a watery sun was making itself known, pushing through the blanket of leaden grey of the past few days. Like an unfamiliar visitor, it threaded its way tentatively into the kitchen, picking up the rich hues of her hair and the smooth, creamy whiteness of her skin.

He stilled as she lowered herself to begin pulling down his jeans, taking his boxers with them until they were at his ankles and he stepped out of them and kicked them to one side.

He couldn't withhold his grunt of intense satisfaction as she began delicately to lick the tip of his erection. He was so aroused that it was painful and as he looked down at the crown of her head, and her pink, darting tongue as it continued to tease him, he became even more aroused.

'You're driving me crazy, woman…' His voice was un-steady, as were his hands as he coiled his fingers into her hair.

Brianna didn't say anything. His nakedness had her firing on all cylinders and his vulnerability, glimpses of which she only caught when they were making love, was the most powerful of aphrodisiacs. She took him in her mouth, loving the way every atom of pleasure seemed to be transmitted from him to her via invisible, powerful pathways. As she sucked and teased, her hands caressed, and she was aware of his big, strong body shaking ever so slightly. How could he make her feel so powerful and so helpless at the same time?

She was so damp, her body so urgent for his, that she itched to rip off her clothes. Her jumper was back in place and it felt heavy and uncomfortable against her sensitised skin. She gasped as he pulled her up, and she obediently lifted her arms so that he could remove the offending jumper. The cool air hit her heated breasts like a soothing balm.

'I can't make it to the bedroom...' He breathed heavily as she wriggled out of the jeans and then he hoisted her onto the kitchen table, shoving aside the remnants of their breakfast—the jar of marmalade, the little ceramic butter dish, the striped jug with milk. Surprisingly, nothing crashed to the ground in the process.

When he stood back, he marvelled at the sight of her naked beauty: her arms outstretched, her eyes heavy with the same lust that was coursing through his bloodstream like an unstoppable virus.

Her vibrant hair streamed out around her, formed a tangle over one breast, and the glimpse of a pink nipple peeping out was like something from an erotic X-rated magazine. Her parted legs were an invitation he couldn't refuse, nor was his body allowing him the luxury of foreplay. As she raised her knees, he embedded himself into her in one hard, forceful thrust and then he lifted her up and drove again into her, building a furious rhythm and somehow ending up with her pressed against the kitchen wall, her legs wrapped around him.

Her hair trailed over her shoulder, down her back, a silky mass of rich auburn. He felt her in every part of him in a way that had never happened with any woman before. He didn't get it, but he liked it. He was holding her underneath her sexy, rounded bottom and as he thrust long and deep into her he looked down at her little breasts bouncing in time to their bodies. The tips of her nipples were stiff and swollen, the big, flattened pink discs encircling them swollen and puffy. Every square inch of her body was an unbelievable turn-on and, even as he felt the satiny tightness of her sheath around him, he would have liked to close his mouth over one of those succulent nipples so that he could feast on its honeyed sweetness.

They came as one, their bodies fused, their breathing mirroring each other.

'That was…indescribable.' He eased her down and they stood facing one another, completely naked. Sanity began restoring itself, seeping through the haze of his hot, replete satisfaction. He swore under his breath and turned away. 'The condom…it seems to have split…'

Brianna's eyes widened with shock. She went over to her bundle of clothes and began getting dressed. He looked horrified. There was a heavy, laden silence as he likewise began getting dressed.

'It's okay. It takes more than one mistake for a person to get pregnant! If you read any magazine there are always stories of women trying for months, *years,* to conceive…' Her menstrual cycle had always been erratic so it was easy to believe that.

Leo shook his head and raked his fingers through his hair. 'This is a nightmare.'

'I won't get pregnant! I'm one-hundred per cent sure about that! I know my body. You don't have to look as though…as though the sky has fallen in!'

Yes, he was a nomad. Yes, he had just jacked in his job to embark on a precarious and unpredictable career. But did he have to look so damned *appalled*? And then, hard on the heels of that thought, came wrenching dismay at the insanity of thinking that a pregnancy wouldn't be the end of the world. God, what was she *thinking*? Had she gone completely *mad*?

She snatched the various bits and pieces left on the kitchen table and began slamming them into cupboards.

'God knows, you're probably right,' he gritted, catching her by the arm and pulling her round to face him. 'But

I've had sufficient experience of the fairer sex to know that they—'

'*What* experience? What are you talking about?'

Leo paused. Money bred suspicion and he had always been suspicious enough to know that it was a mistake to trust contraception to the opposite sex.

Except, how could he say that when he was supposed to be a struggling writer existing on the remnants of his savings from whatever two-bit job he had been in? How could he confess that five years previously he had had a scare with a woman in the dying stages of their relationship. The Pill she claimed to have been on, which she then later denied... Two weeks of hell cursing himself for having been a trusting idiot and, in the end, thankfully there had been no pregnancy. There was nothing he could have done in the circumstances, but a split condom was still bad news.

But how could he concede that his vast financial reserves made him a natural target for potential gold-diggers?

'You must really think that you're such a desirable catch that women just can't help wanting to tie you down by falling pregnant!'

'So you're telling me that I'm *not* a desirable catch?' Crisis over. Deception, even as an acceptable means to an end, was proving unsavoury. He smiled a sexy half-smile, clearing his head of any shade of guilt, telling himself that a chance in a million did not constitute anything to get worked up about.

'There are better options...' The tension slowly seeped out of her although she was tempted to pry further, to find out who these determined women were—the ones he had bedded, the ones who had wanted more.

She tried to picture him in his other life, sitting in a cubicle behind a desk somewhere with a computer in front of him. She couldn't. He seemed so at home in casual clothes; dealing with the snow; making sure the fireplace was well supplied with logs; doing little handyman jobs around the place, the sort she usually ended up having to pay someone to do for her. He now had a stubbly six o'clock shadow on his jawline because he told her that he saw no point in shaving twice a day. He was a man made for the great outdoor life. And yet...

'You were going to tell me about Bridget,' Leo said casually, moving to sit at the table and shoving his chair out so that he could stretch his legs in front of him. 'Before you rudely decided to interrupt the conversation by demanding sex.'

Brianna laughed. Just like that, whatever mood had swept over her like an ugly, freak wave looming unexpectedly from calm waters dissolved and disappeared.

'As I said, you'll like her.' She began unloading the dishwasher, her mind only half-focused on what she was saying; she was looking ahead to the technicalities of keeping the pub shut, wondering how long she could afford the luxury, trying to figure out whether her battered four-wheel drive could make it to the village so that she could stock up on food...

Leo's lips twisted with disdain. 'Funnily enough, whenever someone has said that to me in the past I'm guaranteed to dislike the person in question.' For the first time, he thought of his birth mother in a way that wasn't exclusively abstract, wasn't merely a jigsaw piece that had to be located and slotted in for the completed picture.

What did she look like? Tall, short, fat, thin...? And from whom had he inherited his non-Irish looks? His adoptive parents had both been small, neat and fair-haired. He had towered above them, dark-haired, dark-eyed, olive-skinned…as physically different from them as chalk from cheese.

He stamped down his surge of curiosity and reminded himself that he wasn't here to form any kind of relationship with the woman but merely finally to lay an uncertain past to rest. Anger, curiosity and confusion were unhappy life companions and the faster he dispensed with them, the better.

'You're very suspicious, Leo.' Brianna thought back to his vehement declaration that women couldn't be trusted when it came to contraception. 'Everyone loves Bridget.'

'You mentioned that she didn't have a…partner.' A passing remark on which Brianna had not elaborated. Now, Leo was determined to prise as much information out of her as he could, information that would be a useful backdrop for when he met the woman the following day. It was a given, he recognised, that some people might think him heartless to extract information from the woman he was sleeping with, but he decided to view that as a necessity—something that couldn't be helped, something to be completely disassociated from the fact that they were lovers, and extremely passionate lovers at that.

Life, generally speaking, was all about people using people. If he hadn't learned that directly from his adoptive parents, then he certainly must have had it cemented somewhere deep within his consciousness. Perhaps, and in spite of his remarkably stable background, the fact that he was adopted had allowed a seed of cynicism to run rampant over the years.

'She doesn't talk much about that.'

'No? Why not? You're her…what would you say…confidante? I would have thought that she would find it a comfort to talk to you about whatever happened. I mean, you've known each other how long? Were your parents friends with the woman?'

Brianna laughed. 'Oh, gosh, no!' She glanced round the kitchen, making sure that all her jobs were done. 'Bridget is a relative newcomer to this area.'

'Really...' Leo murmured. 'I was under the impression that she was a valued, long-standing member of the community.' He almost laughed at the thought of that. Valued member of the community? Whilst jettisoning an unwanted child like an item of disposable garbage? Only in a community of jailbirds would someone like that have been up for consideration as a valued member.

'But now you tell me that she's a newcomer. How long has she been living in the area?'

'Eight years tops.'

'And before that?'

Brianna shot him a look of mild curiosity but, when he smiled that smile at her, that crooked, sexy half-smile, she felt any niggling questions hovering on the tip of her tongue disappear.

'You're asking a lot of questions,' she murmured breathlessly. He signalled for her to come closer and she did, until he could wrap his arms around her and hold her close.

'Like I said, I have a curious mind.' He breathed in the clean floral scent of her hair and for a few seconds forgot everything. 'You shouldn't have put your jumper back on,' he remarked in a voice that thrilled her to the core. 'I like looking at your breasts. Just the perfect mouthful...'

'And I have calls to make if I'm to keep the pub shut!' She slapped away his wandering hand, even though she would have liked nothing more than to drag him up to the bedroom to lay claim to him. 'And you have a book to work on!'

'I'd rather work on you...'

'Thank goodness Bridget isn't here. She'd be horrified.'

Leo nearly burst out laughing. 'And is this because she's the soul of prurience? You still haven't told me where she came from. Maybe she was a nun in her former life?' He began strolling out of the kitchen towards the sitting room with the open fire which he had requisitioned as his working space. His computer was shut and there was a stack of novels by the side of it, books he had picked from her collection. He had already started two, abandoned them both and was reaching the conclusion that soul-searching novels with complicated themes were not for him.

'There's no need to be sarcastic.' Brianna hovered by the table as he sat down. She knew that he demanded complete privacy when he was writing, sectioning off a corner of the sitting area, his back to the window. Yet somehow it felt as though their conversation was not quite at an end, even though he wasn't asking any further questions.

'Was I?'

His cool, dark eyes rested on her and she flushed and traced an invisible pattern with her finger on the table. Was there something she was missing? Some important link she was failing to connect?

'You've known this woman for a few years...'

'Nearly seven. She came to the pub one evening on her own.'

'In other words, she has a drinking habit?'

'No! She'd moved to the area and she thought it might be a way of meeting people! We have quiz nights here once a month. She used to come for the quiz nights, and after a while we got chatting.'

'Chatting about where she had come from? Oh no; of course, you know nothing about that. And I'm guessing not many clues as to what she was doing here either? It's a small place for a woman who wants to meet people...'

'It's a community. We make outsiders feel welcome.' She blushed at her unwitting choice of words. 'I felt sorry for her,' Brianna continued hurriedly. 'I started an over-forties' quiz night, ladies only, so that she could get talking to some of them.'

Leo was mentally joining the dots and was arriving at a picture not dissimilar to the one he had always had of the woman who had given birth to him—with a few extra trimmings thrown in for good measure.

A new life and a new start for someone with a dubious past to conceal. Tellingly, no one knew about this past life, including the girl who had supposedly become her anchor in the community.

It didn't take a genius to figure out that, where there were secrets that required concealment, those secrets were dirty little ones. He had received half a picture from Brianna, he was certain of it—the rosy half, the half that didn't conform to his expectations.

'And you did all this without having a clue as to this woman's past?'

'I don't need to know every single detail about someone's past to recognise a good person when I see one!' She folded her arms tightly around her and glared down at him. She should have let him carry on with his writing. Instead, she had somehow found herself embroiled in an argument she hadn't courted and was dismayed at how sick it made her feel. 'I don't want to argue with you about this, Leo.'

'You're young. You're generous and trusting. You're about to give house room to someone whose past is a mystery.' He drew an uneasy parallel with his own circumstance, here at the pub under a very dubious cloud of deceit indeed, and dismissed any similarities. He was, after all, as upstanding and law-abiding as they came. No shady past here.

On the very point of tipping over into anger that he was in the process of dismissing her as the sort of gullible fool who might be taken in by someone who was up to no good, another thought lodged in the back of her mind. It took up residence next to the pernicious feel-good seed that had been planted when she had considered the possibility that he might not be welcoming Bridget because he cherished their one-to-one solitude.

Was he seriously *worried* about her? And if he was… That thought joined the other links in the chain that seemed to represent the nebulous beginnings of a commitment…

She knew that she was treading on very dangerous ground even having these crazy day dreams but she couldn't push them away. With her heart beating like a jack hammer, she attempted to squash the thrilling notion that he was concerned about her welfare.

'Do you think that my friend might be a homicidal maniac in the guise of a friendly and rather lonely woman?'

Leo frowned darkly. Brianna's thoughts about Bridget were frankly none of his concern, and irrelevant to the matter in hand, but he couldn't contain a surge of sudden, disorienting protectiveness.

Brianna had had to put her dreams and ambitions on hold to take charge of her father's failing business, whilst at the same time trying to deal with the double heartbreak of her father's death and her lover's abandonment. It should have been enough to turn her into an embittered shrew. Yet there was a transparent openness and natural honesty about her that had surfaced through the challenging debris of her past. She laughed a lot, she seldom complained and she was the sort of girl who would never spare an act of kindness.

'When people remove themselves for no apparent reason to start a new beginning, it's usually because they're running away from something.'

'You mean the police?'

Leo shrugged and tugged her towards him so that she collapsed on his lap with a stifled laugh. 'What if she turns into an unwanted pub guest who overstays her welcome?' He angled her so that she was straddling him on his lap and delicately pushed up the jumper.

'Don't be silly,' Brianna contradicted him breathlessly. 'You should get down to your writing. I should continue with my stock taking…'

In response to that, Leo eased the jumper off and gazed at her small, pert breasts with rampant satisfaction. He began licking one of her nipples, a lazy, light, teasing with the tip of his tongue, a connoisseur sampling an exquisite and irresistible offering.

'She has a perfectly nice little house of her own.' There was something wonderfully decadent about doing this, sitting on his lap in the middle of the empty pub, watching him as he nuzzled her breast as if he had all the time in the world and was in no hurry to take things to the next level.

'But—' Leo broke off. 'Here…' he flicked his tongue against her other nipple '…she would have…' he suckled for a few seconds, drawing her breast into his mouth '…you…' a few kisses on the soft roundness until he could feel her shiver and shudder '…to take care of her; cook her food…'

He held one of her breasts in his hand so that it was pushed up to him, the nipple engorged and throbbing, and he delicately sucked it. 'Brianna, she might seem perfectly harmless to you.' With a sigh, he leaned back in the chair and gave her tingling breasts a momentary reprieve. 'But what do you do if she decides that a cosy room in a pub, surrounded by people and hands-on waitress service, is more appealing than an empty house and the exertion of having to cook her own food?'

At no point was he inclined to give the woman the benefit of the doubt. In his experience, people rarely deserved that luxury, and certainly not someone with her particular shady history.

Never one ever to have been possessive or protective about the women in his life, he was a little shaken by the fierce streak suddenly racing through him that was repelled by the thought of someone taking advantage of the girl sitting on his lap with the easy smile, the flushed face and tousled hair.

'You need to exercise caution,' he muttered grimly. He raked his fingers through his hair and scowled, as though she had decided to disagree with him even though she hadn't uttered a word.

'Then maybe,' Brianna teased him lightly, 'you should stick around and make sure I don't end up becoming a patsy...'

The journey here should have taken no time at all; his stay should have been over in a matter of a couple of days. There were meetings waiting for him and urgent trips abroad that could only be deferred for so long. It had never been his intention to turn this simple fact-finding exercise into a drama in three parts.

'Maybe I should,' he heard himself say softly. 'For a while...'

'And you can chase her away if she turns out to be an unscrupulous squatter who wants to take advantage of me.' She laughed as though nothing could be more ridiculous and raised her hand to caress his cheek.

Leo circled her slim wrist with his fingers in a vice-like grip. 'Oh, if she tries that,' he said in a voice that made her shiver, 'she'll discover just what a ruthless opponent I could prove to be—and just how regrettable it can be to cross my path.'

CHAPTER FIVE

THE SNOW HAD stopped. As grey and leaden as the skies had been for a seemingly unstoppable length of time, the sun now emerged, turning a bleak winter landscape into a scene from a movie: bright-blue skies and fields of purest white.

Bridget's arrival had been delayed by a day, during which time Leo had allowed the subject of her dubious, unknown past to be dropped. No more hassle warning Brianna about accepting the cuckoo in the nest. No more words of caution that the person she might have considered a friend and surrogate mother might very well turn out to be someone all set to take full advantage of her generous nature and hospitality. There would be fallout from this gesture of putting the woman up while she recuperated; he was certain of that and he would be the man to deal with it. So he might never have specialised in the role of 'knight in shining armour' in his life before, but he was happy with his decision.

London would have to take a little back seat for a while. He was managing to keep on top of things just fine via his computer, tablet and smartphone and, if anything dramatic arose, then he could always shoot down to sort it out.

All told, the prospect of being holed up in the middle of nowhere was not nearly as tedious as he might have

imagined. In fact, all things considered, he was in tre-
mendously high spirits.

Of course, Brianna was a hell of a long way responsible for that. He glanced up lazily from his computer to
the sofa where she was sitting amidst piles of paperwork.
Her hair was a rich tumble over her shoulders and she was
cross-legged, leaning forward and chewing her lip as she
stared at her way-past-its-sell-by-date computer which was
on the low coffee table in front of her.

In a couple of hours the ambulance would be bringing
his destiny towards him. For the moment, he intended to
enjoy his woman. He closed the report in front of him and
stood up, stretching, flexing his muscles.

From across the small, cosy room, Brianna looked up
and, as always happened, her eyes lingered, absorbing the
beautiful sight of his long, lean body; the way his jeans
rode low on his hips; the way he filled out her father's
checked flannel shirt in just the right way. He had loosely
rolled the sleeves to his elbow and his strong, brown forearms, liberally sprinkled with dark hair, sent a little shiver
of pleasurable awareness rippling through her.

'You should get a new computer.' Leo strolled towards
her and then stood so that he was looking down at the col-
umns of numbers flickering on the screen at him. 'Something faster, more up-to-date.'

'And I should have a holiday, somewhere warm and far
away… And I'll do both just as soon as I have the money.'
Brianna sighed and sat back, keenly aware of him looking over her. 'I just want to get all this stuff out of the way
before Bridget gets here. I want to be able to devote some
quality time to her.'

Leo massaged her neck from behind. Her hair, newly
washed, was soft and silky. The baggy, faded pink jumper
was the most unrevealing garment she could have worn

but he had fast discovered that there was no need for her to wear anything that outlined her figure. His imagination was well supplied with all the necessary tools for providing graphic images of her body that kept him in a state of semi-permanent arousal.

'Was the urgent trip to the local supermarket part of the quality-service package?' He moved round to sit next to her, shoving some of the papers out of the way and wondering how on earth she could keep track of her paperwork when there seemed to be no discernible order to any of it.

'I know you don't agree with what I'm doing; I know you think I should just leave her to get on with things on her own but—'

'This conversational road is guaranteed to lead to a dead end,' he drawled smoothly. 'Let's do ourselves a favour and not travel down it.'

'You enjoyed the supermarket experience.' Brianna changed the subject immediately. She didn't want an argument. She didn't even want a mild disagreement, and she knew what his feelings were on the subject of their soon-to-be visitor, even though he had backed off from making any further disparaging remarks about her naïvety in taking in someone whose entire life hadn't been laid out on a plate for her perusal.

'It was…novel.' Actually, Leo couldn't recall the last time he had set foot in a supermarket. He paid someone to deal with the hassle of all that.

'Margaret Connelly has only just opened up that place. Actually, it's not a supermarket as such.'

'I'd noticed.'

'More of a…a…'

'Cosy space filled to overflowing with all manner of things, of which food is only one component? Brussels sprouts nestling next to fishing tackle…?'

'The lay out can seem a bit eccentric but the food's all fresh and locally sourced.'

Leo grinned, swivelled her so that she had her back to him and began massaging her shoulders. 'You sound like an advertisement for a food magazine. I'm going to have to put my foot down if you're thinking of slaving over a hot stove preparing dishes on this woman's whim.'

Brianna relaxed into the massage and smiled with contentment. She felt a thrill of pleasure at the possessive edge to his voice. 'She has to be on a bland diet—doctor's orders.'

'That's irrelevant. You're not going to be running up and down those stairs because someone rings a bell and wants a cup of tea immediately.'

'*You* could always do the running for me if you think I'm too fragile to cope.'

Leo's lips curled with derision and he fought down the impulse to burst into sardonic laughter. 'Running and doing errands for people isn't something I do.'

'Especially not in this instance,' Brianna said, remembering that he *was*, after all, a paying guest despite their unusual arrangement. He had given her a shocking amount of money for his stay thus far, way too much, and had informed her that it was something to do with company expenses owed to him before he'd quit his job. She hadn't quite understood his explanation. Nor had he backed down when she refused to take the full amount.

'Take it,' he had ordered, 'Or I'll just have to find another establishment that will accommodate what I want to pay. And I shall end up having to take taxis here to see you. You wouldn't want to add that further cost to a poor, struggling writer, would you?'

'What do you mean?' Leo stilled now.

'I mean you're a customer. Running up and down stairs

isn't something I would ask you to do. That would be ridiculous. I would never take advantage of you like that.'

'But you *would* take advantage of me in other ways… because I happen to enjoy you taking advantage of me in all those other imaginative ways of yours…'

'Is *sex* all you ever think about?' she murmured, settling back against him and sighing as he slipped his hands underneath her jumper to fondle her breasts.

No. Sex most certainly had never been *all* he thought about. In fact, Leo contemplated with some bemusement, although he had always enjoyed an exceptionally varied and active sex life it had never been at the top of his priorities. Sex, and likewise women, had always taken a back seat to the more important driving force in his life, which was his work.

'You bring out the primitive in me,' he said softly into her ear. 'Is it my fault that your body drives me insane?' He relaxed into the sprawling sofa so that he had Brianna half-lying on top of him, her back pressed against his torso, her hair tangled against his chest. He removed one hand to brush some of her hair from his cheek and returned his hand to her jeans to rest it lightly on her hip. A stray sheet of paper wafted to the ground, joining a disconcerting bundle already there.

Brianna's body was responding as it always did, with galloping excitement and sweet anticipation. She might very well joke that sex was the only thing on his mind, but it certainly seemed to have taken over all her responses as well. Even the problem supplier she knew she had to deal with urgently was forgotten as she undid the button and zip of her jeans.

'Tut, tut, tut; you're going to have to do better than that, my darling. How am I expected to get my hand where it wants to be?'

Brianna giggled softly. He had no hang-ups about where they made love. His lack of inhibition was liberating and it worked in tandem with her own period of celibacy to release an explosion of passion she had never experienced in her life before. She couldn't seem to get enough of him.

She wriggled out of her jeans and he chuckled.

'For someone with a body like yours, I'm always amazed that you've stuck to the functional underwear...' He thought about seeing her in something small, lacy and sexy, lying in his super-king-sized bed in his penthouse apartment in Chelsea.

The thought was random, springing from nowhere and establishing itself with such graphic clarity that he drew in his breath sharply with shock.

Hell, where was his mind going? This was a situation that was intensely enjoyable but it only functioned within very definite parameters. Like it or not, they were operating within a box, a box of his own making, and freedom from that box in any way, shape or form was a possibility that was not to be entertained.

With that in mind, he cleared his head of any inappropriate, wandering thoughts about her being in his apartment. Crazy.

'Is that how you like your women?' Brianna asked casually. He never spoke about his love life. A sudden thought occurred to her and, although this hardly seemed the time for a deep, meaningful conversation, she had to carry on regardless. 'Is that why you're here?'

'What are you talking about?'

Brianna wriggled so that she was on her side, still nestled between his legs, and she looked up at him, breathing in that clean, tangy scent that always seemed to scramble all her thoughts. His hand was curved on her hip, fingers dipping against her stomach. Even that small, casual contact did devastating things to her already hot, aroused body. She was slippery and wet, and it was mad, because she had to get things together before Bridget arrived.

'You know, all the way from London.'

'No clue as to what you're talking about.'

'Never mind. We need to start tidying up.' She sighed. 'Bridget's going to be here soon.'

'Didn't they say that they would telephone you before they left the hospital?'

'Yes, but…'

'No phone call yet.' After the disturbing tangent his thoughts had taken only moments before when he had imagined her in his apartment, the last thing Leo wanted was a heart-to-heart. He wanted to touch her; touching her was like a magic antidote to thinking. Hell, he had worked while he had been here, but his mind had not been on the cut and thrust of business deals with its customary focus. This was as close to a holiday as he had had in years, and the last thing he had expected when he had started on this journey of discovery.

He reached under her knickers, a dull beige with not a scrap of lace in sight, and slid his finger against the wet crease, seeking out the little nub of her clitoris. This was so much better than talking and a damn sight more worthwhile than the sudden chaos of thoughts that had earlier afflicted him.

Brianna moaned softly as he continued to rub. She squirmed and sighed and half-closed her eyes, her nostrils flaring and her breathing thickening the closer she came to a point of no return.

Questions still hovered at the back of her mind like pesky insects nipping at her conscience, refusing to go away, but right now she couldn't focus on any of that. Right now, as the movement of his strong, sure hand picked up speed, she moaned and arched her body and wave upon wave of pleasure surged through her. Lying with her back to him, she couldn't see his face, only his one hand moving inside her while the other was flattened against her thigh and his legs, spread to accommodate her body between them. But she knew that he was watching her body as he brought her to orgasm and the thought of that was wantonly exciting.

She was aware of her uneven, shaky breathing as she lay back and let her heated body return to planet Earth.

For a few seconds, there was silence. Leo linked his fingers on her stomach and absently noted the way they glistened with her honeyed wetness.

'I'm going to start clearing all my paperwork away,' she said eventually. 'I don't seem to have made much progress with our snack supplier. I'm going to have a shower.' She eased herself over his legs and off the sofa, and began tidying the papers which were strewn everywhere. She didn't bother to put on her jeans, instead choosing to scoop them up and drape them over one arm.

It all came down to sex. She knew that she was being silly for objecting to that because this was a situation that was never going to last longer than two minutes. It was something she had jumped into, eyes wide open, throwing caution to the winds and accepting it for what it was, and there was no excuse now for wanting more than what had been laid on the table.

Except…had she thought that this perfect stranger would possess the sort of complex personality that she would end up finding strangely compulsive?

Could she ever have imagined that an unexpected, astounding, elemental physical attraction would turn into something that seemed to have her in its hold? That taking a walk on the wild side, breaking out of the box for just a little while, would have repercussions that struck a chord of fear into her?

She wanted more. She couldn't even begin to think of him leaving, carrying on with his travels. He had entered her life, and what had previously been bland, dull and grey was now Technicolor-bright. She alternated between reading all sorts of things behind his words and actions and then telling herself that she really shouldn't.

'You never said...' Brianna begin heading up the stairs, carrying as much with her as she could: files, her jeans and her trainers, which she didn't bother to stick on completely.

Behind her, Leo scooped up the remainder of the files and began following her.

'Never said what?'

'All those women you're so cynical about...' She paused to look at him over her shoulder. 'The ones who wear lacy underwear...'

'Did I ever say that? I don't recall.'

'You didn't have to. I can read between the lines.' She spun back round and headed towards her suite of rooms, straight to the study, where she dumped all the files she had been carrying. She stood back and watched as he deposited the remainder of them, including her computer, which was as heavy as a barrow full of bricks, and—yes, he was right—in desperate need of updating.

Brianna took in his guarded, shuttered expression and knew instinctively that she was treading on quicksand, even though he hadn't rushed in with any angry words telling her to mind her own business. She could see it on his face. Her heart was beating so fiercely that she could almost hear it in the still quiet of the room.

'I'm going to have a shower,' she mumbled, backing out of the little office. 'On my own, if you don't mind.'

Leo frowned and raked his fingers through his hair, but he didn't move a muscle.

She wanted to *talk*. Talk about what? His exes? What was the point of that? When it came to women and meaningful conversations, they invariably led down the same road: a dead end. He wasn't entirely sure where his aversion to commitment came from and he knew, if he were honest, that his parents would have wanted to see him travel down the traditional route of marriage and kids by thirty—but there it was; he hadn't. He had never felt the inclination. Perhaps a feeling of security was something that developed in a mother's womb and having been given up for adoption, by definition, had wiped that out and the security of making money, something tangible he could control, had taken its place.

At any rate, the minute any woman started showing signs of crossing the barriers he had firmly erected around himself, they were relegated to history.

He told himself that there should be no difficulty in this particular relationship following the same course because he could see, from the look in her eyes, that whatever chat she wanted to have was not going to begin and end with the choice of underwear his women were accustomed to wearing.

He told himself that in fact it would be *easier* to end this relationship because, in essence, it had never really functioned in his real life. It had functioned as something sweet and satisfying within a bubble. And within a day or two, once he had met his birth mother and put any unanswered questions to rest, he would be gone.

So there definitely was *no* point to a lengthy heart-to-,heart. He strolled into the bedroom and glanced down at the snow which was already beginning to thaw.

She emerged minutes later from the shower with a towel

wrapped round her, her long hair piled up on top of her head and held in place with a hair grip. Tendrils had escaped and framed her heart-shaped face. She looked impossibly young and vulnerable.

'What are you doing in my bedroom?'

'Okay. So I go out with women who seem to spend a lot of money on fancy underwear.' He glowered at her. 'I don't know what that has to do with anything.' He watched as she rummaged in her drawers in silence and fetched out some faded jogging bottoms and a rugby-style jumper, likewise faded.

Brianna knew that a few passing remarks had escalated into something that she found unsettling. She didn't want to pry into his life. She wanted to be the adult who took this on board, no questions asked and no strings attached. Unfortunately...

She disappeared back into the bathroom, changed and returned to find him still standing in an attitude of challenging defensiveness by the bedroom window.

'You wanted to talk...' he prompted, in defiance of common sense. 'Are you jealous that I've had lovers? That they've been the sort of women who—?'

'Don't run pubs, live on a shoestring and wear functional underwear from department stores? No, I'm not jealous. Why would I be?'

'Good. Because, personally, I don't do jealousy.' It occurred to Leo that there were a number of things he didn't do when it came to his personal relationships and yet, here he was, doing one of them right now: having a *talk*.

'Have we ended up in bed because you think I make a change?' She took a deep breath and looked him squarely in the face. He was so beautiful. He literally took her breath away. 'From all those women you went out with?' If *she* found him beautiful, if he blew *her* mind away, then why wouldn't he have had the same effect on hordes of other women?

'No! That's an absurd question.'

'Is it?' She turned on her heel and began back down the stairs to the bar area where she proceeded to do some unnecessary tidying. He lounged against the bar, hands in his pockets, and watched her as she worked. She appeared to be in no hurry to proceed with the conversation she had initiated. The longer the silence stretched between them, the more disgruntled Leo became.

Moving to stand directly in front of her, so that she was forced to stop arranging the beer mats in straight lines on the counter, he said, 'If there's any comparison to be done, then you win hands down.'

Brianna felt a stupid surge of pleasure. 'I'm guessing you *would* say that, considering we're sleeping together and you're pretty much stuck here.'

'Am I? The snow seems to be on its way out.' They weren't touching each other, but he could feel her as forcibly as if they had been lying naked on her bed.

'How long do you intend to stay?' She flushed and glanced down at her feet before taking a deep breath and looking at him without flinching. 'I'm going to keep the pub closed for another fortnight but just in case, er, bookings come in for the rooms, it would be helpful for me to know when yours might be free to, er, rent out…'

And this, Leo thought, was the perfect opportunity to put a date in the calendar. It was as obvious as the nose on his face that her reason for wanting to find out when he would be leaving had nothing to do with a possible mystery surge in bookings for the rooms. He didn't like being put in a position of feeling trapped.

'I told you I'd stick around, make sure you didn't get ripped off or taken advantage of by this so-called best buddy of yours,' he said roughly. 'I won't be going any-where until I'm satisfied that you're okay on that score. Satisfied? No; you're not. What else is on your mind, Bri-anna? Spit it out and then I can disappear for a shower and some work and leave you to get on with your female bonding in peace.'

Brianna shrugged. Everything about his body language suggested that he was in no mood to stand here, answer-ing questions. Perhaps, she thought, answering questions was something else he *didn't do* when it came to women. Like jealousy. And yet he wasn't moving. 'Did you end up here on the back of a bad relationship?' she asked bluntly. She shot him a defiant look from under her lashes. 'I know you don't want me to ask lots of questions…'

'Did I ever say that?'

'You don't have to.'

'Because, let me guess, you seem to have a hot line to my thoughts!' He scowled. Far from backing away from an interrogation he didn't want and certainly didn't need, his feet appeared to be disobeying the express orders of his brain. Against all odds, he wanted to wipe that defensive, guarded expression from her face. 'And no, I did not end up here on the back of a bad relationship.' He had ended up here because…

Leo flushed darkly, uncomfortable with where his thoughts were drifting.

'I'm sleeping with you, and I know it's going to end soon, but I still want to know that you're not using me as some sort of sticking plaster while you try to recover from a broken heart.'

'I've never suffered from a broken heart, Brianna.' Leo smiled crookedly at her and stroked the side of her face with his finger.

Just then her mobile buzzed and after only a few seconds on the phone she said to him, 'Bridget's had her final check-up with the consultant and they're going to be setting off in about half an hour. They'll probably be here in about an hour and a half or so. Depends on the roads, but the main roads will all be gritted. It's only the country lanes around here that are still a little snowed up.'

An hour and a half. Leo's lips thinned but, despite the impending meeting with his mother, one which he had quietly anticipated for a number of years ever since he had tracked down her whereabouts, his focus remained exclusively on the girl standing in front of him.

'Everyone has suffered from a broken heart at some point.' She reverted to her original topic.

'I'm the exception to the rule.'

'You've never been in love?'

'You say that as though it's inconceivable. No. Never. And stop looking at me as though I've suddenly turned into an alien life-form. Are you telling me that, after your experience with the guy you thought you would be spending your life with, you're still glad to have *been in love*?'

He lounged against the bar and stared down at her. He had become so accustomed to wearing jeans and an assortment of her father's old plaid flannel shirts, a vast array of which she seemed to have kept, that he idly wondered what it would feel like returning to his snappy handmade suits, his Italian shoes, the silk ties, driving one of his three cars or having Harry chauffeur him. He would return to the reality of high- powered meetings, life in the fast lane, private planes and first-class travel to all four corners of the globe.

Here, he could be a million miles away, living on another planet. Was that why he now found himself inclined to have this type of conversation? The sort of touchy-feely conversation that he had always made a point of steering well clear from? Really, since when had he ever been into probing any woman about her thoughts and feelings about past loves?

'Of course I am,' Brianna exclaimed stoutly. 'It may have crashed and burned, but there were moments of real happiness.'

Leo frowned. Real happiness? What did she mean by that? Good sex? He didn't care much for a trip down happiness lane with her. If she felt inclined to reminisce over the good old days, conveniently forgetting the misery that had been dished up to her in the end, then he was not the man with the listening ear.

'How salutary that you can ignore the fact that you were taken for a ride for years... Are you still in touch with the creep?'

Brianna frowned and tried to remember what the creep looked like. 'No,' she said honestly. 'I haven't got a clue what he's up to. The last I heard from one of my friends from uni, he had gone abroad to work for some important law firm in New York. He's disappeared completely. I was heartbroken at the time, but it doesn't mean that I'm not glad I met him, and it doesn't mean that I don't hope to meet that someone special at some point in the future.'

And as she said that a very clear picture of Mr Special floated into her mind. He was approximately six-two with bronzed skin, nearly black hair and lazy, midnight-dark eyes that could send shivers racing up and down her spine. He came in a package that had carried very clear health warnings but still she had fallen for him like a stupid teenager with more hormones than common sense.

Fallen *in lust* with him, she thought with feverish panic. She hadn't had a relationship with a guy for years! And then he had come along, drop-dead gorgeous, with all the seductive anonymity of a stranger—a writer, no less. Was it any wonder that she had fallen *in lust* with him?

Was that why she could now feel herself becoming *clingy*? Not wanting him to go? Losing all sense of perspective?

'And no one special is on the scene here?' Leo drawled lazily. 'Surely the lads must be queuing up for you...'

Of course there had been nibbles, but Brianna had never been interested. She had reasoned to herself that she just didn't have the time; that her big, broken love affair had irreparably damaged something inside her; that, just as soon as the pub really began paying its way, she would jump back into the dating world.

All lies. She could have had all the time in the world, a fully paid-up functioning heart and a pub that turned over a million pounds a year in profit and she still wouldn't have been drawn to anyone—because she had been waiting for just the moment when Leo Spencer walked through the door, tall, dark and dangerous, like a gunslinger in a Western movie.

'I'm not interested in anything serious at the moment,' she said faintly. 'I have loads of time. Bridget should be arriving any minute now.'

'At least an hour left to go...' How was it possible to shove all thoughts of his so-called mother out of his head? He had almost forgotten that the woman was on her way.

'I need to go and get her room ready.'

'Haven't you already done that? The potpourri and the new throw from the jack-of-all-trades supermarket?'

She had. But suddenly she wanted nothing more than to escape his suffocating masculine presence, find a spot where she could straighten out her tangled thoughts.

'Well, I want to make sure that it's just right,' she said sharply.

Leo stepped aside. 'And I think I'll go and have a shower and do something productive with my time in my room.'

'You don't have to disappear! You're a paying guest, Leo. You can come down and do your writing in your usual place. Bridget and I won't make any noise at all. She'll probably just want to rest.'

'I'll let the two of you do your bonding in peace,' he murmured. 'I'll come down for dinner. I take it you'll be cooking for three?'

'You know I will, and please don't start on the business of me being a mug.'

Leo held up both hands in a gesture of mock-indignation that she could even contemplate such a thing.

Brianna shot him a reluctant smile. 'You wait and see. You'll end up loving her as much as I do.'

'Yes. We'll certainly wait and see,' Leo delivered with a coolness that Brianna felt rather than saw, because his expression was mildly amused. She wondered if she had perhaps imagined it.

Leo remained where he was while she disappeared upstairs to do her last check of the bedroom where Bridget would be staying, doubtless making sure that the sheets were in place with hospital precision, corners tucked in just so.

His mouth curled with derision. The thought of her being taken advantage of filled him with disgust. The thought of her putting her trust in a woman who would inevitably turn out not to be the person she thought she was made his stomach turn. He could think of no other woman whose trusting nature should be allowed to remain intact.

He slammed his clenched fist against the wall and gritted his teeth. He had come here predisposed to dislike the woman who had given birth to him and then given him away. He was even more predisposed to dislike her as the woman who, in the final analysis, would reveal her true colours to the girl who had had the kindness to take her under her wing.

The force of his feelings on this subject surprised him. It was like the powerful impact of a depth charge, rumbling down deep in the very core of him.

He didn't wait for the ambulance bearing his destiny towards him to arrive, instead pushing himself away from the wall and heading up to his bedroom. His focus on work had been alarmingly casual and now, having had a shower, he buried himself in reports, numbers, figures and all the things that usually had the ability to fully engage his attention.

Not now. His brain refused to obey the commands being issued to it. What would the woman look like? Years ago, he could have had pictures taken of her when he had set his man on her trail, but he hadn't bothered because she had been just a missing slot in his life he had wanted to fill. He hadn't given a damn what she looked like. Now, he had to fight the temptation to stroll over to the window and peer out to the courtyard which his room overlooked.

He stiffened when he eventually heard the sound of the ambulance pulling up and the muffled rise and fall of voices which carried up to his room.

Deliberately he tuned out and exerted every ounce of will power to rein in his exasperating, wandering mind.

At a little after five, he got a text from Brianna: a light early supper would be served at six. If he wanted to join them, then he was more than welcome. Sorry she couldn't come up to his room but she had barely had time to draw breath since Bridget had arrived.

She had concluded her text with a smiley face. Who

did that? He smiled and texted back: yes, he'd be down promptly at six.

He sat back and stared at the wall. In an hour he would meet his past. He would put that to bed and then, when that was done, he would move on, back to the life from which he had taken this brief respite.

He had an image of Brianna's face gazing at him, of her lithe, slim body, of the way she had of humming under her breath when she was occupied doing something, and the way she looked when she was curled up on the sofa trying to make sense of her accounts.

But of course, he thought grimly, that was fine. Sure, she would be on his mind. They might not have spent a long time in each other's company but it had been concentrated time. Plenty long enough for images of her to get stuck in his head.

But she was not part of his reality. He would check out the woman who had given birth to him, put his curiosity to bed and, yes, move on...

CHAPTER SIX

LEO WASN'T QUITE sure when the snow had stopped, when the furious blizzards had turned to tamer snowfall, and when that tamer snowfall had given way to a fine, steady drizzle that wiped clean the white horizon and returned it to its original, snow-free state.

He couldn't quite believe that he was still here. Of course, he returned to London sporadically mid-week and was uncomfortably aware of his conscience every time he vaguely intimated that there were things to do with the job he had ditched: paperwork that needed sorting out; problems with his accommodation that needed seeing to; social engagements that had to be fulfilled because he should have returned to London by now.

The lie he had blithely concocted before his game plan had been derailed did not sit quite so easily now. But what the hell was he to do?

He rose to move towards the window and stared distractedly down at the open fields that backed the pub. It was nearly three. In three hours, the pub would be alive with the usual Friday evening crowd, most of whom he knew by sight if not by name.

How had something so straightforward become so tangled in grey areas?

Of course, he knew. In fact, he could track the path

as clearly as if it was signposted. His simple plan—go in, confirm all the suspicions he had harboured about his birth mother, close the book and leave—had slipped out of place the second he had been confronted with Brianna.

She was everything the women he had dated in the past were not. Was that why he had not been able to kill his ill-advised temptation to take her to bed? And had her natural, open personality, once sampled, become an addiction he found impossible to jettison? He couldn't seem to see her without wanting her. She turned him on in ways that were unimaginable. For once in his life, he experienced a complete loss of self-control when they made love; it was a drug too powerful to resist.

And then…his mother. The woman he had prejudged, had seen as no more than a distasteful curiosity that had to be boxed and filed away, had not slotted neatly into the box he had prepared.

With a sigh, he raked his fingers through his hair and glanced over his shoulder to the reports blinking at him, demanding urgent attention, yet failing to focus it.

He thought back to when he had met her, that very first impression: smaller than he'd imagined, clearly younger, although her face was worn, very frail after hospital. He had expected someone brash, someone who fitted the image of a woman willing to give away a baby. He had realised, after only an hour in her company, that his preconceived notions were simplistic. That was an eventuality he had not taken into account. He lived his life with clean lines, no room for all those grey areas that could turn stark reality into a sludgy mess. But he had heard her gentle voice and, hard as he had tried not to be swayed, he had found himself hovering on the brink of needing to know more before he made his final judgement.

Not that anything she had said had been of any importance. The three of them had sat on that first evening and had dinner while Brianna had fussed and clucked and his mother had smiled with warm sympathy and complained about her garden and the winter vegetables which would sadly be suffering from negligence.

She had asked him about himself. He had looked at her and wondered where his dark eyes and colouring came from. She was slight and blonde with green eyes. At one point, she had murmured with a faraway expression that he reminded her of someone, someone she used to know, but he had killed that tangent and moved the conversation along.

Seeing her, meeting her, had made him feel weird, confused, uncomfortable in his own skin. A thousand questions had reared their ugly heads and he had killed them all by grimly holding on to his anger. But underneath that anger he had known only too well that the foundations on which he had relied were beginning to feel shaky. He had no longer known what he should be feeling.

Since that first day, he had seen her, though, only in brief interludes and always with Brianna around. Much of the time she spent in her bedroom. She was an avid reader. He had had to reacquaint himself with literature in an attempt to keep his so-called writer occupation as credible as possible. He had caught himself wondering what books she enjoyed reading.

On his last trip to London, he had brought with him a stack of books and had been surprised to discover that, after a diet of work-related reading, the fiction and non-fiction he had begun delving into had not been the hard work he had expected. And at least he could make a halfway decent job of sounding articulate on matters non-financial.

Where this was going to lead, he had no idea.

He headed downstairs and pulled up short at the sight

of Bridget sitting in the small lounge set aside from the bar area, which Brianna had turned into her private place if she didn't want to remain in her bedroom.

Because of Bridget, the pub now had slightly restricted opening and closing hours. He assumed that that was something that could only be achieved in a small town where all the regulars knew what was going on and would not be motivated to take their trade elsewhere—something that would have been quite tedious, as 'elsewhere' was not exactly conveniently located to get to by foot or on a bike.

'Leo!'

Leo paused, suddenly indecisive at being confronted by his mother without Brianna around as an intermediary. She was sitting by the large bay window that overlooked the back garden and the fields behind the pub. Her fair hair was tied back and the thin, gaunt lines of her face were accentuated so that she resembled a wraith.

'Brianna's still out.' She patted the chair facing hers and motioned to him to join her. 'We haven't chatted very much at all. Why don't you have a cup of tea with me?'

Leo frowned, exasperated at his inability to take control of the situation. Did he want to talk to his mother on a one-to-one basis? Why did he suddenly feel so...*vulnerable* and at odds with himself at the prospect? Wasn't this why he had descended on this back-of-nowhere town in the first place? So things had not turned out quite as he had anticipated, but wasn't it still on his agenda to find out what the woman was like?

He was struck by the unexpectedly fierce urge to find out what had possessed her to throw him to the wolves.

He thought that perhaps the facade she portrayed now was a far cry from the real person lurking underneath, and he hardened himself against the weak temptation to be swept along into thinking that she was innocent, pathetic and deserving of sympathy. Could it be that, without Brianna there to impress, her true colours would be revealed?

'I think I'll have black coffee myself. Would you like to switch to coffee?'

'No, my dear, my pot of tea will be fine, although perhaps you could refresh the hot water. I feel exhausted if I'm on my feet for too long and I've been far too active today for my own good.'

He was back with a mug of coffee and the newly refreshed pot of tea which he rested on the table by her, next to the plate of biscuits which were untouched.

'I'm so glad I've caught you on your own,' she murmured as soon as he had taken a seat next to her. 'I feel I barely know you and yet Brianna is so taken with you after such a short space of time.'

'When you say "taken with me"...' He had told Brianna that he saw it as his duty to keep an eye on her houseguest, to scope her out, because a houseguest with a mysteriously absent past was not a houseguest to be trusted. Was the houseguest doing the same with him? He almost laughed out loud at the thought. As always when he was in her company, he had to try not to stare, not to try and find similarities...

'She's, well, I suppose you know about...'

'About the guy who broke her heart when she was at university?'

'She's locked herself away for years, has expressed no interest in any kind of love life at all. I've always thought it sad for someone so young and caring and beautiful, that she wouldn't be able to share those qualities with a soul mate.'

Leo said something and nothing. He looked at the cane leaning against the chair and wondered what it must feel like to be relatively young and yet require the assistance of a walking stick.

'If you don't mind my asking, how old are you, Bridget?'

Bridget looked at him in surprise. 'Why do you ask?'

Leo shrugged and sipped his coffee.

'Not yet fifty,' Bridget said quietly. 'Although I know I look much, much older.' She glanced away to stare through the window and he could see the shine of unshed tears filming her eyes.

In his head, he was doing the maths.

'But we weren't talking about me,' she said softly.

Leo felt a surge of healthy cynicism and thought that if she figured she could disappear behind a veil of anonymity then she was in for a surprise. There were things he wanted to find out, things he *needed* to find out, and he knew himself well—what he wanted, he got, be it money, women or, in this case, answers. The unsettling hesitancy that had afflicted him off and on, the hesitancy he hated because he just wasn't a hesitant person, thankfully disappeared beneath the weight of this new resolve.

'Indulge me,' he said smoothly. 'I hate one-sided conversations. I especially hate long chats about myself… I'm a man, after all. Self-expression is a luxury I don't tend to indulge very often. So, let's talk about you for a minute. I'm curious. You're not yet fifty, you tell me? Seems very young to have abandoned the lure of city lights for a quiet place like this.' He still could not quite believe that she was as young as she said. She looked like a woman in her sixties.

'What you may call "quiet", by which I take it you mean "dull", is what I see as peace.'

'Brianna said that you've been here a while—quite a few years; you must have been even younger when you decided that you wanted "peace".' He couldn't help thinking that, although their colouring was different, he had her eyes, the shape of them. He looked away with a frown.

She blushed and for the first time he could see her relative youth peep out from behind the care-worn features.

'My life's been…complicated. Not quite the life I ever expected, matter of fact.'

Curiosity was gnawing at him but he kept his features perfectly schooled, the disinterested bystander in whom he hoped she would confide. He could feel in his bones that the questions he wanted answering were about to be answered.

'Why don't you talk about it?' he murmured, resting the cup on the table and leaning towards her, his forearms resting on his thighs. 'You probably feel constrained talking to Brianna. In such a small, close-knit community perhaps you didn't want your private life to be thrown into the public arena?' He could see her hesitate. Secrets were always burdensome. 'Not that Brianna would ever be one to reveal a confidence, but one can never be too sure, I suppose.'

'And who knows how long I have left?' Bridget said quietly. She plucked distractedly at the loose gown she was wearing and stared off through the window as though it might offer up some inspiration. 'My health isn't good: stress, built up over the years. The doctor says I could have another heart attack at any time. They can't promise that the next time round won't be fatal.' She looked at him pensively. 'And I suppose I wouldn't want to burden Brianna with my life story. She's a sweet girl but I would never want to put her in a position of having to express a sympathy she couldn't feel.'

Or pass judgement which would certainly mean the end of your happy times with her, Leo thought with another spurt of that healthy cynicism, cynicism he knew he had to work at.

'But I don't come from here…' he encouraged in a low voice.

'I grew up in a place not dissimilar to this,' she murmured. 'Well, bigger, but not by a lot. Everybody knew everybody else. All the girls knew the boys they would end up marrying. I was destined for Jimmy O'Connor; lived two doors away. His parents were my parents' best friends. In fact, we were practically born on the same day, but that all went up the spout when I met Robbie Cabrera. *Roberto* Cabrera.'

Leo stilled. 'He was Spanish?'

'Yes. His father had come over for a temporary job on a building site ten miles out of town. Six months. He was put into our school and all the girls went mad for him. I used to be pretty once, when I was a young girl of fifteen…you might not guess it now.' She sighed and looked at him with a girlish smile which, like that blush, brought her buried youth back up to the surface.

'And what happened?' Leo was surprised he could talk so naturally, as though he was listening to someone else's story rather than his own.

'We fell madly in love. In the way that you do when you're young and innocent.' She shot him a concerned looked and he hastened to assure her that whatever she told him would stay with him. Adrenaline was pumping through him. He hadn't experienced this edge-of-the-precipice feeling in a very long time. If ever. This was why he was here. The only reason he was here.

From nowhere, he had a vision of Brianna laughing and telling him that there was nothing more satisfying than growing your own tomatoes in summer, and teasing him that he probably wouldn't understand because he probably lived in one of those horrible apartment blocks where you wouldn't be able to grow a tomato if your life depended on it.

He thought of himself, picking her up then and hauling her off to his bedroom at a ridiculous hour after the pub had finally been closed. Thought of her curving, feline smile as she lay on his bed, half-naked, her small, perfect breasts turning him on until his erection felt painful and he couldn't get his clothes off fast enough.

'Sorry?' He leaned in closer. 'You were saying…?'

'I know. You're shocked. And I don't mean to shock you but it's a relief to talk about this; I haven't with anyone. I fell pregnant. At fifteen. My family were distraught, and of course there was no question of abortion, not that we would have got rid of it. No, Robbie and I were committed to one another.'

'Pregnant…'

'I was still a child myself. We both were. We wanted to keep it but my parents wouldn't allow it. I was shipped off to a convent to give birth.'

'You wanted to keep it?'

'I never even held it. Never knew if it was a boy or a girl. I returned to Ireland, went back to school, but from that moment on my parents were lost to me. I had three younger siblings and they never knew what had happened. Still don't. Family life was never the same again.'

'And the father of the child?'

Bridget smiled. 'We ran away. His father ended up on a two-year contract. We skipped town when we were sixteen and headed south. I kept my parents informed of my whereabouts but I couldn't see them and they never lived down the shame of what I'd done. I don't think they cared one way or the other. Robbie always kept in touch with his parents and in fact, when they moved to London, we stayed with them for several months before they returned to Spain.'

'You…ran away…' For some reason, his normally agile mind seemed to be lagging behind.

'We were very happy, Robbie and me, for over twenty years until he died in a hit-and-run accident and then I went back to Ireland. Not back to where I grew up, but to another little town, and then eventually I came here.'

'Hit and run…' The tidal rush of emotions was so intense that he stood up and paced like a wounded bear, before dropping back into the chair.

'We never had any more children. Out of respect for the one I was forced to give up for adoption.'

Suddenly the room felt too small. He felt himself break out in a fine perspiration. Restless energy poured through him, driving him back onto his feet. His cool, logical mind willed him to stay put and utter one or two platitudes to bring the conversation to a satisfactory conclusion. But the chaotic jumble of thoughts filling every corner of his brain was forcing him to pace the room, his movements uncoordinated and strangely jerky.

He was aware of Bridget saying something, murmuring, her face now turned to the window, lost in her thoughts.

There was so much to process that he wasn't sure where to start. So this was the story he had been waiting for and the ending had not been anticipated. She hadn't been the convenient stereotype he had envisaged: she wasn't the irresponsible no-hoper who had given him away without a backward glance. And, now that he knew that, what the hell happened next?

He turned to her, saw that she had nodded off and almost immediately heard the sound of Brianna returning.

'What's wrong?' About to shut the door, Brianna stood still and looked at him with a concerned frown. She had been out shopping and had had to force herself to take her time, not to hurry back, because she just wanted to *see* him, to *be* with him. 'Is…is Bridget all right?' She walked towards him and he automatically reached out to help her with the bags of shopping. Brianna stifled the warm thrill that little slice of pretend domesticity gave her.

'Bridget is fine. She appears to have fallen asleep. Have you ever…?' Leo murmured, reaching to cup the nape of her neck so that he could pull her towards him. 'Thought that you were going in one direction, only to find that the signposts had been switched somewhere along the way and the destination you were heading to turned out to be as substantial as a mirage?'

Brianna's heart skipped a beat. Was he talking about *her*? she wondered with heightened excitement. Was he trying to tell her that meeting her had derailed him? She placed her hand flat on his chest and then slipped it between two buttons to feel his roughened hair.

'What are you saying?' she whispered, wriggling her fingers and undoing the buttons so that she could now see the hard chest against which her fingers were splayed.

'I'm saying I want to have sex with you.' And right at that moment it really was exactly what he wanted. He wanted to drown the clamour of discordant voices in his head and just make love to her. With the bags of shopping in just one hand, he nudged her towards the kitchen.

'We can't!' But her hands were scrabbling over him, hurrying to undo the buttons of his shirt, and her breasts were aching in anticipation of being touched by him. 'Bridget…'

'Asleep.' He shut down the associated thoughts that came with mention of her name.

'I've got to start getting ready to open up.'

'But not for another half-hour. I assure you…' They

were in the kitchen now and he kicked the door shut behind him and pushed her towards the wall until she was backed up against it. 'A lot can be accomplished in half an hour.'

The low drawl of intent sent delicious shivers racing up and down her spine and she groaned as he unzipped her jeans and pushed his hand underneath her panties. Frustrated because his big hand couldn't do what it wanted to do thanks to the tightness of her jeans, he yanked them down, and Brianna quickly stepped out of them.

Bridget, she thought wildly, would have another heart attack if she decided to pop into the kitchen for something. But fortunately her energy levels were still very low and if she was asleep then she would remain asleep at least for another hour or so.

Her fingers dug into his shoulders and she uttered a low, wrenching groan as he pulled the crotch of her panties to one side and began rubbing her throbbing clitoris with his finger.

Her panties were damp with her arousal. She gave a broken sigh and her eyelids fluttered. She could feel him clumsily undoing his trousers and then his thick hardness pushing against her jumper.

This was fast and furious sex.

Where was his cool? Leo was catapulted right back to his days of being a horny teenager lacking in finesse, except he couldn't remember, even as a horny teenager, being as wildly out of control as he was now. He didn't even bother with taking off her jumper, far less his. He hooked his finger under her knickers and she completed the job of disposing of them. He could barely get it together to don protection. His hand was shaking and he swore in frustration as he ripped open the packet.

Then he took her. He hoisted her onto him and thrust into her with a grunt of pleasurable release. Hands under

her buttocks, he pushed hard and heard her little cry of
pleasure with intense satisfaction.

They came together, their bodies utterly united, both
of them oblivious to their surroundings.

He dropped her to the ground, his breathing heavy and
uncontrolled. 'Not usually my style.' But, as he watched
her wriggle back into her underwear and jeans, he figured
it could well become part of his repertoire without a great
deal of trouble.

'You look a little hot and flustered.' He gently smoothed
some tendrils of hair away from her face and Brianna
added that tender gesture to the stockpile she was mentally
constructing. She felt another zing of excitement when she
thought back to what he had said about his plans not going
quite as he had anticipated. She would have loved nothing
more than to quiz him further on the subject, but she would
let it rest for the moment. One thing she had learnt about
him was that he was not a man who could be prodded into
saying anything or doing anything unless he wanted to.

'Right—the bar. I need to get going. I need to check
on Bridget.'

Plus a million and one other things that needed doing,
including sticking away the stuff she had bought. All that
was running through her head as a byline to the pleasurable thought of the big guy behind her admitting to wanting more than a passing fling. A nomad would one day find
a place to stay put, wouldn't he? That was how it worked.
And, if he didn't want to stay put *here*, then she would be
prepared to follow him. She knew she would.

Her mind was a thousand miles away, so it took her a
few minutes to realise that something was wrong when she
entered the little lounge to check on Bridget.

She should have been in the chair by the window. It was
where she always sat, looking out or reading her book. But

she wasn't there. Her mind moved sluggishly as she quickly scanned the room and she saw the limp body huddled behind the chair about the same time as Leo did.

It felt like hours but in fact it could only have been a matter of seconds, and Leo was on it before her brain had really had time to crank into gear. She was aware of him gently inspecting Bridget while barking orders to her at the same time: make sure the pub was shut; fetch some water; get a blanket; bring him the telephone because his mobile phone was in his bedroom, then amending that for her to fetch his mobile phone after all.

'I'll call an ambulance!'

'Leave that to me.'

Such was his unspoken strength that it didn't occur to her to do anything but as he said. She shut the pub. Then it was upstairs to fetch his mobile phone, along with one of the spare guest blankets which she kept in the airing cupboard, only stopping en route to grab a glass of water from the kitchen.

'She's breathing,' was the first thing he said when she returned. 'So don't look so panicked.' He gestured to his phone, scrolled down and began dialling a number. She couldn't quite catch what he was saying because he had walked over to the window and was talking in a low, urgent voice, his back to her. Not that she was paying any attention. She was loosely holding Bridget, talking to her in soft murmurs while trying to assess what the damage was. It looked as though she had fallen, banged her head against the table and passed out. But, in her condition, what could be the ramifications of that?

'Right.' Leo turned to her and slipped the mobile phone into his jeans pocket. 'It's taken care of.'

'Sorry?'

'It's under control. The main thing is to keep her still. We don't know what she's broken with that fall.'

'I'm glad you said that it was a fall. That's what I thought. Surely that must be less serious than another heart attack. Is the ambulance on its way? I've made sure the "closed" sign's on the front door. When I get a chance, I'll ring round a couple of the regulars and explain the situation.'

Leo hesitated. 'No ambulance.'

Brianna looked at him, startled. 'But she's got to go to hospital!'

'Trust me when I tell you that I have things under control.' He squatted alongside them both. The time of reckoning had come and how on earth had he ever played with the thought that it wouldn't? How had he imagined that he would be able to walk away without a backward glance when the time came?

Of course, he certainly hadn't reckoned on the time coming in this fashion. He certainly hadn't thought that he would be the one rescuing his mother because it now seemed that there was more conversation left between them.

'You have things under control?' Brianna looked at him dubiously. 'And yet there's no ambulance on the way?'

'I've arranged to have her air-lifted to the Cromwell Hospital in London,' Leo said bluntly.

'I beg your pardon?'

'It should be here any minute soon. In terms of timing, it will probably get here faster than an ambulance would, even an ambulance with its sirens going.'

In the midst of trying to process what sounded like complete gibberish to her, Brianna heard the distant sound of an overhead aircraft. Landing would be no problem. In fact, there couldn't have been a better spot for an air ambulance to land. The noise grew louder and louder until it felt as though it would take the roof off the pub, and then there was a flurry of activity while she stood back, confused.

She became a mystified bystander as the professionals took over, their movements hurried and urgent, ferrying Bridget to the aircraft.

Then Leo turned to her. 'You should come.'

Brianna looked at him in complete silence. 'Leo... what's going on?' How had he managed to do *that*? Who on earth could arrange for someone to be airlifted to a hospital hundreds of, miles away? She had thought that maybe he had been in computers, but had he been in the medical field? Surely not. She was uneasily aware that there were great, big gaps in her knowledge about him but there was little time to think as she nodded and was hurried along to the waiting aircraft.

'I don't have any clothes.'

'It's not a problem.'

'What do you mean, it's *not a problem*?'

'We haven't got time to debate this. Let's go.'

Brianna's head was full of so many questions, yet something in her resisted asking any of them. Instead she said weakly, as they were lifted noisily into the air and the aircraft swung sharply away, leaving the pub behind, 'Do you think she'll be all right?' And then, with a tremulous laugh, because the detachment on his dark face filled her with a dreadful apprehension, 'I guess this would make a fantastic scene in your book...'

Leo looked at her. She was huddled against him and her open, trusting face was shadowed with anxiety.

This was a relationship that was never going to last. They had both been aware of that from the very start. He had made the position perfectly clear. So, in terms of conscience, he was surely justified in thinking that his was completely clear? But it still took a great deal of effort to grit his teeth and not succumb to a wave of unedited, pure regret for what he knew now lay on the horizon. But this wasn't the time to talk about any of this so he chose to ignore her quip about the book that was as fictitious as the Easter Bunny.

'I think she'll be fine but why take chances?'

'Leo…'

'We'll be at the hospital very shortly, Brianna.' He sighed deeply, pressed his thumbs against his eyes and then rested his head against the upright, uncomfortable seat. 'We'll talk once Bridget's settled in hospital.'

Brianna shivered as he looked away to stare out of the window but she remained silent; then there wasn't much time to do any thinking at all as everything seemed to happen at once and with impressive speed.

Once again she stood helplessly on the sidelines and watched as the machinery of the medical world took over. She had never seen anything like it and she was even more impressed at Leo's handling of the situation, the way he just seemed to take charge, the way he knew exactly what to do and the way people appeared to listen to him in a way she instinctively knew they wouldn't have to anyone else.

Like a spare part, she followed him into the hospital, which was more like a hotel than anything else, a hotel filled with doctors and nurses, somewhere designed to inspire confidence. The smallness of her life crowded her as she watched, nervously torn between wanting to get nearer to Bridget, who had now been established in a room of her own, and wanting to stay out of the way just in case she got mown down by the crisp efficiency of everyone bustling around their new patient.

It felt like ages until Bridget was examined, wheeled off for tests and examined again. Leo was in the thick of it. She, on the other hand, kept her distance and at one point was firmly ushered to a plush waiting room, gently encouraged to sit, handed a cappuccino and informed that she would help matters enormously if she just relaxed, that everything was going to be perfectly fine.

How on earth was she supposed to relax? she wondered. Not only was she worried sick, but alongside all her concerns about her friend other, more unsettling ideas were jostling in her head like pernicious, stinging insects trying to get a hold.

She was dead on her feet by the time Leo finally made an appearance and he, too, looked haggard. Brianna half-rose and he waved her back down, pulled one the chairs across and sat opposite her, legs apart, his arms resting loosely on his thighs.

More than anything else, she wanted to reach out and smooth away the tired lines around his eyes and she sat on her hands to avoid giving in to the temptation which here, and now, seemed horribly inappropriate.

'Leo, what's going on?'

'The main thing is that Bridget is going to be okay. It seems she stood up and fell as she was reaching for her cane. She banged her head against the edge of the table and knocked herself out. They've done tests to make sure that she suffered no brain damage and to ascertain that the shock didn't affect her heart.' He looked at her upturned face and flushed darkly.

'I'm amazed you rushed into action like that when she could have just gone to the local hospital.' She reached out tentatively to touch his arm and he vaulted upright and prowled through the shiny, expensive waiting room of which they were the only occupants.

'Brianna…' He paused to stare down at her and all of a sudden there was no justification whatsoever for any of the lies he had told. It didn't matter whether they had been told in good faith, whether the consequences had been unforeseen. Nor did the rights and wrongs of sleeping with the girl, now staring up at him, come into play.

'It's late. You need to get some rest. But more importantly we have to talk…'

'Yes.' Why was she so reluctant to hear what he had to say? Where was that gut reaction coming from?

'I'm going to take you back to my place.'

'I beg your pardon? You still have a place in London? What place? I thought you might have sold that—you know?—to do your travelling.'

Leo shook his head and raked his fingers through his dishevelled hair. 'I think when we get there,' he said on a heavy sigh, 'some of the questions you're asking yourself might begin to fall into place.

CHAPTER SEVEN

BRIANNA'S FIRST SHOCK was when they emerged from the hospital and Leo immediately made a call on his mobile which resulted, five minutes later, in the appearance of a top-of-the range black Range Rover. It paused and he opened the back door for her and stood aside to allow her to slide into the luxurious leather seat.

Suddenly she was seeing him in a whole new light. He was still wearing the jeans in which he had travelled, a long-sleeved jumper and one of the old coats which he had found in a cupboard at the back of the pub and which he had adopted because it was well lined. But even with this casual clothing he now seemed a different person. He was no longer the outdoor guy with that slow, sexy smile that dragged on her senses. There was a harshness to his face that she was picking up for the first time and it sent a shiver of apprehension racing up and down her spine.

The silence stretched on and on as the car slowly pulled away from the kerb and began heading into central London.

When she looked over to him, it was to quail inwardly at the sight of the forbidding cast of his features, so she pretended to be absorbed in the monotonous, crowded London landscape of pavements and buildings.

It was very late but, whereas in Ireland the night sky

would be dense and black at this hour and the countryside barely visible, here the streetlights illuminated everything. And there were people around: little groups shivering on the pavements, the odd business man in a suit and, the further towards the centre of London the car went, the busier the streets were.

Where one earth were they going? So he had a house in London. Why had he never mentioned that? Her mind scrabbled frantically to come up with some logical reason why he might have kept it a secret. Perhaps he was in the process of selling it. Everyone knew that it could take for ever to sell a property and, if he *was* selling it, then maybe he thought that there was no point mentioning it at all. But when she glanced surreptitiously at his forbidding profile, all the excuses she tried to formulate in her head withered and died.

'Where are we going? I know you said your house, but where exactly is that?'

Leo shifted and angled his body so that he was facing her. Hell, this was a total mess; he could only lay one-hundred per cent of the blame for that at his own door. He had behaved like a stupid fool and now he was about to be stuck handling the fallout.

Brianna was a simple country girl. He had known that the second he had seen her. She might have had the grit and courage to single-handedly run a pub, but emotionally she was a baby, despite her heartbreak. She was just the sort of woman he should have steered clear from, yet had he? No. He had found that curious blend of street-wise savvy and trusting naivety irresistible. He had wanted her and so he had taken her. Of course, she had jumped in to the relationship eyes wide open, yet he couldn't help but feel that the blame still lay entirely on his shoulders. He had been arrogant and selfish and those qualities, neither of which had caused him a moment's concern in the past, now disgusted him.

He harked back to his conversation with Bridget. Before it had turned to the illuminating matter of her past, she had wanted to talk to him about Brianna, had opened the subject by letting on that Brianna hadn't been involved with anyone since her loser boyfriend from university had dumped her. Leo now followed the path of that conversation which had never got off the starting blocks as it turned out.

Had she been on the brink of confiding just how deeply Brianna was involved with him?

Of course she had been! Why kid himself? He might have laid down his ground rules and told her that he was not in the market for involvement, but then he had proceeded to demonstrate quite the opposite in a hundred and one ways. He couldn't quite figure out how this had happened, but it had, and the time had come to set the matter straight.

'Knightsbridge,' he told her, already disliking himself for the explanation he would be forced to give. Less than twenty-four hours ago they had been making love, fast, furious love, her legs wrapped around him, as primitive and driven as two wild animals in heat. The memory of it threatened to sideswipe him and, totally inexplicably, he felt himself harden, felt his erection push painfully against his zip so that he had to shift a little to alleviate the ache.

'Knightsbridge. Knightsbridge as in *Harrods,* Knightsbridge?' The last time Brianna had been to London had been three years ago, and before that when she had been going out with Daniel. She would have had to be living on another planet not to know that Knightsbridge was one of the most expensive parts of London, if not the most expensive.

'That's right.' On cue, the gleaming glass building in which his duplex apartment was located rose upwards, arrogantly demanding notice, not that anyone could fail to pay attention and salute its magnificence.

He nodded towards it, a slight inclination of his head, and Brianna, following his eyes, gasped in shock.

'My apartment's there,' he told her and he watched as the colour drained away from her face and her eyes widened to huge, green saucers.

Before she could think of anything to say, the chauffeur-driven Range Rover was pulling smoothly up in front of the building and she was being ushered out of the car, as limp as a rag doll.

She barely noticed the whoosh of the lift as it carried them upwards. Nor did she take in any of her surroundings until she was finally standing in his apartment, a massive, sprawling testimony to the very best money could buy.

With her back pressed to the door, she watched as he switched on lights with a remote control and dropped blinds with another remote before turning to her with his thumbs hooked into the pockets of his jeans.

They stared at each other in silence and he finally said, the first to turn away, 'So this is where I live. There are five bedrooms. It's late; you can hit the sack now in one of them, or we can talk'

'You actually *own* this place?' Her gaze roamed from the slate flooring in the expansive hall to the white walls, the dark wood that replaced the slate and the edge of a massive canvas she could glimpse in what she assumed would be another grand space—maybe his living room.

'I own it.' He strolled through into the living area, which had been signposted by that glimpse of wall art. Following behind him, Brianna saw that it was a massive piece of abstract art and that there were several others on the walls. They provided the only glimpse of colour against a palette that was uniformly white: white walls, white rug against the dark wooden floor, white leather furniture.

'I thought you were broke.' Brianna dubiously eyed the chair to which she was being directed. She yawned and he instantly told her that she should get some rest.

'I'd prefer to find out what's going on.'

'In which case, you might need a drink.' He strolled towards a cabinet and she looked around her, only to refocus as he thrust a glass with some amber liquid into her hand.

He sat down next to her and leaned forward, cradling his drink while he took in her flushed face. He noticed that she couldn't meet his eyes and he had to steel himself against a wave of sickening emotion.

'We should never have slept together,' he delivered abruptly and Brianna's eyes shot to his.

'What do you mean?'

'I mean…' He swirled his drink round and then swallowed a long mouthful. Never had he needed a swig of alcohol more. 'When I arrived in Ballybay, it was not my intention to get involved with anyone. It was something that just seemed to happen, but it could have and should have been prevented. I blame myself entirely for that, Brianna.'

Hurt lanced through Brianna. Was this the same guy about whom she had been nurturing silly, girlish daydreams involving an improbable future? One where he stuck his hat on the door and decided to stay put, so that they could explore what they had? She felt her colour rise as mortification kicked in with a vengeance.

'And why is that?'

'Because I knew you for what you were, despite what you said. You told me that you were tough, that you weren't looking for anything committed, that you wanted nothing more from me than sex, pure and simple. I chose to believe you because I was attracted to you. I chose to ignore the voice of reason telling me that you weren't half as tough as you claimed to be.' Even now—and he could see her stiffening as she absorbed what he was saying—there was still a softness to her mouth that belied anything hard.

He found that he just couldn't remain sitting next to her. He couldn't feel the warmth she was radiating without all his thoughts going into a tailspin.

'I'm pretty tough, Leo. I've been on my own for a long time and I've managed fine.'

Leo prowled through the room, barely taking in the exquisite, breathtakingly expensive minimalist décor, and not paying a scrap of attention to the Serpentine glittering hundreds of metres in the distance, a black, broad stripe beyond the bank of trees.

'You've taken over your father's pub,' he said heavily, finishing the rest of his drink in one long gulp and dumping the glass on the low, squat table between the sofa and the chairs. It was of beaten metal and had cost the earth. 'You know how to handle hard work, but that's not what I'm talking about and we both know that. I told you from the start that I was just passing through and that hasn't changed. Not for me. I'm…I'm sorry.'

'I understood the rules, Leo.' Her cheeks were stinging and her hands didn't want to keep still. She had to grip the glass tightly to stop them from shaking. 'I just don't get…' she waved her hand to encompass the room in which they were sitting, with its floor-to-ceiling glass windows, its expensive abstract art and weirdly soulless, uncomfortable furniture '…all of this. What sort of job did you have before?'

Leo sighed and rubbed his eyes. It was late to begin this conversation. It didn't feel like the right time, but then what *would* be the right time? In the morning? The following afternoon? A not-so-distant point in the future? There *was* no right time.

'No past tense, Brianna.'

'Sorry?'

'There's no past tense. I never gave my job up.' He laughed mirthlessly at the notion of any such thing ever happening. He was defined by his work, always had been. Apart from the past few weeks, when he had played truant for the first time in his life.

'You never gave your job up...but...?'

'I run a very large and very complex network of companies, Brianna. I'm the boss. I own them. My employees report to me. That's why I can afford all of this, as well as a house in the Caribbean, an apartment in New York and another in Hong Kong. Have another sip of that drink. It'll steady your nerves. It's a lot to take in, and I'm sorry about that, but like I said I never anticipated getting in so deep... I never thought that I would have to sit here and have this conversation with you, or anyone else, for that matter.'

Brianna took a swig of the brandy he had poured for her and felt it burn her throat. She had a thousand angry questions running through her head but they were all silenced by the one, very big realisation—he had lied to her. She didn't know why, and she wasn't even sure that it mattered, because nothing could change the simple truth that he had lied. She felt numb just thinking about it.

'So you're not a writer.'

'Brianna, I'm sorry. No. The last time I did any kind of creative writing was when I was in school, and even then it had never been one of my stronger subjects.' She wasn't crying and somehow that made it all the harder. He had fired a lot of people in his time, had told aspiring employees that their aspirations were misplaced, but nothing had prepared him for what he was feeling now.

'Right.'

Unable to keep still, he sprang to his feet and began pacing the room. His thoughts veered irrationally, comparing the cold, elegant beauty of his sitting room and the warm, untidy cosiness of the tiny lounge at the back of her pub, and he was instantly angry with himself for allowing that small loss of self-control.

He had had numerous girlfriends in the past. He had always told them that commitment wasn't an option and, although quite a few had made the mistake of getting it into their heads that he might have been lying, he had never felt a moment's regret in telling the deluded ones goodbye.

'So what were you doing in Ballybay?' she asked. 'Did you just decide on the spur of the moment that you needed a break from…from the big apartment with the fancy paintings and all those companies you own? Did you think that you needed to get up close and personal with how the other half lives?'

She laughed bitterly. 'Poor Leo. What a blow to have ended up stuck in my pub with no mod cons, having to clear snow and help with the washing up. How you must have missed your flash car and designer clothes! I bet you didn't bank on having to stick around for as long as you did.'

'Sarcasm doesn't suit you.'

But he had flushed darkly and was finding it difficult to meet her fierce, accusatory green-eyed stare. 'I'm sorry,' Brianna apologised with saccharine insincerity. 'I find it really hard to be sweet and smiling when I've just discovered that the guy I've been sleeping with is a liar.'

'Which never made our passion any less incendiary.'

Her eyes tangled with his and she felt the hot, slow burn

of an unwitting arousal that made her ball her hands into angry fists. Unbelievable: her body responding to some primitive vibe that was still running between them like a live current that couldn't be switched off.

'Why did you bother to make up some stupid story about being a writer?' she flung at him. 'Why didn't you say that you were just another rich businessman who wanted to spend a few days slumming it and winding down? Why the fairy story? Was that all part of the *let's adopt a different persona*?' She kept her eyes firmly focused on his face but she was still taking in the perfection of the whole, the amazing body, the strong arms, the length of his legs. Knowing exactly what he looked like underneath the clothes didn't help. 'Well?' she persisted in the face of his silence.

'The story is a little more complex than a bid to take time out from my life here...'

'What do you mean?' She was overwhelmed by a wave of giddiness. She couldn't tear her eyes away from his face and she found that she was sitting ramrod erect, as rigid as a plank of wood, her hands positioned squarely on her knees.

'There was a reason I came to Ballybay.' Always in control of all situations, Leo scowled at the unpleasant and uncustomary sensation of finding himself on the back foot. Suddenly the clinical, expensive sophistication of his surroundings irritated the hell out of him. It was an unsuitable environment in which to be having this sort of highly personal conversation. But would 'warm and cosy' have made any difference? He had to do what he had to do. That was just the way life was. She would be hurt, but she was young and she would get over it. It wasn't as though he had made her promises he had had no intention of keeping!

He unrealistically told himself that she might even *ben-*

efit from the experience. She had not had a lover for years. He had crashed through that icy barrier and reintroduced her to normal, physical interaction between two people; had opened the door for her to move forward and get back out there in the real world, find herself a guy to settle down with…

That thought seemed spectacularly unappealing and he jettisoned it immediately. No point losing track of the moment and getting wrapped up in useless speculation and hypotheses.

'A reason?'

'I was looking for someone.' He sat heavily on the chair facing hers and, as her posture was tense and upright, so his was the exact opposite as he leaned towards her, legs wide apart, his strong forearms resting on his thighs. He could feel her hurt withdrawal from him and it did weird things to his state of mind.

'Who?'

'It might help if I told you a little bit about myself, Brianna.'

'You mean aside from the lies you've already told me?'

'The lies were necessary, or at least it seemed so at the time.'

'Lies are never necessary.'

'And that's a point we can possibly debate at a later date. For now, let me start by telling you that I was adopted at birth. It's nothing that is a state secret, but the reason I came to Ballybay is because I traced my birth mother a few years ago and I concluded that finding her was something I had to do. Not while my adoptive parents were still alive. I loved them very much; I would never have wanted to hurt them in any way.'

Brianna stared at him open-mouthed. It felt as though the connections in her brain were all backfiring so that nothing made sense any more. What on earth was he going on about? And how could he just *sit there* as though this was the most normal conversation in the world?

'You're adopted?' was all she could say weakly, because she just couldn't seem to join the dots in the conversation.

'I grew up in leafy, affluent suburbia, the only child of a couple who couldn't have children of their own. I knew from the beginning that I was adopted, and it has to be said that they gave me the sort of upbringing that most kids could only dream about.'

'But you didn't want to find your real mother until now?'

'*Real* mother is not a term I would use. And finding her would not have been appropriate had my adoptive parents still been alive. Like I said, I owe everything to them, and they would have been hurt had I announced that I was off on a journey of discovery.'

'But they're no longer alive. And so you decided to trace your…your…'

'I've had the information on the woman for years, Brianna. I simply bided my time.'

Brianna stared at him. He'd simply *bided his time*? There was something so deliberate and so controlled about that simple statement that her head reeled.

'And…and…you came to Ballybay and pretended to be someone you weren't because…?'

'Because it was smaller than I imagined,' he confessed truthfully. 'And I wanted to find out about the woman before I passed judgement.'

'You mean if you had announced yourself and told everyone why you were there…what? Your mother—sorry, your *birth* mother—would have tried to…to what?' She looked around her at the staggering, shameless testimony to his well-heeled life and then settled her eyes back on him. 'Did you think that you needed to keep your real identity a secret because if she knew how rich you were she would have tried to latch on to your money?'

Leo made an awkward, dismissive gesture with his hand. 'I don't allow people to latch on to my money,' he said flatly. 'No, I kept my identity a secret, as indeed my purpose in being there in the first place, because I wasn't sure what I would do with the information I gathered.'

'How can you talk about this with such a lack of emotion? I feel as though I'm seeing a stranger.'

Leo sat back and raked his fingers through his hair. He was being honest. In fact, he was sparing no detail when it came to telling the truth, yet he still felt like the guy wrecking Christmas by taking a gun to Santa Claus.

'A stranger you've made love to countless times,' he couldn't help but murmur in a driven undertone that belied his cool exterior. He took a deep breath and tried to fight the intrusive memory of his hands over her smooth, slender body, tracing the light sprinkling of freckles on her collarbone, the circular discs of her nipples and the soft, downy hair between her legs. She was the most naturally, openly responsive lover he had ever had. When he parted her legs to cup the moisture between them, he felt her responding one-hundred per cent to his touch. She didn't play games. She hadn't hidden how he had made her feel.

'And I wish I hadn't.' Brianna was momentarily distracted from the direction of their conversation.

'You don't mean that. Whatever you think of me now, your body was always on fire for mine!'

Again she felt that treacherous lick of desire speed along her nerve endings like an unwanted intruder bypassing all her fortifications. This was not a road she wanted to travel down, not at all. Not when everything was collapsing around her ears.

'And did you find her?' she asked tightly.

'I did,' he answered after only the briefest of hesitations.

'Who is she?'

'At the moment, she's lying in the Cromwell Hospital.'

Brianna half-stood and then fell back onto the chair as though the air had been knocked out of her lungs.

His mother was Bridget. Bridget McGuire. And all of a sudden everything began falling into place with sickening impact. Perhaps not immediately, but very quickly, he had ascertained that she knew Bridget, that she considered Bridget one of her closest friends. Try as she might, Brianna couldn't reference the time scale of this conversation. Had it happened *before* he'd decided to prolong his stay? Surely it would have?

That realisation was like a physical blow because with it came the inevitable conclusion that he had used her. He had wanted to find out about his mother and she had been an umbilical cord to information he felt he might have needed; to soften her up and raise no suspicions, he had assumed the spurious identity of a writer. When he had been sitting in front of his computer, she'd assumed that he had been working on his book. Now, as head of whatever vast empire he ran, she realised he would have been working, communicating with the outside world from the dreary isolation of a small town in Ireland he would never have deigned to visit had he not needed to.

How could she have been so stupid, so naive? She had swooned like a foolish sixteen-year-old the second she had clapped eyes on him and had had no qualms about justifying her decision to leap into bed with him.

She had been his satisfying bonus for being stuck in the boondocks.

'I didn't even know that Bridget had ever had children…

Does she know?' Her voice was flat and devoid of any expression.

That, without the tears, told him all he needed to know about her state of mind. He had brought this on himself and he wasn't going to flinch from this difficult conversation. He told himself that there had never been any notion of a long-lasting relationship with her, yet the repetition of that mantra failed to do its job, failed to make him feel any better.

'No. She doesn't.'

'And when will you tell her?'

'When I feel the time is right.'

'If you wanted to find your mother and announce yourself—if you weren't suspicious that she would try and con money out of you—then why the secrecy? Why didn't you just do us all a favour: show up in your fancy car and present yourself as the long-lost prodigal son?'

'Because I didn't know what I was going to find, but I suspected that what I found would—how shall I put this?— not be to my liking.'

'Hence all your warnings about her when I told you that she was going to be coming to the pub to stay after her bout in hospital...' Brianna said slowly, feeling the thrust of yet another dagger deep down inside her. 'You knew she was hiding a past and you assumed she was a lowlife who would end up taking advantage of me, stealing from me, even. What changed?'

Leo shrugged and Brianna rose to her feet and managed to put distance between them. For a few seconds she stared down at the eerily lit landscape below her, devoid of people, just patches of light interspersed with darkness. Then she returned to the chair and this time she forced herself to try and relax, to give him no opportunity to see just how badly she was affected by what he had said to her.

'So you were using me all along,' she said matter-of-factly. 'You came to Ballybay with a purpose, found out that it wasn't going to be as straightforward as you anticipated—because it's the kind of small place where everybody knows everybody else, so you wouldn't be able to pass unnoticed, without comment—you adopted an identity and the second you found out that I knew your mother…sorry, your *birth mother*…you decided that it would be an idea to get to know me better.'

Leo's jaw hardened. Her inexorable conclusions left a bitter taste in his mouth but he wasn't going to rail against them. What was needed here was a clean break. If she had become too involved, then what was the point in encouraging further involvement by entering into a debate on what he had meant or not meant to do?

His failure to deny or confirm her statement was almost more than Brianna could bear but she kept her voice cool and level and willed herself just to try and detach from the situation. At least here, now; later, she would release the emotion that was building inside her, piling up like water constrained by paper-thin walls, ready to burst its banks and destroy everything in its path.

She could read nothing from his expression. Where was the guy she had laughed with? Made love to? Teased? Who was this implacable stranger sitting in front of her?

How, even more fatally, could she have made such a colossal mistake again? Misjudged someone so utterly that their withdrawal came as complete shock? Except this time it was all so much worse. She had known him for a fraction of the time she had known Daniel. Yet she knew, without a shadow of a doubt, that the impact Daniel had made on her all those years ago was nothing in comparison to what she would feel when she walked away from this. How was that possible? And yet she knew that what Leo had generated inside her had reached deeper and faster and was more profound in a million ways.

'I guess you decided that sleeping with me would be a good way to get background information on Bridget. Or maybe it was just something that was given to you on a silver platter.' Bitterness crept into her voice because she knew very well that what she said was the absolute truth. He hadn't had to energise himself into trying to get her into bed. She had leapt in before he had even finished asking the question.

'We enjoyed one another, Brianna. God, never have I apologised so much and so sincerely.'

'Except I wasn't using you.' She chose to ignore his apology because, in the big picture, it was just stupid and meaningless.

'I...' *Wasn't using you?* How much of that statement could he truthfully deny? 'That doesn't detract from the fact that what we had was real.'

'Don't you mean that the *sex* we had was real? Because beyond that we didn't have anything. You were supposed to be a writer travelling through, getting inspiration.' The conversation seemed to be going round and round in circles and she couldn't see a way of leading it towards anything that could resemble a conclusion. It felt like being in a labyrinth and she began walking on wooden legs towards her coat which she had earlier dumped on one of the chairs.

'Where are you going?'

'Where do you think, Leo? I'm leaving.'

'To go where? For God's sake, Brianna, there are guest rooms galore in this apartment. Pick whichever one you want to use! This is all a shock, I get that, but you can't just run out of here with nowhere to go!' Frustration laced his words with a savage urgency that made him darken and he sprang up, took a couple of steps towards her and then stopped.

They stood staring at one another. Her open transparency, which was so much part and parcel of her personality, had been replaced by a frozen aloofness that was doing all sorts of crazy, unexpected things to his head. He was overcome with an uncontrollable desire to smash things. He turned sharply away. His head was telling him that if she wanted to go, then he should let her go, but his body was already missing the feel of hers and he was enraged with himself for being sidestepped by an emotion over which he appeared to have no control.

Brianna could sense the shift of his body away from her, even though she was trying hard not to actually look at him, and that was just a further strike of the hammer. He couldn't even look at her. She was now disposable, however much he had wanted her. He had found his mother, had had whatever conversation with her that had changed his mind about her, and now he had no further use for the woman he had taken and used.

'Well?' he demanded roughly. 'Where are you going to go at this hour? Brianna, please...'

She wanted to tell him that the last thing she could do was sleep in one of his guest bedrooms. Just the thought of him being under the same roof would have kept her up all night.

She backed towards the door. 'I'm going to go to the hospital.'

'And do *what* there, Brianna? Visiting hours are well and truly over and I don't think they'll allow overnight guests in the common area.' He felt as though he was being ripped apart. 'You have my word that I won't come near you,' he said, attempting to soften his tone. 'I'll leave the apartment, if you want. Go stay in a hotel.'

Did he think that she was scared that he might try and break down her bedroom door so that he could ravish her? Did he honestly imagine that she was foolish enough to fear any such thing after what he had said?

'You can leave or you can stay, Leo.' She gave a jerky shake of her shoulder. 'I don't honestly care. I'm going to the hospital and, no, I won't be trying to cadge a night's sleep on the sofa in the common area. I'm going to leave a letter for one of the nurses to hand to Bridget in the morning, explaining that I've had to get back to the pub.'

'And the reason for that being…?' There were shadows under her eyes. He didn't feel proud to acknowledge the fact that he had put them there. His guilty conscience refused to be reined in. 'What reason could you have for needing to rush back to the pub? Or do you intend to tell Bridget the truth about who I am?'

'I would never do that, Leo, and the fact that you would think that I might just shows how little you know me. As little, as it turns out, I know you. We were just a couple of strangers having fun for a few weeks.' Her heart constricted painfully when she said that. 'I know you think that I'm all wrapped up in you, but I'm not. I'm upset because I didn't take you for a liar and, now that I know what you are, I'm glad this is all over. Next to you, Daniel was a walk in the park!'

For several reasons, none of which she intended to divulge, this was closer to the truth than he could ever imagine and she could see from his dark flush that she had hit home. He had been fond of referring to her distant ex as one of life's great losers.

She stuck her chin up and looked him squarely in the eyes without flinching. 'After I've been to the hospital, I shall find somewhere cheap to stay until I can catch the first train out of London.'

'This isn't Ballybay! London isn't safe at night to be wandering around in search of cheap hotels!'

'I'll take my chances!' Of course he would see no problem with her sleeping in his apartment, she thought with punishing reality. She meant nothing to him, so why on earth would he be affected by her presence? And, if that were the case, then wouldn't it be the same for her? 'And when I leave here I never, ever want to see you again.'

CHAPTER EIGHT

'DIDN'T THIS OCCUR to you at all, Miss Sullivan?'

Her doctor looked at her with the sort of expression that implied this was a conversation he had had many times before. Possibly, however, not with someone who was unmarried. Unmarried and pregnant in these parts was a rare occurrence.

Her head was swimming. It had been over a month since she had walked out of Leo's life for ever and in the interim she had heard not a word from him, although she had heard *about* him, thanks to Bridget, who emailed her regularly with updates on the joys of finding her long-lost son.

Bridget had remained in London in his apartment, where she had all the benefits of round-the-clock care and help courtesy of a man who had limitless funds. She hadn't even needed to fetch any of her clothes, as she was now the fortunate recipient of a brand-new wardrobe.

On all fronts, he was the golden child she thought she had lost for ever.

In between these golden tributes, Brianna never managed to get any answers to the questions she *really* wanted to ask, such as did he ever talk about her? Was he missing her? Was there someone else in his life?

And now *this*.

'No, not really.' Brianna found that she could barely

enunciate the words. Pregnant. They had been so careful. Aside from that one time… She resisted the temptation to put her hand on her still flat stomach. 'I…I didn't even notice that I'd skipped a period…' Because she had been so wrapped up thinking about him, missing him, wishing he was still around. So busy functioning on autopilot that she had missed the really big, life-altering thing happening.

'And what will you do now, Brianna?

Brianna looked at the kindly old man who had delivered her and pretty much everyone her age in Ballybay and beyond.

'I'm going to have this baby, Dr Fallow, and I shall be a very proud, single mother.' She stuck her chin up defiantly and he smiled at her.

'I would have expected nothing less from Annie Sullivan's daughter. And the father?'

And the father…?

The question plagued her over the next few days. He deserved to know. Or did he? He had used her and then dispatched her once her usefulness was at an end. Did a man like that deserve to know that she was having his baby? He had been ultra-careful with precautions. How ironic that despite the best laid plans—because of a split condom, a one-in-a-million chance—here she was, the exception to the rule. And a cruel exception, because having a baby was not on his agenda, least of all with a woman he had used. So what would be his reaction should she show up on his doorstep with the happy news that he was going to be a daddy? She shuddered when she thought of it: horror, rage, shock. And, although there was no way he could blame her, he would still be upset and enraged that fate had dealt him a blow he couldn't deal with.

Yet, how could she *not* tell him? Especially given the circumstances of his adoption? Would he appreciate being left in the dark about his own flesh and blood? Perhaps finding out at some much later date down the road, and being destined forever to imagine that his son or daughter had grown up thinking of him as someone who had not taken enough interest to make contact? Being left in the awful position of wondering whether his own life story had been repeated, except without him even being aware of it?

The pros and cons ran through her head like a constant refrain, although beneath that refrain the one consolation was that she was in no doubt that she was happy about the pregnancy, however much it would disrupt her way of life. In fact, she was ecstatic. She had not thought about babies, having had no guy in her life with whom to have them. And, although she couldn't have chosen a less suitable candidate for the role of father, she was filled with a sense of joyous wonder at the life slowly growing inside her.

A life which would soon become apparent; pregnancy was not a condition that could be kept secret. Within a month or two, she would be the talk of the town, and of course Bridget would know. How could she fail to?

Which pretty much concluded her agonising. Leo would find out and she would have to be the one to tell him before he heard it second-hand.

It seemed the sort of conversation to be held in the evening and, before the bustle of the pub could begin, sweeping her off her feet, she got on the phone and dialled his mobile.

Around her, the pub lacked its usual shine and polish. She would have to start thinking about getting someone in to cover for her on a fairly permanent basis. There was no way she and Shannon could cope but there was also no way she could afford to close the pub, far less find a buyer for it.

Money, she foresaw, was going to be a headache and she

gritted her teeth together because she knew what Leo's solution would be: fling money at the problem. Which would leave her continually indebted to him and that was not a situation that filled her with joy.

But then, she would never, ever be able to break contact with him from here on in, would she?

Even if he just paid the occasional visit in between running those companies of his, he would still be a permanent cloud on her horizon. She would have to look forward to seeing him moving on, finding other women, other women to whom he hadn't fabricated a convoluted story about himself. Eventually, she would have to witness his happiness as he found his soul mate, married her, had children with her. It didn't bear thinking about.

His disembodied voice, deep, dark and lazy, jolted her out of her daydreaming and fired up every nerve in her body. All at once, she could picture him in every vivid, unsettling detail: the way he used to look at her, half-brooding, full of sexy promise; the way he used to laugh whenever she teased him; the way the muscles of his amazing body rippled and flexed when he moved...

'It's me,' she said a little breathlessly, before clearing her throat and telling herself to get a grip.

'I know who it is, Brianna,' Leo drawled. He rose to shut his office door. She had caught him as he had been about to leave. Ever since his mother had arrived on the scene and was recuperating happily at his apartment, he had been leaving work earlier than normal. It was a change of pattern he could not have foreseen in a million years, but he was strangely energised by getting to know his mother a little better. She could never replace the couple who had adopted him, but she was a person in her own right, and one he found he wanted to get to know. It seemed that a genetic link was far more powerful a bond than he could ever have conceived possible.

He thought back to that moment when he had sat next to her at her hospital bed and taken her hand in his. An awkward moment and one he had never envisaged but as she had lain there, frail and bewildered at her expensive private room, it had seemed right.

And he had told her—haltingly at first, trying to find the words to span over thirty years. He had watched her eyes fill up and had felt the way her hand had trembled. He had never expected his journey to take him there and he had been shocked at how much it had changed his way of thinking, had made him see the shades of grey between the black and white. No one could ever replace the wonderful parents he had had, but a new road had opened up—not better, but different—and he had felt a soaring sense of fulfilment at what lay ahead. He had known that they both did.

For a man who had always known the way ahead, he had discovered the wonder of finding himself on a path with no signposts, just his feelings to guide him, and as he had opened up to his mother, asked her questions, replied to the hundreds she had asked him in return, he had turned a corner. The unknown had become something to be embraced.

'How's Bridget?'

'I thought you spoke and emailed daily?' He sat back down at his desk and swivelled his chair so that it was facing the broad floor-to-ceiling glass panes that overlooked the city.

'Why are you calling?' It had been more of a struggle putting her behind him than he could ever have believed possible. Was it because Bridget was staying with him? Because her presence kept alive memories he wanted to bury? He didn't know. Whilst his head did all the right things and told him that she no longer had a place in his life—that what they'd had had been good but it had never been destined to last—some irrational part of him insisted on singing a different tune.

He had found his concentration inexplicably flagging in the middle of meetings. On more than one occasion, he had awoken from a dream-filled sleep to find himself with an erection. Cold showers were becoming the rule rather than the exception. All told, he felt as though he was in unchartered territory. He was taking new steps with his mother and discovering that old ways of dealing with exes did not apply to Brianna.

He knew that she and Bridget were in touch by phone daily and it took every ounce of willpower not to indulge his rampant curiosity and try to prise information out of his house guest. What was she up to? Had she found a replacement for him in her bed? There was no denying that she was hot; what man wouldn't want to try his luck? And she was no longer cocooned within those glacial walls of celibacy. She had stepped out from behind them and released all the unbelievable passion he knew her to be capable of. There was no way that she could ever return to living life like a nun. And, however much she had or hadn't been wrapped up in him, she was ripe for a rebound relationship.

Was that what she was doing right now—engaging in wild sex with some loser from the town or another passing stranger?

He had never considered himself someone who was prone to flights of fancy, but he was making up for lost time now.

All of this introduced a level of coolness to his voice as he stared out of the window and waited for her to come up with an answer.

She damn well wasn't phoning for an update on Bridget, so why was she?

Brianna picked up the unwelcoming indifference in his voice and it stung. Had he *completely* detached from her? How was that possible? And how was he going to greet what she had to tell him, were that the case?

'I…I…need to talk to you.'

'I'm listening. But make it quick. I was on my way out.'

'I need to see you…to discuss what I have to say.'

'Why?'

'Can't you be just a little more polite, Leo? I know you have no further use for me, but the least you can do is not treat me as though I'm something the cat dragged in.'

'Is it money?' His anger at himself for continuing to let her infiltrate his head and ambush his thoughts transferred into a healthy anger towards her and, although he knew he was being unfair, there was no way he was going to allow himself to be dragged down the apology route.

'I beg your pardon?'

'You know how rich I am now. You must know the lifestyle Bridget's enjoying—I'm sure she's told you so. Have you decided that you'd like me to throw some money in your direction for old times' sake?' God, was this *him*? He barely recognised the person behind the words.

Brianna clutched the phone so tightly that she thought she might break it in two. Did he know how insulting he was being right now? Did he care? How could she have misread someone so utterly? Was there some crazy missing connection in her head that allowed her to give everyone the benefit of the doubt, including people who were just bad for her health?

'You mentioned more than once that the place needed updating: new bar stools, new paint job on the outside, less tatty sofas in front of the fire…' The sofas had been damn near perfect, he seemed to recall. The sort of sofas a person could sink into and remain sunk in for hours, remain sunk in for a lifetime. 'Consider it done. On me. Call it thanks for, well, everything'

'How generous of you, Leo.' She reined in her explosive rage and kept her voice as neutral as she possibly could. 'And I suppose this might eventually have something to do with money. But I really need to see you face to face to talk about it.'

Perversely, Leo was disappointed that he had hit the nail on the head. Other women played the money angle. Other women assessed his wealth and expected a good time at his expense. It had never bothered him because, after all, fair's fair. But Brianna… She wasn't like other women. Apparently, however, she was.

'Name the figure,' he said curtly.

'I'd rather not. If you could just make an appointment to see me. I could come to London and take the opportunity to look in on Bridget as well…'

'I have no free time during the day. I could see you tomorrow some time after six thirty, and I'm doing you a favour because that would involve cancelling a conference call.'

'Er…' Money she knew she didn't have disappeared through the window at the prospect of finding somewhere to stay, because there was no way she would be staying at his apartment, especially after she had dropped her bombshell.

'Take it or leave it.' He cut into her indecisive silence. 'I can meet you at seven at a bistro near my office.' He named it and then, from nowhere, pictured her sitting there at one of the tables, waiting for him. He pictured her face, her startling prettiness; he pictured her body, which would doubtless be concealed underneath something truly unappealing—that waterproof coat of hers of indeterminate green which she seemed to wear everywhere.

On cue, his body jerked into life, sourly reminding him of the way just thinking of her could manage to turn him on.

Tomorrow, he resolved, he would rifle through his address book and see whether there wasn't someone he could date, if only as a distraction. Bridget, oddly, had not referred back to that aborted conversation she had had with him at the pub, had made no mention of Brianna at all. She would think there was nothing amiss were he to start dating. In fact, she would think something was amiss if he *didn't*.

'Well?' he said impatiently. 'Will you be there? This is a going, going, gone situation.'

'I'll be there. See you tomorrow.'

Brianna barely slept through the night. She was having a baby! Unplanned, unexpected, but certainly not unwanted.

She was on edge as she finally landed on English soil. The weather had taken a turn for the better but, to be on the safe side, she had still decided to wear her faithful old coat just in case. The deeper into the city she got, the more ridiculously out of place she felt in her clothing. Even at nearly seven in the evening, the streets were packed. Everyone appeared to be dressed in suits, carrying briefcases and in a massive rush.

She had given the address of the bistro to the taxi driver but, when she was dropped off, she remained outside on the pavement, her battered pull-along in one hand, her other hand shoved into the capacious pocket of her coat. Nerves threatened to overwhelm her. In fact, she wanted nothing more than to hop into the nearest taxi and ask it to deliver her right back to the airport.

There were people coming and going from the bistro. She stood to one side, shaking like a leaf, aware of the pathetic figure she cut, and then she took a deep breath and entered with all the trepidation of someone entering a lion's den.

The noise was deafening, exaggerated by the stark-ness of the surroundings and the wooden floor. It was teeming with people, all young, all beautiful. A young woman clacking along in her high heels, with a leather case clutched to her side, tripped over her pull-along and swore profusely before giving her the once-over with contempt.

'Oh God, darling, are you lost? In case you haven't no-ticed, this isn't the bus station. If you and your luggage take a left out of the door and keep walking, you both should hit the nearest bus stop and they can deliver you wherever you're going.'

Brianna backed away, speechless, and looked around desperately for Leo. Right now, he felt like the only safe port in a storm and she spotted him tucked away towards the back of the room, sitting at a table and nursing a drink. A wave of relief washed over her as she began threading her way towards him, her pull-along bumping into ankles and calves and incurring a trail of oaths on the way.

Leo watched her zig-zag approach with brooding in-tensity. Amongst the city folk, snappily dressed and all braying in loud voices that competed to be heard, she was as natural and as beautiful as a wild flower. He couldn't fail to notice the sidelong looks she garnered from some of the men and he quickly knocked back the remainder of his whisky in one gulp.

So she had come here on her begging mission. He would have to do a bit better than stare at her and make favour-able comparisons between her and the rest of the over-paid, over-confident, over-arrogant crowd on show. He signalled to a waiter to bring him another drink. It was a perk of this bar that he was the only one to receive waiter service, but then again, had it not been for his injection of cash years previously, the place would have been run into the ground. Now he owned a stake in it and, as soon as he clicked his fingers, the staff jumped to attention. It certainly saved the tedium of queuing at the bar trying to vie for attention. It also secured him the best table in the house, marginally away from the crowds.

'I'm sorry I'm a little late.' Brianna found that she could barely look at him without her entire nervous system gathering pace and going into overdrive. How had she managed to forget the impact he had on her senses? The way those dark, dark eyes could make her head swim and scramble her thoughts until she could barely speak?

'Sit.' He motioned to the chair facing him with a curt nod and she sank onto it and pulled her little bag alongside her. 'So...' He leant back and folded his arms. She was pink and her hair, which had obviously started the trip as a single braid down her back, was in the process of unravelling.

'I hadn't expected so much noise.' Her eyes skittered away from his face but then returned to look at him with resolve. She had to forget about being out of her depth. She had come here for one reason and one reason only and she wasn't going to let an attack of nerves stand in her way. How much more could he hurt her?

Leo cast a cursory glance around him and asked her what she wanted to drink: a glass of water. He would have expected something a little more stiff to get her through her 'begging bowl' speech, but to each their own. He ordered some mineral water and another stiff drink for himself then settled back with an air of palpable boredom.

Something in him railed against believing the worst of

her, knowing her to be the person that she was, yet he refused to give house room to that voice. He felt he needed to be black and white or else forever be lost. Let it not be forgotten that she had refused to listen to him when he had attempted to explain the reason for his fabrications. She had turned her back and stalked off and for the past month he had seen and heard nothing from her.

She had taken off her coat, the gruesome coat which he was annoyed to discover made inroads into his indifference, because he could remember teasing her that she needed something a little less worn, that waterproof coats like that were never fashion statements.

'What's it like?' Brianna opened the conversation with something as far removed from what she actually needed to say as she could get, and Leo shot her a perplexed glance.

'What's what like? What are you talking about?'

'Having your... Having Bridget in your life. It must be very satisfying for you.'

Leo flushed. No one knew about Bridget, aside from Harry. He had never been the sort of man who spilled his guts to all and sundry and there had been absolutely no temptation to tell anyone about his mother living with him. He had not been dating, so there had been no women coming to his apartment, asking questions. Even if there had been, it was debatable whether he would have confided in any of them or not. He looked at her open, upturned face and found it hard to resurrect his cynicism.

'It's working for me,' he said gruffly. Working for them both. The years had dropped off his mother. She had been to the hairdresser, had her hair styled, had her nails done... She bore little resemblance to the fragile creature he had first set eyes on.

Drinks were brought and he sat back to allow the waiter to fuss as he put them on the table, along with a plate of appetisers which had not been ordered. 'But you didn't come here to talk about my relationship with Bridget.'

'No, I didn't, but I'm interested.' She just couldn't launch into her real reason for coming to London without some sort of preamble.

And, an inner voice whispered, didn't she just want to prolong being in his company, like a thief stealing time that didn't belong to them? Didn't she just want to breathe him in, that clean, masculine scent, and slide her eyes over a body she knew so well even when, as now, it was sheathed in the finest tailored suit money could buy?

'Just tell me why you're here, Brianna. You said something about money. How much are you looking for?'

'It's a bit more complicated than that.'

'What's more complicated than asking for a hand-out?'

Brianna looked down and fiddled with the bottle of water before pouring a little more into her glass. She envied him his stiff drink. She felt that under different circumstances, without this baby inside her, she could have done with a little Dutch courage.

'Leo…' She looked him directly in the eye and felt that this was the last time that she would be seeing him like this: a free man who could do whatever he wanted to do. She could even appreciate that, however dismissive he was of her now, it was an emotion that would soon be overtaken by far more overwhelming ones. Perhaps, thinking about it, it was just as well that they were having this conversation somewhere noisy and crowded.

'I'm pregnant.'

For a few seconds, Leo thought that he might have misheard her, but even as his mind was absorbing her body language—taking in the way she now couldn't meet his eyes, the hectic flush on her cheeks, the way her hand was trembling on the glass—he still couldn't put two and two together.

'Come again?' He leaned forward, straining to catch her every word. There was a buzzing in his ears that was growing louder by the second.

'I'm having a baby, Leo. Your baby. I'm sorry. I do realise that this is probably the last thing in the world you expected to hear, and the last thing you *wanted* to hear, but I felt you ought to know. I did think about keeping it to myself but that would have been impossible. Well, you know how small the place is, and sooner or later Bridget would have found out. In fact, there's no way that I would have wanted to keep it from her.'

Why wasn't he saying anything? She had expected more of an immediate and explosive reaction, but then he was probably still in a state of shock.

'You're telling me that you're having my baby.' The words felt odd as they passed his lips. The thought had taken root now with blinding clarity and he looked down at her stomach. She was as slender as she had always been. He heard himself asking questions: how pregnant was she? Was she absolutely certain? Had it been verified by a doctor? He knew home tests existed but any test that could be done at home would always be open to error...

'I'm not expecting anything from you,' Brianna ended. 'I just thought that you ought to know.'

'You thought that *I ought to know*?' Leo shot her a look of utter incredulity. The impersonal bistro he had chosen now seemed inappropriate. Restless energy was pouring through his body and, as fast as he tried to decipher a pattern to what he was thinking, his thoughts came unstuck, leaving him with just the explosive realisation that in a matter of months he was going to be a father.

'I realise that you might want to have some input...'

'You have got to be kidding me, Brianna. You come here, drop this bombshell on me, and the only two things you can find to say are that you felt I *ought to know* and you realise that I *might want some input*? We have to get out of here.'

'And go where?' she cried.

'Somewhere a little less *full of chattering morons*.'

'I'm not going to your apartment,' she said, refusing to budge and clutching the sides of her chair as though fearful that at any moment he might just get it into his head to bodily pick her up and haul her over his shoulder to the front door, caveman style.

'I haven't said anything to Bridget yet and I'd rather not just at the moment. I...I need time to absorb it all myself so, if you don't mind, I'd quite like to stay here. Not that there's much more for me to bring to the table.'

'And another classic line from you. God, I just don't believe this.'

Brianna watched as he dropped his head to his hands. 'I'm so sorry to be the bearer of unexpected tidings. Like I said, though...'

'Spare me whatever pearls of wisdom are going to emerge from your mouth, Brianna.' He raised his head to stare at her. 'It is as it is, and now we're going to have to decide how we deal with this situation.' He rubbed his eyes and continued holding her gaze with his.

'Perhaps you should go away and think about this. It's a lot to take on board. We could fix a time to meet again.'

'I don't think so.' He straightened and sat back. 'Waiting for another day isn't going to alter this problem.'

Brianna stiffened. 'This isn't your problem, it's mine, and I don't see it as a *problem*. I'm going to be the one having the baby and I shall be the one looking after it. I recognise that you'll want to contribute in some way, but let me assure you that I expect nothing from you.'

'Do you honestly believe that you can dump this on me and I'm going to walk away from it?'

'I don't know. A few weeks ago I would have said that the guy at the pub who helped clear snow wouldn't, but then you weren't that guy at all, were you? So, honestly? I have no idea.' She sat on her hands and leaned towards him. 'If you want to contribute financially, then that would be fine and much appreciated. I don't expect you to give anything to me, but helping to meet the needs of the baby would be okay. They may be small, but they can be very expensive, and you know all too well what the finances at the pub are like. Especially with all the closures of late.'

'I know what you think of me, Brianna, but I'm not a man to run away from my responsibilities—and in this instance my responsibilities don't stop at sending you a monthly cheque to cover baby food.'

'They don't?' Brianna queried uneasily. She wondered what else he had in mind. 'Naturally you would be free to see your child whenever you wanted, but it might be difficult, considering you live in London…' She quailed inwardly at the prospect of him turning up at the front door. She wondered whether the onslaught of times remembered, before she had discovered who he really was, would be just too much for her. Not that she would have any choice. It would be his right to visit his child, whether it made her uncomfortable or not.

'Visiting rights? No, I don't think so.'

'I won't let you take custody of my baby.'

'*Our* baby,' he corrected.

Brianna blanched as her worst imaginings went into free fall. She hadn't even thought that he might want to take the baby away from her, yet, why hadn't that occurred to her? He was adopted. He would have very strong feelings about being on hand as a father because his own real father had not been on hand. And, whatever concoctions he had come up with to disguise his true identity, she knew instinctively that he possessed a core of inner integrity.

And those concoctions, she was reluctantly forced to conclude, had not been fabricated for the sheer hell of it. They had been done for a reason and, once he had embarked on that road, it would have been difficult to get off it.

Would that core of integrity propel him to try and fight her for custody of the baby? He was rolling in money whilst she was borderline broke and, when it came to getting results, the guy who was rolling in money was always going to win hands down over the woman who was borderline broke. You didn't need a degree in quantum physics to work that one out.

'You can stop looking as though you're about to pass out, Brianna. I have no intention of indulging in a protracted battle with you to take custody of our baby.' He was slightly surprised at how naturally the words 'our baby' rolled off his tongue. The shock appeared to have worn off far more quickly than might have been expected, but then he prided himself as being the sort of guy who could roll with the punches and come up with solutions in the tightest of spots.

Brianna breathed a sigh of relief. 'So what are you proposing?'

'We get married. Obvious solution.'

'You have got to be joking.'

'Do I look like someone about to burst into laughter?'

'That's a crazy idea.'

'Explain why.'

'Because it's not a solution, Leo. Two people don't just

get married because, accidentally, there's a baby on the way. Two people who *broke up*. Two people who wouldn't have laid eyes on one another again were it not for the fact that the girl in question happens to find herself pregnant.'

'Brianna, I'm not prepared to take a backseat in the upbringing of my child. I'm not prepared for any child of mine to ever think that they got less of me than they might have wanted.'

'I'm not asking you to take a back seat in anything.'

'Nor,' Leo continued, overriding her interruption as though it hadn't registered, 'am I willing to watch on the sidelines as you find yourself another man who decides to take over the upbringing of my child.'

'That's not likely to happen! I think I've had enough of men to last a lifetime.'

'Of course, you'll have to move to London, but in all events that won't depend on the sale of the pub. In fact, you can hand it over to someone else to run on your behalf.'

'Are you listening to a *word* I'm saying?'

'Are you listening to what *I'm* saying?' he said softly. 'I hope so, because the proposal I've put on the table is the only solution at hand.'

'This isn't a maths problem that needs a solution. This is something completely different.'

'I'm failing to see your objections, aside from a selfish need to put yourself ahead of our child.'

'I could never live in London. And I could never marry someone for the wrong reasons. We would end up resenting one another and that would be the worst possible atmosphere in which to raise a child. Don't you see that?'

'Before you knew who I was,' Leo said tautly, his dark eyes fixed intently on her face, 'did you hope that our relationship would go further?'

He sat forward and all of a sudden her space was invaded and she could barely breathe. 'I knew that you weren't intending on hanging around,' she said and she could hear the choked breathlessness in her voice. 'You said so. You made that perfectly clear.'

'Which doesn't answer my question. Were you hoping for more?'

'I didn't think it would end the way it did,' she threw back at him with bristling defiance.

'But it did, and you may not have liked the way it ended, but what we had…' He watched the slow colour creep up her cheeks and a rush of satisfaction poured through him, because behind those lowered eyes he could *smell* the impact he still had on her.

'This wouldn't be a marriage in name only for the sake of a child. This would be a marriage in every sense of the word because—let's not kid each other—what we had was good.' Her naked, pale body flashed through his mind, as did the memory of all those little whimpering noises she made when he touched her, the way her nostrils flared and her eyelids quivered as her body gathered pace and hurtled towards orgasm. He already felt himself harden at the thought and this time he didn't try to kill it at source because it was inappropriate given she was no longer part of his life. She was a part of his life now, once again, and the freedom to think of her without restraint was a powerful kick to his system.

'What we had was…was…'

'Was good and you know it. Shall I remind you how good it was?' He didn't give her time to move or time even to think about what was coming. He leant across the small table, cupped his hand on the nape of her neck and pulled her towards him.

Brianna's body responded with the knee-jerk response of immediate reaction, as though responding with learned behaviour. Her mouth parted and the feel his tongue thrusting against her was as heady as the most powerful drug. Her mind emptied and she kissed him back, and she felt as though she never wanted the kiss to end. The coolness of his withdrawal, leaving her with her mouth still slightly parted and her eyes half-closed, was a horrifying return to reality.

'Point proven,' he murmured softly. 'So, when I tell you that you need to look outside the box and start seeing the upsides to my proposal, you know what I'm talking about. This won't be a union without one or two definite bonuses.'

'I'll never move to London and I'll never marry you.' Her breathing was only now returning to normal and the mortification of what she had done, of how her treacherous body had *betrayed* her, felt like acid running through her veins. 'I'm going now but I'll give you a call in a couple of days. When you're ready to accept what I've said, then we'll talk again.' She stood up on wobbly legs and turned her back. The urge to run away as fast as she could was overpowering, and she did. Out to the pavement, where she hailed the nearest taxi and instructed him to drive her to a hotel—something cheap, something close to the airport.

She wouldn't marry him. He didn't love her and there was no way that she would ever accept sacrificing both their lives for the wrong reason, whatever he said about the bonus of good sex. Good sex would die and then where would they be?

But she had to get away because she knew that there was something craven and weak in the very deepest part of her that might *just* play with the idea.

And there was no way she was going to give that weak, craven part of her a voice.

CHAPTER NINE

LEO LOOKED AT the sprawling house facing him and immediately wondered whether he had gone for the wrong thing. Too big, maybe? Too ostentatious? Too much land?

He shook his head with frustration and fired a couple of questions at the estate agent without bothering to glance in her direction.

In the space of six weeks, this was the eighth property he had personally seen out in the rolling Berkshire countryside, sufficiently far away from London to promote the idea of clean air, whilst being within easy commuting distance from the city.

Brianna had no idea that he was even hunting down a house. As far as she was concerned, he was the guy she'd refused to commit to who seemed intent on pursuing her even though she had already given him her answer—again and again and again, in varying formats, but all conveying the same message.

No thank you, I won't be getting married to you.

On the upside, he had managed to persuade her temporarily to move to London, although that in itself had been a task of no small order. She had refused to budge, had informed him that he was wasting his time, that they weren't living in the Victorian ages. She had folded her arms, given him a gimlet stare of pure stubbornness. He had been reduced to deviating from his intention to get what he wanted—what was *needed*, at all costs—in favour of thinking creatively.

For starters, he had had to pursue her to Ireland because she'd refused to continue her conversation with him in London. And then, he had had to travel to the pub to see her, because she didn't want him staying under her roof, not given the circumstances. He had refrained from pointing out the saying about horses bolting and stable doors. He had initiated his process of getting what he wanted by pointing out that it made sense.

He had done that over the finest meal to be had in a really very good restaurant not a million miles away from the pub. He had used every argument in the book and had got precisely nowhere. Then he had returned, this time to try and persuade her to see his point of view during a bracing walk by one of the lakes with the wind whipping his hair into disarray and his mega-expensive coat proving no match for the cold. He had tried to remind her of the sexual chemistry that was still there between them, but had cut short that line of argument when she'd threatened to walk back to the pub without him.

He had informed her that there wasn't a single woman alive who wouldn't have chewed off his arm to accept an offer of marriage from him, which had been another tactical error.

He had dropped all talk of anything and concentrated on just making her feel comfortable in his presence, whilst marvelling that she could carry on keeping him at arm's length, considering how close they had been. But by this point he had been clued up enough to make sure that he didn't hark back to the past. Nothing to remind her about how much she clearly loathed him, having found out about his lies.

Never in his life had Leo put this much effort into one woman.

And never in his life had he had so many cold showers. From having given no thought whatsoever to settling down, far less having a child, he now seemed fixated by the baby growing inside her and, the more fixated he became, the more determined he was that she would marry him. He was turned on by everything about her. Turned on by the way she moved, the way she looked at him, by all her little gestures that seemed ingrained inside his head so that, even when she wasn't around, he was thinking about her constantly.

Was it a case of the inaccessible becoming more and more desirable? Was it because she was now carrying his baby that his body seemed to be on fire for her all the time? Or was it just that he hadn't stopped wanting her because it had been a highly physical relationship that had not been given the opportunity of dying a natural death?

He didn't know and he didn't bother analysing it. He just knew that he still wanted her more than he could remember wanting anyone. He wanted her to be his. The thought of some other man stepping into his shoes, doing clever things behind the bar of the pub and having a say in his child's welfare, made him grit his teeth together in impotent rage.

The estate agent, a simpering woman in her thirties, was saying something about the number of bedrooms and Leo scowled.

'How many?'

'Eight! Perfect for having the family over!'

'Too many. And I can look at it from here and see straight away that it would be far too big for the person I have in mind.'

'Perhaps the lucky lady would like to pop along and have a look for herself? It's really rather grand inside...'

Leo flinched at the word 'grand'. He pictured Brianna wiping the bar with a cloth, standing back in her old jeans and sloppy jumper to survey her handiwork, before retiring to the comfy sofa in the lounge which had been with her practically since she'd been a kid. She wouldn't have a clue what to do with 'grand' and he had a gut feeling that if he settled on anything like this she would end up blaming him.

How, he thought as house number nine bit the dust, had he managed to end up with the one woman in the world to whom a marriage proposal was an insult and who was determined to fight him every inch of the way? Even though the air sizzled between them with a raw, elemental electricity that neither of them could deny.

But at least he had managed to get her to London. It was a comforting thought as his Ferrari ate up the miles back to the city centre and his penthouse apartment.

He had appealed to her sense of fairness. He wanted to be there while she was pregnant and what better way than for her to move to London? No need to live in his apartment. He would find somewhere else for her, somewhere less central. It would be great for Bridget as well. Indeed, it would be a blessing in disguise, for Bridget was tiring of the concrete jungle of inner London. She was back on her feet, albeit in a restricted way, and the constant crowds terrified her. They could share something small but cosy in West London. He would personally see to it that a manager was located for the pub...

She had acquiesced. That had been ten days ago and, although he had made sure to visit them both every evening after work, he had ostensibly dropped all mention of marriage.

That aggressive need to conquer had been forced into retreat and he was now playing a waiting game. He wasn't sure what would happen if that waiting game didn't work and he preferred not to dwell on that. Instead, he phoned his secretary and found out what other gems were available on the property market in picturesque Berkshire.

'Too impressive,' he told her about his last failed viewing. It was added to all the other too 'something or other' that had characterised the last eight viewings, all of which had come to nothing. He laughed when she suggested that he send someone in his place to at least narrow the possibilities.

He couldn't imagine anyone he knew having the slightest idea as to what to look for when it came to Brianna. They were people who only knew a London crowd, socialites for whom there could be nothing that could ever be too grand.

'Find me some more properties.' He concluded his conversation with his long-suffering PA. 'And forget about the marble bathrooms and indoor swimming pools. Go smaller.'

He hung up. It wasn't yet two-thirty in the afternoon. He had never taken this much time off work in his life before. Except for when he had voluntarily marooned himself at Brianna's pub. And yet, he was driven to continue his search. Work, meetings and deals would just have to take a back seat.

His secretary called him on his mobile just as he was leaving the M25, heading into London.

'It's a small village near, er, Sunningdale. Er, shall I read you the details? It's just on the market. Today, in fact. Thank goodness for estate agents who remember we exist…'

Leo thought that most estate agents would remember

any client for whom money was no object. 'I'll check that out now.' He was already halfway back to London but he manoeuvred his car off the motorway and back out. 'Cancel my five o'clock meeting.'

'You've already cancelled Sir Hawkes twice.'

'In that case, let Reynolds cover. He's paid enough; a little delegation in his direction will do him the world of good.'

He made it to the small village in good time and, the very second he saw the picture-postcard cottage with the sprawling garden in the back and the white picket fence at the front, he knew he had hit the jackpot.

He didn't bother with an offer. He would pay the full asking price and came with cash in hand. The estate agent couldn't believe his luck. Leo waved aside the man's ingratiating and frankly irritating bowing and scraping and elicited all the pertinent details he needed for an immediate purchase.

'And if the occupants need time to find somewhere else, you can tell them that they'll be generously compensated over and beyond what they want for the house to leave immediately.' He named a figure and the estate agent practically swooned. 'Here's my card. Call me in an hour and we'll get the ball rolling. Oh, and I'll be bringing someone round tomorrow, if not sooner, to look at it. Make sure it's available.' He was at his car and the rotund estate agent was dithering behind him, clutching the business card as though it were a gold ingot.

'What if...?' He cleared his throat anxiously as he was forced to contemplate a possible hitch in clinching his commission. 'What if the sellers want to wait and see if a better offer comes along?'

About to slide into the driving seat, Leo paused and

looked at the much shorter man with a wry expression. 'Oh, trust me, that won't be happening.'

'Sir...'

'Call me——and I'll be expecting a conversation that I want to hear.' He left the man staring at him red-faced, perspiring and doubtless contemplating the sickening prospect of sellers who might prove too greedy to accept the quick sale.

Leo knew better. They simply wouldn't be able to believe their luck.

He could easily have made it back to the office to catch the tail end of the meeting he had cancelled at the last minute. Instead, he headed directly to Brianna's house, which was an effortless drive off the motorway and into London suburbia.

Brianna heard the low growl of the Ferrari as it pulled up outside the house. It seemed her ears were attuned to the sound. She immediately schooled her expression into one of polite aloofness. In the kitchen Bridget was making them both a cup of tea, fussing as she always seemed to do now, clucking around her like a mother hen because she was pregnant, even though Brianna constantly told her that pregnancy wasn't an illness and that Bridget was the one in need of looking after.

'He's early this evening!' Bridget exclaimed with pleasure. 'I wonder why? I think I'll give you two a little time together and have a nice, long bath. The doctor says that I should take it easy. You know that.'

Brianna raised her eyebrows wryly and stood up. 'I don't think chatting counts as not taking it easy,' she pointed out. 'Besides, you know Leo enjoys seeing you when he gets here.' Every time she saw them together, she felt a lump of emotion gather at the back of her throat. However cut-throat and ruthless he might be, and however much of a lying bastard he had been, he was always gentle with Bridget. He didn't call her 'Mum' but he treated her with the respect and consideration any mother would expect from her child. And they spoke of all the inconsequential things that happened on a daily basis. Perhaps they had explored the past already and neither wanted to revisit it.

At any rate, Bridget was a changed person. She looked healthier, more *vibrant*. The sort of woman who was actually only middle-aged, who could easily get out there and find herself another guy but who seemed perfectly content to age gracefully by herself.

She quelled the urge to insist to Bridget that she stay put as the older woman began heading to her bedroom on the ground floor—a timely coincidence because the owners of the house from whom they were renting had had to cater for an ageing relative of their own.

Her stomach clenched as she heard the key being inserted into the front door.

She still wondered how he had managed to talk her into moving to London, a city she hated because it was too fast, too crowded and too noisy for her tastes.

But move to London she had, admittedly to a quieter part of the city, and now that she was here she was in danger of becoming just a little too accustomed to having Leo around. Okay, so he didn't show up *every* evening, and he never stayed the night, but his presence was becoming an addiction she knew she ought to fight.

He had dropped all talk of marriage and yet she still felt on red alert the second he walked through the door. Her eyes still feasted surreptitiously on him and, even though she knew that she should be thanking her lucky stars that he was no longer pursuing the whole marriage thing—because he had 'come to his senses' and 'seen the foolishness of hitching his wagon to a woman he didn't love'—she was oddly deflated by the ease with which he had jettisoned the subject.

As always, her first sight of him as he strode into the small hallway, with its charming flagstone floor and tiny stained-glass window to one side, was one of intense *awareness*. She literally felt her mouth go dry.

'You're here earlier than...um...normal.' She watched as he dealt her a slashing smile, one that made her legs go to jelly, one that made her want to hurl herself at him and wrap her arms around his neck. Every time she felt like this, she recalled what he had said about any marriage between them having upsides, having the distinct bonus of very good sex...

Leo's eyes swept over her in an appraisal that was almost unconscious. He took in the loose trousers, because there was just a hint of a stomach beginning to show; the baggy clothes that would have rendered any woman drab and unappealing but which seemed unbelievably sexy when she was wearing them.

'Is Bridget around?' He had to drag his eyes away from her. Hell, she had told him in no uncertain terms that mutual sexual attraction just wasn't enough on which to base a marriage, so how was it that she still turned him on? Even more so, now that she was carrying his baby.

'She's upstairs resting.'

'There's something I want to show you.' He had no doubt that he would be able to view the property at this hour. He was, after all, in the driving seat. 'So...why don't you get your coat on? It's a drive away.'

'What do you want to show me?'

'It's a surprise.'

'You know I hate surprises.' She blushed when he raised one eyebrow, amused at that titbit of shared confidence between them.

'This won't be the sort of surprise you got two years ago when you returned from a weekend away to find the pub flooded.'

'I'm not dressed for a meal out.' Nor was she equipped for him to resume his erosion of her defences and produce more arguments for having his way…although she killed the little thrill at the prospect of having him try and convince her to marry him.

'You look absolutely fine.' He looked her over with a thoroughness that brought hectic colour to her cheeks. And, while he disappeared to have a few quick words with Bridget, Brianna took the opportunity—cursing herself, because why on earth did it matter, really?—to dab on a little bit of make-up and do something with her hair. She also took off the sloppy clothes and, although her jeans were no longer a perfect fit, she extracted the roomiest of them from the wardrobe and twinned them with a brightly coloured thick jumper that at least did flattering things for her complexion.

'So, where are we going?' They had cleared some of the traffic and were heading out towards the motorway. 'Why are we leaving London?'

Leo thought of the perfect cottage nestled in the perfect grounds with all those perfect features and his face relaxed into a smile. 'And you're smiling.' For some reason that crooked half-smile disarmed her. Here in the car, as they swept out of London on a remarkably fine afternoon, she felt infected with a holiday spirit, a reaction to the stress she had been under for the past few weeks. 'A man's allowed to smile, isn't he?' He flashed her a sideways glance that warmed her face. 'We're having a baby, Brianna. Being cold towards one another is not an option.'

Except, she thought, *he* hadn't been cold towards *her*. He had done his damnedest to engage her in conversation and, thus far, he had remained undeterred by her lack of enthusiasm for engagement. She chatted because Bridget was usually there with them and he, annoyingly, ignored her cagey responses and acted as though everything was perfectly fine between them. He cheerfully indulged his mother's obvious delight in the situation and, although neither of them had mentioned the marriage proposal, they both knew that Bridget was contemplating that outcome with barely contained glee.

'I hadn't realised that I was being cold,' she said stiffly. Her eyes drifted to his strong forearms on the steering wheel. He had tossed his jacket in the back seat and rolled up the sleeves of his shirt to his elbows. She couldn't look even at that slither of bare skin, the sprinkling of dark hair on his arms, without her mind racing backwards in time to when they were lovers and those hands were exploring every inch of her body.

'No, sometimes you're not,' he murmured in a low voice and Brianna looked at him narrowly.

'Meaning?'

'Meaning that there are many times when your voice is cool but the glances you give me are anything but...' He switched the radio on to soft classical music, leaving her to ponder that remark in silence. Did he expect her to say something in answer to that? And what could she say? She *knew* that he had an effect on her; she *knew* that she just couldn't stop herself from sliding those sidelong glances at him, absorbing the way he moved, the curve of his mouth, the lazy dark eyes. Of course he would have noticed! What *didn't* he notice?

She was so wrapped up in her thoughts that she only noticed that they had completely left London behind when fields, scattered villages and towns replaced the hard strip of the motorway, and then she turned to him with confusion.

'We're in the countryside.' She frowned and then her breath caught in her throat as he glanced across to her with amusement.

'Well spotted.'

'It's a bit far to go for a meal out.' Perhaps he wanted to talk to her about something big, something important. Maybe he was going to tell her that he had listened to everything she had said and had come to the conclusion that he could survive with her returning to Ireland whilst he popped up occasionally to see his offspring. Perhaps he thought that a destination far away would be suitable for that kind of conversation, because it would allow her time to absorb it on the return trip back into London.

Had having her at close quarters reminded him of how little he wanted any kind of committed relationship? Had familiarity bred the proverbial contempt? For maybe the first time in his life, he had been tied to a routine of having to curtail his work life to accommodate both her and Bridget. Had he seen that as a dire warning of what might be expected should he pursue his intention of marrying her, and had it put him off?

The more she thought about it, the more convinced she was that whatever he had to say over a charming pub dinner in the middle of nowhere would be...

Something she wouldn't want to hear.

Yet she knew that that was the wrong reaction. She needed to be strong and determined in the road she wanted to follow. She didn't want a half-baked marriage with a guy who felt himself trapped, for whom the only option looming was to saddle himself with her for the rest of his life. No way!

But her heart was beating fast and there was a ball of misery unfurling inside her with each passing signpost.

When the car turned off the deserted road, heading up a charming avenue bordered by trees not yet in leaf, she lay back and half-closed her eyes.

She opened them as they drew up outside one of the prettiest houses she had ever seen.

'Where are we?'

'This is what I wanted to show you.' Leo could barely contain the satisfaction in his voice. He had been sold on first sight. On second sight, he was pleased to find that there was no let-down. It practically had her name written all over it.

'You wanted to show me a *house*?'

'Come on.' He swung out of the car and circled round to hold her door open for her, resisting the urge to help her out, because she had already told him that she hadn't suddenly morphed into a piece of delicate china simply because she was pregnant.

Brianna dawdled behind him as he strode towards the front door and stooped to recover a key which had been placed underneath one of the flower pots at the side of the front step. What the hell was going on? She took a deep breath and realised that, although they were only a matter of forty-five minutes out of West London, the air smelled different. Cleaner.

'This isn't just any house.' He turned to look at her and was pleased at the expression on her face, which was one of rapt appreciation. 'Bar the technicalities, I've bought this house.'

'You've *bought* this house?'

'Come in and tell me what you think.'

'But…'

'Shh…' He placed a finger gently over her parted lips

and the feel of his warm skin against hers made her tremble. 'You can ask all the questions you want after you've
had a look around.'

Despite the fact that he had only looked around the
place once, Leo had no hesitation on acting as tour guide
for the house, particularly pointing out all the quaint features he was certain she would find delightful. There was
a real fire in both the sitting room and the snug, an Aga
in the kitchen, bottle-green bedrooms that overlooked an
orchard, which he hadn't actually noticed on first viewing, but which he now felt qualified to show her with some
pride. He watched as she dawdled in the rooms, staring
out of the windows, touching the curtains and trailing her
finger along the polished oak banister as they returned
downstairs, ending up in the kitchen, which had a splendid view of the extensive back gardens.

The owners had clearly been as bowled over by his
over-the-top, generous offer as he had anticipated. There
was a bottle of champagne on the central island and two
champagne glasses.

'Well? What do you think?'

'It's wonderful,' Brianna murmured. 'I'd never have
thought that you could find somewhere like this so close
to London. Is it going to be a second home for you?'

'It's going to be a first home for us.'

Brianna felt as though the breath had temporarily been
knocked out of her. Elation zipped through her at the
thought of this—a house, the perfect house, shared with
the man she loved and their child. In the space of a few
seconds, she projected into the future where she saw their
son or daughter enjoying the open space, running through
the garden with a dog trailing behind, while she watched
from the kitchen window with Leo right there behind her,
sitting by the big pine table, chatting about his day.

The illusion disappeared almost as fast as it had surfaced because that was never going to be reality. The reality would be her, stuck out here on her own, while Leo carried on working all hours in the city, eventually bored by the woman he was stuck with. He would do his duty for his child but the image of cosy domesticity was an illusion and she had to face that.

'It's not going to work,' she said abruptly, turning away and blinking back stupid tears. 'Nothing's changed, Leo, and you can't bribe me into marrying you with a nice house and a nice garden.'

For a few seconds, Leo wasn't sure that he had heard her correctly. He had been so confident of winning her over with the house that he was lost for words as what she had said gradually sank in.

'I didn't realise that I was trying to bribe you,' he muttered in a driven undertone. He raked his fingers through his hair and grappled with an inability to get his thoughts in order. 'You liked the house; you said so.'

'I do, but a house isn't enough, just like sex isn't enough. That glue would never keep us together.' The words felt as though they had been ripped out of her and she had to turn away because she just couldn't bear to see his face.

'Right.' And still he couldn't quite get it through his head that she had turned him down, that any notion of marriage was over. He hesitated and stared at the stubborn angle of her profile then he strode towards the door. He was filled with a surge of restlessness, a keen desire to be outside, as if the open air might clear his head and point him towards a suitably logical way forward.

It was a mild evening and he circled the house, barely taking in the glorious scenery he had earlier made a great show of pointing out to her.

Inside, Brianna heard the slam of the front door and

spun around, shaking like a leaf. The void he had left behind felt like a physical, tangible weight in the room, filling it up until she thought she would suffocate.

Where had he gone? Surely he wouldn't just drive off and leave her alone here in the middle of nowhere? She contemplated the awkward drive back into London and wondered whether it wouldn't be better to be stuck out here. But, when she dashed out of the front door, it was to find his car parked exactly where it had been when they had first arrived. And he was nowhere to be seen.

He was a grown man, fully capable of taking care of himself, and yet as she dashed down the drive to the main road and peered up and down, failing to spot him, she couldn't stop a surge of panic rising inside her.

What if he had been run over by a car? It was very quiet here, she sternly told herself; what called itself the main road was hardly a thoroughfare. . In fact, no more than a tractor or two and the occasional passing car, so there was no need to get into a flap. But, like a runaway train, she saw in her mind's eyes his crumpled body lying at the kerbside, and she felt giddy and nauseous at the thought of it.

She circled the house at a trot, circled it again and then…she saw him sitting on the ground under one of the trees, his back towards the house. Sitting on the *muddy* ground in his hand-tailored Italian suit.

'What are you doing?' She approached him cautiously because for the life of her she had never seen him like this—silent, his head lowered, his body language so redolent of vulnerability that she felt her breath catch painfully in her throat.

He looked up at her and her mouth went dry. 'You have no intention of ever forgiving me for the lie I told you, have you?' he asked so quietly that she had to bend a little to hear what he was saying. 'Even though you know that I had no intention of engineering a lie when I first arrived. Even though you know, or you *should* know, that what appeared harmless to me at the time was simply a means towards an end. I was thinking on my feet. I never expected to end up painting myself into the box of pathological liar.'

'I know you're not that,' Brianna said tentatively. She settled on the ground next to him. 'Your suit's going to be ruined.'

'So will your jeans.'

'My jeans cost considerably less than your suit.' She ventured a small smile and met with nothing in response, just those dark, dark eyes boring into her. More than anything else she wanted to bridge the small gap between them and reach for his hand, hold it in hers, but she knew that that was just love, her love for him, and it wouldn't change anything. She had to stand firm, however tough it was. She had to project ahead and not listen to the little voice in her head telling her that his gesture, his magnificent gesture of buying this perfect house for her, was a sign of something more significant.

'You were right,' he admitted in the same sort of careful voice that was so disconcerting.

'Right about what?'

'I was trying to bribe you with this house. The garden. Anything that would induce you to give us a chance. But nothing will ever be enough for you to do that because you can't forgive me for my deception, even though it was a deception that was never intended to hurt you.'

'I felt like I didn't know who you were, Leo,' Brianna said quietly. 'One minute you were the man helping out at the pub, mucking in, presumably writing your book when you were closeted away in the corner of the bar…and then the next minute you're some high-flying millionaire with a penthouse apartment and a bunch of companies, and the book you were writing was never a book at all. It was just loads of work and emails so that you could keep your businesses ticking over while you stayed at the pub and used me to get information about Bridget.'

'God, Brianna it wasn't like that...' But she had spelt out the basic facts and strung them together in a way that made sense, yet made no sense whatsoever. He felt like a man with one foot off the edge of a precipice he hadn't even known existed. All his years of control, of always being able to manage whatever situation was thrown at him, evaporated, replaced by a confusing surge of emotions that rushed through him like a tsunami.

He pressed his thumbs against his eyes and fought off the craven urge to cry. Hell, he hadn't cried since his father had died!

'But it was,' she said gently. 'And even if I did forgive you...' *and she had* '...the ingredients for a good marriage just aren't there.'

'For you, maybe' He raised his head to stare solemnly at her. 'But for me, the ingredients are all there.'

CHAPTER TEN

HE LOOKED AT her solemnly and then looked away, not because he couldn't hold her stare, but because he was afraid of what he might see there, a decision made, a mind closed off to what he had to say.

'When I came to search out my mother, I had already presumed to know what sort of person she was: irresponsible, a lowlife, someone without any kind of moral code… In retrospect, it was a facile assumption, but still it was the assumption I had already made.'

'Then why on earth did you bother coming?'

'Curiosity,' Leo said heavily. Rarely given to long explanations for his behaviour, he knew that he had to take his time now and, funnily enough, talking to her was easy. But then, he had talked to her, really talked to her, a lot more than he had ever talked to any other woman in his life before. That should have been a clue to the direction his heart was taking, but it had been a clue he had failed to pick up on.

Now he had a painful, desperate feeling that everything he should have said had been left too late. In his whole life, he had never taken his eye off the ball, had never missed connections. He had got where he had not simply because he was incredibly smart and incredibly proactive but because he could read situations with the same ease with which he could read people. He always knew when to strike and when to hold back.

That talent seemed to have deserted him now. He felt that if he said one wrong word she would take flight, and then where would he be?

'I had a wonderful upbringing, exemplary, but there was always something at the back of my mind, something that needed to fill in the missing blanks.'

'I can get that.'

'I always assumed that…' He inhaled deeply and then sat back with his eyes closed. This was definitely not the best spot to be having this conversation but somehow it felt right, being outside with her. She was such an incredibly outdoors person.

'That?'

'That there must be something in me that ruled my emotions. My adoptive parents were very much in love. I had the best example anyone could have had of two people who actually made the institution of marriage work for them. And yet, commitment was something I had always instinctively rejected. At the back of my mind, I wondered whether this had something to do with the fact that I was adopted; maybe being given away as a baby had left a lasting legacy of impermanence, or maybe it was just some rogue gene that had found its way into my bloodstream; some crazy connection to the woman who gave birth to me, something that couldn't be eradicated.'

Brianna let the conversation wander. She wanted to reassure him that no such rogue gene existed in anyone, that whatever reasons he might have had in the past for not committing it was entirely within his power to alter that.

Except, she didn't want him to leap to the conclusion that any altering should be done on her behalf. She was still clinging to a thread of common sense that was telling her not to drop all her defences because he seemed so vulnerable. He might be one-hundred per cent sincere in wanting her to marry him, but without the right emotions she would have to stick fast to her decision. But it was difficult when her heart wanted to reach out to him and just assure him that she would do whatever it took to smooth that agonised expression from his face.

'As you know, I've been biding my time until I made this trip to find her. I had always promised myself that hunting down my past would be something I would do when my parents were no longer around.'

'I'm surprised you could have held out so long,' Brianna murmured. 'I would have wanted to find out straight away.'

'But then that's only one big difference between us, isn't it?' He gave her a half-smile that made her toes curl and threatened to permanently dislodge that fragile thread of common sense to which she was clinging for dear life. 'And I didn't appreciate just how *good* those differences between us were.'

'Really?' Brianna asked breathlessly. The fragile thread of common sense took a serious knocking at that remark.

'Really.' Another of those smiles did all sorts of things to her nervous system. 'I think it was what drew me to you in the first place. I saw you, Brianna, and I did a double take. It never occurred to me that I would find myself entering a situation over which I had no control. Yes, I lied about who I was, but there was no intention to hurt you. I would never have done that...*would* never do that.'

'You wouldn't?'

'Never,' he said with urgent sincerity. 'I was just passing through then we slept together and I ended up staying on.'

'To find out as much as you could about Bridget.'

'To be with you.'

Hope fluttered into life and Brianna found that she was holding her breath.

'I didn't even realise that I was sinking deeper and deeper. I was so accustomed to not committing when it came to relationships that I didn't recognise the signs. I told myself that I was just having time out, that you were a novelty I was temporarily enjoying but that, yes, I'd still be moving on.'

'And then you met her.'

'I met her and all my easy black-and-white notions flew through the window. This wasn't the lowlife who had jettisoned a baby without any conscience. This was a living, breathing human being with complexities I had never banked on, who overturned all the boxes I had been prepared to stick her in. I wanted to get to know her more. At the back of my mind—no, scratch that, at the forefront of my mind—I knew that I had dug a hole for myself with that innocuous lie I had told in the very beginning—and you know something? I couldn't have chosen a more inappropriate occupation for myself. Reading fiction is not my thing, never mind writing it. I didn't like myself for what I was doing, but I squashed that guilty, sickening feeling. It wasn't easy.'

'And then Bridget had that fall and...'

'And my cover was blown. It's strange, but most women would have been delighted to have discovered that the guy they thought was broke actually was a billionaire; they would happily have overlooked the "starving writer" facade and climbed aboard the "rich businessman" bandwagon. I'm sorry I lied to you, and I'm sorry I wasn't smart enough to come clean when I had the chance. I guess I knew that, if there was one woman on the planet who would rather the struggling writer than the rich businessman, it was you...'

Brianna shrugged.

'And, God, I'm sorry that I continued to stick to my facade long after it had become redundant… I seem to be apologising a heck of a lot.' His beautiful mouth curved into a rueful, self-deprecatory smile.

'And you don't do apologies.'

'Bingo.'

'What do you mean about sticking to your facade after it had become redundant?'

'I mean you laid into me like an avenging angel when you found out the truth about my identity and what did I do? I decided that nothing was going to change; that you might be upset, and we might have had a good thing going, but it didn't change the fact that I wasn't going to get wrapped up in justifying myself. Old habits die hard.'

He sighed and said, half to himself, 'When you walked out of my life, I let you go and it was the biggest mistake I ever made but pride wouldn't allow me to change my mind.'

'Biggest mistake?' Brianna said encouragingly.

'You're enjoying this, aren't you?' He slanted a glance at her that held lingering amusement.

'Err…'

'I can't say I blame you. We should go inside.'

'We can't sit on anything, Leo. We're both filthy. I don't think the owners would like it if we destroyed their lovely furniture with our muddy clothes.'

'My car, then. I assure you that that particular owner won't mind if the seats get dirty.' He stood up, flexed his muscles and then held out his hand for her to take.

She took it and felt that powerful current pass between them, fast, strong and invisible, uniting them. He pulled her up as though she weighed nothing and together they walked towards his car, making sure that the house was firmly locked before they left and the key returned to its original hiding place.

'No one living in London would ever dare to be so trusting,' he said, still holding her hand. She hadn't pulled away and he was weak enough to read that as a good sign.

'And no one where I live would ever be suspicious.'

He wanted to tell her that that was good, that if she chose to marry him, to share her life with him, she would be living somewhere safe, a place where neighbours trusted one another. If he could have disassociated himself from his extravagantly expensive penthouse apartment, he would have.

She insisted that they put something on the seats and he obliged by fetching a rug from the trunk, one of the many things which Harry had insisted would come in handy some day but for which he had never before had any use. Then he opened the back door of the car so that he wasn't annoyed by a gear box separating them.

Brianna stepped in and said something frivolous about back seats of cars, which she instantly regretted, because didn't everyone know what the back seats of cars were used for?

'But you liked the house; you said so.' Had he mentioned that before? Was he dredging up an old, tired argument which she had already rejected? 'It's more than just the house, Brianna, and it's more than just marriage because it makes sense. It's even bigger than my past, bigger than me wanting to do right by this child because of what happened to me when I was a baby.' He rested back and sought out her hand without looking at her.

Brianna squeezed his fingers tentatively and was reassured when he returned the gesture.

'If you hadn't shown up, if you hadn't sought me out to tell me about the pregnancy, I would have eventually come for you because you were more than just a passing relationship. I may have wanted to keep you in that box, but you climbed out of it and I couldn't stuff you back in and, hell, I tried.' He laughed ruefully. 'Like I said, old habits die hard.'

'It means a lot for you to say that you would have come for me,' Brianna said huskily. They weren't looking at one another but the connection was still thrumming between their clasped fingers.

'I wouldn't have had a choice, Brianna. Because I need you, and I love you, and I can't imagine any kind of life without you in it. I think I've known that for a long time, but I just didn't admit it to myself. I've never been in love with any one before, so what were my points of comparison? Without a shred of vanity, I will admit that life's been good to me. Everything I touched turned to gold, but I finally realised that none of the gold was worth a damn when the only woman I've ever loved turned her back on me.'

Brianna had soared from ground level to cloud nine in the space of a heartbeat.

'You *love* me?'

'Which is why marriage may not make sense to you, but it makes sense to me. Which is why all the ingredients are there…for me.'

'Why didn't you say?' She twisted to face him and flung her arms around his neck, which was an awkward position, because they were sitting alongside one another. But as she adjusted her body, so did he, until they were face to face, chest to chest, body pressed tightly against body. Now she was sure that she could feel his heart beating, matching hers.

'I love you so much,' she whispered shakily. 'When you proposed, all I could think was that you were doing it because it was the sensible option, and I didn't want us to be married because it was a sensible option. If I hadn't loved you so much, Leo, maybe I would have jumped at the chance—but I knew that if you didn't love me back that road would only end up leading to heartbreak.'

His mouth found hers and they kissed urgently and passionately, holding on to one another as if their lives depended on it.

'I've never felt anything like this before...' The feel of her against him was like a minor miracle. He wanted just to keep holding her for ever. 'And I didn't have the vocabulary to tell you how I felt. The only thing I could do was hope that my actions spoke on my behalf and, when they didn't, when I thought that I was going to lose everything...'

'You came out there...' She reached up and sighed with pleasure as their mouths met yet again, this time with lingering tenderness. She smoothed her fingers over his face and then through his hair, enjoying the familiarity of the sensation.

'So...' he said gravely. Even though he was ninety-nine per cent certain of the answer she would give him, he still feared that one per cent response he might hear. This, he thought, was what love felt like. It made you open and vulnerable to another person. It turned wanting into needing and self-control into a roller-coaster ride. He could think of nowhere he would rather have been.

'Yes. Yes, yes, yes! I'll marry you.'

'When?' Leo demanded and Brianna laughed with pleasure.

'When do you think? A girl needs time to plan these things, you know...'

'Would two weeks be time enough?'

She laughed again and looked at him tenderly. 'More than enough time!'

* * *

But in the end, it was six long weeks before they tied the knot in the little local church not a million miles away from her pub. The entire community turned out for the bash and, with typical Irish exuberance, the extremely happily wedded couple were not allowed to leave until for their honeymoon until the following morning.

They left a very proud Bridget behind to oversee the running of the pub because Ireland was her home in the end and she had been reluctant to leave it behind for good.

'But expect a very frequent visitor,' she had said to Brianna.

Brianna didn't doubt it. The older woman had rediscovered a joy for living ever since Leo had appeared on the scene, ever since she had rediscovered the baby, now a man, whom she had been compelled to give away at such a young age. She had spent her life existing under a dark cloud from which there had been no escape, she had confided to Brianna,. The cloud had now gone. Being asked to do the job of overseeing the pub, which had been signed over to her, was the icing on the cake.

Now, nearly two days after their wedding, Brianna sat on the veranda of their exquisite beach villa, a glass of orange juice in her hand and her baby bump a little bigger than when she had first headed down to London with a madly beating heart to break the news of her pregnancy to the man who she could hear padding out to join her.

The past few weeks had been the happiest of her life. By the time they returned to England, the house which she had loved on sight would be theirs and what lay ahead glittered like a pathway paved in precious jewels: a life with the man she adored; a man who never tired of telling her how much he loved her; a baby which would be the perfect celebration of their love. And not forgetting Bridget, a true member of their family.

'What are you thinking?'

Brianna smiled and looked up at him. The sun had already set and the sea was a dark, still mass lapping against the sand. It was warm and the sound of myriad insects was harmonious background music: the Caribbean at its most perfect.

'I'm thinking that this must be what paradise is like.'

'Sun, sand and sea but without the alcoholic cocktails?' Leo teased, swinging round so that he could sit next to her and place his hand on her swollen stomach. He marvelled that he never seemed to tire of feeling the baby move. He was awestruck that he was so besotted with her, that he hated her being out of sight, that work, which had hitherto been his driving force, had taken a back seat.

'That's exactly right.' Brianna laughed and then her eyes flared as he slipped his hand under the loose cotton dress so that now it rested directly on her stomach, dipping below the swell to cup her between her legs.

'Have I told you how sexy I find your pregnant body?' he murmured into her ear.

'You may have once or twice, or more!' She lay back, as languorous as a cat, and smiled when he gave a low grunt of pleasure.

'And now...' he kissed the lobe of her ear and felt her smile broaden '...I think there are more pressing things for us to do than watch the sea, don't you?'

He could have added that he too now knew what paradise felt like.

* * * * *

THE MOST EXPENSIVE LIE OF ALL

BY
MICHELLE CONDER

From as far back as she can remember **Michelle Conder** dreamed of being a writer. She penned the first chapter of a romance novel just out of high school, but it took much study, many (varied) jobs, one ultra-understanding husband and three very patient children before she finally sat down to turn that dream into a reality.

Michelle lives in Australia, and when she isn't busy plotting loves to read, ride horses, travel and practise yoga.

This book is dedicated to Amber and Corin for opening up the world of polo for me and doing it with such warmth and generosity. You guys are great.

To a formidable squash champ, Juan Marcos, who promptly responded to my queries about his game.

And also to my lifelong friend Pam Austin, who wrote down every memory she ever had of her visits to Mexico—which could have been a novel in itself.

Thank you!

CHAPTER ONE

'EIGHT-THREE. MY SERVE.'

Cruz Rodriguez Sanchez, self-made billionaire and one of the most formidable sportsmen ever to grace the polo field, let his squash racquet drop to his side and stared at his opponent incredulously. 'Rubbish! That was a let. And it's eight-three *my* way.'

'No way, *compadre*! That was my point.'

Cruz eyeballed his brother as Ricardo prepared to serve. They might only be playing a friendly game of squash but 'friendly' was a relative term between competing brothers. 'Cheats always get their just desserts, you know,' Cruz drawled, moving to the opposite square.

Ricardo grinned. 'You can't win every time, *mi amigo*.'

Maybe not, Cruz thought, but he couldn't remember the last time he'd lost. Oh, yeah, actually he could—because his lawyer was in the process of righting that particular wrong while he blew off steam with his brother at their regular catch-up session.

Feeling pumped, he correctly anticipated Ricardo's attempted 'kill shot' and slashed back a return that his brother had no chance of reaching. Not that he didn't try. His running shoes squeaked across the resin-coated floor as he lunged for the ball and missed.

'*Chingada madre!*'

'Now, now,' Cruz mocked. 'That would be nine-three. My serve.'

'That's just showing off,' Ricardo grumbled, picking himself up and swiping at the sweat on his brow with his sweatband.

Cruz shook his head. 'You know what they say? If you can't stand the heat...'

'Too much talking, *la figura.*'

'Good to see you know your place.' He flashed his brother a lazy smile as he prepared to serve. '*El pequeño.*'

Ricardo rolled his eyes, flipped him the bird and bunkered down, determination etched all over his face. But Cruz was in his zone, and when Ricardo flicked his wrist and sent the ball barrelling on a collision course with Cruz's right cheekbone he adjusted his body with graceful agility and sent the ball ricocheting around the court.

Not bothering to pick himself up off the floor this time, Ricardo lay there, mentally tracking the trajectory of the ball, and shook his head. 'That's just unfair. Squash isn't even your game.'

'True.'

Polo had been his game. Years ago.

Wiping sweat from his face, Cruz reached into his gym bag and tossed his brother a bottle of water. Ricardo sat on his haunches and guzzled it.

'You know I let you win these little contests between us because you're unbearable to be around when you lose,' he advised.

Cruz grinned down at him. He couldn't dispute him. It was a celebrated fact that professional sportsmen were very poor losers, and while he hadn't played professional polo for eight years he'd never lost his competitive edge.

On top of that he was in an exceptionally good mood, which made beating him almost impossible. Remembering the reason for that, he pulled his cell phone from his kitbag to see if the text he was waiting for had come through, frowning slightly when he saw it hadn't.

'Why are you checking that thing so much?' Ricardo queried. 'Don't tell me some *chica* is finally playing hard to get?'

'You wish,' Cruz murmured. 'But, no, it's just a business deal.'

'Ah, don't sweat it. One day you'll meet the *chica* of your dreams.'

Cruz threw him a banal look. 'Unlike you, I'm not looking for the woman of my dreams.'

'Then you'll probably meet her first,' Ricardo lamented.

Cruz laughed. 'Don't hold your breath,' he replied. 'You might meet an early grave.' He tossed the ball in the air and sent it spinning around the court, his concentration a little spoiled by Ricardo's untimely premonition.

Because there *was* a woman. A woman who had been occupying his thoughts just a little too often lately. A woman he hadn't seen for a long time and hoped to keep it that way. Of course he knew why she was jumping into his head at the most inopportune times of late, but after eight years of systematically forcing her out of it that didn't make it any more tolerable.

Not that he allowed himself to get bent out of shape about it. He'd learned early on that the things you were most attached to had the power to cause you the most pain, and since then he'd lived his life very much like a high-rolling gambler—easy come, easy go.

Nothing stuck to him and he stuck to nothing in return—which had, much to everyone's surprise, made him a phenomenally wealthy man.

An 'uneducated maverick', they'd called him. One who had swapped the polo field for the boardroom and invested in deals and stock market bonds more learned businessmen had shied away from. But then Cruz had been trading in the tumultuous early days of the global financial crisis and he'd already lost the one thing he had cared about the most. Defying expectations and market trends seemed inconsequential after that.

What had really fascinated him in the early days was how people had been so ready to write him off because of his Latino blood and his lack of a formal education. What they hadn't realised was that the game of polo had perfectly set him up to achieve in the business world. Killer instincts combined with a tireless work ethic and the ability to think on his feet were all attributes to make you succeed in polo and in business, and Cruz had them in spades. What he didn't have right now—what he *wanted*—was a text from his lawyer advising him that he was the proud owner of one of East Hampton's most prestigious horse studs: Ocean Haven Farm.

Resisting another urge to check his phone, he prowled around the squash court, using the bottom of his sweat-soaked T-shirt to swipe at the perspiration dripping down his face.

'Nice abs,' a feline voice quipped appreciatively through the glass window overlooking the court.

Ah, there she was now.

Lauren Burnside, one of the Boston lawyers he sometimes used for deals he didn't want made public knowledge before the fact, her hip cocked, her expression a smooth combination of professional savvy and sexual knowhow.

'I always thought you were packing a punch beneath all those business suits, Señor Rodriguez. Now I know you are.'

'Lauren.' Cruz let his T-shirt drop and waited for her hot eyes to trail back up to his. She was curvy, elegant and sophisticated, and he had nearly slept with her about a year ago but had baulked at the last minute. He still couldn't figure out why. 'Long way to come to make a house call, counsellor. A text would have sufficed.'

'Not quite. We have a hitch.' She smiled nonchalantly. 'And since I was in California, just a hop, skip and a jump away from Acapulco, I thought I'd deliver the news *mano-a-mano*.' She smiled. 'So to speak.'

Cruz scowled, for once completely unmoved by the flick of her tongue across her glossy mouth.

He knew women found him attractive. He was tall, fit, with straight teeth and nose, a full head of black hair, and he was moneyed-up and uninterested in love. It appeared to be the perfect combination. '*Untameable*,' as one date had purred. He'd smiled, told her he planned to stay that way and she'd come on even stronger. Women, in his experience, were rarely satisfied and usually out for what they could get. If they had money they wanted love. If they had love they wanted money. If they had twenty pairs of shoes they wanted twenty-one. It was tedious in the extreme.

So he ignored his lawyer's honey trap and kept his mind sharp. 'That's not what I want to hear on a deal that was meant to be completed two hours ago, Ms Burnside.' He kept his voice carefully blank, even though his heart rate had sped up faster than during the whole squash game.

'Let me come down.'

For all the provocation behind those words Cruz could tell she had picked up his *not interested* vibe and was smart enough to let it drop.

'She your latest?'

'No.'

Cruz's curt response raised his brother's eyebrows.

'She wants to be.'

Cruz folded his arms as Lauren pushed open the clear door and stepped onto the court, her power suit doing little to disguise the killer body beneath. She inhaled deeply, the smell of male sweat clearly pleasing to her senses.

'You boys have been playing hard,' she murmured provocatively, looking at them from beneath dark lashes.

Okay, so maybe she wasn't that smart. 'What's the hitch?' Cruz prompted.

She raised a well-tended brow at his curtness. 'You don't want to go somewhere more private?'

'This is Ricardo, my brother, and vice-president of Rodriguez Polo Club. I repeat: what's the hitch?'

Lauren's forehead remained wrinkle-free in the face of his growing agitation and he didn't know if that was due to nerves of steel or Botox. Maybe both.

'The hitch,' she said calmly, 'is the granddaughter. Aspen Carmichael.'

Cruz felt his shoulders bunch at the unexpectedness of hearing the name of the female he was doing his best to forget. The last time he'd laid eyes on her she'd been seventeen, dressed in nothing but a nightie and putting on an act worthy of Marilyn Monroe.

The little scheme she and her preppy fiancé had concocted had done Cruz out of a fortune in money and, more importantly, lost him the respect of his family and peers.

Aspen Carmichael had bested him once before and he'd walked away. He'd be damned if he walked away again.

'How?'

'She wants to keep Ocean Haven for herself and her uncle has magnanimously agreed to sell it to her at a reduced cost. The information has only just come to light, but apparently if she can raise the money in the next five days the property is hers.'

Cruz stilled. 'How much of a reduced cost?'

When Lauren named a figure half that which he had offered he cursed loudly. 'Joe Carmichael is not the sharpest tool in the shed, but why the hell would he do that?'

'Family, darling.' Lauren shrugged. 'Don't you know that blood is thicker than water?'

Yes, he did, but what he also knew was that everyone was ultimately out for themselves and if you let your guard down you'd be left with nothing more than egg on your face.

He ran a hand through his damp hair and sweat drops sprayed around his head.

Lauren jumped back as if he'd nearly drenched her designer suit in sulphuric acid and threw an embarrassed glance towards Ricardo, who was busy surveying her charms.

Cruz snapped his attention away from both of them and concentrated on the blank wall covered in streaks of rubber from years of use.

Eight years ago Ocean Haven had been his home. For eleven years he had lived above the main stable and worked diligently with the horses—first as a groom, then as head trainer and finally as manager and captain of Charles Carmichael's star polo team. He'd been lifted from poverty and obscurity in a two-dog town because of his horsemanship by the wealthy American who had spotted him on the *hacienda* where Cruz had been working at the time.

Cruz gritted his teeth.

He'd been thirteen and trying to keep his family from going under after the sudden and pointless death of his father.

Charles Carmichael, he'd later learned, had ambitious plans to one day build a polo 'dream team' to rival all others, and he'd seen in Cruz his future protégé. His mother had seen in him an unmanageable boy she could use to keep the rest of his siblings together. She'd said sending him off with the American would be the best for him. What she'd meant was that it would be the best for all of them, because Old Man Carmichael was paying her a small fortune to take him. Cruz had known it at the time—and hated it—but because he'd loved his family more than anything he'd acquiesced.

And, hell, in the end his mother had been right. By the age of seventeen Cruz had become the youngest player ever to achieve a ten handicap—the highest ranking any player could achieve and one that only a handful ever did. By the age of twenty he'd been touted as possibly the best polo player who had ever lived.

By twenty-three the dream was over and he'd become the joke of the very society who had kissed his backside more times than he cared to remember.

All thanks to the devious Aspen Carmichael. The devious and extraordinarily beautiful Aspen Carmichael. And what shocked Cruz the most was that he hadn't expected it of her. She'd blindsided him and that had made him feel even more foolish.

She had come to Ocean Haven as a lonely, sweet-natured ten-year-old who had just lost her mother in a horrible accident some had whispered was suicide. He'd hardly seen her during those years. His summers had been spent playing polo in England and she had attended some posh boarding school the rest of the year. To him she'd always been a gawky kid with wild blonde hair that looked as if it could use a good pair of scissors. Then one year he'd injured his shoulder and had to spend the summer—her summer break—at Ocean Haven, and *bam!* She had been about sixteen and she had turned into an absolute stunner.

All the boys had noticed and wanted her attention.

So had Cruz, but he hadn't done anything about it. Okay, maybe he'd thought about it a number of times, especially when she had thrown him those hot little glances from beneath those long eyelashes when she assumed he wasn't looking, and, okay, possibly he could remember one or two dreams that she had starred in, but he never would have touched her if she hadn't come on to him first. She'd been too young, too beautiful, too *pure*.

He found himself running his tongue along the edge of

his mouth and the taste of her exploded inside his head. She sure as hell hadn't been pure *that* night.

Gritting his teeth, he shoved her out of his mind. Memory could be as fickle as a woman's nature and his aviator glasses were definitely not rose coloured where she was concerned.

'You okay, *hermano*?'

Cruz swung around and stared at Ricardo without really seeing him. He liked to think he was a fair man who played by the rules. A forgive-and-forget kind of man. He'd stayed away from Ocean Haven and anything related to it after Charles Carmichael had given him the boot. Now his property had come up for sale and objectively speaking it was a prime piece of real estate. The fact that he'd have to raze it to the ground to build a hotel on it was just par for the course.

Of course his kid brother wouldn't understand that, and he wasn't in the mood to explain it. He'd left Mexico when Ricardo had been young. Ricardo had cried. Cruz had not. Surprisingly, after he'd returned home with his tail between his legs eight years ago, he and his brother had picked up from where they'd left off, their bond intact. It was the only bond that was.

'I'm fine.' He swung his gaze to Lauren. 'And I'm not concerned about Aspen Carmichael. Old man Carmichael died owing more money than he had, thanks to the GFC, so there's no way she can have that sort of cash lying around.'

'No, she doesn't,' Lauren agreed. 'She's borrowing it.'

Cruz stilled. Now, that was just plain stupid. He knew Ocean Haven agisted horses and raised good-quality polo ponies, but no way would either of those bring in the type of money they were talking about.

'She'll never get it.'

Lauren looked as if she knew better. 'My sources tell me she's actually pretty close.'

Cruz ignored Ricardo's interested gaze and kept his face visibly relaxed. 'How close?'

'Two-thirds close.'

'Twenty million! Who would be stupid enough to lend her twenty million US dollars in this economic climate?' And, more importantly, what was she using for collateral?

Lauren raised her eyebrows at his uncharacteristic outburst, but wisely stayed silent.

'Hell!' The burst of adrenaline he used to feel when he mounted one of his ponies before a major event winged through his blood. How on earth had she managed to raise that much money and what could he do about it?

'Do you want me to start negotiating with her?' Lauren queried.

'No.' He turned his ordinarily agile mind to come up with a solution, but all it produced was an image of a radiant teenager decked out in figure-hugging jodhpurs and a fitted shirt leaning against a white fencepost, laughing and chatting while the sun turned her wheat-blonde curls to gold. His jaw clenched and his body hardened. Great. A hard-on in gym shorts. 'You focus on Joe Carmichael and any other offers lurking in the wings,' he instructed his lawyer. 'I'll handle Aspen Carmichael.'

'Of course,' Lauren concurred with a brief smile.

'In the meantime find out who Aspen is borrowing from and what exactly she's offering as collateral—' although as to that he had his ideas '—and meet me in my Acapulco office in an hour.'

Ricardo waited until Lauren had disappeared before tossing the rubber ball into the air. 'You didn't tell me you were buying the Carmichael place.'

'Why would I? It's just business.'

Ricardo's eyebrows lifted. 'And *handling* the lovely Aspen Carmichael will be part of that business?'

People said Cruz had a certain look that he got just before a major event which told his opponents they might as well pack up and go home. He gave it to his brother now. 'This is not your concern.'

His brother, unfortunately, was one of the few people who ignored it.

'Maybe not, but you once swore you'd never set foot on Ocean Haven again. So, what gives?'

What gave, Cruz thought, was that old Charlie had kicked the bucket and his son, Aspen's uncle, Joseph Carmichael, couldn't afford to run the estate and keep his English bride in diamonds and champagne so was moving to England. Cruz had assumed Aspen would be going with them—to sponge off him now that her grandfather was out of the picture.

It seemed he had assumed wrong.

But he had no intention of talking about his plans with his overly sentimental brother, who would no doubt assume there was more to it than a simple opportunity to make a lot of money. 'I don't have time to talk about it now,' he said, making a split-second decision. 'I need to organise the jet.'

'You're flying to East Hampton?'

'And if I am?' Cruz growled.

Ricardo held his hands up as if he was placating an angry bear. 'Miama's surprise birthday party is tomorrow.'

Cruz strode towards the changing rooms, his mind already in Hampton—or more specifically in Ocean Haven. 'Don't count on me being there.'

'Given your track record, the only person who still has enough hope to do that is Miama herself.'

Cruz stopped. Ricardo's blunt words stabbed him in the heart. His family still meant everything to him, and he'd help any of them out in a heartbeat, but things just weren't the same any more. With the exception of Ricardo, none of his family knew how to treat him, and his mother constantly threw him guilty looks that were a persistent reminder of the darker days of his youth after he'd gone to the farm.

Charles Carmichael had been a difficult man with a formidable temper who'd liked to get his own way, and Cruz had never been one to back down from a fight until *that* night. No, it had not been an easy transition for a proud thirteen-year-old to make, and if there was one thing Cruz hated more than the capricious nature of the human race it was dwelling on the past.

He glanced back at Ricardo. 'You're going to be stubborn about this, aren't you?'

Ricardo laughed. 'You've cornered the market in stubborn, *mi amigo*. I'm just persistent.'

'Persistently painful. You know, bro, you don't need a wife. You *are* a wife.'

Aspen decided that she had a new-found respect for telemarketers. It wasn't easy being told no time after time and then picking yourself up and continuing on. But like anyone trying to make a living she had to toughen up and stay positive. Stay on track. Especially when she was so close to achieving her goal. To choke now or, worse, give up, would mean failing in her attempt to keep her beloved home and that was inconceivable.

Smiling up at the beef of a man in front of her as if she didn't have a head full of doubts and fears, Aspen surreptitiously pulled at the waist of the silk dress she'd worn to impress the polo patrons attending the midweek chukkas they held at Ocean Haven throughout the summer months.

In the searing sunshine the dress had taken on the texture of a wet dishrag and it did little to improve her mood as she listened to Billy Smyth the Third, son of one of her late grandfather's arch enemies, wax lyrical about the game of polo he had—thankfully—just won.

'Oh, yes,' she murmured. 'I heard it was the goal of

the afternoon.' Fed to him, she had no doubt, by his well-paid polo star, who knew very well which side his bread was buttered on.

Billy Smyth was a rich waste of space who sponged off his father's cardboard packaging empire and loved every minute of it—not unlike many others in their circle. Her ex-husband still continued unashamedly to live off his own family's wealth, but thankfully he'd been out of her life for a long time, and she wasn't going to ruin an already difficult day by thinking about him as well.

Instead she concentrated on the wealthy man in front of her, with his polished boots and his pot belly propped over the top of his starchy white polo jeans. Years ago she had tried to like Billy, but he was very much a part of the 'women should keep silent and look beautiful' brigade, and the fact that she was pandering to his unhealthy ego at all was testament to just how desperate she had become.

When he'd asked her to meet him after the game she had jumped at the chance, knowing she'd dance on the sun in a bear suit if it would mean he'd lend her the last ten million she needed to keep Ocean Haven. Though by the gleam in his eyes he'd probably want her naked—and she wasn't so desperate that she'd actually hawk herself.

Yet.

Ever, she amended.

So she continued to smile and present her plan to turn 'The Farm', as Ocean Haven was lovingly referred to, into a viable commercial entity that any savvy businessman would feel remiss for not investing in. So far two of her grandfather's old friends had come on board, but she was fast feeling as if she was running out of options to find the rest. Ten million was small change to Billy and, she thought, ignoring the way his eyes made her skin crawl as if she was covered in live ants, he seemed genuinely interested.

'Your grandpop would be rolling in his grave at the thought of the Smyths investing in The Farm,' he announced.

True—but only because her grandfather had been an unforgiving, hard-headed traditionalist. 'He's not here anymore.' Aspen reminded him. 'And without the money Uncle Joe is going to sell to the highest bidder.'

Billy cocked his head and considered his way slowly down to her feet and just as slowly back up. 'Word is he already has a winner.'

Aspen took a minute to relax her shoulders, telling herself that Billy really didn't mean to be offensive. 'Yes. Some super-rich consortium that will no doubt want to put a hotel on it. But I'm determined to keep The Farm in the family. I'm sure you understand how important that is, being such a devoted family man yourself.'

A slow smile crept over Billy's face and Aspen inwardly groaned. She was trying too hard and they both knew it.

'Yes, indeed I do.'

Billy leered. His smile grew wider. And when he rocked back on his heels Aspen sent up a silent prayer to save her from having to deal with arrogant men ever again.

Because that was exactly why she was in this situation in the first place. Her grandfather had believed in three things: testosterone, power, and tradition. In other words men should inherit the earth while women should be grateful that they had. And he had used his fearsome iron will to control everyone who dared to disagree with him.

When her mother had died suddenly just before Aspen's tenth birthday and—surprise surprise—her errant father couldn't be located, Aspen had been sent to live with her grandfather and her uncle. Her grandmother had passed away a long time before. Aspen had liked Uncle Joe immediately, but he'd never been much of an advocate for her during her grandfather's attempts to turn her into the perfect debutante.

So far she had been at the mercy of her controlling grandfather, then her controlling ex, and now her misguided, henpecked uncle.

'I'm sorry Aspen,' her Uncle Joe had said when she'd managed to pin him down in the library a month ago. 'Father left the property in my hands to do with as I saw fit.'

'Yes, but he wouldn't have expected you to *sell it*,' Aspen had beseeched him.

'He shouldn't have expected Joe to sort out the mess of his finances either,' Joe's determined wife Tammy had whined.

'He wasn't well these last few years.' Aspen had appealed to her aunt, but, knowing that wouldn't do any good, had turned back to her uncle. 'Don't sell Ocean Haven, Uncle Joe. Please. It's been in our family for one hundred and fifty years. Your blood is in this land.'

Her mother's heart was here in this land.

But her uncle had shaken his head. 'I'm sorry, Aspen, I need the money. But unlike Father I'm not a greedy man. If you can raise the price I need in time for my Russian investment, with a little left over for the house Tammy wants in Knightsbridge, then you can have Ocean Haven and all the problems that go with it.'

'What?'

'What?'

Aspen and her Aunt Tammy had cried in unison.

'Joseph Carmichael, that is preposterous,' Tammy had said.

But for once Uncle Joe had stood up to his wife. 'I'd always planned to provide for Aspen, so this is a way to do it. But I think you're crazy for wanting to keep this place.' He'd shaken his head at her.

Aspen had been so happy she had all but floated out of

the room. Then reality at what exactly her uncle had offered had set in and she'd got the shakes. It was an enormous amount of money to pay back but she *knew* if she got the chance she could do it.

The horn signifying the end of the last chukka blew and Aspen pushed aside her fear that maybe she *was* just a little crazy.

'Listen, Billy, it's a great deal,' she snapped, forgetting all about the proper manners her grandfather had drummed into her as a child, and also forgetting that Billy was probably her last great hope of controlling her own future. 'Take it or leave it.'

Oh, yes and losing that firecracker temper of yours is sure to sway him, she berated herself.

A tiny dust cloud rose between them as Billy made a figure eight with his boots in the dirt. 'The thing is, Aspen, we're busy enough over at Oaks Place, and even though you've done a good job of hiding it The Farm needs a lot of work.'

'It needs some,' Aspen agreed with forced calm, thinking she hadn't done a good job at all if he'd seen through her patchwork maintenance attempts. 'But I've factored all that into the plan.' *Sort of.*

'I just think I need a bit more of a persuasive argument if I'm to take this to my daddy,' he suggested, a certain look crossing his pampered face.

'Like…?' A tight band had formed around Aspen's chest because, really, it was hard to miss what he meant.

'Well, hell, Aspen, you're not that naïve. You *have* been married.'

Yes, unfortunately she had. But all that had done was make her determined that she would never be at any man's mercy again. Which was exactly where arrogant, controlling men like this one wanted their women to be. 'For just you, Billy?' she simpered. 'Or for your daddy as well?'

It took Mr Cocksure a second or two to realise she was yanking his chain and when he did his big head reared back and his eyes narrowed. 'I ain't no pimp, lady.'

'No,' she said calmly, flicking her riot of honey-coloured spiral curls back over her shoulder. 'What you are is a dirty, rotten rat and I can see why Grandpa Charles said your kind were just slime.' *Who gave a damn about proper manners anyway?*

Instead of getting angry Billy threw back his head and hooted with laughter. 'You know. I can't believe the rumours that you're a cold one in the sack. Not with all that fire shooting out of those pretty green eyes of yours.' He reached out and ran a finger down the side of her cheek and grinned when she raised her hand to rub at it. 'Let me know when you change your mind. I like a woman with attitude.'

Before she could open her mouth to tell him she'd mention that to his wife he sauntered off, leaving her spitting mad. She watched him pick up a glass of champagne from a table before joining a group of sweaty riders and willed someone to grab it and throw it all over him.

Of course no one did. Fate wasn't that kind.

Turning away in disgust, she cursed under her breath when a gust of hot wind whipped her hair across her face. Too angry to stop and clear her vision, she would have walked straight into a wall if it hadn't reached out and grabbed her by her upper arms.

With a soft gasp she looked up, about to thank whoever had saved her. But the words never came and the quick smile froze on her face as she found herself staring into the hard eyes of a man she had thought she would never see in the flesh again.

The air between them split apart and reformed, vibrating with emotion as Cruz Rodriquez stared down at her with such cold detachment she nearly shivered.

Eight years dissolved into dust. Guilt, shame and a host of other emotions all sparked for dominance inside her.

'I…' Aspen blinked, her mind scrambling for poise… words…*something*.

'Hello, Aspen. Nice to see you again.'

Aspen blinked at the incongruity of those words. He might as well have said *Off with her head*.

'I…'

CHAPTER TWO

CRUZ STARED DOWN at the slender woman whose smooth arms he held and wished he hadn't left his sunglasses in the car. At seventeen Aspen Carmichael had been full of sexual promise. Eight years later, with her golden mane flowing down past her shoulders and the top button of her dress artfully popped open to reveal the upper swell of her creamy assets, she had well and truly delivered. And he was finding it hard not to take her all in at once.

'You...?' he prompted casually, dropping his hands and raising his eyes from her cleavage.

She glanced down and quickly closed the top of her dress. Clearly only men offering part of their vast fortunes were allowed to view the merchandise. The realisation of his earlier assumption as to what she might be using as leverage to raise her cash was for some reason profoundly disappointing.

'I...' She shook her head as if to clear it. 'What are you doing here?'

'Old Charlie would roll over in his grave if he heard you greeting a polo patron like that,' Cruz drawled. *Even one he didn't think would ever be good enough for his perfect little granddaughter,* he added silently.

Cruz's velveteen voice, with no hint at all of his Mexican heritage, scraped over Aspen's already raw nerves and she didn't manage to contain the shiver this time.

She couldn't tell his frame of mind but she knew hers and it was definitely disturbed. 'My grandfather probably feels like he's on a spit roast at the moment.' She smiled, trying for light amusement to ease the tension that lay as thick as the issues of the past between them.

'Are you implying he's in hell, Aspen?'

He probably was, Aspen thought, but that wasn't what she'd meant. 'No. I just…you're right.' She shook her head, wondering what had happened to her manners. Her composure. Her *brain*. 'That was a terrible greeting. Shall we start again?'

Without waiting for him to reply she stuck out her hand, ignoring the racing memories causing her heart to beat double time.

'Hello, Cruz, welcome back to Ocean Haven. You're looking well.' Which was a half-truth if ever she'd uttered one.

The man didn't look well. He looked superb.

His thick black hair that sat just fashionably shy of his expensive suit jacket and his piercing black eyes and square-cut jaw were even more beautiful than she remembered. He'd always had a strong, angular face and powerful body, but eight years had done him a load of favours in the looks department, settling a handsome maturity over the youthful virility he'd always worn like a cloak.

The apology she'd never got to voice for her part in the acrimonious accusations that had no doubt contributed to him leaving Ocean Haven eight years ago hovered behind her closed lips, but it seemed awkward to just blurt it out.

How could she tell him that a couple of months after that night she had written him a letter explaining everything but hadn't had the wherewithal to send it without feeling a deep sense of shame at her ineptitude? It was little comfort knowing she'd been distracted by her grandfather's stroke at the time, because she knew her behaviour that night had probably brought that on too. After he had recovered sending Cruz a letter had seemed like too little too late, and she'd pushed out of her mind the man who had fascinated her during most of her teenage years.

And maybe he was here now to let bygones be bygones. She didn't know, but why pre-empt anything with her own guilt-riddled memories?

Because it would make you feel better, that's why.

'As are you.'

As she was what? Oh, looking well. 'Thank you.' She ran a nervous hand down the side of her dress and then pretended she was flicking off horse dust. 'So...ah...are you here for the polo? The last chukka just finished, but—'

'I'm not here for the polo.'

Aspen hated the anxious feeling that had settled over her and raised her chin. 'Well, there's champagne in the central marquee. Just tell Judy that I sent—'

'I'm not here for the champagne either.'

Even more perturbed by the way he regarded her with such cool detachment she felt as if she was frying under the blasted summer sun. 'Well, it would be great if you could tell me what you *are* here for because I have a few more people to schmooze before they leave. You know how these things go.'

He looked at her as if he was seeing right inside her. As if he knew all her secrets. As if he could see how desperately uncomfortable she was. *Impossible*, she thought, telling herself to get a grip.

Cruz could almost see the sweat breaking out over Aspen's body and noted the way her cat-green eyes wouldn't quite meet his. He didn't know if that was because he was keeping her from an assignation with Billy Smyth, or someone else, or because she could feel the chemistry that lay between them like a grenade with the pin pulled.

Whatever it was, she wasn't leaving his side until he

had won over her confidence and figured out a way to handle the situation.

His brother's silky question about 'handling the lovely Aspen Carmichael' came into his head. He knew what Ricardo had meant and looking at Aspen now, in her svelte designer dress and 'come take me' heels, her wild hair curling down around her shoulders as if she'd just rolled out of her latest lover's bed, he had no doubt many men had 'handled' her that way before. But not him. Never him.

So far he'd drawn a blank as to how to contain her money-grabbing endeavours without alerting her to his own interest in Ocean Haven. Until he did he'd just have to rein himself in and keep his eyes away from her sexy mouth.

'I'm here to buy a horse, Aspen. What else?'

'A horse?'

Aspen blinked. That was the last thing she had expected him to say, though what she *had* expected she couldn't say.

'You do have one for sale, don't you?' he continued silkily.

Aspen cleared her throat. 'Gypsy Blue. She's a thoroughbred. Ex-racing stock and she's gorgeous.'

'I have no doubt.'

Aspen frowned at his tone, wondering why he seemed so tense. Not that he *looked* tense. In his bespoke suit with his hands in his pockets, his hair casually ruffled by the warm breeze, he looked like a man who didn't have a care in the world. But the vibe she was picking up from him was making her feel edgy—and surely that wasn't just because of her sense of guilt.

'Are you hoping the horse will materialise in front of us, Aspen, or are you going to take me to see her?'

'I…' Aspen felt stupid, and not a little perturbed to be standing there trying not to look at his chiselled mouth. Which was nearly impossible when the memory of the kiss they had shared on that awful night was swirling inside her head. 'Of course.' She glanced around, hoping to see Donny, but knew that was cowardly. It was really *her* responsibility to show him the mare, not her chief groom's.

'She played earlier today, so she should be in the south stables.' It was just rotten luck that she happened to be in the building where she had kissed Cruz on that fateful night. 'Hey, why don't I take you past the east paddock?' she said, using anything as a possible distraction. 'Trigger is out there, and I know he'd remember you and—'

'I'm not here on a social visit, Aspen.'

And don't mistake it for one, his tone implied.

No polo, no champagne, no socialising. Got it.

Still, she hesitated at his sharp tone. Then decided to let it drop and listened to the sound of their feet crunching the gravel as they walked away from the busy sounds of horse-owners loading tired horses into their respective trucks. It was all very normal and busy at the end of the afternoon's practice, and yet Aspen felt as if she was wading through quicksand with Cruz beside her.

She cast a curious glance at him and wondered if he felt the same way. Or maybe he didn't feel anything at all and just wanted to do his business and head out like everyone else. In a way she hoped that was the case, because the shock of seeing him again had worn off and his tension was raising her stress levels to dangerous proportions.

But then he had a reason for being tense, she reminded herself, and her skin flushed hotly as the weight of the past bore down on her. Years ago she had promised herself that she would never let pride interfere with the decisions she made in her life, but in avoiding the elephant walking alongside them wasn't that exactly what she was doing now?

Taking a deep breath, she stopped just short of the stable

doors and turned to Cruz, determined to rectify the situation as best she could *before* they made it inside.

Shading her eyes with one hand, she looked up into his face. Had he always been this tall? This broad? This good-looking?

'Cruz, listen. This feels really awkward, but you took me by surprise before when I ran into you—*literally*.' She released a shaky breath. 'I want you to know that I feel terrible about the way you left The Farm all those years ago, and I'm truly sorry for the role I played in that.'

'Are you?' he asked coolly.

'Yes, of course. I never meant for you to get into trouble.'

Cruz didn't move a muscle.

'I didn't!' Aspen felt her temper flare at his dubious look, hating how defensive she sounded.

She'd gone down to the stables that night because Chad—now thankfully her ex—had stayed for dinner so he could present his idea to her grandfather that he would marry her as soon as she turned eighteen. Aspen remembered how overwhelmed she had felt when neither man would consider her desire to study before she even thought about the prospect of marriage.

She'd known it was what her grandfather wanted, and at the time pleasing him had been more important than pleasing herself. So she'd done what she'd always done when she was stressed and gone down to be with the horses and to reconnect with her mother in her special place in the main stable.

Gone to try and make sense of her feelings.

Of course in hindsight letting her frustration get to her and kicking the side of the stable wall in steel-capped boots hadn't been all that clever, because it had brought Cruz down from his apartment over the garage to investigate.

She remembered that he had looked gorgeous and lean

and bad in dirty jeans and a half-buttoned shirt, as if he had just climbed out of bed.

'What's got you in a snit, *chiquita*?' he'd said, the intensity of his heavy-lidded gaze in the dim light belying the relaxed humour in his voice.

'Wouldn't you like to know?' she'd thrown back at him challengingly.

Inwardly grimacing, she remembered how she had flicked her hair back over her shoulder in an unconscious gesture to get his full attention. She hadn't known what she was inviting—not really—but she hadn't wanted him to go. For some reason she had remembered the time she had come across him kissing a girlfriend in the outer barn, and the soft, pleasure-filled moans the girl had made had filled her ears that night.

Acting purely on instinct she had wandered from horse stall to horse stall, eventually coming to a stop directly in front of him. The warm glow of his torch had seemed to make the world contract, so that it had felt as if they were the only two people in it. Aspen was pretty sure she'd reached for him first, but seconds later she had been bent over his arm and he had been kissing her.

Her first kiss.

She felt her breathing grow shallow at the memory.

Something had fired in her system that night—desperation, lust, need—whatever it had been she'd never felt anything like it before or since.

Looking back, it was obvious that a feeling of entrapment—a feeling of having no say over her future—had driven her into the stables that night, but it had been Cruz's sheer animal magnetism that had driven her into his arms.

Not that she really wanted to admit any of that to him right now. Not when he looked so...*bored*.

'This is old news, Aspen, and I'm not in the mood to reminisce.'

'That's your prerogative. But I want you to know that I told my grandfather the next day that he'd got it wrong.'

'Really?'

'Yes, really.' But her grandfather had cut her off with a look of disgust she hadn't wanted to face. She looked up at Cruz now, more sorry than she could say. 'I'm—'

'Truly sorry? So you said. Have you become prone to repeating yourself?'

Aspen blinked up at him. Was it her imagination or did he hate her? 'No, but I don't think you believe me,' she said carefully.

'Does it matter if I do?'

'Well, we used to be friends.'

'We were never *friends*, Aspen. But I was glad to see your little indiscretion didn't stop Anderson from marrying you.'

Aspen moistened her parched lips. 'Grandfather thought it best if I didn't tell him.'

Cruz barked out a laugh. 'Well, now I almost feel sorry for the fool. If he'd known what a disloyal little cheat you were from the start he might have saved himself the heartache at the end.'

Oh, yes, he hated her all right. 'Look, I'm sorry I brought it up. I just wanted to clear the air between us.'

'There's nothing to clear as far as I'm concerned.'

Aspen studied him warily. He wasn't moving but she felt as if she was being circled by a predator. A very angry predator. She didn't believe that he was at all okay with what had transpired between them but who was she to push it?

'I made a mistake, but as you said you're not here to reminisce.' And nor was she. Particularly not about a time in her life she would much rather forget had ever happened.

She turned sharply towards the stables and kept up a brisk pace until she reached the doors, only starting to feel

herself relax as she entered the cooler interior, her high
heels clicking loudly on the bluestone floor. Her nose was
filled with the sweet scent of horse and hay.

Cruz followed and Aspen glanced around at the worn
tack hanging from metal bars and the various frayed blankets and dirty buckets that waited for Donny and her to
come and finish them off for the day. The high beams of
the hayloft needed a fresh coat of paint, and if you looked
closely there were tiny pinpricks of sunlight streaming in
through the tin roof where there shouldn't be. She hoped
Cruz didn't look up.

A pigeon created dust motes as it swooped past them
and interested horses poked their noses over the stall doors.
A couple whinnied when they recognised her.

Aspen automatically reached into her pocket for a treat,
forgetting that she wasn't in her normal jeans and shirt.
Instead she brushed one of the horses' noses. 'Sorry, hon.
I don't have anything. I'll bring you something later.'

Cruz stopped beside her but he didn't try to stroke the
horse as she remembered he might once have done.

'This is Cougar. Named because he has the heart of a
mountain lion, although he can be a bit sulky when he gets
pushed around out on the field. Can't you, big guy?' She
gave him an affectionate pat before moving to the next
stall. 'This one is Delta. She's—'

'Just show me the horse you're selling, Aspen.'

Aspen read the flash of annoyance in his gaze—and
something else she couldn't place. But his annoyance
fed hers and once again she stalked away from him and
stopped at Gypsy Blue's stall. If she'd been able to afford
it she would have kept her beloved mare, and that only increased her aggravation.

'Here she is,' she rapped out. 'Her sire was Blue Rise,
her dam Lady Belington. You might remember she won
the Kentucky Derby twice running a few years back.' She

sucked in a breath, trying not to babble as she had done over her apology before. If Cruz was happy with the way things were between them then so was she. 'I have someone else interested, so if you want her you'll have to decide quickly.'

Quite a backpedal, Cruz thought. From uncomfortable, apologetic innocent to stiff Upper East Side princess. He wondered what other roles she had up her sleeve and then cut the thought in half before it could fully form. Because he already knew, didn't he? Cheating temptress being one of them. Not that she was married now. Or engaged as far as he knew.

'I've made you angry,' he said, backpedalling himself.

This wasn't at all the way he needed her to be if he was going to get information out of her. It was just this damned place. It felt as if it was full of ghosts, with memories around every corner that he had no wish to revisit. He'd closed the door on that part of his life the minute he'd carried his duffel bag off the property. On foot. Taking nothing from Old Man Carmichael except the clothes on his back and the money he'd already earned.

Of its own accord his gaze shifted to the other end of the long walkway to the place where Aspen had approached him that night, wearing a cotton nightie she must have known was see-through in the glow of his torch. He hadn't been wearing much either, having only thrown on a pair of jeans and a shirt he hadn't even bothered to button properly when he'd heard something banging on the wall and gone to investigate.

He'd presumed it was one of the horses and had been absolutely thunderstruck to find Aspen in that nightie and a pair of riding boots. She'd looked hotter than Hades and when she'd strolled past the stalls, lightly trailing her slender fingers along the wood, he couldn't have moved if someone had planted a bomb under him.

It had all been a ploy. He knew that now. He'd kissed her because he'd been a man overcome with lust. She'd kissed him because she'd been setting him up. It had been like a bad rendition of Samson and Delilah and she'd deserved an acting award for wardrobe choice alone.

His muscles grew taut as he remembered how he had held himself in check. How he hadn't wanted to overwhelm her with the desperate hunger that had surged through him and urged him to pull her down onto the hay and rip the flimsy nightie from her body. How he hadn't wanted to take her *innocence*. What a joke. She'd played him like a finely tuned instrument and, like a fool, he'd let her.

'Like I said before.' She cleared her throat. 'This feels a little awkward.'

She must have noticed the direction of his gaze because her voice sounded breathless; almost as if her memories of that night mirrored his own. Of course he knew better now.

About to placate her by pretending he had forgotten all about it, he found the words dying in his throat as she raised both hands and twisted her flyaway curls into a rope and let it drop down her back. The middle button on her dress strained and he found himself willing it to pop open.

Surprised to find his libido running away without his consent, he quickly ducked inside the stall and feigned avid interest in a horse he had no wish to buy.

He went through the motions, though, studying the lines of the mare's back, running his hands over her glossy coat, stroking down over her foreleg and checking the straightness of her pasterns. Fortunately he was on auto-pilot, because his undisciplined mind was comparing the shapeliness of the thoroughbred with Aspen's lissom figure and imagining how she would feel under his rough hands.

Silky, smooth, and oh, so soft.

Memories of the little sounds she'd made as he'd lost

himself in her eight years ago exploded through his system and turned his breathing rough.

'She's an exceptional polo pony. Really relaxed on the field and fast as a whip.'

Aspen's commentary dragged his mind back to his game plan and he kept on stroking the horse as he spoke. 'Why are you selling her?'

'We run a horse stud, not a bed and breakfast,' she said with mock sternness, her eyes tinged with dark humour as she repeated one of Charles Carmichael's favourite sayings.

'Or an old persons' home.' He joined in with Charles's second favourite saying before he could stop himself.

'No.' Her small smile was tinged with emotion.

Her reaction surprised him.

'You miss him?'

She shifted and leant her elbows on the door. 'I really don't know.' Her eyes trailed over the horse. 'He had moments of such kindness, and he gave me a home when Mum died, but he was impossible to be around if he didn't get his own way.'

'He certainly had high hopes of you marrying well and providing blue stock heirs for Ocean Haven.' And he'd made it more than clear to him after Aspen had returned to the house that night that Cruz wouldn't be the one to provide them under any circumstances.

'Yes.'

Her troubled eyes briefly met his and for a moment he wanted to shake her for not being a different kind of woman. A more sincere and genuine woman.

'So what do you think?'

It took him a minute to realise she was talking about the mare and not herself. 'She's perfect. I'll take her.'

'Oh.' She gave a self-conscious laugh. 'You don't want to ride her first?'

Oh, yes, he certainly did want to do that!

'No.'

'Well, I did tell you to be quick. I'll have Donny run the paperwork.'

'Send it to my lawyer.' Cruz rubbed the mare's nose and let her nudge him. 'I hear Joe is planning to sell the farm.'

She grimaced. 'Good news travels fast.'

'Polo's a small community.'

'Too small sometimes.' She gestured towards the mare. 'She'll ruin your nice suit if you let her do that.'

'I have others.'

So nice not to have to worry about money, Aspen thought, a touch enviously. After the abject poverty she and her mother had lived in after her father's desertion, the wealth of Ocean Haven had been staggering. It was something she'd never take for granted again.

'Where are you planning to go once it's sold?'

'It's not going to be sold,' she said with a touch of asperity, stepping back as Cruz joined her outside the stall. 'At least not to someone else.'

He raised an eyebrow. 'You're going to buy it?'

'Yes.' She had always been a believer in the power of positive thinking, and she had never needed that more than she did now.

Gypsy Blue whickered and stuck her head over the door and Aspen realised her water trough was nearly empty. Unhooking it, she walked the short distance to a tap and filled it.

'Let me do that.'

Cruz took the bucket from her before she could stop him and stepped inside the stall. Aspen grabbed the feed bucket Donny had left outside and followed him in and hooked it into place.

'It's a big property to run by yourself,' he said.

'For a girl?' she replied curtly.

'I didn't say that.'

'Sorry. I'm a bit touchy because so many people have implied more than once that I won't be able to do it. It's like they think I'm completely incompetent, and that really gets my—' She gave a small laugh realising she was about to unload her biggest gripe onto him and he was virtually a stranger to her now. Why would he even care? 'The fact is…' She looked at him carefully.

He had money. She'd heard of his business acumen. Of the companies he bought and sold. Of his innovative and brilliant new polo-inspired hotel in Mexico. He was the epitome of a man at the top of his game. Right now, as he leant his wide shoulders against the stall door and blocked out all sources of light from behind, he also looked the epitome of adult male perfection.

'But the fact is…?' he prompted.

Aspen's eyes darted to his as she registered the subtle amusement lacing his voice. Did he know what she had just been thinking? 'Sorry, I was just…' *Just a bit distracted by your incredible face? Your powerful body? Way to go, Aspen. Really. Super effort.* 'The fact is—' she squared her shoulders '—I need ten million dollars to keep it.'

She forced a bright smile onto her face.

'You're not looking for an investment opportunity, are you?'

CHAPTER THREE

SHE COULDN'T BELIEVE she'd actually voiced the question that had just formed in her mind but she knew that she had when Cruz's dark gaze sharpened on hers. But frankly, with only five days left to raise the rest of the money and Billy Smyth firmly out of the picture, she really was that desperate.

'Give you ten million dollars? That's a big ask.'

Her heart thumped loudly in her chest and her mouth felt dust dry. 'Lend,' she corrected. 'But you know what they say…' She stopped as he straightened to his full height and she lost her train of thought.

He shoved both hands into his pockets. '*They* say a lot of things, Aspen. What is it exactly you're referring to?'

'If you don't ask you never know,' she said, moistening her lips. 'And I'm desperate.'

Cruz's eyes glittered as he looked down at her. 'A good negotiator never shows that particular hand. It puts their opponent in the dominant position.'

Heat bloomed anew on her face as his tone seemed to take on a sensual edge. 'I don't see you as my opponent, Cruz.'

'Then you're a fool,' he returned, almost too mildly.

Aspen felt her hopes shrivel to nothing. What had she been thinking, approaching a business situation like that? Where was her professionalism? Her polish?

But maybe she'd known he'd never agree to it. Not with the way he obviously felt about her.

'What would I get out of it, anyway?'

The unexpected question surprised her and once again her eyes darted to his. Had she been wrong in thinking he wouldn't be interested? 'A lot, actually. I've drawn up a business plan.'

'Really?'

She didn't like his sceptical tone but decided to ignore it. 'Yes. It outlines the horses due to foal, and how much we expect to make from each one, and our plans to purchase a top-of-the-line stallion to keep improving the breed. We also have a couple of wonderful horses we're about to start training—and I don't know if you've heard of our riding school, but I teach adults and children, and— well... There's more, but if you're truly interested we can run through the logistics of it all later.' Out of breath, she stopped, and then added, 'It has merit. I promise.'

'If it has so much merit why haven't any of the financial institutions bankrolled you?'

'Because I'm young—that is usually the first excuse. But really I think it's because unbeknownst to any of us Grandfather hadn't been running his business properly the last few years and—' Realising that yet again she was about to divulge every one of her issues, she stopped. 'The banks just don't believe I have enough experience to pull it off.'

'Perhaps you should have thought about furthering your education instead of marrying to secure your future.'

Aspen nearly gasped at his snide tone of voice. 'I didn't marry to secure anything,' she said sharply. Except perhaps her grandfather's love and affection. Something that had always been in short supply.

Upset with herself for even being in this position, and with him for his nasty comment, Aspen thought about telling him that she was one semester out from completing a degree in veterinary science—and that she'd achieved that while working full-time running Ocean Haven. But she knew that in her current state she would no doubt come across as defensive or whiney, and that only made her angry.

'If you have such a low opinion of me why pretend any interest in my plans for The Farm?' she demanded hotly, slapping her hands either side of her waist. 'Are you planning to steal our ideas?'

That got an abrupt bark of laughter from him that did nothing to improve her temper. 'I don't need to steal your ideas, *gatita*. I have plenty of my own.'

'Then why get my hopes up like that?'

'Is that what I did?'

Aspen stared him down. 'You know that's exactly what you did.'

He stepped closer to her. 'But maybe I *am* interested.'

His tone sent a splinter of unease down her spine but she was too annoyed to pay attention to it. 'Don't patronise me, Cruz. I have five days before The Farm will be sold to some big-shot investment consortium. I don't have time to bandy around with this.'

'Ocean Haven really means that much to you?'

'Yes, it does.'

'I suppose it *is* the easiest option for a woman in your position,' he conceded, with such arrogance that Aspen nearly choked.

Easy? Easy! He clearly had no idea how hard she worked on the property—tending horses, mending fences, keeping the books—nor how important Ocean Haven was to her. How it was the one link she had left with her mother. How it was the one place that had made her feel happy and secure after she'd been orphaned. After her marriage had fallen apart.

She was incredibly proud of her work and her future plans to open up a school camp for kids who'd had a tough start in life. Horses had a way of grounding troubled adolescents and she wanted to provide a place they could come to and feel safe. Just as she had. And she hated that Cruz was judging her—*mocking her*—like every other obnoxious male she had ever come across. That she hadn't expected it from him only made her feel worse.

Hopping mad, she had a mind to order him off her property, but she couldn't quite kill off this avenue of hope just yet. He was supposed to be a savvy businessman after all, and she had a good plan. Well, she hoped she did. 'Ocean Haven has been in my family for centuries,' she began, striving for calm.

'I think the violinist has packed up for the day…'

Aspen blinked. 'God, you're cold. I don't remember that about you.'

'Don't you, *gatita*? Tell me…'

His voice dropped an octave and her heartbeat faltered. 'What *do* you remember?'

Aspen's gaze fell to his mouth. 'I remember that you were…' *Tall. That your hair glints almost blue-black in the sun. That your face looks like it belongs in a magazine. That your mouth is firm and yet soft.* She forced her eyes to meet his and ignored the fact that her face felt as if it was on fire. 'Good with the horses.' She swallowed. 'That you were smart, and that you used to keep to yourself a lot. But I remember when you laughed.' *It used to make me smile.* 'It sounded happy. And I remember that when you were mad at something not even my grandfather was brave enough to face you. I rem—'

'Enough.' He sliced his hand through the air with sharp finality. 'There's only one thing I want to know right now,' he said softly.

If she remembered his kisses? Yes—yes, she did. Sometimes even when she didn't want to. 'What?' she asked, hating the breathless quality of her voice.

'Just how desperate *are* you?'

His dark voice was so dangerously male it sent her brain into overdrive. 'What kind of a question is that?' She shook her head, trying to ward off the jittery feelings he so effortlessly conjured up inside her.

He reached forward and captured a strand of her hair between his fingertips, his eyes burning into hers. 'If I were to lend you this money I'd want more than a share in the profits.'

Aspen felt her chest rising and falling too quickly and hoped to hell he wasn't going to suggest the very thing Billy Smyth had done not an hour earlier.

Reaching up, she tugged her hair out of his hold. 'Such as…?'

His eyes looked black as pitch as they pinned her like a dart on a wall. 'Oh, save us both the Victorian naïveté. You're no retiring virgin after the life you lived with Chad Anderson—and before that, even. You're a sensual woman who no doubt looks very good gracing a man's bed.' He paused, his gaze caressing her face. 'If the terms were right I might want you to grace mine.'

Was he kidding?

Aspen felt her mouth drop open before she could stop it. Rage welled up inside her like a living beast. Rage at the injustice of her grandfather's will, rage at the way men viewed her as little more than a sexual object, rage at her mother's death and her father's abandonment.

Maybe Cruz had a reason for being upset with her after she had failed to correct her grandfather's assumption that they were sleeping together years ago, but that didn't give him the right to treat her like a—like a whore.

'Get out of my way,' she ordered.

His eyes lingered on her tight lips. 'Make sure you don't

burn your bridges unnecessarily, Aspen. Pride can be a nasty thing when it's used rashly.'

She knew all about pride going before a fall. 'It's not rash pride making me reject your offer, Cruz. It's simple self-respect.'

'Whatever you want to call it, I'm offering you a straightforward business deal. You have something I've decided I want. I have something you need. Why complicate it?'

'Because it's disgusting.'

'What an interesting way to put it,' he sneered. 'Tell me, Aspen, would it have been less *disgusting* if I'd first said that you were beautiful before taking you to bed? If I'd first invited you out for a drink? Taken you to dinner, perhaps?' He took a step towards her and lowered his voice. 'If I had gone down that path would you have said yes?' His lips twisted with mocking superiority. 'If I had romanced you, Aspen, I could have had you naked and beneath me in a matter of hours and saved myself a hell of a lot of money.'

Aspen threw him a withering look, ignoring the sudden mental picture of them both naked and tangled together. 'You can save yourself a hell of a lot of money *and* skin right now and get off my property,' she said tightly.

His nostrils flared as he breathed deeply and she suddenly realised how close he was, how far she had to tilt her head back to look up at him. 'And for your information,' she began, wanting to stamp all over his supersized ego, 'I would *never* have said yes to you.'

'Really?'

He stepped even closer and Aspen felt the harsh bite of wood at her back. Caged, she could only stare as Cruz lifted one of her spiral curls again; this time carrying it to his nose. Her hands rose to shove him back but he didn't budge, and almost immediately her senses tuned in to the warm packed muscle beneath the thin cotton of his shirt, to the fast beat of his heart that seemed to mirror her own racing pulse.

A flash of memory took her back eight years to the feel of his mouth on hers. The feel of his tongue rubbing hers. The feel of his hands spanning her waist. Heat pooled inside her and made her breasts heavy, her legs unsteady. She remembered that after they'd been caught she had been so shocked by her physical reaction to him and so scared of her grandfather's wrath she'd fallen utterly silent—ashamed of herself for considering one man's marriage proposal while losing herself in the arms of another. Cruz hadn't raised one word of denial the whole time and she still wondered why.

Not that she had time to consider that now... He leant forward as if her staying hands were nothing more than crepe paper. His breath brushed her ear.

'Let me tell you what I remember, *gatita*. I remember the way your curvy backside filled out those tight jodhpurs. I remember the purple bikini top you used to wear riding your horse along the beach. And I remember the way you used to watch me. A bit like the way you were watching me stroke the mare before.' His hand tightened in her hair. 'You were thinking about how it would feel if I put my hands on you again, weren't you? How it would feel if I kissed you?'

Aspen made a half coughing noise in instant denial and tried to catch her breath. There was no way he could have known she'd been thinking exactly that.

'Have you turned into a dreamer, Cruz?' she mocked with false bravado, frightened beyond belief at how vulnerable she suddenly felt. 'Because really a dream would be the only place I would ever want something like that from you.'

Dreamer?

Cruz felt his jaw knot at her insolent tone. How dared she accuse him of being a dreamer when *she* was clearly the dreamer here if she thought she could buy and hold onto the rundown estate Ocean Haven had become?

Memories of the past swirled around him and bit deep. Memories of how she had felt in his arms. How she had tasted. Memories of how she had stood there, all dazed innocence, and listened to her grandfather rail at him. He'd been accused of ruining her that night but it was her—her and that slimy fiancé of hers, Chad Anderson—who had tried to ruin him. She and her lover who had set him up for a fall to clear the way for Chad to take over as captain of Charles Carmichael's dream team.

There'd been no other explanation for it, and he'd always wondered how far she would have taken things if her grandfather had turned up five minutes later. Because that was all it would have taken for him to twist her nightie up past her hips and thrust deep into her velveteen warmth.

His eyes took her in now. Her defiant expression and flushed face. Her rapidly beating pulse and her moist lips where her pink tongue had just lashed them. Her hands were burning a hole in his shirt and he was already as hard as stone—and, by God, he'd had enough of her holier-than-thou attitude.

'You would have loved it.' Cruz twisted her hair into a knot at the back of her head and pulled her roughly up against him. '*Will* love it,' he promised thickly, wrapping his other arm around her waist and staunching her shocked cry with his mouth.

Her lips immediately clamped together and she pushed against him, but that only brought her body more fully up against his as her hands slipped over his shoulders. She stilled, as if the added contact affected her as much as it affected him, and with a deep groan he ran his tongue across the seam of her lips. He felt a shiver run through her and then she shoved harder to dislodge him. He told himself he wasn't doing his plan any favours by forcing himself on her, but the plan paled into insignificance when compared to the feel of her warm and wriggling in his arms. He wanted her to surrender to him. To admit that the chemistry that had exploded through him like a haze of bloodlust as soon as he had seen her again wasn't just one-sided.

But some inner instinct warned him that this wasn't the way to get her to acquiesce, and years of experience in gentling horses rushed through him. He marshalled some of that strength and patience now and gentled her. Sucking at her lips, nipping, soothing her with his tongue. She made a tiny whimper in the back of her throat and he felt a sense of primal victory as she tentatively opened her mouth under his, aligning her body so that her soft curves were no longer resisting his hardness but melting against him until he could feel every sweet, feminine inch of her.

With a low growl of approval he gentled his hold on her and angled her head so that he could take her mouth more fully. When her lips opened wider and her arms urged him closer he couldn't stop himself from plundering her, couldn't resist drawing her tongue out so that she could taste him in return.

An unexpected sense of completeness settled over him—a sense of finding something he'd been searching for his whole life—and he didn't want the kiss to end. He didn't want this maddening arousal to end.

If he'd had any idea that it would be like this again he wasn't sure that he would have started it. But now that he had he didn't want to stop. *Ever*. She tasted so sweet. So silky. So *good*.

He made a sound low in his throat when she circled her pelvis against his in an age-old request and he couldn't think after that. Could only grab her hips and smooth his hands over her firm backside to mould her against him.

'Yes,' he whispered roughly against her mouth. 'Kiss me, *chiquita*. Give me everything.'

And she did. Without reservation. Her mouth devouring his as if she too had dreamed of this over and over and over. As if she too couldn't live without—

'Ow!'

Her sharp cry of pain echoed his deeper one as something pushed the back of his head and bumped his forehead into hers. He pulled back and glared over his shoulder to where the horse he had just agreed to purchase snorted in disgust.

Aspen blinked dazedly, rubbing at her head. Then the stunned look on her face cleared and he knew their impromptu little make out session had well and truly finished.

'You bastard.'

She raised her arm and slapped his face. The sound echoed in the cavernous stall and he worked his jaw as heat bloomed where her palm had connected.

About to tell her that she had a good arm, he was shocked to see that she had turned white and looked as if she might pass out.

'Aspen?'

She looked at him as if *he* had hit *her*. 'Now look what you made me do!' she cried.

Well, wasn't that typical of her—to blame him?

'I didn't *make* you do anything. You hit me. And if I'm not mistaken all because you enjoyed my kisses just a little too much.'

'Oh!'

She pushed against him with all her might and he was only too glad to step away from her.

'I've already turned down one slimy rat today and now I'm turning down another.' Her glare alone could have buried him. 'Now, get off my property before I have every man available throw you off.'

'I'm flattered you think it would take that many.'

'Oh, I bet you are.' Every inch of her trembled with feminine outrage. 'But I'm not prepared to take chances with a bully like you.'

'I didn't bully you, *chiquita*. You were asking for it.'

'Don't call me that.'

Cruz rubbed his jaw and scowled. 'What?'

'You know what.'

His brain must still have been on a go-slow because he couldn't recall what he'd called her. The thought irked him enough that he said, 'Maybe you should think about the way you act and dress if you don't want men thinking you're free and easy in bed.'

'Oh, my God. Are you serious?'

'Silky dresses that outline every curve, killer heels and just-out-of-bed hair all tell a man what's what.'

Fascinated, he watched her pull herself up to her full five feet and four inches—six in the heels.

'Any man who judges me on the way I look isn't worth a dime. You and Billy—'

Cruz raised his hand, cutting short her dramatic tirade. 'I am not like him,' he snarled.

'Keep telling yourself that, Cruz.' She tossed her head at him. 'It might help you sleep better at night.'

'I sleep just fine,' he grated. 'But if you should decide to change your high and mighty little mind about my offer I'll be staying at the Boston International until tomorrow morning.'

'Don't hold your breath.' She reefed open the stall door and stomped past him. 'I'd have to be crazy to accept an offer like that.'

Cruz ran a shaky hand through his hair and listened to the staccato sound of her high heels hammering her ire against the stone floor.

Her words, 'don't hold your breath' rang out in his head. Hadn't he told his brother the same thing a few hours ago? *Hell*. If he had, he couldn't remember why.

CHAPTER FOUR

'DAMMIT.' ASPEN CURSED as her hair caught around the button she had just wrenched open on the front of her dress. 'Stupid, idiotic hair.'

She yanked at it and winced when she heard the telltale crackle that indicated that she'd left a chunk behind. Then the pain set in and she rubbed her scalp.

God, she was angry. Furious. She pulled at the rest of her buttons and stopped when she caught sight of herself in the free-standing mirror that stood in the corner of her bedroom. Slowly she walked towards it.

An ordinary female figure stared back. An ordinary female figure with a flushed face and a wild mane of horrible hair. And tender lips. She put her fingers to them. They *looked* the same as they always did, but they *felt* softer. Swollen. And there was a slight graze on her chin where Cruz's stubble had scraped her skin.

Her pelvis clenched at the remembered pleasure of his mouth on hers. He hadn't even kissed her like that eight years ago. Then he'd been softer, almost tender. Today he'd kissed her as if he hadn't been able to help himself. As if he'd wanted to devour her. And never before had she kissed someone like that in return. Thank God Gypsy Blue had tried to knock some sense into them.

She had no idea why she'd acted like that with a man who had insulted her so badly. Maybe it was the fact that seeing him again had knocked her sideways. Somehow he had dazzled her the way he'd used to dazzle the women at polo matches. He was so attractive the crowds had always doubled when he had played, because all the wives and girlfriends had insisted that they simply *loved* polo and had to spend the *whole* day watching it. Really, they'd just mooned over him when he'd been on the field and drunk champagne and chatted the rest of the time. He'd dazzled her friends too.

Unconsciously she licked her tender lips and felt his imprint on them. Really she felt his imprint everywhere—and especially in the space between her thighs.

Heaven help her! She would have had sex with him. Had inadvertently *wanted* to have sex with him. The realisation of that alone was enough to shock her. She hated sex!

So why was she currently reliving Cruz's wicked kisses over and over like a hopeless teenager? He hadn't kissed her out of any real passion—he'd kissed her to make a point and to put her in her place and by God she had let him! Putting up a token resistance like the Victorian virgin he had accused her of acting like and then melting all over him like hot syrup.

She scratched the hair at her temples and made her curls frizz. Grabbing the offending matter, she quickly braided it, pulled on her jeans and shirt and stomped down to the stables.

Donny raised a startled eyebrow as she muttered a few terse words in his direction and started work at the other end. The rhythmical physical labour of putting away tack and shifting hay, of bantering with the horses and going through the motions of bedding them down for the night, was doing nothing to eradicate the feeling of all that hard male muscle pressed up against her.

'Make sure you don't burn your bridges unnecessarily, Aspen. Pride can be a nasty thing when it's used rashly.'

Pride? What pride. She had none. Well, she'd had enough to say no to both him and Billy Smyth.

'Oh, Billy Smyth! There's no way I would have slept with him even if he wasn't married,' she told Delta as she brushed her down vigorously.

But you would have with Cruz Rodriguez. Even without the money.

'I would not,' she promised Delta, knowing that if she had sex again with any man it would be too soon.

She stopped and leant her forehead against the mare. She breathed in her comforting scent and stared out over the stall door, looking up when something—a rat, maybe—disturbed a sleeping pigeon.

Her eye was immediately drawn to a rusty horseshoe lodged firmly between two supporting beams. Her mother had told her the story about how it had got there when she was little and it was the first thing Aspen had looked for when she had come to Ocean Haven, missing her mother desperately. Since then, whenever she was in a tricky situation she came out here and sought her mother's advice.

'And, boy, do I need it right now,' she muttered.

Delta nudged her side, as if to tell her to get on with it.

'Yes, I know.' She patted her neck. 'I'm thinking.'

Thinking about how much this place meant to her. Thinking about the dreams she had that would never materialise if she lost it. And she would lose it. To some faceless consortium in five days. Her stomach felt as if it had a rock in it.

Cruz's offer crept back into her mind for the thousandth time. He was right; it was pride making her say no.

So what if she said yes?

No, she couldn't. Cruz was big and overpowering and arrogant. Exactly the type of man she'd vowed to keep well away from.

But you're not marrying him.

No, but she would have to sleep with him. Which was just as unpalatable.

Sighing, she contemplated the peeling paint on the stall door. Her mother's face swam into her mind. Her tired smile. The day she had died she had been so exhausted after working two jobs and caring for Aspen, who had been sick at the time, that she'd simply forgotten that cars drove on the left-hand side of the road in England and she'd stepped out onto a busy road. It had been horrific. Devastating.

Aspen felt a pang of remorse and a deep longing. She had to keep Ocean Haven if only to preserve her mother's memory.

Feeling weighted down by memories, she continued brushing Delta. She had eked out a life here. She felt whole here. Protected. And, dammit, if she could keep it she would. She hadn't worked this hard to lose everything now.

Rash pride.

Rash pride had stopped her grandfather and her mother from reaching out to each other and maybe changing their lives for the better. Rash pride had made her grandfather refuse to listen to her own concerns about Chad after she had mentioned her doubts to him right before the wedding.

Rash pride wasn't going to get in the way of her life decisions any more. If Cruz Rodriguez wanted her body he could damned well have it. She didn't care. She hadn't cared about that side of things for years. And, anyway, once he found out what a dud she was in bed he'd change his mind pretty quickly.

Familiar fingers of distaste crawled up her spine as she recalled her wedding night before she could prevent herself doing it. She swallowed. What surprised her most was that being in Cruz's arms had been nothing like being in Chad's. But then Chad had often been drunk during their brief marriage and the alcohol had changed him. After that first night Aspen had frozen so much on the rare occasions he had approached her that he'd sought solace elsewhere. And made sure she knew about it. Always being deeply apologetic the following day when the alcoholic haze had retreated.

She'd stayed with him for six months and tried to be a better wife, but then he'd unfairly accused her of sleeping with his patron. It had been the final straw and she'd fled to Ocean Haven and never looked back.

She shivered.

'If you should happen to change your high and mighty little mind I'll be staying at the Boston International until tomorrow morning.'

Had she changed her mind?

There was no doubt that Cruz hated her after what had happened eight years ago, but he must also want her to make such an extreme offer. Could she put her concerns aside and sleep with him? She already knew she responded differently with him, felt differently with him, but what if she froze at the last minute as she had with Chad? What if he laughed at her when he learned about her embarrassing problem?

Rash pride, Aspen.

She groaned. To find out was to experiment, and to experiment meant opening herself up to knowing once and for all that *she* had been the problem in the bedroom and not Chad—as she sometimes liked to pretend when she was feeling particularly low.

'Coward,' she said softly.

Delta whickered.

'Oh, not you, beauty.' Aspen fished inside her pocket for a sugar cube. 'You're brave and courageous and would probably not bat an eyelid if I told you that Ranger's Apprentice had paid money to mount you if it meant saving The Farm.'

Aspen unwound Delta's tail from the tight bundle it had been wrapped in for the polo and wondered what would become of her beloved horses if she had to leave. Wondered if they'd be well cared for.

She felt she should warn the unsuspecting mare. 'If I keep The Farm I probably will be putting you in with him next season. I hope you don't mind. He's quite handsome.'

Not that looks had anything to do with the price of eggs.

She sighed as Donny stopped by Delta's stall and said that his lot were all set for the night and he would help out with some of the others if Aspen needed it.

At the rate she was going Aspen would need an army to get the horses done before the week was out.

She smiled at him. He had worked on the farm for six years now and she'd be lost without him. 'You're a gem, but I'm good. You go home to Glenda and the kids.'

'You're sure?' He shifted his gum around in his mouth. 'You seem a little wound up.'

Oh, she was. Ten million dollars wound up.

'Donny, what would you do if everything you loved was being threatened?' she asked suddenly.

He stuck a finger through his belt buckle and considered his shoes. 'You mean like Glenda and Sasha and Lela? Like my home?'

'Yeah,' Aspen said softly. 'Like your home.'

Donny nodded. 'I'd fight if I could.'

Aspen smiled. 'That's what I thought.'

Donny turned to go and then looked back over his shoulder. 'You sure you're all right, boss?'

'Fine. See you Monday.'

Cruz was going crazy. When a man let his ego get in the way of common sense that was the only conclusion to make. And the only one that made sense.

What other explanation could there possibly be when

he had just offered a woman he didn't even like ten million dollars to sleep with him?

And what would he have done if she'd said yes? Because he'd had no intention of going through with it. The very idea was ludicrous. He'd never paid for sex in his life.

So he wanted her? Big deal. It was because she was even more alluring than he remembered. And more stuck-up. Her hair was longer too, her cheekbones more defined, her breasts fuller, her mouth— He laughed. What was he doing? A full inventory? Why? There were plenty of women in his sea. Plenty more beautiful than this one when it came down to it.

And, yes, he liked to pit himself against an opponent for the sheer thrill of it, but making that offer to Aspen Carmichael had felt a bit like riding a nag into the middle of a forty-goal polo game without a bridle or a saddle and telling his opponents to have at him.

He certainly hadn't come anywhere close to finding a way to ensure that she wouldn't be able to raise the money to buy Ocean Haven herself—which had been his original goal.

Cruz poked at the half-eaten steak sandwich on his plate and stuffed an overcooked chip into his mouth. All he'd done instead was lump himself in with the likes of Billy Smyth and he was nothing like his lot.

No, you're worse, his conscience happily informed him. *You'd like to screw her* and *steal her family home out from under her as well*.

Yeah, whatever.

Unused to having a back and forth commentary inside his head about a woman—or about his decisions—he shoved himself to his feet and headed outside to see if the answer to his problem was written in the stars.

Of course it wasn't, but he stood there and let the warm evening air wash over him until memories of the past sailed in on the scent of jasmine and lilac. The sickening ball that had settled in his gut as he'd driven through the stone archway to Ocean Haven returned full force.

Focusing on something else, he listened to the distant murmurs of the light-hearted partying he could hear coming up off the darkened beach. Probably teenagers enjoying yet another stunning summer evening. Light flickered and wisps of smoke trailed in the moonlight. He imagined that many of them would be pairing off before long and snuggling down beside a campfire.

Unbidden, his mind conjured up an image of Aspen flirting with Billy Smyth earlier that day. He'd watched them for a couple of minutes before approaching her, not really wanting anyone to recognise him and start fawning all over him.

Aspen had used all her feminine wiles so the unhappily married Billy would notice her, but it hadn't been until she had let him run his finger down the side of her face and held his cheek afterwards, as if preserving his touch, that real bitterness and anger had rolled through Cruz like an incoming thunderstorm. Would she have let Smyth kiss her and shove her up against the wall of the stable as she had done with him earlier? Had she *planned* to later on?

'Damn her anyway.' He slammed the palm of his hand against the bronze railing and told himself to forget about her. Forget about the way she had caught fire in his arms once again. Forget about the way he had done the same in hers. Unfortunately his body was more than happy to relive it, and he was once again uncomfortably hard as he headed inside and downed the rest of his tequila.

As far as Cruz was concerned the Aspen Carmichaels of the world deserved everything they got. So why was he hanging around his hotel room feeling like the worst kind of male alive?

No reason.

No reason at all.

The hotel phone rang and he crossed to the hall table and picked it up, almost disappointed to find that the number on the display was a local one. Because he knew who it was even before he answered it. And now was the time to tell her that he had no intention of giving her the money in exchange for her delectable body. No intention at all.

But he didn't say that. Instead he threw his conscience to the wind and said, 'I'll pick you up at seven in the morning.'

There was enough of a silence on the other end of the line for him to wonder if he hadn't been mistaken, but then Aspen's husky tones sounded in his ear.

'Why?'

'Because I'm flying back to Mexico first thing in the morning.'

She cleared her throat. 'I can wait until you're next in Boston.'

She might be able to. He couldn't.

'You need that money by Monday, don't you?'

Again there was a pause long enough to fill the Grand Canyon. He waited for her to tell him to go to hell.

'Yes,' she said as if she was grinding nails.

'I'll see you tomorrow, then.'

He hung up before she could say anything else and stood staring at the telephone. He didn't know what shocked him more: the fact that he hadn't rescinded his ludicrous offer or the fact that he had made it in the first place. What didn't shock him was the fact that she had accepted.

He waited for a sense of satisfaction to kick in because he had finally come up with a way to stop her going after anyone else for the money. Instead he felt a sense of impending doom. Like a man who had bitten off more than he could chew. Because he had no intention of lending her the money and he didn't like what that said about him.

Maybe that he needed more tequila.

'Just have a shower, *imbecil,* and get some sleep,' he told himself.

Come Saturday The Rodriquez Polo Club would run the biggest polo tournament in Mexico for the second year and he had a Chinese delegation coming over to view the proceedings. They had some notion that he could form a partnership with them to introduce polo into China via a specialised hotel in Beijing. So he had to be on site for the next three days and be at his charming best.

'Better get rid of the *chica*, then,' he told his reflection grimly as he stripped off and stepped into the shower. Because watching Aspen flick her hair and flirt with everything in pants was not, he already knew, conducive to putting him in a good mood.

Ah, hell, maybe he should just forget the whole thing. Forget buying Ocean Haven. Yes, it was an exceptional piece of land, with those rolling hills and the bluff that looked out over the North Atlantic Ocean. But there were plenty of beautiful spots in the world. What did he really want it for anyway?

He squirted shampoo over his head and rubbed vigorously.

The fact was eight years ago Aspen Carmichael had set him up so that her over-indulged fiancé could take his place on the dream team without batting a pretty eyelash. She'd walked up to him and shyly put her arms around his neck and, like a fool who had fantasised about her for too long, he'd lost control. He would have done anything for her back then because, if he was honest, he'd liked her a little bit himself. Liked her a lot, in fact, and he hated knowing that she'd so easily fooled him.

But not this time. This time he would be the one holding all the cards. He relaxed for the first time that night. And why not? Why not take what she had offered him eight years ago? She was older now, and obviously still prepared to use her delectable body to get what she wanted. *So, okay—game on, Ms Carmichael. Game on.*

And if a small voice in his head said that he was wrong about her—well, he couldn't see how.

So what that she had loved the horses and been kind to everyone she came into contact with? So what if her apology earlier had seemed genuine? She knew how to play the game, that was all *that* said about her, but in the end she'd used him for her own ends just like everyone else in his life had done.

So, no, he didn't owe Aspen-damned-Carmichael any-damned-thing. And if this was fate's way of evening the score between them then, hell, who was he to argue?

CHAPTER FIVE

ASPEN WAS PACKED and ready by six the following morning. She'd told Mrs Randall, their long-time housekeeper, that she was going to Mexico to look over Cruz's horses for future growth opportunities. It was the best explanation she could come up with at short notice, especially when Mrs Randall had looked so pleased at the mention of Cruz's name.

'He missed his family terribly, that boy. Of course he was too proud to show it, but I suppose that was why he left so suddenly when he was a young man. He wanted to get back to them.'

Aspen would have liked to believe that homesickness had contributed to Cruz leaving The Farm eight years ago, but she suspected it was more because she had put him in an untenable situation.

Guilt ate at her, and all the confusing emotions she'd experienced at that time came rushing back. Her desperate need for approval from her grandfather, her fear of the future, her confusing feelings for Chad and the amazing pull she'd always felt towards Cruz.

Fortunately Mrs Randall was doing her Thursday morning market shopping when Cruz drove up in a mean black sports car, because Aspen was sure her confused state would have been on display for the wily older woman to see and that would have only added to her anxiety. Especially when she had decided that the best way to approach the situation was to be optimistic and positive. Treat it as the business transaction it was.

Shielded by the velvet drapes in the living room, she watched as Cruz climbed out of the car and literally prowled towards the front steps of the house, breathtakingly handsome in worn jeans that clung to his muscular thighs and a fitted latte-coloured T-shirt that set off his olive skin tone and black hair to perfection.

Not wanting him to think she was nervous at the prospect of seeing him, Aspen waited a few minutes after he'd pressed the bell before opening the door; glad that just last week she had given the front door a fresh lick of white paint and cleaned down the stone façade of the portico with an industrial hose.

'Good morning.' She hoped he hadn't heard her voice quaver and told herself that if she was really going to go through with this she needed to do better than she was now. 'Did you want coffee or tea?'

His gaze swept over her face and lingered on her chin, and when he unconsciously rubbed his jaw she knew he had noticed the mark—*his* mark—that she had made a futile effort to cover with concealer. Involuntarily her own eyes dropped to his mouth and heat coursed through her; she was mortified and embarrassed when his lips tightened with dismissal and he turned abruptly to scan the rest of the hallway.

'No. My plane's on standby. Let's go.'

Great. She wasn't even going to have the benefit of other commuters to ease the journey.

Turning to pick up her keys from the hallway table, she spotted the document she had spent half the night drafting. She couldn't believe she'd forgotten it. But then rational thinking and Cruz Rodriguez didn't seem to go together for her very well.

'I'd like you to sign this first.'

He looked at it dubiously. 'What is it?'

It was a document stipulating a condition she hoped he'd agree to and also preventing him from reneging on their deal if he found himself dissatisfied with the outcome of their temporary liaison. Which he undoubtedly would. But since this was a business arrangement Aspen wanted to make sure that when their physical relationship failed he was still bound to invest in Ocean Haven.

'Read it. I think it's clear enough.'

He took it from her and the paper snapped in the quiet room. The antique grandfather clock gauged time like a marksman.

It wasn't long before he glanced back at her, and Aspen swallowed as he laughed out loud.

Her mouth tightened as she waited for him to collect himself. She'd had an idea that he might have some objections to her demands but she hadn't expected that he find them comical.

'Once?' His eyes were full of amusement. 'Are you're kidding me?'

She wasn't. *Once*, she was sure, was going to be more than enough for both of them.

'No.'

When he looked as if he might start laughing again Aspen felt her nerves give way to temper.

'I don't see what's so funny?'

'That's because you're not paying the money.'

He circled behind her as if she was some slave girl on an auction block and he was checking her over.

She swung around to face him. 'If you read the whole document it says that I'm planning to pay you back the money anyway, so technically it's free.'

'With what?'

He unnerved her by circling her again, but this time she stood stock-still. 'I don't know what you mean.'

'What are you intending to pay me back with?' he murmured from behind her.

'The profits from The Farm.'

He scoffed, facing her. 'This place will be lucky to break even in a booming market.'

His eyes held hers and the chemistry that was as strong as carbon links every time they got within two feet of each other flared hotly. Aspen took a careful breath in. He was pure Alpha male right now, and his self-satisfied smile let her know that *he* knew the effect he was having on her.

Not that it would help either one of them in the long run. But she had to concentrate. If she didn't there was a chance she'd end up with nothing. Less than nothing. Because she'd lose the only tie she had left to her mother.

'That's your opinion. It's not mine.'

He studied her and she didn't know how she managed not to squirm under that penetrating gaze.

'It would want to be a damned good once, *gatita*.'

Aspen raised her chin. It was going to be horrible.

'It's a good deal.' She repeated what she'd said to Billy Smyth and so many others before him. 'Take it or leave it.'

He regarded her steadily, his eyes hooded. 'I tell you what. You make it one night and I'll agree.'

One night?

'As in the *whole* night?'

His slow smile sent a burst of electrical activity straight to her core. 'What a good idea, *gatita*. Yes, the whole night.'

Bastard.

'What *is* that you're calling me?' she fumed.

His smile was full of sex. '*Kitten*. You remind me of a spitting kitten who needs to be stroked.'

'Fine.' Aspen picked up the pen but didn't see a thing in front of her.

'Wait. Before you make your changes I want to know what this is.' Cruz stabbed his finger at her second point—the one that said he had to pay no matter what happened or didn't happen between them. 'Is this your way of telling me you're going to welsh on me?'

She frowned. 'Welsh on you?'

'Renege. Back out. Break your word.'

'I know what it means,' she snapped, wondering if he wasn't having a go at her character. 'And rest assured I am fully prepared to uphold my end of the bargain. I just want to make sure you do as well.'

Her throat bobbed as he continued to watch her and Cruz wondered if she had guessed that he was stringing her along.

Once!

He nearly laughed again. But he had to hand it to her. The document she had crafted was legally sound and would probably hold up well enough in a court of law.

Something about the way she stood before him, all innocently defiant, like a lamb to the slaughter, snagged on his conscience like an annoying burr in a sock, which you'd thought you'd removed only to have it poke at you again.

He couldn't do it. He couldn't let her go into this blind. 'There's something you should know.'

Her eyes turned wary. 'Like what?'

'I own Trimex Holdings.'

Aspen frowned. 'If that's supposed to mean something to me it doesn't.'

'Trimex Holdings is currently the highest bidder for Ocean Haven.'

He watched a myriad of emotions flit across her expressive face as the information set in. Shock. Disbelief. Anger. Uncertainty.

'So...' She frowned harder. 'This isn't real?'

How much he wanted her? Unfortunately, yes.

He tried not to let his gaze drop once again to the spot on her chin. He'd obviously grazed her with his stubble the day before and, although he'd hate to think that he'd hurt her, there was a part of him that was pretty pleased to see her wearing his mark. The moronic part.

Oh, yeah, it was real enough. But he knew that wasn't what she was referring to.

'My offer?'

'Yes.'

'It's real.'

'That doesn't make sense. Why would you lend me money to buy a property you are trying to buy for yourself?'

'Because I believe I'll win.' And he had just decided to instruct Lauren to keep upping his offer until it was so ludicrously tempting Joe Carmichael would see stars.

Aspen shook her head. 'You won't. Joe is very loyal to me.'

All families were loyal until money was involved. 'Care to back yourself?'

She looked at him as one might a maggot on a pork chop. 'I never realised how absolutely ruthless you are.'

'I'm absolutely successful. For a reason.'

She shook her head. 'You're not going to be this time. But can I trust you?'

The fact that she questioned his integrity annoyed him. 'I didn't have to tell you this, did I?'

'Fine,' she snapped, pacing away from him to the other side of the neat sitting room. She glared at him. Shook her head. Then paced back. Picked up the pen. 'It's not like I have a better option right now.'

Her fingers shook ever so slightly as she put pen to paper and something squeezed inside his chest.

'I'll do it.'

Impatient for this to be finalised, he grabbed the pen and replaced 'once' with 'one night'. Then he scrawled the date and his signature on the bottom of the page.

His gaze drifted down over her neat summer tunic which showed the delicate hollows either side of her collarbones and hinted at her firm breasts before it skimmed the tops of her feminine thighs. She'd been soft and firm pressed up against him yesterday. Svelte, he decided, glancing at her fitted jeans and ankle boots.

His body reacted predictably and he told himself it was past time to stop looking at her.

The flight from East Hampton to Acapulco took five hours. It might as well have been five days. Cruz had barely uttered a word to her since leaving The Farm—not much more than 'This way', 'Mind your step' and 'Buckle up; we're about to take off'. And Aspen was glad. She didn't think she'd be able to hold a decent conversation with the man right now. He wasn't a rat, she decided. He was a shark. A great white that hunted and killed without compunction.

And she was playing the game of her life against him.

Thank heavens she had her uncle on her side. But could she trust Cruz to give her the money? He'd looked startled and not a little angry when she had questioned his integrity. Yes, she was pretty sure she could trust him. His pride alone would mean that he upheld his end of the deal.

The deal. She had just made a bargain to sleep with the devil. She shuddered, glancing across the aisle to where Cruz was seated in a matching plush leather chair and buried in paperwork. It was beyond her comprehension that she should still want him. Which was scary in itself when she considered that she didn't even like sex. And, yes, she'd enjoyed kissing him, but that wasn't sex. She knew if they'd been anywhere near a bed she would have clammed up.

Urgh… She hated the thought of embarrassing herself in front of him. He was so confident. So *arrogant*. She hated that he just had to look at her and she had to concentrate extra hard to think logically. His touching her made her want to do stupid things. Things she couldn't trust.

And she particularly hated the thought of being vulnerable to him. Especially now. Now when he had made it clear that he'd win anyway. That she was doing this for nothing. It just made her more determined that he wouldn't.

Aspen pulled out her textbook. Questioning whether she had done the right thing in coming with him wouldn't change anything now. She'd signed the document she herself had drafted and she'd assured him that she wouldn't 'welsh' on him.

It would mean that her beloved home was hers. It would mean she would have the chance to put all the naysayers who didn't believe that a girl on her own could run a property the size of Ocean Haven in their places. And it would mean that for the first time in her life she would be free and clear of a dominating man controlling her future. That alone would be worth a little embarrassment with the Latin bad boy she had once fantasised about.

It was a thought that wasn't easy to hold onto when the plane landed on a private airstrip and a blast of hot, humid air swept across her face.

Cruz's long, loose-limbed strides ate up the tarmac as if the humid air hadn't just hit him like a furnace. He stopped by a waiting four-by-four and Aspen kept her eyes anywhere but on him as she climbed inside, doing her best to ease the kinks out of shoulders aching with tension.

Still, she noticed when he put on a pair of aviator sunglasses and clasped another man's hands in a display of macho camaraderie before taking the keys from him.

He was just so self-assured, she thought enviously, and she hated him. Hated him and everything he represented. Yesterday she'd been willing to greet him as a friend, had felt sorry for the part she had played in his leaving The Farm. Now she wished her grandfather had horsewhipped him. It was the least he deserved.

But did he?

Just because he wanted to buy her farm it didn't make him a bad guy, did it? No, not necessarily bad—but ruthless. And arrogant. And so handsome it hurt to look at him.

'You know I hate you, don't you?' she said without thinking.

Not bothering to look at her, he paused infinitesimally, his hands on the key in the ignition.

'Probably,' he said, with so little concern it made her teeth grind together.

He turned the key and the car purred to life. Then his eyes drifted lazily over her from head to toe and she felt her heart-rate kick up. He was studying her again. Looking at her as if he was imagining what she looked like without her clothes on.

'But it won't make a difference.'

His lack of empathy, or any real emotion, drove her wild. 'To what?'

'To this.'

Quick as a flash he reached for her, grabbed the back of her neck before she'd realised his intention and hauled her mouth across to his. Aspen stiffened, determined to resist the force of his hungry assault. And she did. For a moment. A brief moment before her senses took over and shut down her brain. A brief moment before his mouth softened. A brief moment before he pulled back and looked at her with lazy amusement. As if he was already the victor.

'He won't sell to you,' she blazed at him.

His smile kicked up one corner of his mouth. 'He'll sell to me.'

Aspen cut her gaze from his. She hated his insolent confidence because she wished she had just a smidgeon of it herself. 'How long till we get there?' she griped.

He laughed softly. 'So eager, *gatita*?'

'Yes,' she fumed. 'Eager to get out of your horrible company. In fact I don't know why we didn't just do this on the plane. Or at The Farm, come to think of it.'

His head tilted as he regarded her. 'Maybe I want to woo you.'

Aspen blew out a breath. 'I wonder what your mother would have to say about your behaviour?'

'Damn.' Cruz forked a hand through his hair, his lazy amusement at her expense turning to disgust.

He cursed again and gunned the engine.

'Problem?' she asked, hoping beyond hope that there was one.

'You could say that.' His words came out as a snarl.

She waited for him to elaborate and sighed when he didn't. This situation was impossible. There was no way she would be able to relax with this man enough to have sex with him. Which was fine, she thought. It would serve him right, all things considered.

Switching her mind off, she turned her attention outside the window. From the air Mexico was an amazing contrast of stark brown mountains and stretches of dried-up desert against the brilliant blue of the Pacific Ocean. On the ground the theme continued, with pockets of abject beauty mixed with states of disrepair. A bit like her own mind, she mused in a moment of black humour.

But gradually, as Cruz drove them through small towns and along broken cobblestoned streets alive with pedestrians and tourists fortified against the amazing heat with wide-brimmed hats, Aspen felt herself start to relax.

She snuck a glance at Cruz's beautiful profile. His expression was so serious he looked as if he belonged on a penny. The silence stretched out like the bitumen in front of them and finally Aspen couldn't take it any longer. 'So you went back to Mexico after you left The Farm?'

He cut her a brief glance. 'You want the low-down on my life story, *gatita*?'

No, she wanted to know if it would take a silver bullet to end his life, or whether an ordinary one would do the trick.

One night, Aspen.

'I was making polite conversation.'

'Choose another topic.'

Okay.

'Why do you want my farm?'

'It's a great location for a hotel. Why else?'

Aspen glared at him. 'You're going to tear it down, aren't you?' Tear down the only home she'd ever loved. Tear down the stables.

'Perhaps.'

'You can't do that.'

'Actually, I can.'

'Why? Revenge?'

She saw a muscle tick in his jaw. 'Not revenge. Money.'

Aspen blew out a breath, more determined than ever that he shouldn't get his hands on her property. 'How much further is it to the hotel?' she asked completely exasperated.

Cruz smiled. 'You sound like you're not expecting to enjoy yourself, *gatita*.'

She didn't answer, and she felt his curious gaze on her as she stared sightlessly out of the window.

'It will be a while,' he said abruptly. 'We have a small detour to make.'

Aspen glanced back at his austere expression. 'What sort of detour?'

'I have to stop at my mother's house.'

'Your mother's house?' She frowned. 'Why would you take me to meet your mother?'

'Believe me, I'm not happy about it either,' he said. 'Unfortunately my brother has arranged her surprise birthday party for today and I promised I'd show up.'

'Your mother's...' She cleared her throat as if she had something stuck in it. 'You could have warned me.'

'I just did.'

She blew out a frustrated breath.

'Don't make a big deal out of it,' he cautioned. 'I'm not.'

'Well, that's obvious. But how can I not? What will she think of me?'

'That you're my latest mistress. What else?'

Cruz saw a flash of hurt cross her face and hated how she made him feel subtly guilty about the situation between them. He had nothing to feel guilty about. She had asked him for money, he had laid down his terms, and she'd accepted. And now that she knew he was in direct competition with her his conscience was clear. Or should have been. Still, it picked at him that he might be making a decision he would later regret. His body said the opposite and he ran his eyes over her feminine, but demure outfit. All that wild hair caught back in a low ponytail just begging to be set free.

'I don't have anything for her,' she said in a small voice.

Cruz forced himself to concentrate on a particularly dilapidated section of road before he had an accident. 'I've got it covered.'

She fell blessedly silent after that as he navigated through the centre of town and he was just exhaling when she spoke again.

'What did you get her?'

'Excuse me?'

'Your present. I would know what it was if I was really your mistress.'

'You *are* my mistress,' he reminded her. 'For one night anyway.'

If possible even more colour drained from her face, and it irritated him to think that she saw sleeping with him as such a chore. By the time he was finished with her she would be screaming with pleasure and begging for more than one night.

'Money,' he said, pulling his thoughts out of his pants.

'Sorry?'

'I'm giving her money.'

'Oh.'

Her nose twitched as if she'd just smelt something foul.

'What's wrong with that?' he snapped.

'Nothing.'

Her tone implied *everything*.

'Money makes the world go round, *gatita*,' he grated.

'Actually, I think the saying is that love makes the world go round.'

'Love couldn't make a tennis ball go round,' he said, knowing from her tight expression that she didn't approve or agree. Well, he didn't give a damn. *She* hadn't been given up as a child. 'Look, my mother sold me to your grandfather when I was thirteen. I think I know what she likes.'

Aspen looked aghast. 'I had heard that rumour but I never actually believed it.'

'Believe it,' he said, hating the note of bitterness that tinged his words.

'I'm sure she didn't *want* to send you away.'

Cruz didn't say anything. She sighed and eventually said, 'I know how you feel.'

'How could you possibly know how I feel?' he mocked.

'You grew up on a hundred-acre property and went to a private school.'

'I wasn't born into that, Cruz. My father left my mother when I was three and she struggled for years to keep our heads above water while she was alive. What I was getting at was that my grandfather paid my father to stay away.'

Cruz frowned. He'd assumed her mother had lived off some sort of trust fund and her father had died. 'Your father was a ski instructor, wasn't he?'

'Yes.'

'Probably better that you didn't have anything to do with him.'

'Because of his profession?'

'No, because he accepted being paid off. A parent should never give up a child, no matter what.'

'I'm sorry that happened to you,' she said quietly.

Cruz didn't want her compassion. Especially not when he understood why his mother had done it. Hell, wasn't that one of the reasons he worked so hard? So that if he did ever marry no wife of his would ever have to face the same decision?

He shrugged it off, as he always did. 'I had a lot of opportunities from it. And worse things happen to kids than that.'

'True, but when a child feels abandoned it's—'

He cut off her sympathetic response. 'You move on and you don't look back.'

Aspen registered the pain in his voice, the deep hurt he must have felt. She experienced a strange desire to make him feel better—and then reminded herself that he was a wealthy man who was determined to steal her home away from her and was so arrogant he was lending her money to challenge him.

'I'd like to stop for flowers,' she said stiffly.

Cruz turned down a side street and cursed when the

traffic came to a standstill along a busy ocean-facing bou-
levard, completely oblivious to the cosmopolitan coastline
that sparkled in the sun.

'What?'

'I'd like to stop for flowers.'

'What for?'

She looked pained—and stiff. 'Your mother's birthday,
for one, and the fact that I'm visiting someone's home and
don't have a gift.'

'I told you I have it covered.'

'And given your attitude to money I'm sure it's very
generous, but I would prefer to give something more personal.'

Cruz ground his teeth together, praying for patience.

Five minutes later he swung the big car onto the side of
the road in front of a group of shops. When she made to
get out of the car, he stopped her. 'I'll get them. You wait
here and keep the door locked.'

'But they're supposed to be from me.'

'Believe me, my mother will know who they're from.'
The last time he'd given her flowers he'd picked wild dahl-
ias by the side of the road when he'd been about twelve.

Not long after that Aspen was relieved when Cruz pulled
into the circular driveway of a large *hacienda,* with fat
terracotta pots either side of a wide entrance filled with
colourful blooms.

She stepped out of the car before Cruz reached her side
and saw his scowl grow fiercer as he unloaded a box of
brightly wrapped presents from the back.

'You told me you were giving your mother money,' she
said, confused.

'I am. These are for my nieces and nephews.'

That surprised her, and she wondered if maybe he had
a heart beating somewhere inside his body after all. The

thought lasted for as long as it took for his eager nieces and nephews to descend on him in a wild flurry.

It was as if Santa had arrived and, like that mythical person, Cruz was treated with deference and a little trepidation. As if he wasn't quite real. Aspen saw genuine affection for him on the faces of his family, but it was clear when no one touched or hugged him that all was not quite right between them.

For his part, Cruz didn't seem to notice. His cool gaze was completely tuned in to the delighted squeals of his six nieces and nephews as they unearthed remote-controlled cars, sporting equipment and several dolls. That was when Aspen realised that the gifts were either an ice-breaker or possibly a replacement for any real affection between them.

'This is Aspen,' he said once the furore had died down. 'Aspen, this is my family.'

Succinct, she thought as each one of his family members warily introduced themselves, clearly unsure how to take her. Deciding to ignore the way that made her feel and make the best of the situation, she smiled at them as if there was nothing amiss about her being by Cruz's side.

'These are from both of us,' she said, handing Cruz's mother the elaborate posy he had purchased and watching as her gentle face lit up with pleasure. She must once have been a great beauty, Aspen thought, but time and life had wearied her, lining her face and sprinkling her thick dark hair with silvery streaks. She gazed up at her son with open adoration and Aspen could have kicked Cruz when he barely mustered a stiff smile in return.

An awkward silence fell over his sisters until his brother, Ricardo, took charge and led them all out to the rear patio, where the scent of a heavenly barbecue filled the air.

Cruz's youngest sister, Gabriella, who looked to be about nineteen, hooked her arm through Aspen's and took it upon herself to introduce her two brothers-in-law, who each had a pair of tongs in one hand and a beer in the other.

Gabriella pointed out the small vineyard her mother still tended, and the lush veggie patch in raised wooden boxes. Three well-fed dogs lazed beneath the shade of a lemon-coloured magnolia tree and the view of the ocean from the house was truly spectacular.

'Cruz has never brought a girlfriend here before,' Gabriella whispered.

Aspen smiled enigmatically. She knew the label hadn't come from Cruz but she wasn't about to correct his sister and embarrass them both. And, anyway, 'girlfriend' sounded much better than mistress to her ears, even if it did mean that she had terrible taste in men.

Returning to the patio, she found Cruz sprawled in a deckchair at the head of the large outdoor table, with his sisters and his mother crowded around him like celebrity minders who were worried about losing their jobs. One after the other they asked if he was okay or if he needed anything with embarrassing regularity, offering him food and drink like the Wise Men bestowing gifts on the baby Jesus.

The two brothers-in-law had cleverly retreated to tend the state-of-the-art barbecue, and Aspen tried her best to appreciate the amazing view of grapevines tripping down the hillside towards the azure sea below.

The conversation was like listening to an uninterested child practising the violin: one minute flowing and easy, the next halting and grating. Nobody seemed to know which topic of conversation to stick to.

Even worse, Cruz's mother kept throwing guilty glances his way, while treating him like a king. Cruz either didn't notice, or pretended that he didn't, conversing mainly with his brother about work issues.

It made her think about what Mrs Randall had said the day before. *He missed his family terribly, that boy.*

Ironically, Cruz didn't look as if he had missed them at all, and yet Aspen sensed from his intermittent glances along the table that Mrs Randall had been right.

What had it been like for him? she wondered. On The Farm, all alone and cut off from his family? And how did one reconnect after that?

Bizarrely, she started to feel sorry for him, and found herself wanting to break through the solid barrier he seemed to have erected around himself.

Thankfully one of the older boys brought out the new basketball Cruz had bought and called for everyone to play Four Square. Gabriella jumped up and mercifully asked Aspen to join in. It was the only time Cruz wasn't asked if he wanted to partake.

One of the children quickly drew out four squares and Aspen patiently waited for a cherubic-looking boy with a mop of curly black hair to explain the rules while his ten-year-old sister tapped her foot impatiently and said, 'We know…we *know*.'

Before long there was a mixed line of adults and kids and Aspen found she was enjoying herself for the first time that day, laughing with the children and jockeying for position as king of the game.

When one of the older children tried a shifty manoeuvre the ball went spinning off towards the stone table. Cruz deftly caught it and threw it back to Aspen.

Some devil on Aspen's shoulder made her toss the ball straight back at him. 'Come and play.'

'No, thanks.'

'He never plays games when he comes,' Gabriella whispered.

Aspen gave her a half-smile, knowing exactly how it felt to hanker after the affection of someone who wouldn't give it. She remembered that her grandfather and her uncle had been far too serious to play games with her and she'd very quickly learned not to ask.

Sensing that Cruz was far too serious as well, and that if he just lightened up a little everyone else could start to as well, she bounced the ball back in his direction.

'Are you afraid you'll lose?' she challenged lightly.

He stood up from the table and placed his beer bottle down with deliberate restraint.

Every member of his family seemed to hold their collective breath—even the two men tending the sizzling barbecue—waiting to see what he would do. If a tree had fallen in Africa they would have heard it.

Aspen saw the moment Cruz became conscious of the same thing and the smile on her lips died as he stared at her with a dangerous glint in his eyes. He came towards her slowly, like a hungry panther, his black hair glinting in the sunlight just as she remembered.

A shiver of awareness skittered over her skin. Her mind told her to run, but her body was on another frequency because it remained rooted to the spot.

Towering over her, Cruz took her hand and carefully placed the ball in it, as if he was handing back a newborn baby—or a bomb about to go off. He leant closer, and Aspen forgot about their audience as his gaze shifted to her mouth.

'I said no.'

When his gaze lifted to hers there was an implicit warning for her to behave deep within his cold regard. Then without a word he spun on his heels and stalked towards the garden.

Aspen released a shaky breath and heard Gabriella do the same.

'Doesn't he scare you when he frowns at you like that?'

His sister was right. His anger should have scared her. Terrified her, in fact. Her grandfather had wielded his temper like a weapon and when Chad had been drunk he had been volatile and moody. But Cruz didn't scare her in that way. Other ways, yes. Like the way he made her feel shivery and out of control of her senses. As if when he touched her he consumed her, controlled her.

That scared her.

Pushing her troubled thoughts aside, she sought to reassure Gabriella. 'No, he doesn't scare me that way. I think his bark—or his look—is more ferocious than his bite.'

The sound of the back door opening drew Aspen's gaze from Cruz's retreating figure and she watched Ricardo back out of the doorway, an elaborate birthday cake resplendent with pink icing and brightly coloured flowers held gingerly in his arms.

'Where's Cruz?' he asked, casting a quick glance at the now vacant chair.

There was a bit of low murmuring that Aspen understood, despite not speaking Spanish, and she felt a guilty flush highlight her cheekbones. It was her fault that Cruz had stalked off.

'I'll go and get him.'

Ricardo looked as if he was about to argue with her but then changed his mind. 'Thank you.'

Following the path Cruz had taken, she found him out by the small vineyard, his head bent towards a leafy vine laden with bunches of purple grapes. The bright sun darkened his olive skin as he stood there, which was extremely unfair, Aspen thought, when her skin was more likely to turn pink and blister.

A bee buzzed lazily past her face and she stepped out of its way.

Cruz must have heard the sound of her steps on the dirt

but he gave no indication of it, putting his hands in his pockets and staring out across the ocean like a god from the days of old. Strong. Formidable. *Impenetrable*.

'I was hoping for a moment's peace,' he said without turning around, his deep voice a master of creation.

'They're about to serve the birthday cake,' Aspen informed him softly.

'So they sent you to find me?'

'No.' She stood beside him and watched tiny waves break further out to sea. 'I volunteered.'

He made a noise that seemed to say she was an idiot. And she was—because she had an overpowering urge to reach out to him.

'They don't know how to treat you, you know.' She glanced up at him, no longer able to ignore what had been going on since they arrived. 'Your mother seems to be suffering. From guilt? Remorse? It's not clear, but it *is* clear that she loves you. They all do.'

Cruz tensed and dug his hands further into his pockets. Aspen had inadvertently picked a scab off an old wound. He knew his mother felt guilty. He'd told her she shouldn't but it hadn't worked. He had no idea what to do about that and it made being around his family almost impossible, because he knew that without him around they would be up singing and dancing and having a great time.

'Don't start talking about what you can't possibly understand,' he grated harshly.

'I understand that you're upset…maybe a little angry about what happened to you,' she offered gently.

He swung around to face her. 'I'm not angry about that. When my father died it was my job as the eldest boy to take care of my family while the girls ran the house. It's what we did. Rallied around each other and banded together.'

'Oh, dear, that must have made it even harder for you to leave them.'

Cruz scowled down at her. 'It's not like I had a say in it. Old Man Carmichael offered my mother money and she preferred to send me away than to let me provide for the family my way.'

'Which was…?'

Mostly he'd worked at a nearby *hacienda* and tended rich people's gardens. Sometimes he'd done odd jobs for the men his father had become involved with, but he hadn't been stupid enough to do anything illegal. Anything criminal.

'Boring stuff.'

'And your mother didn't work herself?'

'She cleaned houses when she could, but I have one brother and four sisters. All were under ten at the time. My father's family were what you would politely term dysfunctional, and my mother had been an only child to elderly parents. If I hadn't stepped up, nobody else would have.'

'I'm sorry, Cruz. That's a lot for a child to have heaped on his shoulders. You must have really struggled.' She grimaced. 'I guess that's why they treat you like you're a king now.'

He looked at her sharply. 'They don't treat me like a king. They act like it didn't happen. They tiptoe around me as if I'm about to go off at them.'

She paused and Cruz caught the concern in her gaze. Something tightened in his chest. What was he doing, spilling his childhood stories to this woman? A person he didn't even *like*.

As if sensing his volatile thoughts she murmured half to herself and he had to strain to capture the words. '…not real.'

'Excuse me?' He glanced at her sharply. 'Are you saying my feelings for my family are not real?'

'Of course not. Though it might help them relax a bit if you scowled a little less.' She shot him a half-smile. 'I can see that you love your family. Which is strangely reassuring though I don't know why. But there's no hugging. No touching.' Her pause was laden with unwanted empathy. 'Truthfully, you remind me of my grandfather. He found it tough to let anyone get close to him as well.'

His eyes narrowed. Nobody in his family talked about the past—not even Ricardo. Cruz had come back from Ocean Haven eight years ago angry—yes, by God, *angry*—and he'd stayed that way. And he liked it. Anger drove him and defined him. Made him hungry and kept him on his guard.

He looked at Aspen. Unfortunately for her he was *really* angry now. 'I don't remember reading anywhere in that makeshift document of yours that pop psychology was part of our deal.'

Her eyes flashed up at him. 'I was only trying to help. Though I don't know why,' she muttered, half under her breath, inflaming his anger even more.

'Helping wasn't part of it either. There's only one thing I want from you. Conversation before or after is not only superfluous, it's irrelevant.'

She gave him that hurt look again, before masking it with cool hauteur, and he felt his teeth grind together.

Dammit, why couldn't he look at her without feeling so…so *much*?

All the time.

Lust, anger, disappointment, hunger. A deep hunger for more—and not just of that sweet body which had haunted more dreams than he cared to remember.

He reminded himself of the type of woman she was. The type who would use that body to further her own interests.

She'd used it to good effect to deceive him years ago and hadn't cared a damn for his feelings. That was real. That was who she was. And once he'd had her in his bed, had slaked his lust for her—*used* her in return—then she'd be out of his life and his head.

Hell, he couldn't wait.

CHAPTER SIX

It was early evening by the time Cruz turned onto the long stretch of driveway that led to the Rodriquez Polo Club. A hotel, Aspen had heard it said, that was a hotel to end all hotels.

She didn't care. She was too keyed-up to be impressed. And, anyway, it was just a hotel.

Only it wasn't *just* anything. It was magnificent.

A palatial honey-coloured building that looked about ten storeys high, it curved like a giant horseshoe around a network of manicured gardens with a central fountain that resembled an inverted chandelier.

As soon as their SUV stopped a uniformed concierge jumped to attention and treated Cruz with the deference one usually expected only around royalty.

Expensively clad men and women wandered languidly in and out of the glassed entrance as if all their cares in the world had disappeared and Aspen glanced down at her old top and jeans. Despite the fact that her grandfather had once been seriously wealthy, Ocean Haven hadn't done well for so long that Aspen couldn't remember the last personal item she'd bought other than deodorant. Now she felt like Cinderella *before* the makeover, and it only seemed to widen the gulf between her and the brooding man beside her.

'Well, I can see why it's rated as seven stars and I

haven't even seen inside yet,' she said with reluctant admiration. 'And, oh…wow…' she added softly. A row of bronzed life-sized horses that looked as if they were racing each other in a shallow pool with shots of water trickling around them glowed under strategically placed lights, adding both pizazz and majesty to the entrance. 'There's so much to see. I almost don't want to go inside.'

'Unfortunately we're not allowed to serve meals on the kerb so you'll have to.'

Aspen switched her gaze to Cruz at his unexpected humour and her pulse skittered. He was just so handsome and charismatic. What would it feel like, she wondered, to be with him at the hotel because she *wanted* to be there and he *wanted* her to be there with him?

The unexpected thought had her nearly stumbling over her own feet.

Why was she even thinking like that?

The last thing she needed was to become involved with a man again. And Cruz had told her in no uncertain terms that he expected sex and nothing else. No need to pretty it up with unwanted emotion.

How had she convinced herself that she'd be able to do this? Not only because of her own inherent dislike of sex but because it was so cold. What would happen once they got upstairs? Did they go straight to the bedroom? Undress? Would he undress her? No. Probably not.

Fortunately she didn't have much time to contemplate the sick feeling in the pit of her stomach as the doorman swept open the chrome and glass doors and inclined his head as Cruz strode inside. Aspen scurried to keep up and couldn't help but notice the lingering attention Cruz garnered with effortless ease.

Another deferential staff member in a severely cut suit descended on him and Aspen left them to stroll towards a circular platform with a large wood carving of a polo player on horseback.

'Aspen?'

Having finished up with his employee, Cruz waited impatiently for her to come to him but Aspen couldn't help returning her gaze to the intricate carving.

'Did you do this?'

He looked startled. 'Why would you think that?'

'I just saw some smaller versions in your mother's house and they reminded me of the wood carvings you used to do in your spare time. Were they yours?'

He paused and Aspen felt a little foolish.

'I haven't done one of those in years.'

It was the most he'd said to her since leaving his mother's and her curiosity got the better of her. 'You don't play polo any more either. Why is that?'

For a minute she didn't think he had heard her.

'Other things to do.'

'Do you miss it?' she asked, imagining that he couldn't not, considering how good he was.

'Mind your step when you come down,' he said, turning away from her.

Right. That would be the end of yet another conversation, she thought, wondering why she'd even bothered to try and engage him. Her natural curiosity and desire to help others was clearly wasted on this man.

She thought back to his angry response to her gentle prodding at his mother's house and shook her head at her own gumption. What did she really know, anyway? Her own relationship history wasn't exactly the healthiest on the planet.

Following Cruz to the bank of elevators, she decided to keep her mouth shut. It was hard enough contemplating what she was about to do without adding to it by trying to come up with superfluous conversation.

When the lift opened directly into Cruz's private suite Aspen gasped at the opulence of the living area, but Cruz ignored it all, striding into the room and throwing his wallet and keys onto a large mahogany table with an elaborate floral arrangement in the centre. With barely a pause he pushed open a set of concertina glass doors that led to a long balcony. Beyond the doors Aspen could just make out a jewel-green polo field.

Stepping closer, she saw that beyond the field there was an enormous stone stable with an orange tiled roof and beyond that white-fenced paddocks holding, she knew, some of the finest polo ponies in the world.

'Wow….' She breathed hot evening air that carried the scent of freshly mown grass and the lemony scent of magnolia with it. 'Is that a swimming pool out there to the right?'

'Yes.' Cruz had his hands wedged firmly in his pockets as he stood behind her. 'It's a saltwater pool the horses use to cool off in.'

'Lucky horses.'

'If you take ten steps to your left and look around the corner you'll see a pool and spa *you* can use.'

Happy to move out of his commanding orbit, Aspen followed his directions.

'Oh…' She stared at a sapphire-blue lap pool which had a large spa at the end of it. The pool was shielded on one side by a thick hedge and from above by a strategically placed cloth sail that would block both the sun and any paparazzi snooping around. 'You don't do things by halves, do you?'

'Mexico is a hot place.'

Then why did she feel so cold?

Shivering, she glanced back at him, her attention caught by piercing black eyes and the dark stubble that highlighted his square jaw. Those broad shoulders…

She shivered again, and tossed her head to cover her reaction. 'Time to get this party started, I'd say.'

'Party?' He raised a cool eyebrow at her. 'In the pool?'

Aspen cast a quick glance at the inviting water, alarmed as an image of both of them naked and entwined popped into her head. It was so clear she could almost see them there—his larger, tanned body holding her up, the silky feel of the water lapping at her skin as it rippled with their movements, her arms curved over his smooth shoulders as she steadied herself, his hands stroking her heavy breasts....

She felt her face flame. She had the romantic—the *fantasy*—version of sex in her mind. The real version, she knew from experience, could never live up to it.

'Of course not.'

'Have you ever made love in the water, Aspen?'

Had he moved closer to her? She glanced at him with alarm but he hadn't moved. Or hadn't appeared to.

She inhaled and steeled her spine. 'The pool doesn't appeal to me.'

'Pity. It's a nice night for it.'

Aspen didn't want to complicate this. A bed was more than adequate for what was about to happen between them. And she could close her eyes more easily in a bed.

'A bed is fine.'

She wondered if Cruz would put a towel down, the way Chad had done.

A muscle ticked in Cruz's jaw and he stared at her as if trying to discern all her deepest thoughts. Then he turned abruptly away. 'Actually, I find I don't enjoy making love on an empty stomach.'

'This has nothing to do with love,' Aspen reminded him assertively.

Halfway to returning indoors, Cruz stopped and his

black eyes smouldered. 'When I touch your body, Aspen, you'll think it does.'

Oh, how arrogant was *that*? If only he knew that all his Latin charm was wasted on her.

Aspen hurled mental daggers at his broad back and wondered why he didn't want to get this over with as soon as possible. By all accounts he seemed to want her—but then so had Chad in the beginning. Oh, this was beyond awful. She hated second-guessing Cruz's desire. Hated hoping that with him it would be different. She knew better than to count on hope. It hadn't brought her mother or her father back into her life. It hadn't made her grandfather love her for herself in the end.

This time when she looked around the vast living area she noticed a bottle of champagne in a silver ice bucket on the main dining table. Maybe that was what she should do. Get drunk.

As if reading her mind, Cruz tightened his mouth. 'Come—I'll show you to your room.'

Aspen felt her heart bump inside her chest. *He's just showing you the room, you fool, not asking you to use it.*

Yet.

Standing back to let her pass, Cruz indicated towards a closed door. 'The bathroom, which should be stocked with everything you'll need, is through there.'

Aspen nodded, feeling completely overwhelmed.

When it became obvious she wasn't going to say anything Cruz turned to go. 'I'll leave you to freshen up.'

She noticed a book on the bedside table. 'This is your room,' she blurted out.

'You were expecting someone else's?'

'No. I…' She spared him a tart look. 'I thought you might like your own space.'

'I like my bed warm more.'

Right.

'Dinner should be served in twenty minutes.'

After he closed the door behind him Aspen sagged against the silk-covered king bed and wondered how long it would be before he realised she was a dud.

Feeling completely despondent, she picked up the novel beside the bed and noticed it was one of her favourites. Surprised, she flicked through it. Could he really be reading it or was it just for show? Just to impress the plethora of mistresses who wandered in and out of his life?

An hour later she was wound so tight all she could do was pick at the delicious Mexican dinner that for once didn't include *tacos* and *enchiladas*.

'Something wrong?'

Her eyes slid across Cruz's powerful forearms, exposed by his rolled shirtsleeves.

Was he serious? She was about to embarrass herself with a man who didn't even like her in order to save her home. Of *course* there was something wrong.

'Of course not,' she replied, feigning relaxed confidence.

He frowned down at her plate. 'Is it the *birria*? If it's too hot for you I can order something else.'

Oh, he'd meant the food. 'No, no, the food's lovely.'

He put down his fork and brought his wine glass to his lips. Now, *there* was relaxed confidence, she thought a little resentfully.

'Then why is most of it still on your plate?'

He licked a drop of red wine from his lower lip and Aspen couldn't look away. Remembered pleasure at the way his mouth had taken hers in the most wonderful kiss vied with sheer terror for supremacy. Unfortunately sheer terror was winning out, because he looked like a man who would expect everything and the kitchen sink as well.

'I…um…I ate a lot at the party.'

'No, you didn't. You barely touched a thing.'

'I'm not a big eater at the best of times.'

'And these are far from the best of times—is that it, Aspen?'

It was more of a statement than a question and Aspen wondered if perhaps he felt the same way. 'You could say that,' she said carefully.

'Is that because you're still in love with Anderson?'

'Sorry?' She knew her mouth was hanging open and she snapped it closed. '*No*. No, that was a disaster from the start.'

'So you're not still pining for him?'

'No.'

His eyes narrowed thoughtfully. 'Why was it a disaster?'

Had she really just told him being married to Chad had been a disaster? 'Don't ask.'

'I just did.'

'Yes, well, I'd rather not talk about it, if it's all the same to you.'

He sat staring at her and Aspen wished she knew what to say next. His unexpected question about Chad had completely derailed her.

'Come here.'

The soft command made her senses leap and she felt her breath quicken with rising panic. He was trying to control her, and she knew she couldn't let him do that.

She tossed her hair back behind one shoulder. 'You come here.'

Despite the fact that he hadn't moved she could sense the tightly coiled tension within him. It radiated outward across the table and stole the breath from her lungs. And for all her dismissive tone she still felt like a puppet on his string—despite her resolve not to be.

He watched her with heavy-lidded eyes and she was

totally unprepared for the scrape of his chair on the terra-cotta tiles as he stood up.

Aspen's heart jumped as if she'd been startled out of a trance.

Determined to remain neutral—outwardly at least—she didn't move. Couldn't, if the truth be told. Her limbs were completely paralysed—by his laconic sensuality as much as her own blinding insecurities.

'You have amazing hair.'

She snatched in a quick breath to feed her starving lungs. She could feel the heat emanating from his strong thighs beside her shoulders and even though he hadn't touched her she started to tremble. Her only saving grace was that he couldn't possibly be aware of her inner turmoil, and she stared straight ahead as she felt him roll a strand of her hair between his fingers as if it were the finest silk.

She couldn't do this. Already she was freezing up, and to put herself at another man's mercy was truly frightening.

Chad's roughness crowded her mind and permeated her soul, and it was as if Cruz ceased to exist in that moment.

'Dammit, Aspen. What is wrong with you?'

Cruz's dark, annoyed voice only added fuel to the raging fire of Aspen's insecurities. Panic enveloped her and galvanised her into action.

Gouging the floor tiles with her chair, she forced it back and moved in the opposite direction from the one Cruz was in. Unfortunately that only brought her to the balustrade. She gripped the iron railing, enjoying the coolness of the metal against her overheated palms, and pretended rapt attention in the glowing lights that outlined the low boards around the darkened polo field.

'What bothers you the most about this?' he grated. 'The money aspect or the fact that it's me you'll be sleeping with?'

Aspen knew he stood close behind her—every fibre of

her being felt as if it was attuned to every fibre of his—but she didn't turn around. Honestly, she should have known that when it came to the crunch she would fall at the first hurdle. But of course she needed to do this—her mind was so fogged that she couldn't comprehend any other way to save her farm.

'It's not the money.' She tilted her gaze to take in the starry sky. She was planning to pay him back every cent he loaned her, plus interest, so she'd reconciled that in her mind before he'd even picked her up. No, it was... 'It's—'

'Me?' The single word sounded like a pistol-shot.

Interesting, she thought, holding a conversation with someone you couldn't see. It made her other senses come alive. Her sense of hearing that was so in love with the deep timbre of his voice, the feel of the heat of his body that seemed to reach out like a beckoning light, his smell... Unconsciously she rubbed at the railing and felt the smooth texture of the iron beneath her sensitive fingertips.

'It's more the fact that you don't like me,' she said on a rush.

She hadn't realised how true that was until the words left her mouth. A beat passed and then she felt his hands on her shoulders, gently turning her. Embarrassed by the admission, she forced herself to meet his gaze. Because she knew she was right.

He stared at her, not saying anything, his large hands burning into the tops of her shoulders, his thumbs almost absently caressing her collarbones. It was hard to read his expression with only a candle flickering on the table and a crescent moon ducking behind darkened clouds. It was even harder when he lowered his gaze to his hands, his inky lashes shielding them.

He gently slid those large hands up her neck to the line of her jaw, setting off a whole host of sensations in their wake. Aspen stiffened as she felt the pad of one of his thumbs slowly graze her closed mouth. His eyes locked on her lips as he pressed into the soft flesh, making them feel gloriously sensitised.

They were both utterly still. The only movement came from his thumb as it swept back and forth, back and forth, across her hyper-sensitive flesh. Back and forth until her lips started to buzz and gave beneath the persuasive pressure, allowing him to reach the moisture within. Aspen trembled as he spread her own wetness along her bottom lip and then opened her lips wider, until he was touching her teeth. He traced their shape just as thoroughly, only they weren't as malleable as her lips and stayed firmly closed.

She should have known that he wouldn't stop there. Unfairly he was bringing his fingers into play, to knead the side of her neck, pressing firmly into her nape. On a rush of heat her senses were overloaded and her teeth parted, giving him greater liberties.

Only he didn't immediately take them, and without even realising it Aspen tilted her head, seeking to capture his thumb between her teeth, silently inviting him inside. Still he hung back, and with a small sound in the back of her throat she couldn't stop her mouth from closing around his thumb and sucking on his flesh, couldn't stop her tongue from wrapping itself around it as she sought to taste him.

Cruz didn't know if he'd ever experienced anything as erotic as Aspen drawing his thumb into her wide mouth, her cheeks hollowing as she sucked firmly and then softening as she used her tongue to drive him wild. With every stroke his erection jerked painfully behind his zipper and, unable to hold back any longer, he pulled his thumb from her mouth and replaced it with his own.

She immediately latched onto his mouth as if she was just as desperate as he was, and he backed her against the cast iron balustrading and didn't stop until he was hard up against her.

Incapable of thought, he let his instincts take over and hooked one of her legs up over his hip so he could settle into the cradle of her thighs, all the time ravaging her mouth until she fed him more of those hot little moans.

The deep neckline of her otherwise demure dress, which had tantalised him all night, was no barrier to his wandering hands and he deftly moved the soft jersey aside and cupped her, squeezing her full breasts together. He strummed his thumbs over her lace-covered nipples and felt exalted when she arched into him, moaning more keenly as he slowly increased the pressure.

He groaned, licked his way to her ear, bit it, and then trailed tiny kisses down over her neck, sucking on her soft skin. She smelled like flowers and tasted like honey and he knew he'd never experienced anything so sweet. So heady.

Her leg shifted higher as she sought a deeper contact, and her fingers dug into his shoulders as if she was trying to hold herself upright.

'Cruz, please....'

Needing no further invitation, he pushed her bra aside and leant back so that he could look at her.

'Perfect. You fit perfectly into my hands.'

He moulded her fullness, watching her beautiful raspberry-coloured nipples tighten even more as they anticipated his mouth on them. His body throbbed as it anticipated the same thing, and he tested the weight of each breast before drawing his thumb and fingertips together until he held just the tips of each nipple between his fingers, his touch too light to fully satisfy.

She cried out and arched impossibly higher, as if in pain, and he bent his head and gave her what he knew she needed, soldering his lips to one peak and pulling her turgid flesh deeply into his mouth while rubbing firmly over the other.

'Cruz! Oh, my God!'

She buried her hands in his hair and clung—and thank goodness she did. The taste of her made his knees feel weak and his hunger to be buried deep inside her impossibly urgent.

Wrapping one arm around her waist, he lifted her and ground his hardness against her core, his self-control shredded by her wild response. 'I want you, Aspen.' He smoothed his hand down the silky skin of her thigh and rode her skirt all the way up. 'Tell me you want me, *mi gatita*. Tell me this has nothing to do with money.'

He registered the rigidity in her body at the same time as his rough words reverberated inside his head, and both acted like a bucket of cold water on his libido.

What was he saying? More importantly, what was he *asking*?

'I...'

She looked up at him, flushed with passion. Dazed. Beautiful. The breeze whispered over her hair.

'I'm sorry,' she whispered breathlessly.

Sorry?

So was he.

The last time he had wanted something this badly he had lost everything. And he couldn't take her like this.

Couldn't take her because he was paying her.

Once again the image of a lustful Billy Smyth with his hand stroking her face clouded his vision. Up to yesterday Cruz would have said that he wasn't a violent man, but just the thought of her sleeping with anyone else curdled his blood. If he hadn't offered her this deal where else might she be tonight—and who with?

The question just added ice to the bucket and he unwound her arms from around his neck.

'Cruz...?'

Was he crazy? He had a hot woman in his arms so why was he hesitating? He couldn't explain it; he just knew it didn't feel right.

His hard-on pressed insistently against his fly, as if to say it had felt very right ten seconds ago, and he stepped away from her so he wouldn't be tempted to pull her back into his arms.

Something of his inner turmoil must have shown on his face, because she blanched and he thought she might throw up.

'Steady.'

He went to grab her but she pulled back sharply and quickly righted her dress as best she could before wrapping her arms around herself.

'I can't believe it. I've ruined it,' she muttered, more to herself than him.

On one level he registered the comment as strange, but part of him had already agreed with her—because, yes, she *had* ruined it. She was ruining everything.

His desire to buy Ocean Haven.

His peace of mind.

'That sounds like revenge,' she'd said earlier.

'Go to bed, Aspen,' he said wearily, upset with himself and his unwelcome conscience.

Her eyes were uncertain pools of dark green when she looked at him. 'But what about—?'

'I'm not in the mood.'

He turned sharply and tracked back into the penthouse before he threw his aggravating conscience over the balcony and did what his body was all but demanding he do.

Aspen stood on the balcony, the night air cooling her over-heated skin as the realisation that he was rejecting her sank in. She swallowed heavily, her mind spinning back to those last few moments. She felt like an inept fool as memories of Chad's hurtful rejection of her years ago tumbled into her mind like an avalanche. His repulsed expression when he'd told her to go out and buy a bottle of lube.

At the time she'd been so naïve about sex she hadn't even known what he was talking about. So he'd clarified. *'Lubrication. You're too dry. It's off-putting.'*

Completely mortified, she'd searched the internet and learned that some women suffered dryness due to low oestrogen levels. She hadn't investigated any further. She'd shame-facedly done what he'd asked, but they'd never got round to using it. He hadn't wanted to touch her after that.

And no matter how many times she told herself that Chad's harsh words were more to do with his own inadequacies in the bedroom than hers it didn't matter. She didn't believe it. Not entirely. There was always a niggle that he was right.

Don't go there, she warned herself, only half aware that she had pressed her hand to her stomach. *Chad's long gone and you* knew *this was going to happen with Cruz so, okay, deal with it. And quickly. Then you can go home to Ocean Haven and be safe again.*

Fortifying her resolve, she moved inside and found Cruz pouring a drink, his back to her.

'You still have to lend me the money,' she said, glad that her voice sounded so strong.

Cruz felt his shoulders tense and turned slowly to face her.

She was a cool one, all right. Haughty. Dismissive. *Way too good for him.*

Slowly he folded himself into one of the deep-seated sofas. 'No, I don't,' he said, wanting to annoy her.

'Yes, you do. You signed—'

'I know what I signed.' He swirled his drink and ice clinked in the glass as he watched her. Her eyes were cool to the point of being detached. Damn her. That was usually *his* stock in trade.

'Then you know that if it turns out you don't want...' She stopped whatever it was she was about to say and raised her chin. 'I trusted you.'

He ignored the way those words twisted his gut. Her soft declaration was making his conscience spike again. 'The agreement didn't stipulate which night.' He waited for his words to sink in and it didn't take long. 'Consider yourself off the hook for tonight. As I told you, I'm not in the mood.'

She frowned. 'When *will* you be in the mood?'

Right now, as it happens.

'I don't know,' he said roughly, annoyed with his inability to control his physical response to her.

Of course that answer wasn't good enough for her.

'And if *I'm* not in the mood when you decide you are?'

This wasn't going to work. If he stayed here he'd damned well finish what he had started outside.

He sprang to his feet and those green eyes widened warily. And well they might. He stalked towards her and wrapped one hand around that glorious mane of hair. He tilted her face up so that she was forced to meet his steely gaze, unsure if he was angry with her or himself or just in general.

'When I decide to take you, Aspen, rest assured you'll be in the mood.'

Then he kissed her. Long and deep and hard.

Aspen held the back of her hand against her throbbing mouth as Cruz marched out through the main door to the lift.

And good riddance, she wanted to call out to his arrogant back. Except she didn't. She felt too shattered. Lack of sleep last night, the roller coaster of a day today. It all crashed in on her.

Not wanting to wait around in case he suddenly reappeared, she fled to the bedroom, hoping sleep would transport her back to East Hampton. Literally.

Only it wasn't her room she was in, and she quickly snatched her things together and headed to one of the spare bedrooms.

Ha—she would show him who wasn't 'in the mood'.

She let out a low groan as those words he had flung at her came rushing back. The embarrassing thing was she couldn't have been more in the mood if he had lit scented candles and told her he loved her.

And he had seemed to be totally in the mood.

When she found herself trying to analyse the exact moment it had all gone wrong she pulled herself up. That was a one-way street to anxiety and sleeplessness and she wouldn't go there again. Not for any man.

By the time Cruz let himself back into the penthouse his frame of mind had not improved. He'd gone down to the stables—something he'd always done when he felt troubled—but it hadn't made him feel any better.

In fact it had made him feel worse, because now that Aspen had walked back into his life—or rather he had walked back into hers—he couldn't get her out of his head.

Worse, he couldn't get the game he was playing with her out of his head. He'd had a lot of time to think about things since he'd picked her up, and although he'd like to be able to say that it had started out as an underhand way of getting what he wanted the truth was it hadn't even been that logical. He'd taken one look at her and wanted her. Then he'd made the mistake of touching her. Kissing her. He'd never felt so out of control. Something he hadn't anticipated at all.

He'd convinced himself that he could sleep with her for one night and send her home.

So much for that.

The reality was that right now he wanted her in his bed—and not because he was paying her a pit full of money but because she wanted to be there. And didn't that make his head spin? The last time he'd wanted something from a Carmichael he'd been kicked in the teeth, and he was about as likely to let that happen again as the sun rising in the west.

He thought about her comment about his family treating him like a king. He'd been so caught up in his own sense of betrayal and, yes, his anger at missing out on *knowing* them that he hadn't considered his own involvement in continuing that state of affairs. Now he saw it through Aspen's eyes and it made him want to cringe. Yes, he held himself back. But distance made things easier to manage.

But she had understood that as well, hadn't she? *'That's a lot for a child to have heaped on his shoulders. You must have really struggled.'*

Yes, it had been a lot. Particularly when Charles Carmichael had been such an exacting and forbidding taskmaster. Maybe others understood what he had gone through but no one had dared say it to his face.

And her suggestion that he could scowl a little less…?

He scowled now. Maybe he should just go and find her, have sex with her and be done with her. But something about that snagged in his unconscious. Something wasn't right about her hot and cold responses but he couldn't put his finger on what it was.

'I can't believe it. I've ruined it.'

Why would she have said that? If anything he'd ruined it by stopping. But she hadn't questioned that, had she? She'd had a look on her face that was one of resigned acceptance and moved on.

And hard on the heels of that thought was her comment about her marriage to Anderson being a disaster. He'd wanted to push her on that but had decided not to. Now he wished he had. There was something about the lack of defiance in her eyes when she had mentioned her ex that bothered him. Almost as if she'd been terribly hurt by the whole thing.

He frowned. The truth was he shouldn't give a damn about Aspen Carmichael, or her feelings, or her comments, and he didn't know why he did.

Throwing off his tangled thoughts, he tentatively pushed open his bedroom door and stopped short when he found the room empty. His wardrobe door lay open and a stream of feminine clothing crossed his room like a trail of breadcrumbs where she had obviously dropped them as she'd carried her things out.

Gingerly he picked them up and placed them on the corner chair. She'd no doubt be upset to realise she'd dropped them. Especially the silky peach-coloured panties. He rubbed the fabric between his thumb and forefinger and his body reacted like a devoted dog that had just seen its master return after a year-long absence.

'Not tonight, Josephine,' he muttered, heading for the shower.

A cold one.

Cruz rubbed his rough jaw and picked up his razor. Unbidden, Charles Carmichael's rangy features came to his mind. Initially he had admired his determination and objectivity. His loyalty. Only those traits hadn't stacked up in the end. The man had been ruthless more than determined, cold rather than objective, and his loyalty had been prejudiced towards his own kind.

Had *he* degenerated into that person? Had *he* become a hollow version of the man he'd thought he was? He stopped

shaving and stared at the remaining cream on his face.
Why did his life suddenly feel so empty? So superficial?

Hold on. His life wasn't empty or superficial. He barked
out a short laugh. He had everything a man could want.
Money. Power. Women. Respect.

His razor nicked the delicate skin just under his jaw.
Respect.

He didn't have everyone's respect. He didn't have Aspen's. And he didn't have his own right now, either.

He thought again about the night Aspen had set him up.
He supposed he could have defended himself against Carmichael's prejudiced accusations and changed the course
of his life, but something in Aspen's eyes that night had
stayed him. Fear? Devastation? Embarrassment? He'd
never asked. He'd just felt angry and bitter that she had
stolen his future.

Only she hadn't, had she? He'd disowned it. He'd thrown
it all in. Nobody made a fool of a Rodriguez—wasn't that
what his *padre* would have said?

He took a deep steadying breath, flexed his shoulders
and heard his neck crack back into place.

So, okay, in the morning he would tell Aspen to go
home. He wouldn't sleep with her in exchange for the
money. She could have it. But she still wasn't getting The
Farm. He wanted it, and what he wanted he got.

End of story.

CHAPTER SEVEN

WHEN SHE WOKE the next morning and decided she really couldn't hang out in her room all day Aspen ventured out into the living area of Cruz's luxury penthouse and breathed a sigh of relief to find it empty. Empty bar the lingering traces of his mouth-watering aftershave, that was.

After making sure that he really had gone she sucked in a grateful breath, so on edge she nearly jumped out of her skin when the phone in her hand buzzed with an incoming text.

Make yourself comfortable and charge whatever you want to the room. We'll talk tonight.

'About a ticket home?' she mused aloud.

The disaster of the previous night winged into her thoughts like a homing pigeon.

In the back of her mind Aspen had imagined that they would try to have sex, she would freeze, Cruz might or might not laugh, and Aspen would return home. Then she would get on with her life and never think of him again.

Only nothing was normal with Cruz. Not her inability to hate him for his ruthlessness or her physical reaction to him. Because while she had been in his arms last night she had forgotten to be worried. She'd been unable to do anything but feel, and his touch had felt amazing. So amazing that she'd mistakenly believed it might work. That this time she would be okay. Then she'd panicked and he'd stopped. And she really didn't want to analyse why that was.

'Urgh.' She blew out a breath. 'You weren't going to replay that train wreck again, remember?'

Right.

Determinedly she dropped her phone into her handbag and poured herself a steaming cup of coffee from the silver tray set on the mahogany dining table.

There was an array of gleaming dome-covered plates, and as she lifted each one in turn she wondered if Cruz had ordered the entire menu for breakfast and then realised that he wasn't hungry. Her own stomach signalled that she was ravenous and Aspen placed scrambled eggs and bacon on a plate and tucked in.

Unsure what do with herself, she checked in with Donny and Mrs Randall and then decided to do some studying. She was doing a double load at university next semester, so she could qualify by the end of the year, and she needed to get her head around the coursework before assignments started rolling in.

But she couldn't concentrate.

A horse whinnied in the distance and another answered. *The call of the wild,* she mused with a faint smile. She walked out onto the balcony and leant on the railing. The grooms in the distance were leading a group of horses through their morning exercises and the sight made her feel homesick.

It was probably a mistake to go looking for her, but after three hours locked in a business meeting with his executive team, who had flown in from all over the States for a strategy session, Cruz's brain was fried. Distracted by a curly-haired blonde. He told his team to take an early lunch, because he knew better than to push something when it wasn't working. Once he'd found Aspen and or-ganised for her to return to Ocean Haven he'd be able to think again. Until then at least the members of his team could find something more productive to do than repeat every point back to him for the rest of the day.

But, annoyingly, Aspen wasn't anywhere he had ex-pected her to be. Not in his penthouse, nor the hotel bou-tiques, not one of the five hotel restaurants, nor the day spa. When he described her to his staff they all looked at him as if he was describing some fantasy woman.

Yeah, your fantasy woman.

Feeling more and more agitated, he stopped by the con-cierge's desk in case she had taken a taxi into town on her own. It would be just like her to do something monumen-tally stupid and cause him even more problems. Of course the concierge on duty knew immediately who he was talk-ing about and that just turned his mood blacker.

'The strawberry blonde babe with the pre-Raphaelite curls all the way down to her—?'

'Yes, that one,' Cruz snapped, realising that someone—him—had neglected to inform his staff that she was off-limits.

Oblivious to his mounting tension, the concierge con-tinued blithely, 'She's in the stables. At least she was a couple of hours ago.'

And how, he wanted to ask the hapless youth, *do you know that?* His mind conjured up all sorts of clandestine meetings between her and his college-age employee.

Growling under his breath, Cruz stalked across the wide expanse of green lawn that had nothing on her eyes to-wards the main stable. He reminded himself that if he'd waited around for her to wake up he would now know where she was and what she was up to.

Survival tactics? his conscience proposed.

Busy, Cruz amended.

He heard the lovely sound of her laughter before he saw her, and then the sight of her long legs encased in snug jeans came into view. He couldn't see the rest of her; bent as she was over the stall door, but frankly he couldn't take his eyes off her wiggling hips and the mouthwatering curve of her backside.

Another giggle brought his eyes up and he had to clear his throat twice before she reared back and stood in front of him. Cruz glanced inside the stall in time to see one of his men stuffing his wallet into his back pocket, a guilty flush suffusing his neck.

Unused to such testy feelings of jealousy, and on the verge of grabbing his very married assistant trainer by the throat and hauling him off the premises, Cruz clenched his jaw. 'I believe your services are required elsewhere, Señor Martin.'

'Of course, sir.' His trainer swallowed hard as he opened the stall door and ducked around Aspen. 'Excuse me, *señorita*.'

'Oh, we were just—' Aspen stopped speaking as Luis turned worried eyes her way, and she glanced at Cruz to find his icy stare on the man. He might have been wearing another expensive suit, but he looked anything but civilised, she noted. In fact he looked breathtakingly *un*-civilised—as if he had a band of warriors waiting outside to raid the place.

Irritated both by his overbearing attitude and the way her heart did a little dance behind her breastbone at the sight of him, Aspen went on the attack. 'Don't tell me.' She arched a brow. 'You've suddenly decided you're in the mood?'

'No.'

His expression grew stormier and he stepped into her space until Aspen found herself inside the stall with the almost sleeping horse Luis had been tending to.

'What are you up to, Aspen?' he rasped harshly, blocking the doorway.

Wanting to put space between them, Aspen stepped lightly around the mare and picked up the discarded brush Luis had been using to groom her.

'I feel bad that Luis didn't get to finish in here because of our conversation so I thought I'd brush Bandit down for him.'

'I meant *with* him?'

She paused, not liking the tone of his voice. 'If you're implying what I think you are then, yes, I did offer to sleep with Luis—but unfortunately he only has a spare nine million lying around.' She shrugged as if to say, *What can you do?*

'Don't be smart.'

Aspen glared at him. 'Then don't be insulting.'

He looked at her as if he was contemplating throttling her, but even that wasn't enough to stop the thrilling buzz coursing through her body at his closeness.

Aspen shook her head as much at herself as him. 'You really have a low opinion of me, don't you, Cruz?'

'Look at it from my point of view.' He balled his hands on his hips. 'I come out here to find you giggling like a schoolgirl and one of my best trainers stuffing his wallet back into his pocket. What am I supposed to think?'

Aspen's gaze was icily steady on his. 'That he was showing me pictures of his children being dragged along by the family goat.'

A beat passed in which she wouldn't have been surprised if Cruz had turned and walked away as he had the night before. It seemed to be his *modus operandi* when confronted with anything remotely emotional. Only he didn't.

'I'm sorry,' he said abruptly, raking a hand through his hair. 'I might have overreacted.'

Aspen had never had a man apologise to her before and it completely took the wind out of her sails. 'Well, okay…'

For the first time in her dealings with him he looked a tad uncomfortable. 'I didn't come here to quarrel with you.'

'What *did* you come here for? If you're checking on Bandit's cankers I had a look at the affected hoof before and it's completely healed.'

Cruz frowned. 'That's for the vet to decide, not you.'

'The vet was busy and I know what I'm doing. I'm one semester away from becoming a fully qualified vet. Plus, I've treated a couple of our horses for the disease. So,' she couldn't resist adding, 'not just marrying to secure my future, then.'

A muscle ticked in his jaw. 'You enjoyed telling me that, didn't you?'

'It did feel rather good, yes.'

They stared at each other and then his mouth kicked up at the corners. 'I suppose you want another apology?'

What she wanted was for him to stop smiling and scowl again so she could catch her breath. 'Would it be too much to hope for, do you think?'

'Probably.'

Aspen couldn't hold back a grin and quickly ducked down to pick up Bandit's rear hoof and clean it.

'You've changed,' he said softly.

She looked up and he nodded to the tool in her hand.

'You used to be much more of a princess type.'

'Really?' Her green eyes sparkled with amusement. 'That's how you saw me?'

'That's how all the boys saw you.' He shrugged. 'We got your horse ready and you rode it and then we brushed it down at the end. Back then you wouldn't have even known how to use one of those.'

Aspen grimaced and went back to work on the horse. 'That was because my grandfather wouldn't let me work with the horses. He had very clear ideas on a woman's place in the world. It was why my mother left. She didn't really talk to me about him, but I remember overhearing her talking to a friend and saying that he didn't understand anyone else's opinion but his own.'

Satisfied that the horse's feet were clean, Aspen patted her rump and collected the wooden toolbox. 'You're done for the day, girl.'

She glanced up as Cruz continued to block the doorway. The sound of someone moving tack around further along the stable rattled between them.

'Why did you set me up that night?'

The suddenness of the question and the harshness of his tone jolted her.

'What are you talking about?' She couldn't think how she had set him up, but—

'Eight years ago. You and your *fiancé*.'

'Fiancé?'

She frowned and then realised that he was talking about the night her grandfather had found them. She had no idea what he meant by setting him up, but it shocked her that he thought she'd been engaged to Chad at the time. Then she recalled her grandfather's vitriolic outburst. Something she'd shoved into the deepest recess of her mind.

She grimaced as it all came rushing back. 'Chad and I weren't actually engaged that night,' she said slowly.

'Your grandfather certainly thought you were.'

'That's because I later learned that he had accepted Chad's proposal on my behalf.'

Cruz swore. 'You're saying he forced you to go along with it?'

Aspen hesitated. 'No. I could have turned him down.'

'But you didn't?'

'No, but I certainly didn't consider myself engaged when I walked into the stables and saw you there.'

'How about when you kissed me?'

Aspen shifted uncomfortably. 'No, not then either.'

'That still doesn't answer my question.'

Aspen couldn't remember his question, her mind so full of memories and guilt. 'What question?'

'Why you set me up.'

She shook her head. 'I don't really understand what you mean by that.'

Cruz took in her wary gaze, frustration and desire biting into him like an annoying insect. 'You're saying it was a coincidence that your grandfather just *happened* to come across us and then just *happened* to kick me off the property, thereby paving the way for Anderson to take over as captain of the dream team?'

Her eyes widened with what appeared to be genuine shock. 'I would never...' She blinked as if she was trying to clear her thoughts. 'Grandfather said it was your decision to leave Ocean Haven.'

Cruz scoffed at the absurdity of her statement. 'It was one of those "you can go under your own steam or mine" type of offers,' he said bitterly.

But he could admit to a little resentment, couldn't he? He'd given Charles Carmichael eleven years of abject devotion that had been repaid with anger and accusations and the revocation of every promise the old man had ever made him.

Memories he'd rather obliterate than verbalise turned his tone harsh. 'He accused me of *deflowering* his precious *engaged* granddaughter and you let him believe it.'

'I don't remember that,' she said softly. 'I told him afterwards that we hadn't been together.'

Cruz wasn't interested in another apology. 'So you said.'

'But you still don't believe me?'

'It's irrelevant.'

'I don't think it is. I can hear in your voice that it still pains you and I don't blame you. I should never have let him think what he did. Not even for a second.'

'What you can hear in my voice is not pain but absolute disgust.'

He stepped closer to her, noting how small and fragile she looked, her shoulders narrow, her limbs slender and fine. He knew the taste of her skin, as well as her scent.

'When it happened…' He forced himself to focus. '*Then* I was upset. Devastated, if you want to know the truth. I thought your grandfather and I were equals. I thought he respected me. Maybe even cared for me.' He snorted out a breath and thrust his hand through his hair. 'I thought wrong. Do you know what he told me?'

Cruz had no idea why he was telling her something so deeply private but somehow the words kept coming.

'He told me I wasn't good enough for his granddaughter. He didn't want your lily-white blood mixing with that of a second-class *Mexicano*.'

'But my blood isn't lily-white. My mother saw to that in a fit of rebellion. My grandfather could never get past her decision and because they were both stubborn neither one could offer the other an olive branch. My mother wanted to go home to The Farm *so* many times.'

Aspen swallowed past the lump in her throat.

'But my grandfather had kicked her out. It was the same with you. Two days after you left he had a stroke and I'm sure it was because he had lost you. Of course no one outside the family knew about it, but I knew it had to do with what happened and I felt terrible. Ashamed of myself. But I was scared, Cruz.'

She looked at him with remorseful eyes and no matter what he thought of her it was impossible to doubt her sincerity.

'You know my grandfather's temper. I didn't know what he'd do to me.'

'Nothing,' Cruz bit out. 'He was angry at me, not you. He thought the world of you.'

'As long as I did what he wanted.' She shivered. 'I was so frightened when I arrived at Ocean Haven. I'd heard about the place from my mother and I'd loved it from a small child. I'd never met my grandfather before and I was determined that he wouldn't hate me. And he didn't. But nor did he like me questioning him or going against his wishes. At first that was okay, because I was little, but as I got older it became harder to always be agreeable. That night...' She stopped and looked at him curiously. 'Why didn't you defend yourself against him? Why didn't you tell him that it was *me* who had kissed *you*?'

'It hadn't exactly been one-way.' He ran a hand through his hair. 'And you looked...frightened.'

Aspen gave him a small smile. 'I was that, all right. I'd never seen him in such a rage. I didn't know what to do and I froze. It's a horrible reaction I've never been able to shake when I'm truly petrified. That night, if he had found out that I instigated things with you after he'd told me I was expected to marry Chad, I thought...I thought...'

Cruz briefly closed his eyes. 'You thought he'd disown you like he had your mother.'

The truth of what had happened that night was like a slap in the face.

'It seems silly now, but...'

'It was like history repeating itself. Your mother with the ski instructor...you with the lowly polo player.'

'*I* didn't think that, but he was so angry.' She shuddered at the memory. 'And I never wanted to leave the one place my mother loved so much. She used to talk about it all the time. Do you know that skewed horseshoe wedged between two roof beams in the stable?'

Cruz knew it. Old Charlie had grumbled about it whenever he was in a bad mood.

'Apparently years ago Mum and Uncle Joe were playing hooky with a bunch of them and when she was losing she got in a terrible snit and aimed one at his head.' Aspen laughed softly, as if she were remembering her mother recounting the story. 'Unfortunately she was a terrible shot and released it too soon. It went shooting up towards the roof and somehow it got stuck. Which was lucky for my uncle because she obviously put her back into it.' She smiled. 'Every time I see it, it's as if she's still here with me.'

She looked at him.

'That night I was so angry with my grandfather for ignoring my wishes that I went to the stable to talk to her. When you showed up and you weren't dressed properly I... I can't explain it rationally.'

Her eyes flitted away and then she seemed to force them back to his.

'I had wanted to kiss you for so long and I wasn't thinking clearly. I know you don't want to hear this but I am sorry, Cruz. I should have stood up for you. But I was selfishly worried about myself and—'

Cruz cupped her face in his hands and kissed her. Lightly. 'It's okay. I remember his temper.'

Aspen gave him a wobbly smile. 'I think I inherited that from him.'

He shook his head, his thumbs stroking her cheekbones. 'You're not scary when you're angry. You're beautiful.'

She made a noise somewhere between a snort and a cough and he couldn't resist kissing her again, his lips lingering and sipping at hers.

This time the noise she made was one of pleasure, and Cruz slid his hand into her hair to hold her head steady, nudging the toolbox out of his way with his knee so that he could shift closer. She pressed into him and he wrapped his other hand around her waist, deepening the kiss. Slowly.

Deliberately drawing out the sweet anticipation of it for both of them.

Aspen's arms rose, linked around his neck and time passed. How much, he couldn't have said.

Slowly she drew back, lifting her long lashes to reveal eyes glazed with passion. 'Wow...' she whispered.

Wow was right.

She moistened her lower lip, her eyes flitting from his, and he frowned. He could have sworn he saw a touch of apprehension in them. He nipped at her lower lip, kissed her again.

With a thousand questions pounding through his head—not least why she seemed nervous when it came to intimacy—he reluctantly ended the searing kiss and leant his forehead against hers. Their breaths mingled, hot and heavy.

'I don't hate you, Aspen,' he said, answering her question of the previous night. Her bewitching green eyes returned to his and he found himself saying, 'I have a formal dinner at the hotel tonight. Come with me.'

Aspen felt dazzled. By the conversation. By his sweet, tender kisses. By the piercing ache in her pelvis that made a mockery of her previous experiences with Chad. 'I'd like that...'

And she did—right up until she found an emerald-green gown laid out on her bed next to black stiletto sandals still inside their box.

Standing stock-still in the centre of the spare room Aspen stared at the exquisite gown.

'Don't wear that. You look awful in it. Here. Put this on.'

Aspen shivered. Chad's voice was so clear in her head he might as well have been standing beside her.

Cruz wasn't Chad. She knew that. But somehow her stomach still felt cramped. Because the dress symbolised some sort of ownership. Some sort of control. And she knew she couldn't give him that—not over her.

It made her realise just what she'd been thinking when he had invited her to the dinner. She'd been thinking it was a date. That it was real.

But this wasn't real. She wouldn't even be here if it wasn't for the deal he had offered her. A deal she had accepted and still hadn't fulfilled. Which she needed to do to keep Ocean Haven. How had she forgotten that? How had she forgotten that he was trying to steal it away from her?

But she knew how. He'd kissed her so tenderly, so reverently, it had been as if eight years had fallen away between them. And she couldn't think like that. Because as much as she hated the coldness of the deal they had struck she also knew that she couldn't afford to feel anything. She couldn't afford to want anything from him other than money. That way was fraught with disaster. It would turn her from an independent woman in charge of her own destiny back into the people-pleaser she had tried to be for her grandfather. For Chad.

She stared at the dress. Cruz was an extraordinarily wealthy man who was used to getting what he wanted. For some reason he had decided that he wanted her. For a night. But that didn't mean she had to wear clothes he'd chosen as well.

Before she could think too much about it she strode out into the living room. The sun was hanging low in the sky and it illuminated his fit body as he stood in front of the window, talking into his cell phone.

As if sensing her presence he turned, scanned her face and the dress she was holding, and told whomever he was talking to that he had to go.

She held the dress out to him. 'I can't wear this.'

He frowned. 'It doesn't fit?'

'No. Yes. Actually, I don't know. I haven't tried it on.'

He smiled. 'Then what's the problem?'

'The problem is—' She dropped her hand and paced away from him. 'The problem is that I'm not a possession you can dress up whenever you like. The problem is I'm an independent woman who has some idea about how to dress herself and doesn't need to be told what to wear by some high-powered male who has to own everything.'

A heavy silence fell over the room as soon as her spiel had finished but somehow her words hung between them like a hideously long banner dragged through the sky by a biplane.

'I take it your grandfather didn't like your choice in outfits?' He dropped into a plush sofa. 'Or was it Anderson?'

For a minute his astute questions floored her. 'Chad has *nothing* to do with this,' she bit out.

His beautiful black eyes glittered with confidence and Aspen was suddenly embarrassed to realise that she had just exposed a part of herself she hadn't intended to.

'At some point we need to talk about him.'

Aspen felt her heart hammer inside her chest. 'We so do not.'

His eyes became hooded. 'We will, but not now. As to the other.' He waved his hand at the emerald silk crushed in her hand. 'It's just a dress, Aspen. I assume you didn't pack anything formal?'

'No.' Deciding to ignore her embarrassment, she forged on. 'But I can buy my own clothes if I need to.'

Clearly exasperated, he looked at her from under long thick lashes. 'Fine. I'll forward you the bill.'

Aspen could tell he had no intention of doing that. 'You may have bought a night with me, Cruz, but that doesn't mean you own me.'

'I don't want to own you.' He laid his arm along the back of the sofa. 'Wear it. Don't wear it. It's irrelevant to me.'

'What *is* relevant to you?' she asked, goaded by his

nonchalant attitude. 'Because it seems to me that you've cut yourself off from everything that could have meaning in your life other than work. Your family. Your polo playing—' Aspen stopped, breathlessly aware that he had risen during her tirade and that he was nowhere near as relaxed as he had appeared.

'The dress was a peace offering.' He grabbed his suit jacket from the back of the nearby chair. 'But you can bin it for all I care.'

Feeling all at sea as he stalked out of the penthouse, Aspen returned to her room and leant against the closed door.

A peace offering?

She felt stupid and knew that she had acted like a drama queen. And she knew why. She was tense. The thought of sex with Cruz was hanging over her head like a stalactite. And felt just as deadly.

Glancing at the bed, she ignored the tight feeling in her chest and tossed the dress onto it. Then she stripped off and scalded herself with a hot shower, all the while knowing that as she plucked and preened and soaped herself with the delicious vanilla-scented soap that she was doing so with Cruz in mind. Which made her feel worse. This wasn't a romance. It was a deal.

A deal that would end as soon as they'd slept together.

A deal that could still go wrong if her uncle decided that he needed the money Cruz was willing to part with to turn Ocean Haven into a horrible hotel.

Trying not to dwell on that, she rolled her eyes at herself when she realised she'd changed her hairstyle five times. She looked at the spiralling mess. All her fiddling had turned her hair to frizz. *Great.*

Salvaging it as best she could, she stomped back into the bedroom and spied the offending gown she had flung onto the bed. Even skewed it rippled, and dared any woman not to want to wear it.

And given the contents of her suitcase what choice did she really have? None. And she hated that because she'd had so little choice in what had happened to her growing up on Ocean Haven. After Chad she had vowed she'd never be beholden to anyone again—especially not a man. But one night with Cruz didn't make her beholden to him, did it?

Once he'd lent her the money and she'd paid him back, as she would the other investors, they would be back on an equal footing. She exhaled. One night, straight up, and then she was home free.

Why did that leave her feeling so empty?

She looked again at the dress. Grimaced. Trust him to have such superb taste.

CHAPTER EIGHT

'ARE YOU EVEN listening to what I'm saying?'

Cruz glanced at Ricardo, who was debriefing him on who was attending the formal dinner that night and how impressed the Chinese delegation were with the facilities. The Sunset Bar, where they had decided to catch up for a drink before the evening proceedings, was full to bursting with excited players and polo experts from all over the globe.

'Of course,' he lied. 'Go on.'

Ricardo frowned, but thankfully continued working his way through the list.

Cruz studied it also, but his mind was elsewhere. More specifically his mind was weighing up how he was going to steal The Farm out from under Aspen's gorgeous fingertips when he now knew the truth about that fateful night.

He took a healthy swig of his tequila. He'd been *so* sure she had done him wrong eight years ago he'd been blind to any other possibility. *Tainted*, he realised belatedly. Tainted by his own deep-seated feelings of inferiority and hurt pride.

Hell.

He couldn't escape the knowledge that seeing Aspen again had unearthed a wealth of bitterness he hadn't even realised he'd buried deep inside himself—resentments he'd let fester but that no longer seemed relevant.

What is *relevant to you?*

Hell, that woman had a way of working her way inside his head. But as much as he hated that he knew in good conscience he couldn't take Ocean Haven away from her. He'd never be able to face himself in the mirror again if he did. But what to do? Because if he also let her continue with her foolhardy plan to borrow thirty million dollars to keep it she'd be bankrupt within a year.

Of course that wasn't his problem. She was an adult and could take care of herself. But some of that old protectiveness he had always felt towards her was seeping back in and refused to go away. He wanted to fix everything for her, but she was so fiercely guarded, so intent on doing everything herself. It was madness. But so was the fact that he couldn't stop thinking about her. That he even *wanted* to fix things for her in the first place.

Realising that Ricardo was waiting for him to say something, Cruz nodded thoughtfully. 'Sam Harris is playing tomorrow. Got it.'

'Actually,' Ricardo said patiently, 'Sam Harris is sick. Tommy Hassenberger is taking his place.'

'Send Sam a bottle of tequila.'

'I already sent flowers.'

Cruz shook his head at his brother. 'And you think you need a *wife*?'

Normally his brother would have returned his light ribbing, but to Cruz's chagrin he didn't this time.

'What's up?' he said instead.

Cruz rubbed his jaw and realised he should have shaved again. 'Nothing.'

'You're a million miles away. It wouldn't have anything to do with Aspen Carmichael, would it?'

Bingo.

'If I say no, you'll assume I'm lying, and if I say yes, you'll want to know why.'

Ricardo shook his head and laughed. '*Dios mio*, you've got it bad.'

Cruz dismissed Ricardo's comment. He *wanted* her badly, yes, and he was happy to admit that, but he didn't *have* it bad in the way his brother was implying.

A hush fell over the bar at the same time as the skin on the back of his neck started to prickle. Then Ricardo let out a low whistle under his breath.

'*Mi, oh, mi....*'

Slowly Cruz turned his head to find Aspen framed in the open double glass doorway of the bar like something out of a 1950s Hollywood extravaganza, the silky green gown he'd bought her flowing around her slender figure like coloured water. His mouth went dry. The halterneck dress was deceptively simple at the front but so beautifully crafted it lovingly moulded to her shape exactly as it was supposed to. She'd pinned her hair up in a soft, timeless bun—which must mean she had a fair amount of skin showing, as he was pretty sure the dress dipped quite low at the back.

Okay, make that completely backless, he corrected, fighting a primitive urge to bundle her up in his arms and return her to his room. His bed.

She hadn't spotted him yet, and when a male voice called out her name Cruz watched her turn her head, the wispy tendrils of hair she had left to frame her face dancing golden beneath the halogen lighting. Her expression softened as she spied a few of his polo players lounging in the club chairs that circled a small wooden table.

She walked towards them and Cruz tried not to react, but it was impossible to stop his gut from tightening as the men watched her with unrestrained lust in their eyes.

She looked so delicate.

So sensual.

So *his*.

The need to stamp his ownership all over her took hold and he didn't bother to contain it. For right now, for tonight, she was his—and he didn't care who knew it. In fact, the more who did the better. It would save him from having to keep tabs on her during dinner, and the four European jocks already halfway to being tanked would, he knew, be the best candidates to spread the news.

As conversation once again resumed in the bar he ignored Ricardo's keen gaze and went to her.

She had her back to him and he felt her jump as his thigh lightly grazed her hip. She looked up and he bent his head, let his eyes linger on her mouth, gratified by her quick intake of breath.

If it were possible, the more time he spent with her the more time he *wanted* to spend with her. It was a sobering thought, if he'd been in the mood to care.

He cupped Aspen's elbow in his palm. 'Gentlemen, if you'll excuse us?'

Slowly each man registered Cruz's proprietorial manner, but only Tommy Hassenberger had the nerve to look disgruntled. 'Looks like I'm too late,' he complained.

'You were too late when you were born, Tommy,' one of his friends joked, making the others laugh.

Aspen grinned, said she'd catch up with them at the formal dinner, and then felt intoxicated as Cruz placed his hand on the small of her back to guide her from the room, the heat of his palm scorching her bare skin.

She hadn't known what to expect when she had entered the bar but she had decided to try and relax. To try and forget about their deal and her fears and just brave it out. Cruz had invited her to dinner—a formal event, not a date—and for all she knew that was a peace offering as well.

'You wore the dress,' he said, his gravelly voice stroking her already heightened senses.

'Yes. I couldn't not in the end. Thank you.'

'You look stunning in it.'

The look he gave her made her burn.

Aspen took in his superbly cut tuxedo. 'You look—'
Simply divine. 'Nice too,' she croaked.

He gave her a small smile. 'Aspen, I need to tell you
something.'

Cruz gazed down at the utterly stunning woman at his
side and a ball of emotion rushed through him. Seeing her
like this…having her beside him…all the animosity of the
past fell away and he just wanted to take her upstairs and
make love to her with a need that floored him.

'What is it?'

Aspen tilted her head and Cruz heard a roaring in his
ears as their eyes connected. Reality seemed suspended
and—

'Señor Rodriguez, sir, the first lot of guests are assembled in the Rosa Room.'

Cruz turned towards his head waiter. 'Thank you, Paco.
I'll be along in a minute.'

'Certainly.'

The waiter inclined his head and left and Cruz lifted
Aspen's fingers to his lips. He could see her pulse racing
and his did the same.

'I wish I'd never planned this idiotic dinner.'

'It's not idiotic.' She smiled up at him, her eyes almost
on a level with his chin because she was wearing the stilettos. 'It's to welcome honoured guests to your flagship
hotel for tomorrow's tournament. It's important.'

Not half as important as what he wanted to be doing
with her upstairs right now.

His nostrils flared as he fought to control the urge to
drag her into the nearest darkened corner. On one level
he thought he should be concerned about the intensity of
his hunger for her, but on another he just couldn't bring

himself to examine it. There was something about her that sent his baser instincts off the scale.

Nothing a night of straightforward, short-term hot sex wouldn't cure.

He smiled at the thought and, with the situation once again under his control, he tucked her elegant hand in the crook of his elbow and prayed for the evening formalities to fly by.

The dinner took all night. As it was supposed to.

The first course had been Mushroom-something. Aspen couldn't remember and Cruz, possibly noticing her picking at it dubiously, had swapped it for his goat's cheese soufflé. Then there'd been the main course. Beef or chicken. This time Aspen had swapped with him when she'd seen him eyeing her steak.

He'd smiled, grazed her chin with his knuckles and then resumed talking to two well-dressed Asian men, who'd nodded with polite restraint. Now and then he'd twined his fingers with hers when she'd left her hand on the tabletop while he talked, as if it was the most natural thing in the world for him to do. As if this really was a date.

Aspen had chatted to the wife of the Mayor, who was very down to earth and full of Latin passion, and their daughter who was studying to be a doctor. They'd swapped war stories of bad essay topics, boring lecturers and horror exams and then it had been time for dessert.

She was full. Even though she'd hardly eaten a thing.

Her dinner companions excused themselves, and Aspen was just contemplating whether she should move to the other side of the table to speak with an older woman who sat on her own when Cruz slid his fingers through hers again. His hand was so much bigger than hers, his skin tone darker, the hairs on the back of his wrists absurdly attractive.

He stroked his thumb over her palm and goosebumps raced themselves up her arm.

He glanced in her direction, brought her hand briefly to his lips and then answered one of the Asian men's questions.

The Mayor's daughter returned and Cruz dropped Aspen's hand as the girl produced a photo of her horse on her phone. Aspen made polite responses, all the time disturbingly aware of the man beside her.

Something had changed between them since she'd come downstairs. He was behaving as she imagined a man in love would behave. Little intimate glances, tucking her hair behind her ear, pouring her water, holding her hand...

Chad had seemed nice in the beginning too. Wooing her. Treating her lovingly. Somehow it had all come unstuck the year Cruz had left and her grandfather had been too sick to send the team to England. Chad had been unable to get a permanent ride that year and had started drinking more. By the time their wedding had rolled around she'd barely recognised him as the man who had courted her and treated her so deferentially. He'd moved back home when his father had threatened to halve his trust fund, and his father had used the opportunity to encourage Chad to get a real job. Aspen had tried to smooth things over but that had only seemed to make him resentful.

On their wedding night— No, she didn't want to remember that.

She glanced at Cruz to find him deep in conversation. Would he be rough? She swallowed, her gaze drawn to his hands, wrapped around a wine glass. He stroked the slender stem with the pad of his thumb. Aspen recalled how he had stroked her lips the same way and heat erupted low in her belly. For a man with such size and strength he had been gentle. Suddenly his thumb stopped moving and Aspen felt the air between them shift even before her eyes connected with his.

Her mouth dried and her heart thumped. Fear and desire commingled until she felt emotionally wrung out.

'Aspen?'

She glanced up but didn't really see him.

'Everything okay?'

Oh, God, that deep, sensual voice so close to her ear. She couldn't help it. She trembled. Then pulled herself together.

'Fine.' *Just me being a nincompoop.*

Nincompoop? Her mother had used that word when she'd been laughing at herself.

A wave of sadness overtook her and immediately made her think of Ocean Haven. Her horses. Her mother. Aspen had gained wealth by moving in with her grandfather but not love, and certainly not security.

Cruz moved his hand to the back of her chair. 'You look miles away.'

A wave of panic washed through her and she made the mistake of glancing up at him.

As soon as their eyes met his sharpened with concern. 'Hey, what's wrong?'

'Nothing.' She forced a smile. 'I just need to go to the bathroom.'

He scanned her face but thankfully didn't push her. 'Don't be long. We'll go when you get back.'

Oh, help.

She got up, stumbled and snagged the tablecloth with her leg. Cruz leaned over and held it while she straightened up. The deliciously sexy gown he had bought her swayed around her body and settled. She felt his eyes on her as she started to walk away, the dress floating around her legs as light as butterfly wings. Of course that was nothing compared to the butterflies using her belly as a trampoline.

Once in the bathroom she told herself to calm down and splashed cold water on her wrists, dabbed it on her cheeks. She checked her make-up, shocked to see her face so flushed. It was because every time he touched her she thought of sex.

A woman smiled at her in the mirror and Aspen dropped her gaze lest the woman accurately read her mind. Then she realised how rude that was and raised her eyes only to find the person had gone.

She let out a shaky laugh at her absurd behaviour. She felt like… She felt like… She frowned. She couldn't remember ever feeling this nervous.

Well, maybe she could. On her wedding day. She'd had a similar fluttering feeling in her stomach then that had turned out to be a bad omen.

She stared at herself. Fear knotted her insides. She couldn't do this. Her eyes looked like two huge dots in her face. She just couldn't do it. She was so anxious she'd probably throw up all over him.

An older woman entered the bathroom and Aspen pretended to be wiping her hands.

She'd have to tell Cruz.

Would it mean she'd still get the money if she backed out?

Oh, who cares about the money? This was no longer about the money. This was now about self-preservation. This was about going back to the wonderful, predictable life that she loved.

Yes, but there won't be that life if you don't go through with this.

She'd backed herself into a corner and the only way out was through Cruz. A man who, for all his surface arrogance, genuinely cared about his family and was smart. And also ruthless. He would chew her up and spit her out without a backward glance if she let him.

'Let's not forget why you're here, Aspen,' she told her reflection softly.

He was pitting himself against her for Ocean Haven. Her farm. She should hate him for that alone but she didn't, she realised. She didn't hate him at all. Because she had come to understand him a little better. Understand what he had thought of her. What had shaped him as a boy. What had shaped him as a man.

How did you hate someone you instinctively sensed was good underneath? And what did that even matter?

Shaking her head at her reflection, she refastened a few loosened strands of hair and wondered where all her positive self-talk had run off to.

Maybe down the toilet.

She smiled at her lame attempt at humour and nearly walked straight into Cruz where he leant against the wall opposite the ladies' room.

'You were taking so long I got worried. I was just about to go in but I didn't want to surprise you.'

'I would have been okay.' She let out a shaky breath. 'It's the old lady in the cubicle you might have had some trouble with.'

Cruz laughed and it broke the tension. He held out his hand. 'Shall we go?'

She looked at his perfect, handsome face. Then his hand, palm up. He was strong, maybe stronger than Chad, but he wasn't nasty. Even when he'd thought she had done him wrong he still hadn't picked on her the way Chad would have done. No, Cruz was arrogant and controlling, but he was honest and straight down the line. A straight arrow. Black and white. No shades of grey.

'Aspen?'

She saw hunger and desire in his eyes and it made her feel hot all over. Maybe she could do this. *Maybe.*

She glanced at his hand, wondered if she was as crazy as her uncle had suggested and placed hers in it.

He smiled.

She swallowed.

It wasn't until they were halfway across the foyer that she saw a familiar figure—a man—leaning against the reception desk. He had his back to her, so she couldn't see his face, but he was average height with blond hair and a slightly stocky bodybuilder's physique.

Chad?

Cruz pressed the lift button and Aspen's attention was momentarily snagged by their reflection in the gold-finished doors. They looked good together, she thought. He was tall and broad, and she looked feminine and almost otherworldly in the beautiful green dress.

His eyes met hers and she couldn't look away.

Then the lift doors opened. Aspen snuck another quick glance over her shoulder but the man she had spotted wasn't there. She let out a relieved breath. After their last acrimonious argument Chad had kept to his own part of the world and she to hers.

Still, she stabbed repeatedly at the penthouse button and only realised how questionable her behaviour looked when she noticed Cruz's bemused expression and realised he hadn't swiped his security tag across the electronic panel.

His eyebrows rose and Aspen's gaze dropped to the space between their feet, her heart beating too fast. Seeing the man who might or might not have been her ex-husband had been terrible timing. Just when she'd begun to think maybe her night with Cruz would be all right it was as if the powers that be had sent her a message to take care.

To remind her that being in a man's control was when a woman was at her most vulnerable.

As the lift ascended Cruz pushed away from the mirror-panelled wall and invaded her space, startling her out of her dark reverie when he placed his warm hands either side of her waist.

'Okay, talk to me. You're as nervous as a pony facing the bridle for the first time. The same as you were last night.'

Aspen gave a low laugh at his analogy and jumped when his thumbs stroked her hip bones through the dress. She couldn't tell him she thought she'd just seen Chad. That would raise a whole host of questions that she did not want to answer. And what if she was wrong? Then she'd just look stupid. Or paranoid.

'I'm fine.'

'You're shaking.'

Was she?

He gave her a look. 'Is it the deal? Because—'

'It's not the deal. Actually I'd forgotten all about that again.'

Her answer seemed to please him but she didn't have time to consider his satisfied—'Good.'—because the lift doors opened.

When he'd released her he placed his hand on the small of her back as he ushered her through to the living room. The housekeeper had been and the room was cast with shadows by the floor lamps that had been switched on for their convenience.

'Do you want a drink?'

'Yes, please.'

She'd said that too loudly and his eyes narrowed.

'Of…?'

Aspen forced a smile. 'Gin and tonic.' She winced. She hated gin and tonic.

She wandered over to the wall to study one of the paintings she'd admired the evening before but never taken the time to look at. An overhead light outlined it perfectly and she gasped.

'That's a Renoir.'

'I know.'

He was right behind her and she heard the tinkle of ice as he handed her the drink she didn't want.

'You're not having one?'

'No.' He perched on the arm of a nearby sofa, watching her. 'Something wrong with it?'

'What?'

He motioned patiently towards the highball in her hand. 'Your drink?'

'No. It's fine. At least, I'm sure it's fine.' It was all about maintaining control. If she did that she could get through this. 'Look, maybe we should just…start.'

'Start?'

Aspen could have kicked herself, and she moved towards a side table so she could let out a discreet breath and put the drink down. She knew he hadn't taken his eyes off her and she told herself that he wanted her. She'd felt how aroused he had been last night, and again in the stable that day. He had felt huge!

So why had he stopped? Was he struggling to maintain an erection with her as Chad had done? She shuddered. On those occasions Chad had been particularly vile.

Cruz tilted his head and looked as if he was about to say something, and then he changed his mind. Instead he uncurled his large frame and came towards her until he practically loomed over her. Then he reached for her hair.

She didn't mean to do it, of course, but she flinched and his hand stilled. 'I'm just going to take your hair down.'

She stared at his chest and tried to slow her heartbeat.

'Is that okay?'

She nodded, not trusting herself to speak.

'Turn around.'

It took all of her willpower to give him that modicum of control, but when she did turn around he stroked her shoulders.

'You have a beautiful back. Lean and supple. Strong.'

He kneaded the bunched muscles either side of her neck and her involuntary sigh of pleasure filled the quiet room.

'That feels so good. I know I must be really tight.'

Cruz groaned inwardly, knowing she hadn't meant that comment the way his depraved mind had interpreted it. Yes, she did feel tight. Too tight. Too nervous.

He wanted to ask her what was wrong, but she moaned softly and her head lolled on the graceful stem of her neck and the question died in his throat.

All through dinner he'd imagined doing this. Touching her, tasting her. He'd been harder than stone all night and he wasn't sure if he'd committed to five hotels in China or fifty. Nor did he care. Right now he'd put a hundred on Mars if someone asked him to.

Aspen moaned again and shifted beneath his pressing thumbs.

'Harder or softer?' he asked, the rough timbre of his voice reflecting his deep arousal.

He heard her breath catch, and then his did as well as her gorgeous bottom brushed his fly.

'Harder,' she whispered, and a shudder ripped through him.

The musky perfume of her skin was ambrosia to his senses and he trailed soft kisses across her shoulders. Her head fell forward and she braced her hands on the side table in front of her. Cruz registered her position on a purely primal level and knew all he'd have to do was lift that long silk skirt, tear whatever excuse for a pair of panties she was hiding underneath, bend her a little more forward and slide right into her—and he very nearly did.

But he wanted more of her taste in his mouth first, and with unsteady hands he gripped the side of her waist and trailed tiny moist kisses down the column of her spine until he reached the small of her back.

She undulated for him, arching backwards, and unable to hold himself back any longer he rose, spun her around to face him and slanted his mouth across hers. Not softly, as he had done earlier in the stables—he was too far gone for that—but hard, with barely leashed power and a deep driving hunger to be inside her.

She opened for him instantly, her fingers impatient as they delved into his hair to anchor him to her. That was okay with him. He barely noticed the bite of her short nails, concentrating instead on the throbbing sense of satisfaction as his tongue filled her mouth. He tasted coffee and cream and couldn't suppress a groan.

Somehow some of her earlier hesitation seeped into the minute part of his brain that still functioned on an intellectual level and he attempted to steady himself—before he just dragged her to the floor and had done with it.

Then her tongue stroked his and his mind gave out. Sensation hot and strong coursed through him, just as it had every other time he'd kissed her, and he couldn't help curving her closer so that they touched everywhere.

The silky fabric of her dress slid against his jacket in an erotic parody of skin on skin. Which was what he wanted. What he needed. And, keeping his mouth firmly on hers, he shucked out of it and then lashed at the buttons on his shirt.

She moaned, her warm hands pushing the fabric off his body as she shaped his arms and his shoulders before clinging once more around his neck.

Cruz reached behind her neck. His fingers felt clumsy in his desperation as he finally managed to undo the two pearl-like buttons that held the top of the dress together.

Aroused to an unbearable pitch, he smoothed a hand down to the small of her back, his lips cruising along her jawline until he could tug on the lobe of her ear. She was wearing tiny gold studs and he tongued one as he bit down gently on her flesh and brought his hands around to cradle both breasts in the palms of his hands. She trembled delightfully and her responsiveness rocked him to his core.

His thumb caught her nipple and she cried out, gripping him tighter. Cruz knew that neither of them was going to make it to the bedroom so he didn't even try. Instead he lifted her onto the side table and hoped it would hold.

It did, and he pulled back and looked down at her.

Her nipples pebbled enticingly beneath his lingering gaze and he plumped one breast up. 'You're so beautiful,' he breathed, taking the rosy tip into his mouth.

Arousal beat through his body, hot and insistent, and he urged her thighs wider so that he could settle his erection between her legs. Unfortunately the table wasn't high enough for him to take her on it and he knew he'd have to lift her onto him when the time came.

'Thank heavens you're wearing a dress,' he growled around her tight, wet nipple, his impatient hands delving beneath the reams of fabric to find her.

Moments later he felt her panic in the stiffening of her thighs and the press of her fingernails on his shoulders.

'Wait!'

His blurred mind tried to take in the change and he mentally pulled back.

'We might need some lubricant,' she blurted out against his neck.

Lubricant?

Cruz stilled, and was struck by how slight and vulnerable her body felt compared to his much larger frame curved over her. Instantly his libido cooled as he recalled those times she had flinched away from him when he'd reached for her. He frowned. Had she *never* experienced pleasure during sex?

He brought one hand up between them to cup her jaw and brought her eyes to his. 'Aspen, what's wrong?'

'I'm just…' She licked her lips, her mortified gaze flitting sideways. 'I don't have much natural lubrication. I should have told you earlier.'

Stunned, Cruz could only stare at her. He could tell she was serious but he had briefly felt her moist heat through her panties and knew she needed extra lubrication the way Ireland needed rain.

As if taking his prolonged silence as a rejection, she shoved his chest hard enough to dislodge him and desperately scooted off the table.

Only her stilettos must have come off when he'd lifted her because her feet tangled in the fabric of her dress and she pitched forward.

Cursing, Cruz grabbed hold of her before she fell. 'Aspen, wait.'

'No. Let me go.'

Ignoring her attempts to break free, he gently tugged her back into his embrace. She immediately buried her head against his neck and he brought one hand up to stroke her hair. His heart thundered in his chest as his dazed mind tried to process what was happening.

He waited until he felt her breathing start to even out and then he leaned back so he could look at her face.

'Who told you that you didn't have any natural lubrication?'

She groaned and burrowed even more fully against him.

Cruz cupped her nape soothingly. 'I know you're embarrassed. Was it Anderson?'

'It happens to some women.'

Cruz had no doubt she was correct, but he had already felt how damp she was through her lace panties and, whatever problems she had, he very much doubted this was one of them.

'I'm sure it does *chiquita*, but it hasn't happened to you.'

She pulled back. 'You're wrong. Chad and I... Can we not talk about this?'

He was going to kill the moron.

Cruz nudged her chin up until her baleful glare met his. He nearly smiled at her thorny gaze but this was too serious. 'Did he hurt you?'

She wet her lips, dropped her eyes.

'Aspen?'

'Oh, all right.' She sighed. 'On our wedding night Chad was... I was anxious. Chad had been drinking heavily and I knew I had made a mistake. Actually, I knew I'd made a mistake even before the wedding, but it became bigger than I was and I didn't know how to stop it. And Chad could be charming.' She gave an empty laugh. 'You might not know that, being a man, but my friends thought he was wonderful. But the alcohol changed him and that night...' She swallowed. 'That night...'

'He raped you,' he said flatly.

'No. It was my fault. I was nervous.'

Cruz barely held himself in check. 'Do *not* blame yourself.' He guided her eyes back up to look at him. 'He would have known that you were nervous.' He cursed under his breath. 'Hell, Aspen. You were all of eighteen.'

She gave him a wobbly smile and Cruz enfolded her in his arms. He held her until he felt her trembling subside.

'He didn't mean to, Cruz. It just wasn't easy.'

Uh-huh. When he did kill him he'd do it slowly.

'It's fine. I knew this would happen anyway. You can let me go.'

Let her go?

She tried to pull away, and when he looked at her she had that same resigned look on her face that she'd had the previous night.

'When I first arrived at Ocean Haven to work for your grandfather,' he began tentatively, 'I missed my family so much I cried myself to sleep every night for a month and I felt pathetic. You were right yesterday when you said it was a lot for a kid to take on. At the time, though, I thought I just needed to man up.'

'Oh, Cruz.'

Her hand curled around his forearm, and even though he knew he was sharing the memory with her to take her mind off her own past part of him still soaked up the comfort of her touch.

'I thought my mother was turning her back on me. That I was an embarrassment to the family.'

'No.' Aspen shook her head fiercely. 'I only met her yesterday but I *know* that can't be true.'

'Probably not. And what Anderson told you isn't true either.' When her eyes fell to the side Cruz tipped her chin up. 'Aspen, you're a beautiful, sensual woman and I want to prove that to you if you'll let me.'

She frowned. 'I don't see how.'

He cupped her face in his hands, halting her words. 'I want you, Aspen. I want to kiss you and touch you and make love to you until all you can think about is how good you feel. The question is, do *you* want that to happen?'

The question might also be what the hell was he talking about? It was one thing to make a woman feel good in bed. It was quite another to want to slay her demons for her.

Ignoring the fact that he had never donned the white knight suit before, and what that meant, Cruz waited for her answer.

And waited.

Finally, still clutching her dress to her chest, her eyes wide and luminous in the over-bright room, she nodded. 'I think so.'

'Then relax and let me take care of you. And, Aspen...?' He waited for her to look at him from beneath the fringe of her dark lashes. 'If you want me to stop at any time, then we'll stop. Understand?'

She paused and her green eyes opened a little wider. 'You'd really do that, wouldn't you?'

For a brief moment Cruz savoured all the ways he would break every bone in Chad Anderson's body, starting with his pompous head and working his way down.

'In a heartbeat, *mi chiquita*. No questions asked.'

CHAPTER NINE

ASPEN BREATHED IN Cruz's warm, musky scent as he carried her to his bedroom and told herself to relax. But it was impossible. She was too embarrassed. Her old panic had returned full force when she'd felt Cruz's warm hand slide between her thighs and now she clung to his neck like a spider monkey as he laid her on the bed.

'Aspen?'

The bedcover was cool at her back and his naked chest was hot at her front as he tried to prise her hands from around his neck. In her earlier fantasies about sex it was romantic and sensual. Dreamy and wonderful. Hot and desperate. This felt awkward and tense.

She didn't look at him as he turned onto his side, visualising how gauche she must appear, with her hair spread out around her and her body partially exposed, with the bodice of her dress undone and metres of silk twisted up around her waist. Keeping her eyes scrunched tight, she adjusted the skirt down her legs.

'Can you turn out the light?' She could feel it burning holes in her retinas even though her eyes were clamped shut.

'I will if it makes you more comfortable, but I won't be able to see you if I do that.'

'That would be the general idea.'

'Open your eyes, *gatita*.'

'Is it a prerequisite?'

His low chuckle had her squinting up at him. He looked lazy and indolent with his head propped in his hands, his gaze extremely male and hot as it met hers. Well, clearly only one of them was feeling awkward and tense.

'You're very comfortable with this, aren't you?'

'You will be too, very soon,' he promised. 'More than comfortable.'

He brought his hand up to her face and started drawing lazy patterns with his finger over her cheeks and nose and down the side of her neck to her collarbone. It wasn't easy for her to give him control, but Aspen lay as still as a stone, slowly recognising that her skin was tingling with a pleasant sensation and that goosebumps had risen up along her upper arms.

'How much pleasure have you actually had during sex, *mi chiquita*?'

She swallowed and would have turned from him then, but his magical finger edged along the loose side of her dress and feathered across her nipple. She sucked in a shallow breath, letting it out on a rush. 'Not much,' she answered honestly. *None* seemed too big an admission to make.

'Mmm...' Cruz ducked his head to her shoulder and trailed a line of kisses to the sensitive curve of her neck. 'Then we'll have to change all that. I am now taking it as my personal mission to teach you about pleasure.'

He shifted closer so that she could feel the heat of his body burn into the side of hers.

'Nothing but pleasure.'

He looked at her as if he wanted to devour her. As if he couldn't think of anything else but her. The thought frightened her, because her desire for him had grown exponentially over the course of a couple of days and she didn't know how that had happened.

He had invaded her thoughts and her dreams and seemed to make a mockery of her declaration that she would never again be at any man's mercy. Because here she was, lying nearly naked on his bed and feeling way out of her depth. And yet as scary as that thought was, as she looked at him like this, his face half in shadow from the bedside lamp, he looked amazing. His strong features and wide shoulders promised to fulfil all of her hidden desires and she felt utterly and completely safe with him, she re-alised with astonishment. Something she would have said she would never feel again in a man's arms.

Warmth returned deep inside her. Warmth and a sense of wonder that made her feel hot and restless. Her gaze fell to where her hands rested on his gorgeous chest and then she slowly returned her eyes to his. The look in his was both tender and hungry and it made her insides melt.

Reaching up, she stroked the sexy stubble already lin-ing his jaw. 'Make love to me, Cruz. Please.'

As if he'd been waiting for her to say those exact words he took one of her hands and brought her palm to his lips. His answer, 'It will be my pleasure…' rumbled through his chest and arrowed straight into her heart.

His next kiss was hot and deep and sensation swamped her, sending sparks of excitement everywhere, cutting off her ability to think. Her inhibitions and worries seemed to be caught up with some primal desire and this time de-sire won out.

There was just no room to consider anything other than Cruz's big hands on her body, stroking her, adoring her. His whispered words of encouragement as he discarded her dress and moved her tiny thong down her thighs raised her level of anticipation to an unbearable pitch.

Within seconds she was naked beneath him and his mouth was tracking a path to her breast. Aspen held still, already anticipating the heady pleasure his mouth would bring. And she wasn't disappointed. Cruz drew the tight bud gently into his mouth, licked, circled, nipped and did things to her nipple that were surely illegal. Aspen felt dizzy and her hazy mind didn't even register when his hand slid over the outside of her thighs. Then every neuron in her brain tightened and focused as she felt his hand drift inwards.

'Still with me, *chiquita*?' he asked, blowing warm air across her moist breast.

'Yes, oh, yes.' She curled her hands around the defined muscles in his shoulders. 'But you're still partially dressed.'

'Not for long,' he assured her. 'But let's take care of something first.' He gently pressed her upper body back down on the bed. 'Lie back, *gatita*. This is all for you.'

Aspen complied, but she still tensed when his hand returned to her closed thighs. She half expected him to open them and maybe move over the top of her, to push himself inside her. What she didn't expect was that he would bend one of her knees up and start stroking her leg as one might a domestic cat. Or a startled horse.

And then she couldn't think at all, because he brought his mouth back to her breast and laved the tip with his tongue. She pressed closer, husky little sounds urging him on, and her lower body clenched unbearably with every tug of his lips on her nipple. Then his hand started circling higher on her leg. Slowly. So slowly it was sheer torture. She couldn't stop herself from restlessly trying to turn towards him. She needed weight, she realised, and pressure.

'Patience, *chiquita*,' he implored, his breathing heavy.

'I don't have any,' she groaned, and then gasped as his fingers lightly grazed over the curls between her legs before circling her belly and dipping down again, this time lingering a little longer and pressing a little lower.

Unbelievably Aspen shifted her legs a little wider of her

own accord and knew in that moment that she truly wanted this to happen. That she wanted more. That she wanted all of him. Inside her. Her fear of disappointing him, of failing, of him hurting her was completely eradicated as need spiralled through her and drove everything else out of her mind. If it didn't work out she no longer cared. She just needed *something*. Him!

She waited breathlessly as his finger ran along the seam between her legs again, only to exhale as it continued moving up to link with one of hers.

'Cruz, please…' She curled her free hand around his neck and dragged his mouth back to hers.

'You want me to touch you, *chiquita*?' he said against her lips.

'You know I do.' Then she had a horrid thought. 'Don't you want to?'

He stilled and held her gaze as he brought the hand he held down to the front of his pants. He was huge. That was Aspen's first thought. And her second was that she wanted to see him, touch him.

'Never doubt it,' he said fiercely. 'Never.'

His kiss was hard and hungry and then he wrenched his mouth from hers.

'But I'm trying to go slow. Make sure you're totally ready for me.' He took her hand in his again, linking his fingers over the back of hers. 'And I have something to show you.'

He laid her hand palm-down on her belly and then slowly guided her hand over her silky curls.

'Open your legs wider, *chiquita*,' he murmured beside her ear. 'No. More. Yes, like that…'

And then he directed her hand even lower until, with a gasp, Aspen felt herself as she never had before.

'Oh, my God—that feels…'

'Wet?'

Cruz ran the tip of his tongue around the whorl of her ear and she nearly came off the bed.

He pressed her hand downwards. 'Silky? Sexy?'

Yes!

Lost in a maelstrom of sensation, Aspen closed her eyes and let her feelings take over. She didn't know what to focus on as her fingers slipped over her body, making her want to press upwards.

'And now...' Cruz shifted until he lay on his stomach between her splayed legs, his olive skin dark against the cream bedcovers. 'Now I'm going to taste you.'

Aspen tried to close her legs in a hurry. 'Cruz, you can't.'

He looked up, the skin on his face tight as he held his hands still on her open thighs.

'Let me, Aspen. Remember? I promised you nothing but pleasure.'

Tensing just a little, she let him move her legs wider again and closed her eyes as he dipped down and opened her with his skilled tongue.

She'd heard of men doing this, of course. She had been to an all-girls school, and she knew that some girls liked it and some didn't. She had always put herself in the latter camp. Cruz's low groans of pleasure as he licked and lapped at her sensitive flesh shifted her firmly to the former.

She thought maybe he asked if she was okay, but by that stage he had brought his fingers into play and Aspen couldn't breathe, let alone answer. Her whole body was burning and intensely focused on something that seemed just out of reach. She writhed and twisted beneath him, delighting in the scrape of his stubble against her tender skin, not even registering that she was calling his name until he moved over her.

'It's okay, *chiquita*. Let go.'

Let go? Of what?

And then it happened. Somehow the gentle stroking of his fingers sped up and they moved in such a way that she felt something inside her shift. Within seconds her body had exploded into a thousand tiny pieces.

Distantly she was aware that he had moved down her body again, but she was in such a blissful state of completion she felt as if she was floating.

'Aspen, open your eyes.'

Were her eyes closed again?

Opening them, she saw Cruz watching her.

'How was that?'

She smiled. 'That was the most exquisitely pleasurable experience of my whole life.'

'And I'm just getting started,' he drawled arrogantly.

Aspen laughed, and then her breath caught as he rose over her with latent male grace; his powerful biceps bunched as he completely covered her and took her mouth with his again.

She felt the heavy weight of his erection against her stomach and unbelievably her lower body clenched, needing pressure again. She squirmed upwards, opening her legs automatically.

Groaning, Cruz rolled off her, yanked his pants off in a rustle of fabric and reached into the side drawer for a condom. She watched, completely motionless, as he tore the wrapper apart with his teeth and then held his hard length with one hand while he applied it.

'You keep looking at me like that, *mi gatita*, and I'll have no need for protection,' he husked, his gravelly voice rolling straight to her pelvis.

Aspen felt herself blush, but she didn't look away. He was too mesmerising. Too...

'Beautiful,' she said. 'You're beautiful.'

She ran her hand over his tanned back, briefly marvelling at the smooth heated texture of his skin and the way he trembled beneath her touch. Had *she* done that? Her eyes flew to his and she noticed the sheen of perspiration lining his forehead.

A smile of abject female joy slowly crossed her face. He saw it and groaned. Captured her mouth with his and pushed her onto her back, coming over the top of her in a position of pure male dominance. For once it didn't scare her. Because in that moment she felt a sense of feminine power she'd never known she had. And it was exhilarating. Drugging. *Freeing*.

'Hook your legs around my waist,' he instructed gruffly.

She did, and immediately felt the smooth rounded head of his penis at her entrance. Totally caught up in the wonder of it, she dug her hands into the small of his back as she pulled him closer.

He hesitated and for a moment her old fear returned, her nerves tightening in anticipation of possible pain, and then he nudged her so sweetly her breath rushed out on a sob. She clasped his head and brought his mouth down to hers, tears burning the backs of her eyes as he slowly eased inside her body.

She easily accommodated him at first, but then she did feel too full. Too stretched.

'Relax, *amada*,' he crooned against her lips 'I've got you.'

He kissed her hungrily and withdrew almost all the way, before slowly pushing forward again, his tongue filling her mouth and mimicking his lower body's movements until Aspen felt as if she was melting into the bed.

He raised his face above hers and he looked intense. Focused. 'You feel amazing.'

He adjusted his weight and Aspen moaned, arching towards him.

'But you're so tight. I feel like I'm hurting you.'

'No.' She flexed her hips and rubbed against him, gasping as she felt him lodge deeper. 'It feels sensational. *You* feel sensational.'

Cruz groaned and seemed to praise God as he started moving inside her, his strokes smooth and slow before gradually picking up pace. Every time his big body pushed into hers Aspen clung harder to his damp shoulders, her body growing tighter and tighter until with a sudden pause she felt another rush of liquid heat, right before her body convulsed into a paroxysm of pleasure.

Dimly she was aware of Cruz still moving inside her, of her pleasure being completely controlled by the powerful movements of his. And it was endless as he drove into her, over and over and over, until with a pause of his own he tilted her bottom and surged into her with controlled power. Once, twice more, until she cried out and felt him rear his head back and fall over the edge with her.

Again time seemed endless as Aspen stared at the ceiling, slowly coming back into her body. She felt wonderful. Blissfully, sinfully wonderful. Her body was a sweaty, sensual mass of completion. Her hand lifted to Cruz's hair and she caressed the silky strands, enjoying his harsh breaths sawing in and out against her neck.

A smile curved her mouth as she recalled the moment Cruz had guided her hand between her legs so she could feel how wet she was. And she had been. Unbelievably wet—and soft. It had been like touching somebody else's body.

Unbidden, Chad's drunken taunts came to mind and she realised that it had been he who was unable to perform, not her. Deep down, and in moments of total confidence, she had told herself that exact thing, but believing it to be true was something else entirely. Especially when he was such a gregarious and charming person when he wasn't drinking. He was like a Jekyll and Hyde character, she realised, but after tonight what had happened in the bedroom with him would never haunt her again. She wouldn't let it.

Hours later Cruz woke and used the remote console beside his bed to open the curtains. The sky was pale blue outside so he knew it wasn't much after dawn.

Slightly disturbed by the whirring sound of the drapes, Aspen snuggled deeper beneath the covers he'd pulled over them both some time during the night.

Cruz's arm tightened around her shoulders. Last night had blown his mind. First finding out that Aspen had clearly had a poor excuse of a sex-life before him, and second, realising that *he* had had a poor excuse of a sex-life before her. Hell, he'd never come so hard or so often as he had last night, and he was half expecting to be rubbed raw.

He glanced at her delicate features softened by sleep. Her rosy cheeks and the dark sweep of her lashes. He grew hard just thinking about last night.

One night.

He frowned as their deal slid back into his mind like an insidious serpent. Her damned document. At the time one night had seemed like more than enough. He'd thought she was a vacuous princess type he had once lusted after and needed to get out of his system. He'd thought he'd take her to bed, slake his lust for her and move on.

Of course he'd still move on, but...

He thought about the hotel he'd planned to build on Ocean Haven. Last night he'd given up on that plan and, surprisingly, he didn't care. Aspen had been as much a victim of Charles Carmichael's warped ideas about what was right and wrong as he had been—maybe more so.

And the truth was he didn't need Ocean Haven and she did. Ergo, she should have it. Which seemed to be what her uncle thought as well, because he was still obstinately refusing Lauren's increasing offers on Cruz's behalf. He smiled. Stubborn old goat—he might not be as sanctimonious as his old man, but he'd inherited that attribute from him, all right.

And good for him—because as soon as Cruz got up he would tell Lauren to pull out of that particular race. Aspen had won and for once he didn't mind losing. One day he'd share that with Ricardo. Have a laugh. One day when he understood it better.

But for now he had to face facts.

Fact one: Aspen would want to return to Ocean Haven some time soon. Fact two: he was supposed to be flying to China to check out the site of the first of his—what was it?—fifty new hotels first thing tomorrow. Fact three…

Fact three was that he wanted neither of those things to happen. Fact four was that he didn't know why that was, and fact five was that she felt divine curled up against his side. Fact six was that he was definitely going crazy because he was yapping to himself again.

His throat felt as if he had a collar and tie around it.

Previously, making sure that he was rolling in money had been all that he could think about. He'd put his polo career on hold indefinitely to achieve it. After he'd left Ocean Haven he could have picked up any number of wealthy patrons who would have happily paid any fee to have him play for them, but he would still have been at their beck and call. Still disposable. Still an outsider in a world of rank and privilege. So he'd worked hard to change that. And, although many might say he had now achieved his goal, pride—or maybe that old sense of being vulnerable—drove him onwards.

But was it enough now? Hadn't he started to question how much satisfaction he actually derived from pushing himself so hard? Hadn't that old feeling of wanting a family started poking into his mind again? Wasn't that one of the reasons he'd tried not to visit his own family? And here was fact seven: he hated that feeling of being the one left out. Maybe Aspen was right about that. Maybe if he became more human around his family they might be the same with him.

Madre de Dio.

He was doing it again.

Cruz closed his eyes and let himself absorb the slender length of the woman who was pleasantly draped over his side like a human rug. Gently, so as not to disturb her, he stroked her hair. She shifted and the rustle of the sheets carried her scent to his nose. She smelled good. Superb.

His mind conjured up how she had looked last night, spread out beneath him while he made her come with his mouth. His body hardened and he had to bite back a groan. He wasn't sure he could do it again, and he was damned sure she was probably too sore, but his body had other ideas.

Trying to stanch the completely normal reaction of his body to the closeness of a naked woman, Cruz carefully extricated himself from under Aspen's warm body. Better he get up now, have a shower and start the day. It was going to be a busy one. First a round of meetings to finalise what he hadn't done yesterday, and then the polo matches would start just before lunch and run till the afternoon.

He would have made it too— except Aspen chose that moment to move again and attached herself to him like scaffolding on a building site. She moaned and smoothed her hand over his chest.

Cruz had closed his eyes, his senses completely focused on the southerly trajectory of her hand, when she suddenly snatched it back.

'I'm sorry. I...' She sat up and pushed the tangled mass of curls back from her face.

Fact eight: she looked adorable when she woke up. All

soft and pink, with her lips still swollen from where they had ravaged each other.

Unable to help himself, he dropped his eyes to her chest and she gave a small squeak, quickly dragging the sheet up over her nakedness. But not before he'd had a good glimpse of creamy breasts that wore grazes from his beard growth.

For some reason her obvious distress eradicated his own desire to put as much distance between them as possible. Which was surprising when he recalled how he had opened up about his childhood last night. That alone should have had him eating dust. But her loser ex had done her a disservice when it came to intimacy, and Cruz wasn't about to make that worse because he had itchy feet.

'Good morning.'

She turned wild eyes up at him. Dampened her lips. 'Good morning.'

Silence lengthened between them and Cruz realised he had no idea what to say. This was the equivalent of a one-night stand and, while he'd never had what could be considered a long-term relationship, he didn't indulge in one-night stands either.

'This is—'

'Awkward?'

She let out a shaky breath. 'Yes, but last night was…'

'Wonderful.'

She pulled a pained face. 'You don't have to say that. I mean yes, it was good, great for me but…oh, never mind.'

Cruz felt a well of rage at Anderson for hurting her. He wanted to reassure her that he was actually being honest, but he suspected she'd see his words as hollow.

'Spend the day,' he found himself saying instead.

'Why?' Her shocked eyes flew to his and he made sure his own surprise at his invitation didn't show on his face. But why shouldn't she spend the day? He had a first-rate polo tournament starting in a few hours. She loved polo. She ran a horse stud.

'I thought you were busy today?' she said.

'I am.' Her reserved response had him putting the brakes on the surge of pleasure he'd experienced at the thought of her staying with him. 'But there's plenty for you to stay for. The polo, for one. It's going to be an incredible event.'

She gave him a wan smile that made his teeth want to grind together. 'I don't want to complicate things.'

Confused by his own reaction to her reticence, he took refuge in annoyance. 'And how is watching a polo tournament complicating things?'

'Our deal—'

'Forget the deal.' He got out of bed. 'Stay because you want to. Stay because the sun is shining and because there's going to be a world-class polo tournament here that's sold out to the general public. Stay because you work too hard and you need a break.'

'Well, when you put it like that…'

Torn between wanting to kiss her and sending her home, Cruz nearly rescinded his offer when the cell phone on his bedside table rang.

They both looked at it.

'What's your decision?'

She dampened her lips. 'Yes, okay, I'd like to watch the polo.'

Aspen stood on the penthouse balcony and stared out over the shiny green polo field. Horse floats, white marquees, riders, grooms, horse-owners and hotel employees scurried about as they readied themselves for the day ahead.

Yet despite the heady anticipation in the air that preceded a major event all Aspen could think about was what she was still doing here.

Replaying their awkward morning-after conversation in her head, she cringed. When Cruz had first asked her to stay Aspen had felt her heart jump in her chest at the thought of spending the day with him. Then he'd confirmed that he'd be busy and she'd felt like an idiot. Of course he was busy. He had invited her to watch the polo, not to spend the day with *him*.

When his phone had rung she had automatically said yes because he'd looked beautiful and sleep-tousled and she hadn't wanted to leave.

Now she didn't think she could leave fast enough.

Because last night had changed her. She felt it deep within her bones. Last night had been everything she'd ever dreamed making love could be, because Cruz had taken the time to make it that way for her and she could already feel herself wanting to make more out of it than it was. Wanting to make it special, somehow. But what woman *wouldn't* want to do that when she'd just been so completely loved by a man like Cruz Rodriguez?

No, not loved, she quickly amended. Pleasured.

God.

She buried her forehead against her arms, which were resting on the balustrading.

It was beyond clear that Cruz had asked her to stay out of politeness or—worse—pity. She, of course, had said yes out of desire. Desire to spend more time with him. Desire to experience his lovemaking again. Desire to re-experience the pleasure she felt sure only he could give her.

But he was as much of a Jekyll and Hyde character as Chad when it came down to it, because he had come to Ocean Haven specifically to try and take her farm.

She had forgotten that. *Again.*

Was she a glutton for punishment? Was she so used to having men control her that she'd gladly fall in with the plans of another self-interested, power-hungry male?

Because while Cruz might have shown her the best night of her life, it didn't change the reality of why she was even here.

'Forget the deal,' he'd all but snarled.

Last night she had. This morning it was impossible to do so in the cold light of day.

Or course last night she had been in the grip of a wonderful sense of feminine power with Cruz that could easily become addictive if she let it. A smile curved her lips, only to fade away just as quickly. Cruz had freed her from years of feeling as if there was something wrong with her and she'd be forever indebted to him for that. He was also trying to buy her home out from under her, and that was like a sore that wouldn't heal. If she stayed today it would be for the wrong reasons. It would be because she was hoping for more from him. Something she didn't want from any man. Did she?

Aspen groaned. How could she even think about staying longer under the shade of such conflicting emotions?

The simple answer was that she couldn't. And dwelling on it wasn't going to make it any different.

Decision made, she spun on her heel and went to pack her suitcase.

Cruz looked up, annoyed, as his PA opened the door to his meeting. It was taking him all that he had to concentrate as it was, without yet another irritating interruption.

'What is it, Maria?'

He frowned as he heard Aspen's hasty, 'It's okay…don't interrupt…' in the background.

Maria glanced over her shoulder. 'Ah, Señorita Carmichael wishes to speak with you.'

'Send her in.'

Aspen materialised in the doorway and Cruz saw her suitcase by the side of the door.

He frowned harder. 'What's going on?'

'I can see you're busy.' She threw a quick glance around the room at his executive team. 'It can wait.'

'No, it can't.' He pinned her with a hard look, unaccountably agitated as he registered her intention to leave him. 'Is something wrong?'

'No, no. I just came to say goodbye. I didn't want to leave without letting you know I was going.'

'I thought you had decided to stay?'

She swallowed. 'Our deal was concluded this morning and—'

Cruz swore. 'I thought I'd already told you to forget the deal. It's not relevant. I'm not going to buy Ocean Haven any more. It's yours free and clear.'

A myriad of emotions crossed her lovely face, not completely unlike the morning when he had first told her that he *was* going to challenge her for The Farm.

Disbelief, shock, wariness, a tentative joy...

Three days ago he wouldn't have conceived of giving up something he wanted as much as he had wanted Ocean Haven, but a lot had changed in three days. He'd found out the truth about the night he'd left The Farm and he'd made love to Aspen. Held her in his arms all night. Woken with her still in his arms in the morning. When he looked at her he felt things he'd never felt for any woman before her. Feelings he was still unable to categorize.

'Really?' She took a hesitant step towards him. 'You're serious? It's mine?'

'Yes,' he said gruffly, wondering why it was that he couldn't look at her without wanting to strip her clothes off.

'Oh, Cruz...'

She looked as if she might cry, and just when he was about to back away she gave a gurgle of laughter and rushed over to him, jumping up to wind her arms around his neck. Instinctively Cruz grasped the backs of her thighs, and it seemed completely natural to raise her legs and lock them around his hips.

In an instant the chemistry between them ignited and he filled his hands with her taut curves as he sought to steady them both.

'Thank you, thank you… This means so much to me. You have no idea.'

Before he could formulate a sane response she leant forward and kissed him, her silky tongue sneaking out to wrap around his. Cruz held in a groan and took charge of the kiss. This was what he'd wanted from the minute he'd woken up this morning.

Then he'd held himself back. Now, with her honeyed taste on his tongue, he didn't bother. Her mouth was the greatest aphrodisiac he'd ever known.

She moved her hips and Cruz pressed himself more snugly against the seam of her jeans. She murmured something and he almost ignored it, but the words 'We're not alone…' and 'Everyone is watching…' somehow permeated his addled brain.

He glanced around at his stunned executive team. She was right. Not one of them had looked away and he couldn't say he blamed them. He was just as shocked that he'd forgotten they were still in the room as they were at seeing him with a woman locked in his arms.

He released a careful breath.

'Excuse me, everyone. I'm going to have to adjourn this meeting. Again.'

He held Aspen as still as a statue until the door snicked closed. Then he devoured her, pulling at her clothes and unzipping his jeans. He shoved aside the laptop on the mahogany table and laid her down. Her shirt was open around her and her breasts were heaving against the delicate cups of her plain white bra. She looked wild and wanton, her hair spilling out of the French braid she had secured it in.

His hands skimmed her, claimed her, and she arched up off the table towards him.

'That door isn't locked,' she got out between gasps of pleasure.

'No one will come through it unless they want to start looking for a new job.'

'This is…'

'Madness?' His hands felt clumsy as he yanked her jeans down her legs. 'You need to start wearing skirts more,' he complained.

She let out a husky laugh, and then her breath hitched as he ripped her panties aside and parted her legs. She was already slick and ready and he growled his appreciation.

'I've never wanted a woman as much as I want you.'

He ducked his head down and bathed her silky wetness with his tongue. Her legs fell further apart and he saw her watching him as he licked and sucked on her sweetness. The picture of his dark head nestled between her creamy thighs nearly unmanned him, and when he felt her inner walls start to tremble with her imminent release he rose up and pulled her towards the edge of the table.

'Not without me, *mi gatita*. I want to feel you come around me.'

Quickly applying a condom, Cruz hooked her legs over his forearms and drove into her. Her gasp was raw and shocked and, given everything she had revealed to him last night, he tried to check himself.

'No, don't stop. Please.'

Her hands clutched his forearms, urging him closer, and Cruz closed his eyes and pumped himself into her, grazing her clitoris with his thumb to maximise her pleasure. She came hard and fast at exactly the moment he did. Pleasure turned him inside out. The world might have ended at that moment and he wouldn't have had a clue.

CHAPTER TEN

'You do miss it.'

'What?'

'Playing polo.'

'What makes you say that?'

'Oh, I don't know.' Aspen smiled up at Cruz. 'The wistful look on your face right now, perhaps.'

They were leaning on the fence post of one of the stable yards, watching the grooms and riders put the finishing touches to their horses before the main tournament got under way.

'I'm assessing the state of the horses.'

Aspen cocked her head and studied his profile, shadowed from the sun by a baseball cap. His hair curled sexily at the sides. 'Why did you give it up?'

He turned his head, his black eyes piercing. 'Money.'

'Ah. I'm sensing there's a theme here.' She laughed.

'No theme,' Cruz growled without heat. 'I didn't have much when I left Ocean Haven and I knew that polo wasn't going to give me what I needed.'

Aspen nodded. 'Money gives you the security that Ocean Haven gives me, but it's our loss. Watching you play polo was like watching poetry in motion.'

He looked at her strangely and then gave her a small smile. 'Those days are long gone now. And, while I did miss it, my life is full enough as it is. By the way...' His tone turned serious. 'Anderson is here. He was injured last month in Argentina so he wasn't expected to turn up. I told him to keep away from you.'

Aspen reeled. So it *had* been Chad she had glimpsed last night in the hotel foyer. She sucked in a deep breath and let it out slowly. She hadn't seen him in years, and while she really didn't want to she didn't want Cruz feeling as if he had to defend her just because she had unexpectedly opened up to him.

'You don't have to fight my battles for me, Cruz.'

He shook his head as if he knew better and tapped the tip of her nose affectionately. 'Somebody has to.' He took off his cap and fitted it to her head. 'You need a hat if you're going to stay out in the sun, *mi gatita*. Excuse me for a minute.'

He headed off inside the stable, his long stride and two-metre frame seeming to strike sparks in the air as he moved. Aspen tried to feel annoyed at his high-handedness, but after last night and then this morning on his conference table it was hard to stay irritated with him over anything. It had been so long since she had felt this good.

So long since she had just enjoyed herself without the pressure of work and bills getting in the way.

So long since she had felt the freedom of truly being in charge of her own destiny.

And it was exhilarating. She grinned to herself. Almost—but not quite—as exhilarating as feeling Cruz move inside her body. She smiled again. Almost as exhilarating as feeling his mouth on her breasts, between her legs.

As soon as she had *that* thought liquid heat turned her insides soft and her smile widened, because now that she recognised the sensation she could actually feel herself growing moist. She glanced around surreptitiously, just to make sure no one else could see that she was turning herself on.

Her newly awakened desire was like a runaway train. And while part of her knew she should probably try and put the brakes on it, another part of her wanted to roll around in it like a cat in the sun.

Mi gatita. His kitten.

Aspen rolled her eyes. She shouldn't get so much joy out of the pet name but she did.

Her cell phone beeped an incoming message and she snatched it out of her pocket, hoping it was her uncle returning her call. Earlier she had left an excited message on his answering machine, informing him that she had raised the money they had agreed upon for her to buy The Farm. She wondered if he had got it yet and whether he was surprised, wishing she could have told him in person. Unfortunately a trip to England was not in the cards for her in the next twenty-five hours. Although, seventy-two hours ago she would have said a trip to Mexico wasn't, either.

Checking her phone, she saw it was just Donny, informing her that he'd organised for Matty, one of the local teenagers who attended her riding school, to relieve him for the day. Aspen quickly texted back to tell him to have a great day off with his family.

Family...

That sounded so nice.

'Catch.'

Cruz's voice broke her reverie and Aspen looked up just in time to grab the bundle of clothes he had tossed at her and to see a smirk on his handsome face. 'What's this?'

'You're my new groom. How soon can you change?'

Aspen didn't miss a beat. 'Five minutes.'

'See Luis over there?' Cruz pointed with his free hand towards the players' area.

'Yes.'

'Meet me there in two.'

Aspen felt deliriously happy. She reached out and grabbed

his arm as he made to walk past, a thrill of excitement racing through her. 'You're really going to play?'

He paused, cocked his head. 'You wanted to see poetry in motion, didn't you?'

Aspen shook her head, smiling at his cockiness.

It was dangerous to feel this much happiness because of a pair of jeans and a shirt, but it wasn't that. It was the man.

She'd fallen in love with him, she realised with a sinking feeling.

He must have sensed her regard because he turned and met her gaze.

'One minute left,' he drawled.

Totally in love, she thought, and she had no idea what to do about it.

He was in love.

The thought gripped him by the throat in the middle of the game just as he was about to make a nearside forehand shot and he nearly fell off his horse and landed on his behind. Fortunately years of training and a horse that could play blind saw him come out of the offensive strike still in the saddle.

He pulled up and let one of his team members carry the ball to the goalposts.

He couldn't be in love with her. It was impossible. He didn't want to be in love with anyone. Not yet. It wasn't part of his plan.

Surely it was just the exhilaration of being out on the polo field again that was sending weird magnetic pulses to his brain? The sense of fun he hadn't felt in far too long?

He glanced towards the players' area and his eyes effortlessly zeroed in on Aspen standing beside one of his players. She wore his Rodriquez Polo cap and her flyaway blond curls billowed out at the sides. She'd put on his team colours and she looked curvy and edible as she clapped her hands wildly.

The horn went, signalling the end of the game, and Cruz trotted towards her almost hesitantly.

Unaware of his thoughts, she beamed up at him. 'You are such a show-off. Congratulations on the win.'

He returned her smile. She was gorgeous. Gorgeous and smart and funny and hot-headed. And, yes, he was in love with her.

Other players thumped him on the back and congratulated him and he could hear the commentators waxing lyrical about his statistics and his comeback—not that this *was* a comeback, more a hiatus in his normal working life—but he wasn't really paying attention to anything other than Aspen.

He hadn't had any idea that he was falling in love with her but now that he had acknowledged it, it made perfect sense. Probably he had always loved her.

And he couldn't wait to tell her because last night and earlier, when he should have been concentrating on work, she had looked at him in such a way that he was confident she felt the same as he did.

Not that he would tell her here. He'd do it in private. Maybe over an elaborate dinner. He smiled, already anticipating the moment.

Aspen took Bandit's reins and he dismounted. 'That last goal was simply brilliant.'

'I thought so.'

He readjusted his helmet and Aspen automatically pushed some of his hair out of his eyes. 'You need a haircut,' she admonished.

He stilled, his gaze holding hers. 'I have something I need to tell you.'

'What is it?'

'Not here.' He shook his head. 'I promised Ricardo I'd

check in with the Chinese delegation I have apparently neglected all day. How about we meet back in the suite in thirty minutes?'

'This sounds serious.'

'It is. Here, let me take Bandit back to the stables for Luis to get her cleaned up.' He mounted and reached down for the mallet Aspen was holding for him. Instead of taking it he gripped her elbow, raised her onto her toes and kissed her soundly. 'Very serious.'

Aspen watched Cruz canter back towards the stables, her fingers pressed to her throbbing lips.

'Now, that was really touching.'

Aspen swung around at the sound of a mocking voice behind her. For a moment all she could do was stare blankly, her mind frozen as if she'd just been zapped.

'Chad,' she finally managed to croak out.

His smile was charming and boyish. 'One and the same, babe, one and the same.'

CHAPTER ELEVEN

Hoping Chad was just an apparition, Aspen blinked rapidly and then gave a sharp gasp as her vision cleared and she saw him properly. 'What happened to your eye?'

He fingered the puffy purple skin of his eye socket. 'I ran into your *boyfriend*. Didn't he tell you?'

Yes, he had, but he'd neglected to say that he'd done anything but talk to him. A warm glow spread through Aspen's torso. As much as she abhorred violence, the fact that Cruz had reacted on her behalf did make her feel good. Special.

'Are you okay?'

'Do you care?' he sneered.

'Of course.' Memories flooded in, preventing her from saying anything else. The unexpectedness of seeing him causing her heart to beat heavily in her chest.

He stood before her, the typical urban male, with his designer haircut, stubble and trendy sportswear. She knew it took him hours to achieve that casually dishevelled appearance, and that he'd always hated the fact that she didn't pay more attention to her own appearance.

'Can't you straighten your hair sometimes? It's a mess.'

'I didn't expect to see you so far from Ocean Haven.'

His words snapped her attention back to him and slowly she started breathing properly again.

'I'm…here on…business.' She stumbled over the words

and furtively looked around for Cruz. Then she felt angry with herself. She was no longer the naïve eighteen-year-old girl who had mistaken friendship for love and had thought that wealth was synonymous with decency. She didn't *need* Cruz to protect her. She didn't need any man to do that.

'Some digs,' Chad continued, looking back at the hotel. 'The stable boy has come a long way.'

'What do you want, Chad?'

'To say hello.'

'Well, now you've said it, so…'

'What?' He held his hands wide as if in surprise. 'That's all you're going to say?'

'We haven't spoken for a long time. I don't see any point in changing that.'

'What if I do?'

Aspen felt her mouth tighten. 'I believe Cruz told you not to come near me.' And she hated pulling that card.

Chad's lip curled. 'See, Boy Wonder would like to think he controls everything, but he doesn't control me. Does he control you, Assie?'

Aspen's mouth tightened. There was no way she was playing mind games with her ex-husband again. She'd done that enough when they had been married.

'Goodbye, Chad.'

She turned on her heel, intent on walking away from him. but it seemed he had other ideas.

'Aspen, wait.' He jogged after her. 'I didn't mean to upset you.'

'No?'

'No. I wanted to apologise to you, actually.'

Aspen stopped. 'For…?'

'For being such an idiot when we got married. I was in a bad way and—'

Aspen held up her hand like a stop sign. 'Don't, Chad.' She knew his game. She had heard his apologies a thousand times before. Usually they amounted to nothing. 'It doesn't matter anymore.' And amazingly it didn't. Cruz had seen to that.

Cruz who was *nothing* like Chad. Cruz who was proud, but gentle. Cruz who was smart and masterful and possessive. And it thrilled her. *He* thrilled her. And she couldn't wait to see him. Maybe even to tell him that she loved him if she had the courage.

She looked at Chad now. Really looked at him. He couldn't hurt her anymore and it made her feel a little giddy.

'Chad, I'm sorry, but I don't want to see you or talk to you. Whatever you have to say is irrelevant.' She smiled inwardly as she borrowed one of Cruz's favourite expressions.

'I just want to be friends, Aspen, put things behind us.'

Aspen felt petty in refusing him, but he had hurt her too much for her ever to consider him as a friend. 'I'd like to put things behind us too, but we can't ever be friends, Chad.'

'Because of *Rodriguez*?' Chad sneered. 'He won't want you for long. His heart belongs to his horses and nothing else.'

Aspen shook her head. This was the Chad she knew too well.

'Is it serious between you?'

'That's none of your business.'

'You're in love with him.' Chad spat on the ground. 'You always were.'

'I wasn't. I thought I loved you.'

'But you didn't, did you? It was him all along. I told your grandfather. That night.'

Aspen frowned. 'It was you who sent him out after me?'

'I watched you chase him like one of his fawning groupies. Did you have sex with him? Your grandfather would never say.'

God, this was awful, but Aspen wasn't sure if she was more appalled that he had talked to her grandfather so intimately about her or that he was talking to her about it now.

'Why do you hate Cruz so much?' She couldn't help asking.

Chad shrugged and stared at her mulishly. 'He was an arrogant SOB who never saw me as competition. He never took me seriously except where you were concerned.'

Aspen gave a sharp, self-conscious laugh. 'And there I was, thinking that you wanted Ocean Haven.'

Chad shook his head. 'I didn't. But he did. And he's won that too, I hear.'

An uneasy sensation slipped down Aspen's spine and she told herself to ignore him. To walk away. 'What is that supposed to mean?'

He looked at her like a hyena scenting a wounded animal. 'Boy Wonder bought The Farm. Not literally—unfortunately—but... You didn't know?'

Aspen knew better than most not to listen to anything Chad said, not to place any importance on his words, but she couldn't make herself leave. Not with her mother's cautionary advice that if something looked too good to be true it usually was ringing loudly in her ears.

'How would you know anything about the sale of The Farm?'

'My daddy wanted to buy it. He had high hopes of swooping in at the last minute and picking it up for a song.'

Aspen's head started to hurt. 'Well, it's not true. Cruz hasn't bought Ocean Haven. Your father has his facts wrong.'

Chad shrugged. 'I guess the guy brokering the deal is the one who has it wrong. My father did wonder when he heard Rodriguez had paid more than double the value of the property.'

More than double?

Aspen felt a burning sensation in the back of her throat. 'Yes, I'd say he's wrong. Excuse me.'

She pushed past Chad, only to have him grab her arm.

'He's not worth it, you know. You can't see it, but he won't hang around for long.'

Hardly in the mood for any more of Chad's snide comments, Aspen turned on him sharply. 'That's not your business, is it?'

Chad reeled back and covered the movement with a disbelieving laugh. 'You've changed.'

'So I've been told.'

She said the words automatically but Aspen knew that if there was any truth to Chad's words then she hadn't changed at all. Because if Cruz had bought The Farm out from under her it would mean that she had fallen into the same trap she had in the past— wanting the love and affection of a man who wouldn't think twice before walking all over her.

Telling herself to calm down, she stabbed the button on the lift to the penthouse and used the temporary access card Cruz had given her.

Chad had admitted that he hated Cruz, so this could just be trouble he was stirring up between them. But how would he know it would cause trouble? He couldn't. No one knew about the private deal she had struck with Cruz. No one but her knew that this morning Cruz had promised her he had decided not to buy Ocean Haven.

Calm, Aspen, she reminded herself, desperately trying to check her temper.

When the lift doors opened her eyes immediately fell on an immaculately dressed woman who looked like a supermodel.

For a minute she thought she was in the wrong suite, but deep down she knew she wasn't.

'I'm sorry…' She frowned. 'I'm looking for Cruz.'

'He's in the shower,' the woman said.

Was he, now?

Aspen swallowed down the sudden feeling of jealousy. The woman was dressed, for heaven's sake. 'And you are…?'

The woman held out her hand. 'I'm Lauren Burnside. Cruz's lawyer. Would I be right in assuming that you're Aspen Carmichael?'

The fact that his lawyer knew of her wasn't a good sign in Aspen's mind. 'Yes. Would *I* be right in assuming you're here about the sale of Ocean Haven?'

The lawyer's eyes flickered at the corners and an awkward silence prevailed over the room. 'You would have to ask Cruz about that.'

Cruz, not Mr Rodriguez, Aspen noted sourly. How well did this woman know him? And why did the thought of this woman running her hands all over Cruz's naked body hurt her so much?

Because you love him, you nincompoop.

Aspen moved to the side table beside the Renoir and placed her hands lightly on the wood-grained surface. Memories of the last time she had stood in this exact position, with Cruz behind her, kissing her neck, murmuring tender words of encouragement to her, lanced her very soul. Yes, she loved him—and that just took this situation from bad to completely hideous.

'His heart belongs to his horses and nothing else.'

Chad getting inside her head did nothing to stave off her temper either. But still she tried to convince herself that she didn't know the facts. That she wouldn't jump to conclusions as Cruz had done about her eight years ago.

'Lauren. Aspen!'

Aspen turned as Cruz entered the room. Pleasure shot through her at the sight of him fresh from the shower in worn jeans and a body-hugging white T-shirt.

He smiled at her.

She looked away, but he had already transferred his attention to the other woman.

'You have the contracts?'

'Right here.'

Aspen turned and leant against the side table, blocking all memories of the intimacies they had shared, blocking the pain of his betrayal, her foolish feelings for him.

'They would be the contracts to finalise the sale of my farm?' she said lightly.

Cruz's eyes narrowed and Aspen knew. She *knew*!

'When were you going to tell me?'

Her casual tone must have alerted him to her state of mind because he didn't take his eyes off her. 'Can you excuse us, please, Lauren?'

'Of course. I'll leave the contracts on the table.'

She threw Cruz an intimate glance and Aspen felt her cheeks heat at having witnessed it.

'So, here we are, then...' Aspen strolled across the room and stopped beside the urn of flowers on the dining table. She stroked the soft rose petals and thought how impervious they were to the fact that she felt like hoisting them up and hurling them across the room.

'Yes. And to answer your earlier question I was going to surprise you over dinner.'

Surprise her? Aspen's mouth hit the floor and her temper shot through the roof. *Surprise her!*

'Dinner? *Dinner?*' She laughed harshly. 'You filthy, gloating bastard.'

'Aspen—'

'Don't.' Disappointment coalesced into rage and she just needed to get away from him. 'Don't say a word. I don't want to hear it. I don't want to hear anything from you. I hate you.'

She whirled away and would have walked out of the room—no, run out of the room—but he was on her in a second.

'Aspen, let me explain.'

'No.' She shoved against him and beat her fists against his chest in her anger. 'You tricked me. You lied to me. You told me you weren't trying to buy Ocean Haven any more but you were.'

'Dammit, Aspen.' He bound her wrists in one of his hands but she broke loose and tried to slap him. 'Stop it, you little hellcat. Dammit. *Ow!* Listen to me. I left a message for Lauren to pull the pin on the sale but she didn't get it,' he said, breathing hard.

As suddenly as her rage had swept over her it left her, and Aspen felt deflated and appalled that she had hit him. She *hated* violence. 'Let me go, Cruz,' she said flatly.

He frowned down at her. 'It's the truth.'

Aspen sighed and pushed away from him, feeling shivery and cold when he released her. 'It doesn't matter.'

'Of course it matters.' Cruz moved to the table and picked up the wad of paper Lauren had left behind. 'Look at this.'

Aspen glanced at it warily. 'What is it?'

'As soon as I found out that your uncle had accepted my offer I had Lauren organise the immediate transfer of the deeds into your name. It's all here in this contract.'

'What?'

'That was what I was going to tell you over dinner.'

Aspen frowned. 'So you're saying our deal is still on?'

Cruz glowered at her. 'Of *course* the deal is not still on. I don't expect you to pay me back. I'm giving you the property.'

'You're giving…' She shook her head. 'You mean lending me the money to buy it?'

'No, I mean giving it to you.'

'Why would you do that?'

'Because this way you have security.'

'Security?'

'You would have been bankrupt within the year if you'd borrowed all that money.'

Scowling, she moved away from him. 'That's not true. I have a great business plan to get Ocean Haven out of trouble and—' She stopped as he shook his head at her as if she didn't have a clue.

'Aspen, there's no way you can carry that kind of debt and survive,' he said softly.

His words registered in her brain as if she was sitting at the back of a large lecture theatre and trying to read off a tiny whiteboard. 'So you're just giving it to me?'

'It's just a property, Aspen.'

It's just a dress.

It's just her self-worth.

Just her *heart.*

'I don't want you to give it to me,' she said.

'Why are you being so stubborn about this?'

Why? She didn't know. And then she did. For years she'd thought that all she wanted was security, but really—really what she wanted was validation. Trust in her judgement. What she wanted was to know that she could direct her own future. Her way. But somewhere in the last couple of days Cruz had become the centre of her world. Just as both her grandfather and Chad had been at one stage.

Hadn't she once pinned her hopes and dreams for the future on both of them and been let down?

She shook her head. 'I don't want it that way.'

'What way? *Hell!*' Cruz raked a hand through his hair. 'I don't see what the problem is.'

'I want to do it my way.'

'So do it your way,' he almost roared in frustration. 'Debt-free.'

'I would have thought you of all people would understand,' she said, completely exasperated. 'You hated that your mother didn't trust you to do things your way when you were a teenager.'

'This is not that same thing.'

'It is to me.'

'You're being stupid now.'

Aspen rounded on him. 'Do not call me stupid. I had one man put me down. I won't take it from another.'

'*Dios mio*, I didn't mean it like that.' He turned his back on her and then swung back just as quickly. 'Aspen, I'm in love with you.'

Aspen wrapped her arms around her chest as if she was trying to hold her heart in. Was this some backhanded way for him to get Ocean Haven? She stared at him, her emotions in turmoil, a terrible numbness invading her limbs.

'You're not.'

Cruz swore. 'I've just spent over two hundred million dollars on a property I'm prepared to give you. What would you call it?'

'Crazy.'

'Well, it is that…'

'What would you buy me for my birthday?' she asked suddenly.

Cruz frowned. 'Your birthday is…two months away.'

'You have no idea, do you?'

'How is that relevant?'

It was relevant because she knew if he presented her with an envelope full of cash it would break her heart. It was relevant because if he really loved her for who she was he *would* have some idea.

His eyes narrowed on her face. 'What is this? Some kind of test?'

'And if it is?'

A calmness seemed to pervade his limbs. 'You're being ridiculously stubborn about this. I'm giving you everything that you want. Most women would be on their knees with gratitude right now.'

Aspen wasn't sure if he meant sexually, but the fact that she thought it startled her. She wanted to be on her knees in front of him. She wanted to do all sorts of things to his body until he was as out of control as she was. But that wasn't right. His power over her was so much stronger than Chad's. Or her grandfather's. If she stayed, if she accepted his *gift*, she knew she would do anything for him. Would accept anything from him. And that scared her to death. She would be completely at his mercy and a shadow of herself. A woman seeking the approval of a man who didn't listen to her. It wasn't how she wanted to live her life. Nor was he the type of person she wanted to share her life with. Not again.

'I don't play those games, Aspen,' he warned.

'And I don't play yours. Not anymore. Goodbye, Cruz. I hope you never run out of money. You'll be awfully lost if you do.'

Thankfully the lift doors opened just as she pressed the button, but it wasn't divine intervention finally looking out for her. Ricardo was inside. His wide smile of greeting faltered when he glimpsed her expression and a stilted silence filled the space between them as she waited for the lift doors to close.

Once they had, Ricardo turned to his brother. 'What was that all about?'

Cruz let out a harsh laugh. 'That was Aspen Carmichael making me feel like a fool. Again.'

CHAPTER TWELVE

EXACTLY ONE WEEK to the day later Cruz sat on the squash court beside his brother after a particularly gruelling game. Both of them were sweat-soaked and exhausted and Cruz relished the feeling of complete burnout that had turned his muscles to rubber.

His phone beeped an incoming message and since he was right there he checked it.

Frustration warred with disappointment when he saw that it was from Lauren Burnside. Well, what had he expected? Aspen Carmichael to send him a message telling him how much she missed him?

Right. She'd rejected him. How many ways did he need to be kicked before he got the message?

'Now the woman sends me a text,' he muttered.

'Who?'

'My lawyer.'

Maybe if she'd dropped in he would have taken her up on her offer to get up close and personal with his abs. He wouldn't mind losing himself in a woman right now. Smelling her sweet floral scent with a touch of vanilla. Winding his hands through her tumble of wild curls. Hearing her laugh.

'You're muttering,' Ricardo said unhelpfully.

That was because he needed to visit a loony bin so that he could undergo electroshock therapy and once and for all convince his body that Aspen Carmichael was *not* the woman to end all women. Bad enough that he'd thought he had been in love with her. That he'd told her.

He clamped down on the unwanted memory. It had been a foolish thought that had died as soon as she'd walked out through the door. A foolish thought brought on by an adrenaline rush after the polo match.

Feeling spent, he scrolled through Lauren's text. 'Idiot woman.'

'I thought she looked quite smart.'

'Not Lauren. Aspen.'

'Ah.'

Cruz scowled. 'This is not a dentist, *amigo*. Close your mouth.'

Ricardo smiled. 'Are you going to tell me what she'd done now?'

'According to Lauren, she's signed Ocean Haven over to me.'

'Shouldn't you be happy about that? I mean, isn't that what you wanted?'

'No.' He ignored the interested expression on his brother's face. 'I don't want anything to do with that property ever again.' Scowling, he punched a number into his phone. 'Maria, get the jet fuelled up and cancel any meetings I have later today.'

'I thought you just said you didn't want anything to do with that property ever again?'

'I won't after I handle this.'

'Ah, *hermano*, I hate to point out the obvious, but this didn't end so well for you last week.'

Cruz picked up his bag and shoved his racquet inside. 'Last week I was too attached to the outcome. I'm not now.'

Aspen was in a wonderful mood. Super, in fact. Her chores were almost done for the day and all that was left was to bed Delta down in her stall. Now that the polo season was over there was less pressure on her and Donny to have the place ready for Wednesday night chukkas and there were fewer students. That was a slight downside, but Aspen found that as winter rolled around the lessons veered more towards dressage, with her students preferring to practise in the indoor arena rather than get frostbite in the snow.

Pity about the leak.

'Or not,' she said, to no one in particular. Roofs and their holes, walls and their peeling paint, fences and their rusted nails were no longer her problem. And she couldn't be happier.

'Ow!' Aspen glanced down at her thumb and winced. 'Damn thing.'

She looked at her other fingers with their newly bitten nails. When had that happened? When had she started biting her nails again? She hadn't since she was about thirteen and her grandfather had painted that horrible-tasting liquid on the ends of them.

Rubbing at the small wound, she picked up the horse rug she planned to throw over Delta and headed for her stall.

Delta whickered.

'Hello, beauty,' Aspen crooned. 'I see you've finished dinner. Me? I'm not hungry.'

Which was surprising, really, because she couldn't remember if she'd even eaten that day.

'Who needs food anyway?' She laughed. Who needed food when you didn't have any will to live? 'Now, that's not true,' she told Delta. 'I have plenty to live for. Becoming a vet, a new beginning, adventure, never having to see Cruz Rodriguez ever again.'

She leant against the weathered blanket she'd tossed over Delta's back. He'd told her he loved her but how could you love someone you didn't know? And she'd nearly convinced herself that she had loved him too.

'It's called desire,' she informed the uninterested mare. 'Lust that is so powerful it fries your brain.'

But she wasn't going to think about that. Had forbidden herself to think about it all week. And it had worked. Sort of.

Aspen took in a deep breath and revelled in the smell of horse and hay and Ocean Haven. Her throat constricted and tears pricked at the back of her eyes, her energy suddenly leaving her. She would miss this. Miss her horses. Her school. But things changed. That was the only certainty in life, wasn't it?

'The man who now owns you is big and strong and he'll take care of you.' Delta tossed her head. 'I'm serious. He loves horses more than anything else.'

'Is that right?'

Aspen spun around. Stared. Then swallowed. Cruz stood before her, wearing a striking grey suit and a crisp white shirt. 'What are you doing here?'

'I think you know why I'm here this time.'

She straightened her spine. 'Boy, that lawyer of yours works fast.'

'She should. She's paid enough. Now, answer my question.'

Aspen straightened Delta's already straight blanket over her rump. Better that than looking at Cruz and losing her train of thought. 'I would have thought it was obvious. You bought Ocean Haven so it's yours, not mine.'

'I told you that was a mistake,' he bit out. 'The whole thing happened while I was playing polo.'

Aspen shook her head. 'You really expect me to believe that?' she scoffed. 'That supermodel of yours wouldn't blink without your say-so.'

'Supermodel?'

'We *are* talking about the brunette who happened to know you were in the shower, aren't we?'

Cruz narrowed his gaze and Aspen stared him down. Then he smiled. A full-on toothpaste-commercial-worthy smile. 'I've never slept with Lauren.'

'Like I would care.' She jerked her head. 'Mind moving? I'm tired of you blocking my way. No pun intended.'

Cruz continued to smile. 'None taken.'

But he didn't move.

'You're right about Lauren acting under my instructions,' he began. 'Unfortunately they were my *old* instructions. My *new* ones were caught up somewhere in cyberspace when her firm's e-mail system went down.'

'I don't care. I'm moving on.'

'Where to?'

'I don't know.' She shrugged. 'Somewhere exciting.'

'And what about your mother's horseshoe?'

'It's gone.' She'd cried over that enough when she'd returned last week. 'And before you ask I don't know where and nor does Donny. When I came back last week it wasn't here.' She sniffed. 'I'm taking it as a sign.'

'A sign of what?'

His voice was soft. As gentle as it had been the night she had told him about Chad. It made a horrible pain well up inside her chest. 'A sign that I've put too much store in The Farm for too long. I thought I needed it, but it turns out I needed something else more.'

He stepped closer to her. 'What?'

'It's irrelevant. You know what *that* means, don't you, Cruz?'

Unfortunately he ignored her blatant dig. Blast him.

'Try me.'

'No.' She moved away from him and fossicked with Delta's feed bucket. 'I've discovered that I do have some pride after all, so…no.'

Cruz grabbed the feed bucket and took it out of her numb fingers. Aspen accidentally took a deep breath and it was all him. When he took her hands she closed her eyes to try and ward off how good it felt to have him touch her. She swallowed. Yanked her hands out of his.

'I'm going to finish my vet course and take an internship somewhere, start over,' she said quickly.

Not taking the hint that she didn't want him to touch her, he slid his hand beneath her chin and raised her eyes to his. 'Start over with me?'

Aspen jerked back. 'I didn't know you were looking for a new vet?'

'I don't mean professionally and you know it,' he growled. Then his voice softened. 'I've missed you, *mi gatita*. I love you.'

'I—'

'You don't believe me?' He blew out a breath. 'Kind of ironic that a week ago it was me who didn't believe you, wouldn't you say?'

Aspen's chest felt tight. 'No. I wouldn't.' Nothing seemed ironic to her right now. More like tragic.

Cruz pushed a hand through his hair and Aspen wished he was a thousand miles away. So much easier to deny her feelings when he wasn't actually right beside her.

'I know you're angry, Aspen, and I don't blame you. I thought I knew about human nature, I thought I had it all covered. But you showed me I was wrong. After your grandfather kicked me out I vowed never to need anyone again. I saw money as the way to ensure that I was never expendable. I was wrong. I understand why you didn't want me to give you The Farm now, and if you want we'll consider it a loan. You can pay me back.'

Aspen felt a spurt of hope at his words. But that didn't change their fundamental natures. She couldn't afford to be in love with him. She'd become needy for his affection and he'd do it again. At some point he wouldn't listen to her and they'd be right back where they started. Better to save herself that pain now.

'I can't.'

'I know you were hurt, Aspen. By your grandfather's expectations, by the lucky-to-still-be-breathing Anderson. Me. But I promise if you give me a chance I won't hurt you again.'

Aspen shook her head sadly. 'You will.' Her cheeks were damp and Cruz brushed his thumbs over the tears she hadn't even known she was shedding. 'You won't mean to, because I know deep down you're kind-hearted, but—' She stopped. Recalled what she had said to Delta. He *would* take care of her. But could she trust his love? Could she trust him to listen to her in the future? Could she trust that she wouldn't get lost in trying to please him? 'I'm not great in relationships.'

'Then we really are perfect for each other because I'm hopeless. Or at least I was. You make me want to change all that. You make me feel human, Aspen. You make me want to *embrace* life again.'

Aspen's nose started tingling as she held back more useless tears.

'I know you're scared, *chiquita*. I was too.'

'Was?' She glanced at him.

Cruz leaned towards her and kissed her softly. 'Was.' He gave a half smile and reached inside his jacket pocket. He pulled out a small red velour pouch. 'You asked me last week what I would get you for your birthday and I had no idea. It took me a while, but finally I realised that I was imposing my way of fixing things over yours.'

Aspen gazed at the small pouch he'd placed in her hand.

'One of my flaws is that I see something wrong and I want to fix it. My instinct is to take care of those around me. The only way I knew how to do that without getting hurt was to remain emotionally detached from everything.

But no matter how hard I tried I couldn't do that with you. You fill me up, Aspen and you make me feel so damned much. You make me want so much. No one else has ever come close.'

Aspen's mouth went dry as she felt the hard piece of jewellery inside the pouch. She'd guessed what it was already and she honestly didn't know what her response should be. She wanted to be with Cruz more than anything else in the world but the ring felt big. Huge, in fact. Oh, no doubt it would be beautiful, but it wouldn't be *her*. It wouldn't be something she would ever feel comfortable wearing—especially with her job—and it was just one more sign that they could never make a proper relationship work.

'Open it. It's not what you think it is.'

Untying the drawstrings with shaky fingers, Aspen carefully tipped the contents of the pouch into her hand.

'Oh!' Her breath whooshed out of her lungs and she stared at a tiny, delicate wood carving of a horse attached to a thin strip of leather. 'Oh, Cruz, its exquisite.' Her shocked eyes flew to his. 'It's just like the ones I saw lined up on your mother's mantelpiece. You *did* do them for her, didn't you?'

'I did,' he confirmed gruffly.

Studying him, she was completely taken aback by the raw emotion on his face and her lips trembled as her own deep feelings broke to the surface. 'You *do* love me.'

Cruz cupped her face in his hands and lifted her mouth to his for a searing kiss. 'I do. More than life itself.'

'Oh.' Aspen clutched Cruz's shoulders and welcomed the fold of his strong embrace as the hot tears she had been holding at bay spilled recklessly down her cheeks. 'You've made me cry.'

'And me.'

Aspen looked up and found that his eyes were wet. She

touched a tear clinging to the bottom of his lashes. 'When did you make this?'

'During the week. I couldn't concentrate on anything and my executive team were just about ready to call in the professionals with white coats. I have to say it took a few attempts before my fingers started working again.'

Aspen clutched the tiny horse. 'I'll treasure it.'

'And I'll treasure you. Turn around,' he commanded huskily.

Aspen let out a shaky breath, happiness threatening to burst right out of her. She clasped the tiny horse to her chest as he gently moved her hair aside and tied the leather strap around her neck. Then she turned back to face him.

He looked down to where the horse lay nestled between her breasts. 'You do know that in some countries this binds you to me for ever?'

Aspen smiled. 'For ever?'

'Completely. And in case you're at all unsure what I mean by that I have something else.'

He produced a small box and Aspen knew this time it would be a ring. She also knew that no matter how ostentatious it was she would accept it from him, because she knew it had come from a place of absolute love.

Smiling, she opened it and got the third shock of the day. Inside, nestled on a bed of green silk, was the most exquisitely formed diamond ring she had ever seen. And by Cruz's standards it must have seemed—

'It's tiny! Oh, I'm sorry.' She clapped her hand over her mouth. 'That came out wrong.'

Cruz grimaced and slid the beautiful ring onto her finger. 'It wasn't my first choice, believe me, but I knew if I got you anything larger you'd think it was impractical.'

Aspen laughed and flung herself into his arms, utter joy flooding her system at how well he *did* know her. 'I love it!'

Cruz grunted and then lifted her off the ground and

kissed her. 'I'm getting you matching diamond earrings next, and they're so heavy you won't be able to stand up.'

'Then I'll only wear them in bed.' Smiling like a loon, she rained kisses down all over his face. 'Oh, Cruz, it's perfect. *You're* perfect.'

'So does that mean you're going to put me out of my misery and tell me you love me? Because I know you do.'

'How do you know that?'

'You called my lawyer a supermodel.'

Aspen pulled back. 'You think I was jealous of her?'

'I hope so. Now, please, *mi chiquita*, say yes and become indebted to me for the rest of your life?'

'You'll really lend your wife money and let her pay you back?'

'If she ever gets around to telling me that she loves me I'll let her do whatever she wants, as long as she promises to only do it with me.'

'Yes, Cruz.' Aspen nuzzled his neck and basked in the sensation of safety and love that enveloped her. 'I love you and I will be indebted to you for the rest of my life.'

Cruz touched the tiny horse that lay between her breasts. 'And I you, *mi gatita*. And I you.'

* * * * *

THE MAGNATE'S MANIFESTO

BY
JENNIFER HAYWARD

Jennifer Hayward has been a fan of romance and adventure since filching her sister's Mills & Boon novels to escape her teenaged angst.

Jennifer penned her first romance at nineteen. When it was rejected, she bristled at her mother's suggestion that she needed more life experience. She went on to complete a journalism degree and intern as a sports broadcaster before settling into a career in public relations. Years of working alongside powerful, charismatic CEOs and traveling the world provided perfect fodder for the arrogant alpha males she loves to write about and free research on the some of the world's most glamorous locales.

A suitable amount of life experience under her belt, she sat down and conjured up the sexiest, most delicious Italian wine magnate she could imagine, had him make his biggest mistake and gave him a wife on the run. That story, *The Divorce Party*, won her Harlequin's *So You Think You Can Write* contest and a book contract. Turns out Mother knew best!

A native of Canada's gorgeous east coast, Jennifer now lives in Toronto with her Viking husband and their young Viking-in-training. She considers her ten year old book club, comprising some of the most amazing women she's ever met, a sacrosanct date in her calendar. And some day they will have their monthly meeting at her fantasy beach house, waves lapping at their feet, wine glasses in hand.

You can find Jennifer on Facebook and Twitter.

A big thanks to Rebecca Avalon of *Strip and Grow Rich*, the original stripper school, for taking me inside the life and mind of a dancer and helping me bring Bailey to life.

I can't thank you enough!

CHAPTER ONE

THE DAY THAT Jared Stone's manifesto sparked an incident of international female outrage happened to be, unfortunately for Stone, a slow news day. By 5:00 a.m. on Thursday, when the sexy Silicon Valley billionaire was reputed to be running the trails of San Francisco's Golden Gate Park, as he did every morning in his connected-free beginning to the day, his manifesto was dinner conversation in Moscow. In London, as chicly dressed female office workers escaped brick and steel buildings to chase down lunch, his outrageous state of the union on twenty-first-century women was on the tip of every tongue, spoken in hushed, disbelieving tones on elevator trips down to ground level.

And in America, where the outrage was about to hit hardest, women who had spent their entire careers seeking out the C-suite only to find themselves blocked by a glass ceiling that seemed impossible to penetrate stared in disbelief at their smartphones. *Maybe it was a joke*, some said. *Someone must have hacked into Stone's email,* said others. *Doesn't surprise me at all*, interjected a final contingent, many of whom had dated Stone in an elusive quest to pin down the world's most sought-after bachelor. *He's a cold bastard. I'm only surprised his true stripes didn't appear sooner.*

At her desk at 7:00 a.m. at the Stone Industries building in San Jose, Bailey St. John was oblivious to the firestorm her boss was creating. Intent on hacking her way through her own glass ceiling and armed with a steaming Americano with which to do so, she slid into her chair with as much grace as her pencil skirt would allow, harnessed a morning dose of optimism that today would be different, and flicked on her PC.

She stared sleepily at the screen as her computer booted up. Took a sip of the strong, acrid brew that inevitably kicked her brain into working order as she clicked on her mail program. Her girlfriend Aria's email, titled "OMG," made her lift a recently plucked and perfected brow.

She clicked it open. The hot sip of coffee she'd just taken lodged somewhere in her windpipe. *Billionaire Playboy Ignites International Incident With His Manifesto on Women*, blared the headline of the variety news site everyone in Silicon Valley frequented. *Leaked Tongue-in-Cheek Manifesto to His Fellow Mates Makes Stone's Views on Women in the Boardroom and Bedroom Blatantly Clear.*

Bailey put down her coffee with a jerky movement and clicked through to the manifesto that had already generated two million views. *The Truth About Women,* which apparently had never been meant for anyone other than Jared Stone's inner circle, was now the salacious entertainment of the entire male population. As she started reading what was unmistakably her boss's bold, eloquent tone, she nearly fell off her chair.

Having dated and worked with a cross-section of women from around the globe, and having reached the age where I feel I can make a definitive opinion on the subject matter, I have come to a conclusion. Women lie.

They say they want to be equals in the boardroom, when in reality nothing has changed over the past fifty years. Despite all their pleas to the contrary, despite their outrage at the limits the "so-called" glass ceiling puts on them, they don't really want to be hammering out a deal, and they don't want to be orchestrating a merger. They want to be home in the house we provide, living the lifestyle to which they've become accustomed. They want a man who will take care of them, who gives them a hot night between the sheets and diamond jewelry at appropriate intervals. Who will prevent them from drifting aimlessly through life without a compass...

Drifting aimlessly through life without a compass? Bailey's cheeks flamed. If there was any way in which her life couldn't be described, it was that. She'd spent the last twelve years putting as much mileage between her and her depressing low-income roots as she could, doing the impossible and obtaining an MBA before working herself up the corporate ladder. First at a smaller Silicon Valley start-up, then for the last three years at Jared Stone's industry darling of a consumer electronics company.

And that was where her rapid progression had stopped. As director of North American sales for Stone Industries, she'd spent the last eighteen months chasing a vice president position Stone seemed determined not to give her. She'd worked harder and more impressively than any of her male colleagues, and it was generally acknowledged the VP job should have been hers. Except Jared Stone didn't seem to think so—he'd given the job to someone else. And that hurt coming from the man she'd been dying to work for—the resident genius of Silicon Valley.

Why didn't he respect her as everyone else did?

Her blood heated to a furious level; bubbled and boiled and threatened to spill over into an expression of uncontrolled rage. *Now she knew why.* Because Jared Stone was a male chauvinist pig. The worst of a Silicon Valley breed.

He was...*horrific.*

She forced a sip of the excessively strong java into her mouth before she lost it completely and slammed the cup back down on her desk. Flicked her gaze back to her computer screen and the "rules" on women Jared had also gifted the male population with.

> *Rule Number 1—All women are crazy. And by that I mean they think in a completely foreign way from us that might as well come from another planet. You need to find the least crazy one you can live with. If you elect to settle down, which I'm not advocating, mind you.*
>
> *Rule Number 2—Every woman wants a ring on her finger and the white picket fence. No matter what she says. Not a bad thing for the state of the nuclear family or for you if you're already on that trajectory. But for God's sake know what you're getting yourself into.*
>
> *Rule Number 3—Every woman wants a lion in the bedroom. She wants to be dominated. She wants you to be in complete control. She doesn't want you to listen to her "needs." So stop making that mistake. Be a man.*
>
> *Rule Number 4—Every woman starts the day with an agenda. A cause, an item to strike off her list, the inescapable conclusion of a campaign she's been running. It could be a diamond ring, more of your time, your acknowledgment that you will indeed agree to meet her mother... Whatever it is, take it from me, just say yes or say goodbye. And know that saying goodbye might be a whole hell of a lot cheaper in the long run.*

Bailey stopped reading for the sake of her blood pressure. Here she'd been worrying that the personality conflict she and Jared shared, which admittedly was intense, was the problem. The thing that had been holding her back. Their desire to rip each other apart every time they stepped foot in a boardroom together was legendary within the company, but that hadn't been it. No—in actual fact, he disrespected *the entire female race.*

She'd never even had a chance.

Three years, she fumed, scowling at her computer screen as she pulled up a blank document. Three years she'd worked for that egocentric jerk, racking up domestic sales of his wildly popular cell phones and computers... For what? It had all been a complete waste of time in a career in which the clock was ticking. A CEO by thirty-five, she'd vowed. Although that vision seemed to be fading fast....

She pressed her lips together and started typing. *To whom it may concern: I can no longer work in an organization with that pig at the helm. It goes against every guiding principle I've ever had.* She kept going, wrote the letter without holding back, until her blood had cooled and her rage was spent. Then she did a second version she could hand in to HR.

She wasn't working for Jared Stone. For that beautiful, arrogant piece of work. Not one minute longer. No matter how brilliant he was.

Jared Stone was in a whistling kind of mood as he parked in the Stone Industries lot, collected his briefcase and made his way through the sparkling glass doors. A five-mile run through the park, a long hot shower, a power shake and a relatively smooth commute could do that for a man.

He hummed a bad version of a song he'd just heard on the radio as he strode toward the bank of elevators that ran up the center of the elegant, architecturally brilliant building. When life was this good, when he was on top of his game, about to land the contract that would silence all his critics, cement his control of his company, he felt impermeable, impenetrable, *unbeatable,* as if he could leap tall buildings in a single bound, solve all the world's problems, bring about world peace even, if given the material to work with.

A gilded ray of brilliance for all to follow.

He stuck his hand between the closing elevator doors and gained himself admittance on a half-filled car. Greeted the half dozen employees inside with the megawatt smile the press loved to capture and made a mental note of who was putting in the extra effort coming in early. Gerald from finance flashed him a swaggering grin as if they shared an inside joke. Jennifer Thomas, PA to one of the vice presidents, who was normally a sucker for his charm, did a double take at his friendly "good morning" and muttered something unintelligible back. The woman from legal, what *was* her name, turned her back on him.

Strange.

The weird vibe only got worse as the doors opened on the executive floors and he made his way through the still-quiet space to his office. Another PA gave him the oddest look. He looked down. Did he have power shake on the front of his shirt? Toothpaste on his face?

Power shake stains ruled out, he frowned at his fifty-something PA, Mary, as she handed him his messages. "What is *wrong* with everyone today? The sun is shining, sales are up…"

Mary blinked. "You haven't been online, have you?"

"You know my theory on that," he returned patiently. "I spend the first couple hours of my day finding my center. Seven-thirty is soon enough to discover what craziness has befallen the world."

"Right," she muttered. "Well, you might want to leave your Buddhist sojourn by the wayside and plug in quickly before Sam Walters arrives. He'll be here at eleven."

Jared brought his brows together at the mention of the

chairman of the Stone Industries board. "I have nothing scheduled with him."

"You do now," she said. "Jared—I—" She set down her pen and gave him a direct look. "Your *document*, your manifesto, was leaked on the internet last night."

He felt the blood drain from his face. He'd only ever written two manifestos in his life. One when he'd started Stone Industries and put down his vision for the company, and the second, the private joke he'd shared with his closest friends last night after a particularly amusing guys' night out on the town.

It had not been intended for public consumption.

From the look on Mary's face, she was *not* talking about the Stone Industries manifesto.

"What do you mean leaked?" he asked slowly.

She cleared her throat. "The document…the whole document is all over the Net. My mother emailed it to me this morning. She asked what I was doing working for you."

The thought crossed his mind that this was all impossible because his buddies would never do that to him. Not over a joke intended for their eyes only…. *Had someone hacked into his email?*

He looked down at the wad of messages in his hand, his chest tightening. "How bad is it?"

Her lips pursed. "It's everywhere."

Thinking he might finally have taken his penchant for stirring things up too far, he knew it for the truth when his mentor and adviser Sam Walters walked into his office three hours later, Jared's legal and PR teams behind him. The sixty-five-year-old financial genius did not look amused.

Jared waved them into chairs and attempted a preemptive strike. "Sam, this is all a huge misunderstanding. We'll put out a statement that it was a joke and it'll be gone by tomorrow."

His vice president of PR, Julie Walcott, lifted a brow. "We're at two million hits and climbing, Jared. Women are threatening to boycott our products. This is not going away."

He leaned back against his desk, the abdomen he'd worked to the breaking point this morning contracting at his appalling lack of judgment in ever putting those words on paper. But one thing he never did was show weakness. Particularly not now when the world wanted to eat him alive. "What do you suggest I do?" he drawled, with his usual swagger. "Beg women for their forgiveness? Get down on my knees and swear I didn't mean it?"

"Yes."

He gave her a disbelieving look. "It was a *joke between friends*. Addressing it gives it credence."

"It's now a joke between you and the entire planet," Julie said matter-of-factly. "Addressing it is the only thing that's going to save you right about now."

The sick feeling in his stomach intensified. Sam crossed his arms over his chest. "This has legal implications, Jared. Human rights implications… And furthermore, as I don't need to remind you, Davide Gagnon's daughter is a charter member of a woman's organization. She will not be amused."

Jared's hands tightened around the wooden lip of his desk. He was well aware of Micheline Gagnon's board memberships. The daughter of the CEO of Europe's largest consumer electronics retailer, Maison Electronique—with whom Stone Industries was pursuing a groundbreaking five-year deal to expand its global presence—was an active social commentator. She would *not* be amused. But really…it had been a *joke*.

He let out a long breath. "Tell me what we need to do."

"We need to issue an apology," Julie said. "Position it as a private joke that was in bad taste. Say that it has nothing to do with your real view of women, which is actually one of the utmost respect."

"I *do* respect women," he interjected. "I just don't think they're always honest with their feelings."

Julie gave him a long look. "When's the last time you put a woman on the executive committee?"

Never. He raked a hand through his hair. "Give me a woman who belongs on it and I'll put her there."

"What about Bailey St. John?" Sam lifted his bushy brows. "You seem to be the only one who thinks she hasn't earned her spot as a VP."

Jared scowled. "Bailey St. John is a special case. She isn't ready. She thinks she was *born* ready, but she isn't."

"You need to make a *gesture*," Sam underscored, his tone taking on a steely edge. "You are on thin ice right now, Jared." *In all aspects,* his mentor's deeply lined face seemed to suggest. "Give her the job. *Get* her ready."

"It's not the right choice," Jared rejected harshly. "She still needs to mature. She's only twenty-nine, for God's sake. Making her a VP would be like setting a firecracker loose."

Sam lifted his brows again as if to remind him how sparse his support on the board was right now. As if he needed *reminding* that his control of the company he'd built from a tiny start up into a world player was in jeopardy. *His company.*

"Give her the job, Jared." Sam gave him an even look. "Smooth out her raw edges. Do not blow ten years of hard work on your penchant for self-ignition."

Antagonism burned through him, singeing the tips of his ears. He'd stolen Bailey from a competitor three years ago for her incredibly sharp brain. For the potential he knew she had. And she hadn't disappointed him. He had no doubt he'd one day make her into a VP, but right now, she was the rainbow-colored cookie in the pack. You never knew what you were going to bite into when she walked into a room. And he couldn't have that around him. Not now.

Sam gave him a hard look. "Fine," Jared rasped. He'd figure out a way to work the Bailey equation. "What else?"

"Cultural sensitivity training," his head of legal interjected. "HR is going to set it up."

"That," Jared dismissed in a low voice, "is not happening. Next."

Julie outlined her plan to rescue his reputation. It was solid, what he paid her for, and he agreed with it all, except for the cultural sensitivity training, and ended the meeting.

He had way bigger fish to fry. A board's support to solidify. His own job to save.

He paced to the window as the door closed behind the group, attempting to digest how his perfect morning had turned into the day from hell. At the root of it all, the abrupt end to his "relationship" with his trustworthy 10:00 p.m. of late, Kimberly MacKenna. A logical accountant by trade, she'd sworn to him she wasn't looking for anything permanent. So he'd let his guard down, let her in. Then last Saturday night, she'd plopped herself down on his sofa, declared he was breaking her heart and turned those baby blues on him in a look he'd have sworn he'd never see.

Get serious, Jared, they'd said. He had. By 10:00 a.m. on Monday she'd had his trademark diamond tennis bracelet on her arm and another one had bitten the dust.

He'd been sad and maybe a touch lonely when he'd written that manifesto. But those were the rules. No commitment. His mouth twisted as he pressed his palm against the glass. Maybe he should have given his PR team the official line on his parents' marriage. How his mother had bled his father dry... How she'd turned him into half a man. It would have made him much more sympathetic.

Better yet, he thought, Julie could devote more of her

time to controlling the industry media that wanted to lynch him before he'd even gotten his vision for Stone Industries' next decade off the ground. When you'd parlayed a groundbreaking new personal computer created on your best friend's dorm room floor into the most successful consumer electronics company in America, a NASDAQ gold mine, you didn't expect the naysayers to start calling for the CEO's head as soon as the waters got rough. You expected them to trust your vision, radically different though it might be from the rest of the industry, and assume you had a plan to revolutionize the connected home.

A harsh curse escaped his lips. They would rather tear him down than support him. They were carnivores waiting for the kill. Well, it wasn't going to happen. He was going to go to France, tie up this exclusive partnership with Maison Electronique, cut his competitors off at the knees and deliver this deal signed and sealed to the board at his must-win executive committee meeting in two weeks.

All he had to do was present his marketing vision to Davide Gagnon and secure his buy-in, and it was a done deal.

Spinning away from the window, he stalked to the door and growled a command at Mary to get Bailey St. John in his office *now*. He would promote her all right. But he wasn't a stupid man. He would leave himself a loophole so when she proved herself too inexperienced for the job, he could put things back where they belonged until she *was* ready.

His last call was to his head of IT. Whoever had hacked into his email was going to rue the day they'd crossed him. He promised them that.

Bailey had cooled her heels for fifteen minutes outside Jared Stone's office, resignation in hand, when Mary finally motioned her in. Her ability to appear civil at an all-time low, she pushed the heavy wooden door open and moved into the intensely masculine space. Dominated by a massive marble-manteled fireplace and floor-to-ceiling windows, it was purposefully minimalistic; focused like its owner, who preferred to roam the hallways of Stone Industries and work alongside his engineers instead of sitting at a desk.

He turned as her heels tapped across the Italian marble, and as usual when she was within ten feet of him, her composure seemed to slide a notch or two. She might not pursue his assets like every other female in Silicon Valley, but that didn't mean she could ignore them. The piercing blue gaze he turned on her now was legendary for divesting a woman of her clothes faster than she could say "only if you respect me in the morning." And if that didn't do it for you, then his superbly toned body in the exquisitely tailored suit and his razor-sharp brain would. He supplemented his daily running routine with martial arts, and there was a joke going around the Valley that it was no coincidence his name was Stone. As in All-Night Jared Stone.

Heat filled her cheeks as he waved her into a chair, his finely crafted gold cuff links glinting in the sunlight. She started to sink into the sofa, obeying him like his mindless disciples, before she checked herself and straightened. "I'm not here to socialize, Jared. I'm here to resign."

"Resign?" His usual husky, raspy tone held an incredulous edge.

"Yes, resign." She pushed her shoulders back and walked toward him, refusing to let the balance of power shift in his favor as it always did. When she was a few inches away from him, she stopped and lifted her chin, absorbing the impact of that penetrating blue gaze. "I'm tired of *drifting aimlessly* through this company with you lying to me about where I'm headed."

His gaze darkened. "Oh, come on, Bailey. I would think you of all people could take a joke."

She sank her hands into her hips. "You meant every word of that, Jared. And to think I thought it might be our personality conflict that's been holding me back."

The corner of his mouth lifted, the scar that sliced through his upper lip whitening as skin stretched over bone. "You mean the fact that every time we're in a boardroom together we want to dismantle each other in a slow and painful manner?" His eyes took on a smoky, deadly hue. "That's the kind of thing that gets me out of bed in the morning."

The futility of it all sent her head into an exasperated shake. "I think I've always known what your opinion of women is, but stupid me, I thought you actually respected me."

"I do respect you."

"Then why has everything I've done over the past three years failed to impress you? I was a star at my last company, Jared. You recruited me because of it. Why give Tate Davidson the job I deserved?"

"You weren't ready," he stated matter-of-factly, as much in control as she was out of it.

"In what way?"

"Your maturity levels," he elaborated, looking down his perfect nose at her. "Your knee-jerk reactions. Right now is a good example. You didn't even think this through."

Antagonism lanced through her, setting every limb of her body on fire. "Oh, I thought it through all right. I've had three years to think it through. And forgive me if I don't take the maturity criticism too hard after your childish little stunt this morning. You wanted to make every male in California laugh and slap each other on the back? Well, you've succeeded. Good on you. Another ten steps backward for womankind."

His hooded gaze narrowed. "I put women in the boardroom when they deserve it, Bailey. But I won't do it for appearance's sake. I think you're immensely talented and if you'd get over this ever-present need to prove yourself, you'd go far."

She refused to let the compliment derail her when he was never going to change. Pushing her hair out of her face, she glared at him. "I've outperformed every male in this company over the past couple of years, and that hasn't been enough. I'm through trying to impress you, Jared. Apparently the only thing that would is if I was a D cup."

His mouth tipped up on one side in that crooked smile women loved. "I don't think there's a man in Silicon Valley who would find you lacking in any department, Bailey. You just don't take any of them up on it."

The backhanded compliment made her draw in a breath. Sent a rush of color to her cheeks, heating her all over. She'd asked for it. She really had. And now she had to go.

"Here," she said, shoving the letter at him. "Consider this my response to your manifesto. And believe me, this was *draft two*."

He curled his long, elegant fingers around the paper and scanned it. Then deliberately, slowly, his eyes on hers, tore it in half. "I won't accept it."

"Be glad I'm not filing a human rights suit against you," she bit out and turned on her heel. "HR has the other copy. I'm giving you two weeks."

"I'm offering you the VP marketing job, Bailey." His words stopped her in her tracks. "You've done a phenomenal job boosting domestic sales. You deserve the chance to spread your wings."

Elation flashed through her, success after three long years of brutally hard work overwhelming her, followed almost immediately by the grounding notion of exactly what was happening here. She turned around slowly, pinning him to the spot with her gaze. "Which member of your team advised you to leverage me?"

If she'd blinked she would have missed the muscle that jumped in his jaw, but she didn't, and it made the anger already coursing through her practically flammable. "You want me," she stated slowly, "to be your poster child. Your token female executive you can throw in the spotlight to silence the furor."

His jaw hardened, silencing the recalcitrant muscle. "I want you to become my vice president of marketing, Bailey. Full stop. You've earned the opportunity, now take it. Don't be stupid. We're due at Davide Gagnon's house in the south of France the day after tomorrow to present our marketing plan, and I need you by my side."

She wanted to say no. She desperately wanted to throw the offer back in his face and walk out of here, dignity intact. But two things stopped her. Jared Stone was offering her the one thing she'd sworn she'd never stop working for until she got it—the chance to sit on the executive committee of a Fortune 500 company. And despite everything that he was—an impossible, arrogant full-of-himself jerk—he was the most brilliant brain on the face of the planet. And everyone knew it. If she worked alongside him as his equal she could write her ticket. Ensure she never went back to the life she'd vowed to leave behind forever.

Survival was stronger than her pride. It always had been. And men having all the power in her world wasn't anything unusual. She knew how to play them. How to beat them. And she could beat Jared Stone, too. She knew it.

She stared at him. At the haughty tilt of his chin. It was almost irresistible to show him how wrong he was. About her. About all women. This would be her gift to the female race…

"All right. On two conditions."

His gaze narrowed.

"Double my salary and give me the title of CMO."

"We don't have a chief marketing officer."

"Now we do."

His eyes widened. Narrowed again. "Bailey…"

"We're done then." She turned away, every bit prepared to walk.

"Fine." His curt agreement made her eyes widen, brought her swinging back around. "You can have both."

She knew then that Jared Stone was in a great deal of trouble. And she was in the driver's seat. But her euphoria didn't last long as she nodded and made her way past Mary's desk. There was no doubt she'd just made a deal with the devil. And when you did that, you paid for it.

CHAPTER TWO

BY THE TIME newly minted CMO Bailey threw herself into a cab twenty-four hours later, bound for San Jose Airport and a flight to France, the furor over Jared Stone's manifesto had reached a fever pitch. Two feminist organizations had urged a full boycott of Stone Industries products in the wake of what they called his "irresponsible" and "repugnant" perspective on women. The female CEO of the largest clothing retailer in the country had commented on a national business news show, "It's too bad Stone didn't put this much thought into how he could balance out his board of directors, given that the valley is rife with female talent."

In response, a leading men's blog had declared Stone's manifesto "genius," calling the billionaire "a breath of fresh air for his honest assessment of this conflicted demographic."

It was madness. Even now, the cabbie's radio was blaring some inane talk show inviting men and women to call in with their opinions. She listened to one caller, a middle-aged male, praise Jared for his "balls" to take the bull by the horns and tell it like it was. Followed by a woman who called the previous caller "a caveman relic of bygone days."

"Please," Bailey begged, covering her eyes with the back of her hand, "turn it off. Turn the channel. Anything but him. I can't take it anymore."

The cabbie gave her an irritated glance through his grubby rearview mirror, as if he were fully on board with Jared's perspective and *she* was the deluded one. But he switched the channel. Bailey fished her mobile out of her purse and dialed the only person she regularly informed of her whereabouts in case she was nabbed running through the park some night and became a statistic.

"Where are you?" her best friend and former Stanford roommate, Aria Kates, demanded. "I've been trying to get you ever since this Jared Stone thing broke."

"On my way to the airport." Bailey checked her lipstick with the mirror in her compact. "I'm going with him to France."

"*France?* You didn't *quit?* Bailey, that memo is outrageous."

And *designed* for shock value. She shoved the mirror back in her purse, sat back against the worn, I've-seen-better-days seat, and pursed her lips. "He made me CMO."

"I don't care if he made you head of the Church of England…. He's an ass!"

Bailey stared at the lineup of traffic in front of them. "I want this job, Aria. I know why he promoted me. I get that he wants me to be his female executive poster child. I, however, am going to take this and use it for what it's worth. Get what I need, and get out."

Just as she'd done her entire life: clawed on to whatever she could grasp and used her talent and raw determination to succeed. Even when people told her she'd never do it.

She heard Aria take a sip of what was undoubtedly a large, extra-hot latte with four sweeteners, then pause for effect. "They say he's going to either conquer the world or take everyone down in a cloud of dust. You prepared for the ride?"

Bailey smiled her first real smile of the day. "Did I ever tell you why I came to work for him?"

"Because you're infatuated with his brain, Bails. And, I suspect, not only his brain."

Bailey frowned at the phone. "Exactly what does that mean?"

"I mean the night he hired you. He didn't start talking to you because he detected brilliance in that smart head of yours. He saw your legs across the room, made a bee-line for you, *then* you impressed him. You could almost see him turn off that part of his brain." Her friend sighed. "He may drive you crazy, but I've seen the two of you to-gether. It's like watching someone stick the positive and negative ends of a battery together."

She wrinkled her nose. "I can handle Jared Stone."

"That statement makes me think you're delusional.... Where in France, by the way?"

"Saint-Jean-Cap-Ferrat in the south."

"Jealous. Okay, well, have fun and keep yourself out of trouble. If you can with him along..."

Doubtful, Bailey conceded, focusing on the twelve hour flight ahead with the big bad wolf. Admittedly, she'd had a slight infatuation with Jared when she joined Stone Indus-tries. But then he'd started acting like the arrogant jerk he was and begun holding her back at every turn, and after that it hadn't taken much effort at all to put her attraction aside. Because she was only at Stone Industries for one thing: to plunder Jared Stone's genius and move on.

The master plan hadn't changed.

Traffic went relatively smoothly for a Friday afternoon. Bailey stepped out of the cab in front of the tiny terminal for private flights, ready to soak up the quiet luxury from here on in. Instead she was blindsided by a sea of light, crisscrossing her vision like dancing explosions of fire. *Camera flashes*, her brain registered. She was stumbling to find her balance, her pupils dilating against the white lights, when a strong hand gripped her arm. She looked up to see Jared's impossibly handsome face set in grim lines.

"Good God," she muttered, hanging on to him as his security detail forged a path through the scrum. "Do you regret your little joke now?"

"I regretted it the minute it was broadcast to the world," he muttered, shielding her from a particularly zealous photographer. "But basking in regret isn't my style."

No, it wasn't…although looking amazing in the face of adversity was. Because in the middle of the jostling reporters, acting like a human shield for her, he looked all-powerful and infinitely gorgeous. His fitted dark jeans molded lean, powerful legs, topped by a cobalt-blue sweater that made his piercing blue eyes glitter in the late afternoon sun. And then there was his slicked-back dark hair he looked like he'd raked his hands through a million times that gave him a rebellious look.

When you tossed in the pirate-like scar twisting his upper lip, you ended up with a photo that would undoubtedly make front page news.

A photographer eluded Jared's two bodyguards, stepped in front of them and stuck a microphone in Bailey's face. "Kay Harris called you a figurehead this morning on her talk show. Any comment?"

One hundred percent true. Bailey gave the reporter an annoyed look as Jared started to push her forward. She leaned back against his arm, stood her ground and ignored his warning look. "I think," she stated, speaking to the cameras that had swung to her, "Mr. Stone made an error in judgment he apologized for earlier today and that's the end of the matter." She waved her hand at the man at her side. "I work for a brilliant company that is on a trajectory to become the world's top consumer electronics manufacturer. I couldn't be prouder of what we've accomplished. And I," she forced out, almost choking on the words, "have the utmost professional respect for Jared Stone. We have a great working relationship."

The questions came at her fast and furious. She held up a hand, stated they had a flight to catch, and let Jared propel her forward, hand at her back.

"Since when did you become such a diplomat?" he muttered, ushering her through the glass doors into the terminal.

"Since you created that *zoo* out there." She came to a halt inside the doors, took a deep breath and ran a hand over herself, straightening her clothing.

Jared did the same. Before the airline staff could spirit them off, he squared to face her. "Thank you. I owe you one."

Her gaze flickered away from the intensity of his. Looking at Jared was like observing all the major forces of the world stuffed inside the human form—charging him with an energy, a polar pull that was impossible to ignore. She'd felt it that night he'd headed purposefully across that bar and ended up hiring her. But she didn't need it now. Not when she'd gotten used to avoiding it. Not when she had to spend twelve hours crammed into a private jet with him absorbing it all.

"It was nothing," she muttered. "Don't make me regret saying it."

"I'm sure you already do...." His taunting rejoinder brought her head up. The dark glint in his eyes reminded her that there was still a line in this détente of theirs. And she knew there was. She really did. She just couldn't help it with him.

"After you," he murmured, extending his arm toward the exit to the tarmac. She swished past him out the doors and up the stairs of the sleek ten-person Stone Industries jet. She'd been on it once before, the decor a study in dark male sophistication. An official boarded the plane for a cursory check of their passports, and Bailey settled into one of the sumptuously soft leather seats and buckled up.

They took off, the powerful little jet racing down the runway, leaving San Jose behind in a blur of bright lights. As soon as the seat belt lights were turned off, Jared unpacked a mountain of paperwork and suggested they rehearse the presentation. He wanted it perfect—was determined to rehearse until they'd nailed every last key message. Given that it was new material to her, it might be a long night.

It was. Their styles were completely opposite. She liked to wing it. Jared, emphatically not. Not to mention how intimidating he was when his passion for the subject took over. She could usually hold her own with the best of them, but he was too smart, too intense and too sure of himself to make it easy. So she resorted to her default mechanism of asking a million questions. Knowing the material inside out. What was the logic behind that statistic? Why were they making that particular point here? And wasn't this information coming too soon? Shouldn't they save it to drive the stake in at the end?

Four hours and four rounds of the presentation later, Jared flung himself into the chair opposite her and rubbed his hands over his eyes. "This isn't working. You are the queen of going off script."

"It makes it believable," she countered, sinking down into her chair. "I'm playing off you, taking your lead. You're the one who keeps losing the thread."

He gave her a disbelieving look. "*I'm* following the slides."

She blew out a breath as her head pounded like a jackhammer. "You are stuck on *process*. Try loosening up. It works beautifully. It's even better when I have an audience."

He dropped his head into his hands. "That idea scares me. Greatly."

She looked longingly up at the flight attendant as she came to hover by them with an offer of predinner drinks. "I'm having a glass of wine. I've earned it."

"Whiskey," Jared muttered to the attendant, then sat back and watched her from beneath lowered lashes. The *longest* lowered lashes she'd ever encountered. Divine, really.

He opened them. "What is it about falling in line you have a problem with?"

Bailey widened her eyes. "I fall in line when I need to. Witness the press a few hours ago, for instance."

"You are challenging everything I say," he growled.

"I'm challenging everything that doesn't make sense," she countered. "I haven't seen the material before. I'm an objective eye."

"It's *perfect*."

"It *would be* perfect if everyone in the world thought exactly like you. Davide Gagnon has a creative streak. You need to appeal to that side of him."

"An expert on him already?" he asked darkly.

"I did my homework." She tore open the can of cashews she'd brought with her and shoved some in her mouth. "What value would I be adding if I fell into line like a trained seal?"

His expression inched darker. "A lot of value right now, given that this is the only rehearsal time we're going to get. Davide is famous for his social lifestyle. You can bet he'll have things lined up every night."

She winced inwardly. Although her research had told her all about Davide Gagnon's lavish lifestyle and love of a good party that tended to include the who's who of Europe, and she'd packed accordingly, it was the type of lifestyle she abhorred. She'd seen too much of it when she'd danced in Vegas. The destructive things money and power could do. And although she'd been the girl who'd always gone home after the show rather than take advantage of the high rollers who'd wanted to lavish hefty doses of it on her, she'd seen—*experienced*—enough of it for a lifetime.

Focus on her studies, fast-track her business degree and get the hell out. That had been her mantra.

"Bailey?"

Jared was looking at her, an impatient look on his face. She blinked. "Sorry?"

"I was saying Davide has a fondness for blondes." He folded one long leg over the other and popped a handful of the cashews into his mouth. "I consider you my secret weapon."

Hostility flared through her, swift and sharp, spurred by a past she couldn't quite banish. "If you're suggesting I flirt with him, that's not going to happen. And I can't believe you would even say that considering that your reputation is hanging by a thread and I'm the only thing keeping it afloat."

He gave her a long look as the attendant set their drinks on the table. "I was asking you to charm him, Bailey, not sleep with him."

She gave him a black look. "Forgive me for misinterpreting. We women apparently don't have a use beyond securing ourselves a rich man and keeping ourselves within the style *to which we've become accustomed*. So I just wanted to make the point."

A muscle jumped in his jaw. "You were the one who just said I'd made my apology and bygones should be bygones. Perhaps you can walk the walk, no?"

"That was for public consumption." She pulled the glass of deep ruby-red wine toward her. "Know that in my head, my respect for you personally is at an all-time low."

His eyes darkened to a wintry, stormy blue. "As long as your professional respect is intact, I'm not worried about your personal opinion."

And there it was. The man who cared about nothing but his driving need for success. He was legendary for it and she couldn't fault it because she was his mirror image.

She took a sip of the rich, velvety red, her palate marking it a Cabernet/Merlot blend. "I am curious about one thing, though."

He lifted a brow.

"What *is* your real opinion of women?"

His sexy, quirky mouth turned up on one side. "If you think I'm answering that, you consider me a stupider man than I am."

'No, really," she insisted, waving her glass at him. "Utterly open conversation. I want to know."

His long-lashed gaze held hers for a moment, then he shrugged. "I think the science of relationships goes back as far as time. As far as the cavemen… We men—we hunt, we gather. We provide. Women want us for what we can offer them. And as soon as we can't, as soon as they get a better offer," he drawled, "we are expendable."

She was shocked into silence. Considering that her mother had been the only thing keeping her family afloat with her alcoholic father off work more than on, that seemed ludicrous. "You can't really mean that," she said after a moment. "It's crazy to lump all women together like that."

He lifted a shoulder. "I never say anything I don't mean. You wonder who's really in the power position, Bailey? Think about it."

She frowned. "What about women who can provide for themselves? Women who bring equal billing to a relationship?"

"It doesn't survive. There is *always* a balance of power in a relationship. And when a woman has that power, the relationship is never going to last. Women *need* us to dominate. To be the provider."

She stared at him. "That's ridiculous. You are impossible."

His white smile glittered in the muted confines of the jet. "I've been called worse this week. Come on, admit it, Bailey. A strong woman like you must like a man to take control. Otherwise you'd walk all over him."

A warning buzzed its way along her temple, signaling dangerous territory she wasn't about to traverse. She lifted her chin, met his magnetic blue gaze head-on. "On the contrary. I like to be in control, just like you do, Jared. *Always*. Haven't you figured that out already?"

His lashes lowered, studying, *analyzing*. "I'm not sure I have one-fifth of you figured out."

The air between them suddenly felt too hot, too tight in the close confines of the jet that pulsed with the powerful throb of the engines. She took a jerky sip of her wine. "Should we get back to rehearsing?"

"After dinner." He nodded toward her glass. "Enjoy your wine. Be social."

She searched for something in the safe zone to talk about and when that didn't materialize, pulled her purse toward her, searched for her lipstick and fished it out to reapply.

"Don't."

Her hand froze midway to her face. "Sorry?"

"Don't reapply that war paint. You look perfect the way you are."

Heat spread through her, confusing in its intensity. He'd probably used that line on a million women. Why it made her drop the lipstick back into her purse and reach for her lip balm instead was unclear to her.

Jared sat back in his chair, tumbler balanced on his knee, hand sliding over his dark-shadowed jaw. "There's never a hair out of place, Bailey. Never a cuff that isn't perfectly turned or posture that isn't ramrod straight even after four hours of rehearsing." He angled an inquisitive brow at her. "Why the facade? What are you afraid people might find out if you relax?"

She angled her chin at him. "I work in the male-dominated, testosterone-driven world of Silicon Valley. Men will walk all over me if I show weakness. You of all people should know that."

"Perhaps," he agreed. "Is that why you turn them all down? Let them crash and burn for all to see?"

She looked him straight in the eye. "That would be their stupidity if I wasn't showing interest. And *this* would be my personal life. Which doesn't have any part in this conversation."

"Oh, but it does," he said softly, his gaze holding hers. "We need to go into this presentation like a well-oiled machine. Know each other inside out, anticipate each other's needs, move together seamlessly until we are a well-orchestrated symphony. Trust each other implicitly so no matter what they throw at us we've got it. But right now, we're a disjointed mess. The trust is lacking, and I don't feel like I know the first thing about you."

A chill stole through her. No one *knew* her. Except perhaps Aria. They knew Bailey St. John, the composed, successful woman she'd created by sheer force of will. A female version of the Terminator...and not even bulldog Jared was going to uncover the real her.

Which necessitated an act. And a good one. She cradled her wineglass against her chest, leaned back in her seat and slid into the interview persona she'd perfected over the years. "Ask away, then. What do you want to know?"

Jared leaned back in his seat and took in Bailey's deceptively relaxed pose. He had no doubt from her evasive answers that she was going to give him only half the story. But something was more than nothing, and their disastrous rehearsals necessitated some kind of synergy. They weren't connecting on any level except to strike sparks off each other. Which might be fine, desirable even, in the bedroom, but it wasn't helping here with the board breathing down his neck, the press all over him like a second skin and the most important presentation of his life looming.

If he and Bailey walked into that room right now and did the presentation, they would go down like the Titanic. Slowly and painfully. Davide Gagnon might have handpicked them as partner, but it didn't mean they could afford to miss one detail about why he should work with them.

He took a long sip of his whiskey, considered her while it burned a comforting trail down his throat, then rested the glass on his thigh. "I was reviewing your résumé. Why the University of Nevada-Las Vegas for your undergrad? It seems an odd choice given your East Coast upbringing. Florida, right?"

She nodded.

"Did you win a scholarship?"

The closed-off look he'd watched her perfect over the years made a spectacular reappearance. "I'm from a small city outside Tampa called Lakeland. Population less than a hundred thousand. I wanted to go away to school, and UNLV had a good business program."

"So you chose Sin City?"

"Seemed as good a place as any."

"Did it have something to do with the fact that you aren't close to your family?"

"Why would you say that?"

"You never go home for the holidays and you never talk about them. So I'm assuming that's the case."

Her cool-as-ice blue eyes glittered. "I'm not particularly close to them, no."

Definitely a sore point. "After UNLV," he continued, "you did your MBA at Stanford, my alma mater, then went straight to a start-up. Did you always want to work in the Valley?"

She nodded. "I loved technology. I would have been an engineer if I hadn't gone into business."

"They're in high demand," he acknowledged. "Where did the interest come from? A parent? School?"

She smiled. "School. Science was my favorite class. My teachers encouraged me in that direction."

"And your parents," he probed. "What do they do?"

If he hadn't been watching her, studying her like a hawk, he would have missed the slight flinch that pulled her shoulders back. She lifted her chin. "My father is a traveling salesman and my mother is a hairdresser."

His eyes widened. Her less-than-illustrious background didn't faze him. The complete incompatibility with the woman in front of him did. He would have pegged her as an aristocrat. As coming from money. Because everything about Bailey was perfect. Classy. From the top of her glamorous platinum-haired head, to her finely boned striking features, to her long, lean thoroughbred limbs, she was all sophistication and impeccable taste.

"So no man, no family," he recounted. "Who do you spend your time with when you're not at work? Which is always..." he qualified.

"You should be happy I do that. It's why your sales numbers are so impressive."

"I like my employees to have a life," he countered drily. "Maybe you have a man tucked away none of us know about?"

"I have friends," she said stiffly.

"Pastimes? Hobbies?"

Silence. He watched her mind work, coming up with a suitable answer, not the real one. "I like to read."

"Ah yes," he nodded. "So home on a Friday night with a book in your hand? That sounds awfully dull."

"Maybe I import my men," she offered caustically. "Ship them in for a hot night, then send them home."

His mouth twisted. "Lucky guys."

"Jared…" She exhaled heavily. "Are you ever politically correct?"

"Hopefully this weekend, yes."

She smiled at that. "Is that enough information so we can move on to *your* fascinating backstory?"

"It'll do for now." He poured her another glass of wine, intent on loosening her up.

She shifted, tucked her legs underneath her. He kept his eyes off her outstanding calves with difficulty. "Is it true," she asked, running a finger around the rim of her glass, "that you got your love of electronics tinkering in the garage with your father?"

He nodded. "My father was an investment banker, but his true love was playing with a car's engine until the sun came down. I would go out to the garage and work alongside him until my mother made me come in."

She frowned. "You said *was*. Did your father pass?"

"No." He felt his defenses sliding into place like a cell door at Alcatraz, but opening up was a two-way street, and he needed to give, too. "He embezzled money from the bank, from his personal circle of friends, got himself in way too deep and tried to win it all back in a high-stakes game in Vegas."

Her eyes widened. "And they chewed him up?"

"Yes."

"I'm so sorry. I didn't know."

His mouth twisted. "It's not exactly in my bio. The bank did a good job of hushing it up, and only those close to it ever knew."

Her gaze moved uncertainly over his. Wondering why he'd told her.

"Trust," he said softly. "You shared with me. I need to

share with you. I meant what I said, Bailey. This is the most important presentation of Stone Industries' history. There are no second chances. We have to nail it. We have to trust each other completely walking into that room or we don't do it at all."

She chewed ferociously on her lower lip. He kept his gaze on hers. "You have to be all-in, Bailey."

She nodded. "I'm in."

His shoulders settled back into place, his relief palpable. "Good. Let's try to streamline that second section so it sings…"

She leaned forward to grab her notebook. "Ouch."

"What?"

She pressed her fingers to her neck. "I slept the wrong way last night. I've got the worst kind of kink."

She'd been struggling with it throughout their rehearsals, he realized. He'd thought her funny faces had been grimaces about the material but instead, she'd been in pain.

"Come here."

She looked blankly at him.

He held up his hands. "These are magic. Let me work it out so you can concentrate."

She shook her head. "It'll work itself out. Let's just figure that p—"

He got to his feet and pointed at the chair. "We need to nail this and you obviously can't concentrate. Five minutes."

She came then, taking the chair he'd vacated, as if she knew further resistance was futile. "Here," she told him, pointing to the spot. He sat down on the side of the chair, ran his fingers over her skin lightly, then with increasing pressure.

"Here?"

"Yes," she groaned. "Be careful. It's killing me."

"Trust, remember?" He set about working the immobilized muscles, on the outer edges first, loosening them up so he could find his way to the source of the pain. He felt her relax, let him in. But only so much. And he wondered how often, if ever, this woman allowed herself to be vulnerable?

I like to be in control, just like you do, Jared. Always.

Kink worked fully, he brought his hands down to her shoulders and started to work out the knots from where she'd held herself stiff from the pain. He expected her to protest. Say that was fine. But she didn't. And why the hell did he still have his hands on her?

The scent of her perfume filled his nostrils, light but heady. *Like her...* It made a fist coil tight in his chest. The air thickened around them, his hands slowing as he finished the job. She must have felt it too, this undeniable connection between them, because her breathing changed, quickened, a flush stained her alabaster skin, and she was completely pliable beneath his hands.

She wanted him.

Bailey St. John—queen of the brush-off—wanted him.

The vaguely shattering discovery took him to a place it wasn't wise to go. The woman every man in Silicon Valley coveted was not impenetrable. *No pun intended.* She was far from asexual as some had suggested jokingly, and perhaps bitterly. And it struck him that maybe he'd been avoiding working with her, promoting her, because he'd been afraid of *this*. Because they'd have to work hand in hand. Because he'd wanted to unravel the mystery that was Bailey St. John from the first day she'd walked into his office.

Correction. From the night he'd hired her...

His body tightened with an almighty surge of testosterone. Not particularly admirable, but there it was. And how had he not realized it sooner? Hadn't he learned this in grade school? You only fought with the girls you liked. And on a much more adult level, he realized he wanted

Bailey in his bed. *Under him* as he peeled back layer upon layer.

He would not be the one to crash and burn...

"Bailey?"

"Mm?" Her husky, pleasure-soaked tone rocked him to the core.

"I think I've figured out our issue."

"Our issue?"

"Mmm." He slid his fingers to the racing pulse at the base of her neck. "This."

CHAPTER THREE

BAILEY YANKED HERSELF out from under Jared's hands so fast she pretty much redid all the damage he'd just undone. Her hazy brain wasn't firing on all cylinders as she met her boss's glittering blue gaze, focused and intent, containing the same heated sexual awareness that had been fueling her unspeakable fantasy.

Hot and uncensored, it had been outrageously good...

"We— I—" She started to talk. Anything to deny what was happening.

Jared held up a hand. "There's only one thing that's called, Bailey: pure, unadulterated sexual attraction."

Her pulse racing, hectic color firing her cheeks, it was really pointless to deny it. But it would be insanity not to. "There goes your out-of-control ego again, Jared," she taunted, raising her chin. "You *antagonize* me, you drive me crazy, but you do not attract me."

His jaw hardened. The glitter in his eyes morphed into a spark of pure challenge as his *I am man*, chest-beating need to prove his masculinity roared to life. Her breath stopped in her lungs, her irrational desire to see what would happen if he did lose it mixing with her common sense to create a complete state of inertia. Then his dark lashes came down to shield his eyes, that superior control he exerted over himself sliding back into place. "I think," he said softly, "this is a case of semantics. Antagonize... Attract... What-

ever you want to call it—it's an issue. And we need to figure it out if we're going to make this presentation work. If
we're going to make this *partnership* work."

She pulled in a silent breath, using the reprieve to
steady herself. To regain her equilibrium. He was right.
She needed to figure this antagonism/attraction thing out
before she made a complete fool of herself. Before she destroyed this opportunity she'd been handed.

"How about," she offered, with as cool a gaze as she
could muster, "you try to be a little looser, go with the flow,
and I'll pay more attention to the script? I'm sure even *we*
can meet somewhere in the middle."

His mouth tilted up on one side. "It's worth a shot."

They dined on a delicious meal of filet mignon and
salad, Bailey severely curtailing her consumption of the
delicious wine so her head was clear. She'd made a serious
mistake in ever thinking she could let her defenses down
in front of Jared. In tipping her hand and revealing an attraction she hadn't even fully admitted to herself. But she'd
learned her lesson. And she wasn't about to do it again.

Their final rehearsal wasn't perfect, but it was a heck of
a lot better than their earlier attempts. She toned it down,
made a concerted effort to follow Jared's lead, and they
made it through in a fairly civilized way. Jared, being the
generous soul that he was, gave her a couple of hours'
sleep before they landed in the sparkling, glittering South
of France.

Just how luxurious their trip was going to be was apparent when upon their arrival in the Nice airport, they were
not met by a car, but a shiny silver helicopter flown by
Davide Gagnon's personal pilot. He jumped down under
the slowing, still-whirling helicopter blades, greeted them,
stowed their luggage in the back of the aircraft, and took
them on their way.

Their trip across the sun-kissed Côte d'Azur to the legendary Peninsula of Billionaires, in between Nice and Monaco, featured some of the most exclusive properties on the French Riviera. Bailey, who'd done the South of France on a budget in her backpacking days with Aria, was googly-eyed. Luxurious villas sat in secluded coves behind high cliffs that sheltered them from the wind. And the colors were glorious, brilliant fuchsia and purple-soaked gardens bordering the sparkling turquoise sea.

Jared gave her an amused look as she chatted with the pilot, extending her twenty-question strategy to him. It was presently a balmy twenty-one degrees Celsius, the pilot told them as he set the chopper down on the Gagnon property's private landing pad, expected to get much hotter over the weekend, just in time for film festival season in the South of France.

They were met outside the low, cream-colored sprawling villa that sat directly on the bay by Davide Gagnon's head housekeeper, who informed them their host was en route home from a business meeting and would greet them that night at the party. Until then, they were free to explore the grounds and beach and enjoy some lunch. Bailey forced some salad into her jet-lagged body, took one look at her oceanfront suite—situated directly beside Jared's at one end of a wing—and elected for a face-plant into the three-hundred-count Egyptian cotton sheets and an afternoon nap.

When she woke, the brilliant afternoon sun had faded into early evening, and a sensual pink-orange sunset was streaking its way across the sky. She yawned, padded to her terrace and watched as it deepened into a hot-pink fire laced with smoky gray-blue. She would have done just about anything to be able to sit there and enjoy the magnificent view with a glass of the wine on ice in her suite, but it was already close to six. She needed to shower, dress and face the jeweled, exquisitely coutured guests of Davide Gagnon in a half hour. And hope she had learned enough over the years to fake it so her lowbrow, uncouth roots didn't show through like an ugly weed in a sea of mimosa and lavender.

Put her in a boardroom matched against the world's nastiest deal-maker, and she was rock solid. Put her in a social situation like tonight, and she needed all her acting skills to survive. Etiquette training had only taught her which fork to use. Which wine to drink with what. It didn't make her one of them. And it never would.

She gazed out at the explosion of color in the sky and reminded herself parties like this were about working a room. If there was anything she'd learned as a dancer, it was that. How to get what she wanted out of the men who'd come to watch her so she could make a different life for herself. And tonight was no different. She needed to focus on the prize, Davide Gagnon. Use what she'd learned about him, what she knew of men like him, to convince him a Stone Industries partnership was his ticket to European sales domination.

Show Jared he'd been overlooking a valuable asset for a very long time.

Once she got over her nerves...

She reluctantly abandoned the gorgeous view and stepped inside. She might not be able to enjoy the sunset, but she *could* indulge in a glass of wine to ease the tension. Pouring herself a glass, she took it into the stunning marble bathroom, stepped under a hot shower, and systematically washed away the old Bailey and installed the new one in her place.

Wrapping herself in the thick, soft robe that hung on the door, she padded into the dressing area and ran her fingers over the whisper-soft silks and taffetas she'd hung in the wardrobe. But there was never any question as to which she'd pick. She pulled the just-above-the knee beaded champagne-colored cocktail dress from the hanger and slipped it on. The dress was the softest silk, hugging every curve with just the right amount of propriety. Sexy but conservative at the same time.

She surveyed herself in the floor-length mirror. There was nothing cheap about the woman who looked back at her. This was not the twenty-dollar designer knockoff dress that had once been the only thing she could afford. And it showed.

Working her hair into a smooth, shimmering mass of curls with a round brush and a dryer, she topped it with minimal eye makeup and gloss. Enough to highlight her features. She had just added a dash of perfume to her pulse points when a knock sounded at the connecting door. *Jared.*

She moved across the room, undid the bolt and opened the door. The sight of her boss in an exquisitely tailored black tux might have been more intimidating than the prospect of the evening ahead. From the tip of his slicked-back dark hair to his freshly shaven jaw and long-limbed masculinity, he was devastating.

Jared followed Bailey into her suite, her barefoot, wine-in-her-hand invitation to come in doing something strange to his insides. Her dress—what would you call it, champagne-colored?—hugged every curve as if it had been sewn onto her. Curves that could burn themselves into your memory if you let them. Her hair fell in smooth gold waves to her shoulders, one side pushed back with a diamond butter-fly clasp. Her exquisite face held only the faintest trace of war paint. But she was the most beautiful woman he'd ever stepped foot into a room with. That he knew.

He attempted to divert his wayward thoughts with a thoughtful look down at the floor tapestry, and instead treated himself to a perfect view of her long golden legs, ruby-tipped toes sinking into the carpet. And felt himself lose the plot completely. If she'd been a woman he was dating, he would have skipped the cocktails entirely. Insisted she share her wine while they watched the sunset together, taken the dress off her with his teeth and made her come at least twice before they joined the others.

And that didn't take into account what he would have done to her after the night was over.

He would have had her until sunrise.

"Jared?"

He coughed and lifted his gaze to hers. "Sorry?"

A pink stain stole over her cheeks. "The gold or champagne shoes?"

He looked at the two pairs of sky-high heels dangling by her fingertips and decided either of them would make every man in the room tonight want to bed her.

"Gold," he muttered. "It'll contrast with the dress."

"Right." She tossed the other pair on the carpet, braced her hand against the wall and slipped the stilettos on. As his hormone-clouded brain cleared, he noticed the tight set of her face. The way her ramrod straight posture seemed to have pulled up another centimeter. How she picked up the glass of wine and downed the remainder with a jerky movement reminiscent of his father on the nights he'd had to attend the bank functions he'd never been comfortable with, except his drink had been scotch.

The chink in her armor confounded him. "Are you nervous? You know the plan. We find out Maison's strategy when it comes to the environment and we're all set. It's the last missing piece."

A stillness slipped across her fine-boned face. Indecipherable. "I've got the plan down, Jared. I'm fine."

He didn't buy it for a second. Her revelations on the plane had illuminated one thing about Bailey. She hadn't been born into this lifestyle. She did a good job making it look as though she had, but she hadn't.

He stepped closer, something about her vulnerability touching him deep down inside. "Don't you know?" he said softly, looking down at her. "You're always the most beautiful woman in the room, Bailey. *And* the smartest."

A small smile twisted her lips before she wrinkled her nose at him. "I'll bet that line works wonders for you."

"You have no idea." His answering grin was self-effacing. "But I've never meant it more than I do now. So be yourself tonight, and you'll knock them dead."

She studied him for a moment. Nodded. "We should go."

For what reason he didn't know, he braved her prickly exterior and wrapped his fingers around her delicate hand instead of offering his arm.

"Ready?" he asked roughly.

"Ready."

They emerged on the buzzing wraparound terrace of the villa, ablaze with light and laughter on the warm Mediterranean night, where perhaps close to fifty people had already gathered, cocktails in hand. As Jared cased the crowd, he noticed an Academy Award-winning producer to his left, a high-profile A-list Hollywood couple to his right, and wasn't that Roberto Something-or-other, the Italian film director known for his sprawling epics, straight ahead? The big personalities had, apparently, all made it into town.

He grabbed a couple of glasses of champagne from a passing waiter's tray and handed one to Bailey. Gagnon had spared no expense: a quartet playing in a corner of the large, floodlit deck, black-jacketed staff circulating like an efficient swarm of bees, and from what he'd heard, a well-known French singer slated to play later in the evening, purportedly a mistress to one of the French cabinet ministers. But Jared had only one goal in mind. To corner Davide Gagnon and get the information he needed to develop that final, crucial piece of strategy.

He did not miss the attention every man at the party paid to the woman by his side as he picked out Gagnon, placed a palm to Bailey's back and led her through the crowd. There were a lot of beautiful, stunning even, women at the party. Bailey outshone them all, glittering like a glamorous Hollywood icon brought forward to the present, outclassing even the real Hollywood A-listers in attendance if you were to ask his opinion. But in true Bailey style, she ignored them all and focused on their target.

Davide Gagnon detached himself from the group he was standing with and came toward them, his sun-lined, handsome, younger-looking-than-he-was face breaking into a wide smile as he took Bailey's hand and brought it to his mouth. "My pilot told me you were lovely," he murmured gallantly. "I think he erred on the conservative side."

Bailey gave their host a warm smile and returned his greeting. *In French.* In perfectly accented, lilting Parisian French that sounded so sexy Jared's jaw dropped open.

"I think I'm in love," Davide murmured, hanging on to her hand. "What are you doing with the most controversial man in the room, *ma chère?*"

"And the most brilliant," Bailey returned smoothly as she drew back, an amused sparkle lighting her blue eyes. "I'm with him for his brain."

Jared's gaze tangled with hers. She appreciated a lot more than his brain, he was sure of it. And he suddenly had the burning urge to make her admit it. Maybe it was the look of pure male appreciation on Davide's face. Maybe it had been the scene with the shoes. Regardless, it was out of the question. He had to be a good boy. He was on a very short leash with no room for error.

"You have an absolutely magnificent home," he murmured appreciatively, when Davide finally deigned to let go of Bailey's hand and offer him his. "Thank you for the invitation to join you."

"It only increased the desirability of my guest list," the distinguished Frenchman said in a wry tone. "Like you or hate you, they all want to meet you."

Jared caught the disapproval the Frenchman lobbed him loud and clear. "It was a personal joke that should never have been made public," he asserted.

"But it was," Davide drawled. "And now you've alienated fifty percent of the population."

Tension tightened his jaw. "It will blow over."

Gagnon's eyes glinted. "That's what Richard Braydon thought when his comments about the French were broadcast on YouTube." His gaze was deliberate. "It destroyed his business."

A fist reached in and wrapped itself around his heart. Gagnon could not have missed the business stories depicting him teetering on a high-wire when it came to retaining control of his company. His radical push in a direction few dared to go. The Frenchman's deal would push him over the edge one way or another, and Davide knew it.

"It *will* blow over," Jared reiterated harshly. "And when you see what we have in our marketing plan, you will not have any doubts, I promise you."

The other man inclined his head. "I expect brilliance from you, Stone. It's the wild cards you throw my way I'm not so sure about."

Jared gritted his teeth as Gagnon blew off the conversation and turned to introduce them around. Turned to introduce *Bailey* around, if he were to be accurate. With himself in Davide's bad books, she apparently was a more enticing draw.

He spent the rest of the cocktail hour deflecting conversation of his manifesto, which truly seemed to have struck a global note. Heartily sick of it and inordinately

annoyed with himself, he was then seated next to Gagnon's daughter, Micheline, for dinner. Whether a joke
or penance on Davide's part, Jared thought he'd died and
gone to hell by the main course. Micheline had not let up
over the soup and appetizers about how damaging his effort "to be cute" was to women. How much it denigrated
everything she'd worked for.

By the time the Cornish hens came, he would have
laid down on the floor and allowed her to stick needles in
every part of him if she would have stopped. *Just stopped.*

Bailey, of course, had been placed beside Davide. She
spent the evening chatting away to him in that perfect
French he didn't understand so he couldn't follow their
conversation. Apparently, she had lost her nerves.

Micheline glanced over at her father and Bailey, her
thin mouth curving in a cynical smile. "She was a brilliant
stroke of strategy on your part, Jared, no doubt about it.
You know Daddy can't resist a beautiful blonde."

"She's extremely smart," Jared muttered. And annoying. *He needed* to be in on that conversation. But it didn't
happen. Dessert stretched into liqueurs and no one moved.
Finally, the French singer took the stage on the terrace, the
band backing her up, and Jared seized the opportunity to
grab his CMO.

"Care for a dance?" he requested on a slightly belliger-
ent note, holding out his hand.

She nodded and excused herself from Davide's side.
Jared's long strides ate up the distance to the dance floor
set up on a corner of the balcony. He slid an arm around
Bailey's waist, laced his fingers through hers and pulled
her to him.

"When were you planning on including me in your
little party?"

She absorbed that, absorbed his frustration, then sighed.
"You told me to work him, Jared. That's what I'm doing."

"*Awfully* well."

She sealed her bottom lip over her top.

"When were you going to tell me you spoke French?"

"That was also on my résumé," she said pointedly. "Along with the fact that I speak Spanish and Italian."

"I have a feeling that résumé of yours isn't worth the paper it's printed on," he said darkly, inhaling that trademark floral scent of hers. Trying to ignore what she'd look like stripped of that dress, what his psyche had been working on all evening. "What other tricks do you have up your sleeve? Just so I have a heads-up."

Her perfectly arched brows came together. "I know it must be disconcerting that Davide's being a bit cool with you, but you can't blame me for that."

"I'm not blaming you, I'm wondering *who you are*. You whip out this perfect French I didn't know you speak then you're off talking about Plato over dinner."

"I studied that in college. He's Davide's favorite philosopher."

"Of course he is. He's also clearly besotted with you."

Her calm look hardened until she was matching him stare for stare. "I am using my brain, Jared. Something the women you consort with likely don't do. I can understand why you would find that hard to appreciate."

"*I* appreciate your brain."

"Right." She echoed his skepticism. "He's revealing a lot. I'm getting some good insight into how his brain works. I've run some ideas by him and—"

"You've *run some ideas by him?*" Fury twisted his insides. "I don't want you running ideas by him, I want you *sticking to the script*."

Her lips pressed together. "He liked them. Loved them, in fact."

He kept a leash on himself as the urge to explode like an overdue volcano rolled over him. "Which ideas are we talking about? The ones in our presentation or your rogue *thoughts?*"

Hot color dusted her cheeks. "One of mine—the one about the kiosks in the yoga studios…"

He uttered a curse. "That is not in our plan. It is nowhere in our plan, nor is it going to be. You need to put a leash on yourself."

She lifted her chin, her blue eyes a stormy gray. "He loved the idea, Jared. He said it was exactly where his head was at. So maybe *you* need to open your mind. Use your imagination."

"I am using my imagination," he came back shortly, his gaze sliding over the dress, the *curves* every man in the room hadn't been able to take his eyes off of all night. "And I don't like where it's taking me."

She swallowed, a visible big gulp. "Do not do that. We are negotiating a business deal here, remember? Focus."

"I am focusing," he countered silkily. "Like every other male at this party, you have my complete attention in that dress. Now what are you going to do with it?"

Her eyes widened. Fire arced between them, swift and strong. It made his blood tattoo through his veins in a triumphant march. Sent heat lancing through his body. Bailey stared back at him like a deer caught in the headlights for a long moment. Then she blinked and stepped out of his arms.

"Walk away," she said softly. "You know the magazines are right about you, Jared. You're the one who needs a leash. You *are* out of control. You *have* lost your focus. You might think about getting it back. Think about what's actually going to win this rather than your own ego."

He stood there, hands clenched by his sides with the need to strangle her. She started off, then turned back with a final, parting shot.

"Green is only a peripheral strategy for Davide. He recognizes the importance to consumers, but he also knows they aren't willing to pay a premium for it. It's the price of entry."

She left before he could say anything. Wound her way back through the crowd. And he wondered if she was right. Was he out of control? Had he lost the thread? Because all he'd ever wanted to do was build a company that created great products. That made the impossible possible. But now that he'd done that, now that he was close to the pinnacle of success, he was doing everything but. He was glad-handing politicians, massaging a board's ego, weighing in on a marketing strategy he shouldn't have to worry about. About as far from the business of inspiration as you could get.

It was making him crazy.

He acknowledged one more thing before he bit out a curse and followed Bailey through the crowd. The yoga kiosk idea was brilliant. He'd thought that when she'd mentioned it, but final rehearsals weren't any time to be going off script.

Hell. He'd told Sam this would happen. He should have listened to his instincts.

Bailey spent the rest of the evening trying to manage the thundercloud that was Jared. She had the distinct feeling Davide Gagnon was administering a slap on the hand to her boss by giving him the cold shoulder, because there was no doubt that he respected Jared immensely.

She felt as if she was doing damage control on all sides. She also felt that she was the missing piece of the puzzle. The link between Jared's brilliance and Davide's creative side. Davide *loved* her ideas. He thought they were grass-roots, buzz-inducing genius. And it made her feel just this side of cocky as she stood at the two men's sides for a last brandy as the crowd dwindled on the star-strewn terrace.

She felt *empowered*.

"My son, Alexander, has been delayed until tomorrow night," Davide updated them, pointing his glass at Jared. "Since he will be assuming the mantle at Maison upon my retirement next year, I want him to take the lead on this partnership decision. Why don't you enjoy the day tomorrow, meet Alexander at dinner and we can hear the presentation on Sunday?"

Jared, who had been raring to get the presentation nailed and over with, nodded congenially as if that were the greatest idea in the world.

"You're planning on stepping back over the next few months and transitioning, then?"

Davide nodded. "But I will still be very involved. My son is nothing if not ambitious and aggressive, but he'll need guidance." He shot Jared an amused look. "You'll like him. He likes to win as much as you do."

Jared smiled. "Not a bad trait." But his eyes were blazing with a plan. Four or five more hours of endless rehearsal? She almost groaned out loud at the thought. She might kill him first.

"I should say goodbye to a guest," Davide observed, "then I think I'm going to turn in. I'll see you in the morning for breakfast."

Bailey couldn't imagine anything better than bed. It was 2:30 a.m., her feet were killing her from the heels, she was jet-lagged, and the mental exhaustion of maintaining such a perfect facade all night, of using the French she hadn't practiced in years, had fried her brain. And then there was Jared, who moved silently beside her into the house like a quiet, lethal animal ready to strike.

She stayed quiet because taunting the animal was never a good strategy. And she'd slipped during that dance. Had gotten caught up in him for a split second before she'd walked away.

She didn't think that was helping their harmony.

The hallway stretched long and silent ahead of them. Jared stopped in front of her door, turned the handle and pushed it open. She came to a halt beside him, tension raking over her as she risked a look up at him. Latent, unresolved antagonism stretched like a live wire between them, Jared's penetrating stare making her shift her weight to the other foot. *Away* from him.

She pulled in a breath. "I shouldn't have said wh—"

Her heart sped into overdrive as he leaned forward and braced a hand against the wall behind her, his intent, purposeful look stopping the breath in her chest.

"Add the yoga idea to the deck, Bailey. Blow it out big and make it sing. And don't ever, *ever* run a strategy by a client without my approval first. Or you'll have the shortest tenure an executive at Stone Industries has ever seen."

He had removed his hand from the wall, stepped back and slammed his way into his room before her breath started moving again. She stood there, frozen for about five good seconds, then closed the door behind her. She backed up against the wood frame and finally let a triumphant smile curve her lips.

She had won. She had forced Jared Stone to acknowledge her ideas had merit. Not only had merit—they were going to present them to Davide Gagnon.

The smile faded from her lips, adrenaline pounding through her, licking at her nerve endings. Just now, outside that door, for a split second, she'd been convinced Jared was going to kiss her. Worse, for a fraction of that second, she had been unbearably excited by the idea.

Pulling in a breath, she wiped the back of her hand against her mouth. Since when had she become a fan of Russian roulette? Because surely that's what tonight had been.

With her own career at stake.

She might want to start thinking up alternative strategies.

CHAPTER FOUR

BAILEY WOKE UP full of "piss and vinegar" as her mother would have said, ready to attack the presentation, slot in her yoga idea and rehearse it until it sparkled. She pulled on shorts and a knit top, her mouth curving at the thought of her colorful mother. She may have limited her exposure to the family who'd turned her out when she'd started dancing, *stripping* as her father had bitingly referred to it, but it didn't mean she didn't have *some* good memories of her childhood.

She'd often spent Saturdays sitting on one of the worn, ripped leather chairs in her mother's hair salon rather than face the uncertain mood of her father—who could be even-keeled if he hadn't drunk too much that day, or downright mean if he had. She'd finish her homework, then sit fascinated as her mother's less-than-polished clientele talked about men, other women in an often catty fashion and anything else on their mind they felt needed to be aired. Eye-opening and illuminating conversation for a ten-year-old, to be certain. She'd made sure she didn't miss one juicy detail.

Unfortunately the glow hadn't lasted. As she'd gotten older, it was her mother's quietness she'd noticed. How she would listen but not talk much. Smile but not really. And she'd wondered if her mother knew what *she* knew. That her husband was not only a violent drunk who couldn't get over the loss of his high school football glory, but he'd also been unfaithful to her while on the road selling vacuum cleaners across the state. Bailey had answered one too many phone calls at home while her mother was working from a supposed "customer" named Janine not to put two and two together when her father subsequently ordered her out of the room and a hushed conversation ensued.

As a teenager, the glow had disappeared completely. What did it matter if her mother treated her to hot rollers on Saturday, if on Monday the clothes you wore to school were falling apart? When no one wanted to hang out with you because you were the epitome of poor *uncool?*

The memories floated in the window of her beautiful Cap-Ferrat suite, in blinding contrast to her current circumstances. She pressed her lips together, secured her hair in an elegant pile on top of her head, a hairstyle her mother would have called "hoity-toity," then made her way downstairs to join Davide and Jared in the breakfast room. The two men were discussing a trip into Nice to visit an art gallery. Davide stood, brushed a kiss across both of her cheeks and held a chair out for her. "Would you like to come with us, *ma chère?* The Chagalls are phenomenal."

"It's tempting," she responded, taking a seat. "But no thank you, I have work to do."

Jared murmured a greeting. She slid him a wary glance as she reached for the coffeepot. He was freshly shaven and annoyingly edible in a pair of jeans and a T-shirt that hugged his muscular chest and shoulders in all the right places. And more relaxed this morning if the softer edges of his face were anything to go by. She poured herself a full cup of the strong French brew. He'd probably been up at five doing his Buddhist meditation thing. Rumor had it he'd spent three months as a college dropout in India studying with a Zen master, and practiced it regularly. She'd even heard some of the engineers moan that Jared was on another tangent with his simplicity-inspired principles and they might never leave the lab with an end product if he didn't back off.

She removed her gaze from all that drool-inducing masculinity and focused on buttering a croissant. Rule number one when it came to her new strategy of handling Jared. No drooling. At all. Ignore him completely.

He and Davide took off to Nice in one of the Frenchman's vintage sports cars. Seduced by the spray of the waves and the chance to be outdoors, Bailey settled herself on one of the terraces overlooking the ocean, slid on some sunscreen and set to work building her slides.

By early afternoon, she had fleshed out her ideas into a compelling global strategy to catch consumers where they spent their free time. The kiosks to sell Stone Industries' wearable technologies—pulse monitors, odometers, fitness watches—onsite at yoga studios was only the first niche she was proposing. She added in examples of other health and fitness environments it could replicated in, reviewed the slides, then called it done with a satisfied nod.

This was her chance to shine. She'd forced Jared's hand in allowing her to include her ideas, now she had to make them worthy.

Turning her face up to the sun, she allowed herself a bit of downtime until the men came back.

Jared returned from Nice in his best mood of the week. He had bonded with Davide over their mutual love of art and managed to convince him that no, he was not dangling over the side of a cliff at Stone Industries with the board ready to cut him loose. He had also gone a long way to convincing him that there was little danger of long-term fallout from his manifesto with female consumers. People had short memories. Stone Industries would come out with its next big product and women would flock to it for its cool factor as they always did. And all of this would be a blip on the radar of a soon-to-be successful partnership.

The only thing that *was* messing with his superior mood was the email he'd gotten from his head of IT earlier this morning about the leak of his manifesto. It had literally stopped him in his tracks to discover after a cyber-chase of epic proportions, the email hack had been traced to the servers of Craig International. Which could only mean that Michael Craig, one of his most vocal critics on the Stone Industries board, was behind it. Had meant to bury him at a time of weakness. And for that, he decided, mouth set, stomach hard, as he went outside in search of Bailey, he would pay richly. He had never liked or trusted Michael Craig, had never felt they were playing on the same team. He would use this opportunity to get rid of him.

A growl escaped his throat as he headed toward the ocean-side terrace. You didn't mess with a man's lifeblood. That was way, way over the line.

He found Bailey on the terrace in a sun chair, laptop on her thighs, eyes closed, face turned up to the sun. Davide had gone on about how much he liked her on the drive to Nice. Not surprising after last night, but what *had* caught him off guard was that the collector of women, who'd lost his wife to illness at forty-five, had been focused not on Bailey's looks, but on her intelligence. Her creativity. He loved her—that much was obvious.

His mouth twisted as he surveyed her deceptively re-laxed pose on the lounger, long legs kicked out in front of her. He had no doubt her mind was going a mile a minute under those closed lids. That she wasn't sleeping but strat-egizing. And a sour feeling tugged at his gut. He'd side-lined her. Put her aside as a problem he didn't have time to deal with when it was his attraction to her that had been the issue all along. It wasn't like him to put the personal before business, and he hated that he had.

She opened her eyes, the wariness he'd witnessed this morning making a reappearance. "Did you have a good trip?"

"I did." He sank into the chair opposite her and poured himself a glass of her mineral water. "I owe you an apology."

Her eyes rounded. "For what?"

"For underestimating you. For letting you languish in a role that was beneath you."

She pushed herself up in the chair, her gaze meeting his. "We haven't done the presentation yet."

"I've seen your ideas." He took a long swallow of the water and sat back, resting the glass on his thigh. "I was wrong about you. I should have given you a voice." He lifted his shoulders. "Maybe you were right last night. Maybe my judgment has been off. It's been a David-and-Goliath battle with the board."

She pushed her finger into her cheek, a slow smile curving her lips. "I think I'm just going to say thank you and leave it at that. Are you sure you're feeling all right?"

A wry smile edged his mouth. "As a matter of fact, I am. You got me thinking last night. In a good way."

A frown marred her brow. "I might have been a bit harsh."

He shrugged. "I needed to hear it. I haven't had any time to think lately, and that's when I get myself into trouble."

She pointed toward her computer screen. "Want to see my slides?"

He nodded. "I've heard Alexander is a stickler for detail. He likes to wade into the minutiae—a bit of a control freak. So I want to ensure all our ducks are in order."

They went through the slides. He loved the way she'd laid them out, made a few suggestions of his own, and in a feat that could be classified as the eighth wonder of the world, they did a perfect run-through.

Satisfied the presentation was as smooth and as flawless as it was going to get, he challenged Bailey to a tennis game. She wasn't half bad. What she lacked in skill, she made up for in determination. Which seemed to be her modus operandi. She'd used the incredibly sharp brain she'd been born with, worked brutally hard and taken herself places.

He studied her as he waited for her to serve, concentration written across her face. Pictured her slugging it out at the local café, serving coffee all evening to put herself through school. Selling fifty pairs of shoes a day at the local mall to secure her future. And he couldn't help but admire her.

There was a lot of substance to Bailey St. John.

Bailey was still on a high when she pulled on white capri jeans, a body-hugging tank and a gauzy sheer blouse over it for their dinner at sea. Alexander Gagnon, Maison Electronique's director of international development and soon-to-be CEO, had flown in by helicopter while she'd been showering, the whir of the blades deafening as he'd touched down with two of Maison's other senior marketing staff. Tonight they would get to know the three executives over dinner on Davide's yacht, in a trip up the coast to Cannes. And tomorrow they would present their ideas to the group.

Much more comfortable with the intimate choice of setting this evening, Bailey slipped on strappy, glittery sandals, spritzed on a headier perfume for nighttime and met Jared *outside* his door. A slow smile curved his mouth when he opened it, denting his cheeks with those to-die-for almost-dimples. "You aren't going to let me pick your shoes?"

She resolutely ignored the sexy indentations. "I had it under control tonight."

His gaze swept over her, smooth and all-encompassing. "You look like you're channeling Grace Kelly."

She shifted her weight to the other foot. "I'll take that as a compliment."

The hand he placed at her back to ostensibly guide her down the hallway burned into her skin. "Do that," he murmured, bending so his softly spoken words rasped across the sensitive skin behind her ear. He looked pretty gorgeous himself in casual black pants and a short-sleeved dark blue shirt that made the most of his eyes. But she'd keep that to herself.

A small powerboat was waiting at the dock to take them out to the yacht. All the others were already on board, the crew member told them, firing the motor. Bailey took it all in, eyes wide. Growing up on a swamp in Florida, she'd been around boats her whole life. She'd seen the cruise ships lined up in Tampa when they'd visited the city. But that was a world away from this. Davide's yacht was at least seventy feet in length, they were about to cruise to Cannes during film festival time, and it frankly seemed unreal.

As they neared the sleek yacht painted in the blue, white and red colors of the French flag, the powerboat slowed to a crawl. They pulled alongside the yacht and were helped aboard by crew members. The rosy sky descended low over them, the lights of Saint-Jean-Cap-Ferrat twinkling from the shore as she stood looking back from the deck. It was glorious.

Davide greeted them, then turned to introduce them to the three men beside him. She greeted the two marketing executives who had flown in from Paris, then Alexander Gagnon, a tall, distinguished male with dark hair and cold-as-flint gray eyes.

Her pulse flatlined as Alexander stepped forward. She teetered on her sandals and would have stumbled backward if Jared hadn't placed a hand to her back and steadied her. *It couldn't be. It could not be.*

Her gaze moved over him, hungry to prove herself wrong. But the cold, hard eyes that had studied her, eaten her up with an unflinching need to have her those nights in Vegas almost ten years ago, were unmistakable. And he didn't miss a beat.

"How lovely to meet you...*Bailey*," he murmured, taking her hand to brush a kiss across her knuckles. "Alexander Gagnon."

Her breath constricted in her chest, a solid lump that threatened to choke her. She had never told him her real name. Had never told any of the men she danced for her real name. And now he knew it. She registered the fact with the almost hysterical need to turn around, jump off the boat and swim for shore.

Whether her body actually turned in that direction or whether Jared felt the shudder that went through her at the touch of Alexander Gagnon's lips on her skin, she wasn't sure. He released her for a moment to shake the other man's hand, then returned his palm to her back and kept it there. Alexander's gaze tracked the movement, then moved back to her face.

"I'm looking forward to your presentation tomorrow," he drawled. "Davide has been telling me about your great ideas."

Bailey's knees were shaking so hard she had to lean into Jared to keep herself upright. She felt his gaze hard on her, but kept hers focused straight ahead. Alexander was staring at her, waiting for a response. "Yes, well, we—" she stumbled "—we're hoping you'll like them."

"We know you'll *love* them," Jared corrected firmly, his palm pressing into her spine.

Alexander's lips twisted in a smile that didn't quite reach his eyes. "I've spent some time in the States. Davide mentioned you did your MBA at Stanford," he said to Bailey. "Where did you do your undergrad?"

He knew exactly where she'd done her undergrad. A fine sheen of perspiration broke out on her brow. Her voice dry, more gravelly than she'd ever heard it, she forced out, "At UNLV."

He snapped his fingers. "That must be it. I feel we've met before, but I can't place it. I've entertained a lot of clients in Vegas."

Every muscle in her body froze. The dark glitter in his eyes chilled her to the bone. "You must be mistaken," she rasped, finding her voice. "I'm quite sure we've never met."

Gauntlet laid, she lifted her chin. Alexander inclined his head. "My mistake, then."

She let out the breath she'd been holding. Requested a martini for the pure, unadorned hit of alcohol it would provide. Jared leaned down to her. "What is *wrong* with you?"

"I'm just not feeling...quite right."

His penetrating blue gaze ate through her. "A martini might not be the best thing, then. Let me get you some water."

"I'm fine," she said sharply. "It's probably just the boat. I'll get over it."

The martini helped. She sipped it, feeling the alcohol inject itself into her bloodstream, bite into the unreality gripping her. She had to find a way through this that didn't involve jumping off the boat and getting as far away from that man as she could. She had to pull herself together. *But how?* He had definitely recognized her. Her mind riffled through the options, desperately, not entirely clearly. She had to continue to pretend she'd never met him. Treat him as if he was just a business acquaintance. But it was just her luck that Alexander was seated across from her at dinner. And the red shirt he had on made it impossible to forget the last time she'd seen him.

She'd danced in her signature red lace dress and underwear as Kate Delancy that night at the Red Room—the highest-end strip club in Vegas, legendary for its beau-tiful women and sumptuous interiors. To wear red and dance last meant she was the owner's favorite, the most requested dancer of the week. Which wasn't unusual for her. She pulled in a ton of regulars who came to see her cool, untouchable beauty uncovered; to watch the sensual, erotic transformation unfold.

None of them could have known it was all an act for their benefit. That it was as far from the real Bailey as you could get.

Alexander Gagnon had sat in the front row that night. As he had every night for the past three. She'd felt his eyes on her, dark and unmoving. Despite the fact that there had been at least a hundred and fifty other men in the club, she had only been conscious of him. Of the tall, dark figure who had approached her each night to have a drink with him and whom she'd turned down flat despite the money he'd thrown at her, because there was something about the exquisitely dressed stranger with his thousand-dollar ties that said red light to her.

That night she had retreated to the dressing room, strangely affected by the intensity of the experience. The magnitude of the tip Alexander had left her. Her fellow dancers had showered and dressed in a mad rush to hit the town. Since she'd just been heading home to study for an exam the next day, Bailey had taken her time, sat at her dressing table and removed her thick, dramatic makeup. At some point she'd looked up to find the tall dark stranger standing inside the doorway. That all the other girls had gone. If you were to look past the dangerous edge to him that smoldered just below the surface, she would have called him inordinately handsome. Distinguished. But all she could smell was the scent of her own fear as she got to her feet, heart pounding.

"You can't be in here."

He'd lifted a brow. "Bruno owes me one. He gave us five minutes."

Her manager had let him in? "Get out."

He'd leaned back against the doorway, his gaze moving over her so slowly, so assessingly, she'd had to fight the urge to pull the edges of her blouse together. "After I give you my proposition, *Kate*."

She should have walked to the door then and had him thrown out, but she'd been afraid of him.

"You've rejected my requests to join me for a drink three nights in a row," he'd murmured, eyes glittering as he pushed away from the door and walked toward her. "I figured I'd try another strategy." She'd backed up until her behind was against the dressing table, trying hard not to show her fear. "I know you're a student, Kate. I'm offering you fifty thousand dollars for a night. Any hard limits, I'll respect them."

She had stared at him, shocked. Shocked that anyone would pay that much for a night with someone. Shocked that that person would be *her*. She was the woman men shoved money at in a dirty, covetous thrill. Not a high-priced escort.

For a second, for one split second, it had crossed her mind that fifty thousand dollars would cover her tuition and living expenses for the year. She could spend the days going to school and studying like a normal student. She wouldn't have to be exhausted all the time turning her nights and days upside down…snatching a couple hours' study before she passed out at night. She could leave the backbreaking pain of her four-inch heels behind. Just like that.

Then hot shame had flooded through her. *How could she even be considering it?*

She'd pointed to the door. "Get the hell out of my dressing room."

He'd just stood there. "Everyone has a price, Kate. Name it."

"That's where you're wrong." She'd walked past him to the door and flung it open. "I don't."

He must have seen the hatred burning in her eyes, because he'd left. Afterward, Bruno had denied involvement, then had been fired a few weeks later for stealing money from the club.

Alexander Gagnon had shown up for the next two nights to see if she'd changed her mind. It had been the hardest two nights of her working career, her ability to concentrate nonexistent.

"Bailey?"

Davide was frowning, eyeing her plate. "You didn't enjoy your meal?"

She looked up to see the waitstaff hovering by her side, ready to remove the seafood salad sitting practically untouched in front of her. "I'm so sorry," she murmured. "I'm just a little off."

"Perhaps you got too much sun today," he suggested in French. "You are so fair."

"Perhaps," she agreed. "I'm sure I'll be fine after a good night's sleep."

Jared hadn't taken his eyes off her the entire meal. It could have been because she didn't seem able to add any intelligent insights to the conversation, or alternatively, *ask* any valuable questions. Either way, it felt hard to breathe and she needed to escape.

She excused herself and made a beeline for the ladies' room. It was downstairs, off the opulent drawing room, done in royal-blue marble with gold accents. She pulled in some deep breaths, splashed water on her ashen face, then pressed one of the thick, luxurious hand towels to her face.

Could a nightmare actually come to life? Because this was hers...

She applied some lipstick and pinched her cheeks to give them color, but she still looked deathly pale as she left her sanctuary and headed back upstairs. She had just stepped on deck when Alexander cut her off at the pass.

"You've done well for yourself, Bailey." He leaned his arm on the railing and blocked the way back to the others. "Or should I say Kate? What *is* your real name?"

Bailey gave him a blank look, fighting to keep her composure. "I'm afraid I have no idea what you're talking about."

"You think I don't remember you?" He rested his gaze on her face, as chilling and unnerving as it had been that night he'd sat in the audience watching her. "I remember every curve, every dip of your mind-blowing body. How you seduced every man in that room and left them begging for more."

A fresh wave of perspiration broke out on her brow. "You have the wrong woman," she rasped. "And this is not at all appropriate."

"I don't think I do." He pushed away from the railing and took the last couple of steps toward her. Bailey's heart knocked against her ribs. A cool Mediterranean breeze flitted over her but she felt vaguely feverish. "I saw it on your face that night. You wanted to say yes."

"I don't know you," she bit out and started to brush by him. He curled his fingers around her arm and brought her to a halt.

"They don't know, do they?" His smoky gaze heated with challenge. "You've moved on. Gone to a great deal of trouble to put your past behind you…"

Yes. And she wasn't going back there now.

"Get your hands off her, Gagnon."

Jared's low, menacing command came from behind them. She twisted around and found him watching them, hands clenched by his sides, tall, lean body coiled like a cat ready to pounce. Her heart zigzagged across her chest, threatening to explode right out of it. *God, no. He couldn't know about this.*

Alexander lifted his hand from her arm and stepped back. "Cool your jets, Stone. We were just having a conversation."

Jared took a step closer until he was toe-to-toe with Alexander. "I don't particularly like the nature of it. And neither does Bailey from the looks of it. So perhaps we should all return to the table for dessert?"

Alexander stared him down, just for the fun of it, Bailey guessed semi-hysterically. Her airways seemed closed to oxygen. Alexander lifted his hands in the air. "Beautiful, isn't she? Can't blame you. Ask her about the sexy mole on her hip, Stone. It's quite something...or maybe you already know that?"

Bailey's heart sank into the deck. A trickle of perspiration rolled down her neck as Alexander turned and sauntered off. *He had not just said that.*

Jared's gaze moved over her face. It was the stillness, the absolute stillness about him that got to her. "What is he talking about, Bailey? And how do you know him?"

She shook her head, in full denial. "I don't know him." And that was true. She didn't know anything about him. *Except he was now the key player who would decide their fate in the biggest deal of her life. Of Jared's life.*

Jared stepped closer to her. "Then why are you white as a ghost? Why have you been off since the moment you saw him?"

Her brain swirled in a desperate attempt to make this go away. Heart thumping painfully hard against her chest, she looked up at him. "He is an obnoxious jerk who has mistaken me for someone else. I am not good with boats, Jared. Never have been. And I don't want to make it an issue for Davide, who has been kind enough to take us on this lovely sail. So I think we should get back to the others before he worries."

She brushed past him before he could stop her and headed back to the table where dessert was being served. Somehow she managed to spoon a few mouthfuls of the undoubtedly delicious chocolate mousse into her mouth. But she tasted nothing. How could she when the world felt as if it was unraveling around her?

Alexander's cool, unruffled composure across the table was utterly unnerving. As if they'd been trading old war stories rather than him throwing her past in her face.

The night thankfully ended an hour later when Davide, she figured, took pity on her and suggested they do a final nightcap back at the villa. He insisted she rest rather than join them, and Bailey didn't protest. She brushed off Jared's intention to walk her to her room. "I'm fine."

He came anyway, wearing a frown.

"I'll be back to check on you," he said when they'd reached her room, planting a hand against the wall and looking her over. "Are you sure you're okay?"

"I'm fine." She pressed a hand to her pounding head, which was making her feel distinctly nauseous now. "Don't bother. I'll be asleep."

He stared her down. "I'll be back in half an hour."

Bailey forced some painkillers down her throat with a glass of water and paced her beautiful, airy suite. The more she paced, the more her head pounded. The two lives she'd so carefully kept light-years apart for so long had just crashed together with debilitating consequences. And the chances she was going to be able to keep them apart any longer were slim. Alexander Gagnon had offered her fifty thousand dollars to sleep with him almost ten years ago. And now she had to face him, *to pitch to him* over a boardroom table?

What if she had to work with him afterward?

The trails of perspiration rolling down her nape made her feel hot, feverish. She had not spent years of her life building her reputation in the business world to let a man like Alexander Gagnon destroy it. To assume he knew what she was when she wasn't anything like that.

I remember every curve, every dip of your mind-blowing body. How you seduced every man in that room and left them begging for more...

Alexander's words, cutting, accusatory, washed over her. Suddenly she felt dirty, so dirty. Hands shaking, she ripped off her jeans and tops. Found her bathing suit, threw it on and took the back stairs to the beach. The sea was dark and strewn with moonlight. The surf was up, eating into the sand with swift currents. She ignored how the darkness made it look dangerous, walked into it and struck out to a place unknown. To a place where the past couldn't find her.

Jared knocked on Bailey's door forty-five minutes later. He'd nursed a final brandy with Davide and the others, fought the urge to put his fist through Alexander Gagnon's face and ultimately restrained himself. He didn't believe Bailey for a second when she'd said she didn't know him. She'd had a violent reaction the minute she'd seen him. He'd *felt* it.

They don't know, do they? You've moved on. Gone to a great deal of trouble to put your past behind you.

What had Gagnon been talking about?

He knocked again on the door, his mouth tightening. *Nothing.* He waited five more seconds, knocked again and turned the knob. The door was open, a table lamp flooding the drawing room with light. No Bailey. He strode across the room, pushed her bedroom door open and saw the bed hadn't been touched. Her clothes were lying in a heap on the floor, which raised his antennae because Bailey was obsessively, compulsively neat.

He walked out onto the floodlit terrace and found it empty. Scanning the grounds, he searched for her. On the beach below a flash of white in the water caught his eye. Bailey's pale skin in the moonlight. *There*. He stripped off his shoes and socks and went after her.

She was so far out in the waves, he almost dived in fully clothed. But her pace was steady and her strokes sure, so he waited her out instead, his heels sinking into the sand. When she reached shore, she headed toward her towel, not fifteen feet from him, but she didn't notice him at all.

He allowed himself to enjoy the view while she toweled off. He'd had his fair share of women in his life. Some would say gone through them much more carelessly than a man should. But he'd never seen a woman look so utterly...goddess-like in a bathing suit.

The spotlights on the beach rendered those never-ending legs of hers a work of art. The product of gently rolling hips, they were slim enough to look delicate, curved enough to be irresistible. His hungry gaze moved upward, over her slim waist and more than ample chest, the perfection of which made his mouth go dry. She might not be a D cup, but she was exquisite.

She reached up and pulled her hair back into a ponytail, squeezing the water from it. It threw her delicate, unforgettable beauty into perfect spotlight. She looked untouchable...*haunted*.

It reminded him why he was here. He started toward her. She bent over to dry her calves. Her mouthwatering backside was not something to be missed. The round, dark mark on the curve of her buttock wasn't either. He froze. It was unmistakably a mole. A mole Alexander Gagnon knew intimately enough to call out.

He was across the sand and in her face so fast it made

his own head spin. Bailey looked up, her pale face catching the moonlight. Her hands slapped the towel around her hips but he was faster, spinning her around and pointing at the mark.

"You lied to me," he snarled. "You don't know him but he knows about intimate marks on your body? What exactly is going on?"

She tried to twist out of his hold, but he was stronger, his fingers digging into her upper arms. Her eyes flashed dark, almost gray in the moonlight, contrasting with her chalk-white cheeks. "Get your hands off me, Jared. Or are you no better than him?"

He let her go then, fury singeing his nerve endings. "We are negotiating a deal worth tens of millions of dollars a year, Bailey. I want the truth and I want it *now*."

She took a step back. Wrapped her arms around herself. "I told you the truth. I don't *know* him. I met him once when I lived in Vegas. He came on to me, I turned him down. That's it."

"That's it?" He slapped his palms against his temples, biting out a curse. Seconds passed, three, maybe four. Then he pinned his gaze on her face. "How did he know about the mole if you turned him down?"

She went even paler. "There's nothing further you need to know that has anything to do with this deal." Her chin came up. "That's all I'm answering and this conversation is done."

His blood fired. Raced in his veins. And he realized his fury had nothing to do with the deal. He wanted to know why that snake had an intimate knowledge of Bailey's behind. "I don't think so." He took a step closer, and this time she didn't back up. She stood her ground, eyes flashing. "You turn every man in Silicon Valley down. You act like you are untouchable…and yet that arrogant jerk, *known for his womanizing*, has had his hands on you… I don't get it."

She stepped up to him, her heat fusing with his until they were in danger of a spontaneous combustion. "What's the matter, Jared? You can't stand that it wasn't you? That Mr. Manifesto has met his match?"

He raked his gaze over her. "You know what, Bailey? You're right. I can't. Because if it had been me, you wouldn't have walked away."

She opened those luscious lips of hers to say something not very nice. He kissed her before she made it there. And by God, she was the sweetest female he'd ever tasted. Hot, honeyed perfection he savored for about two seconds before she raised her hand to slap him. He caught it in his and slid his other behind her nape, tangling it in her wet hair. Changed the kiss into a persuasive, seductive assault on her senses. The kind that always, without fail, worked.

Bailey wanted to fight but somewhere along the way, somewhere along the edges of the soul-destroying assault Jared was laying on her, she found escape. *Needed* it.

When he cupped the back of her head and angled her to take the kiss deeper, she let him. Moaned her approval when he brought his tongue into play and stroked her deeply. He smelled insanely good and he tasted better. Of cognac and expensive cigars. And she wanted more of him. A lot more.

He muttered something under his breath. Slid his hard thigh between her wet, shaking ones and brought her closer. So close his heart pounded beneath her palm. His hand at her back dragged her against his chest, urged her softness against his hardness. Her cool, air-tightened nipples brushed against him through the fine material of his shirt, and the heat that flooded her core came hot and hard. Like nothing she'd ever felt before.

He cursed again and dragged his mouth down the column of her throat, pressing openmouthed kisses against her damp skin. "Bailey," he breathed. "Who is he to you?"

Reality hit her like the hard slap of the night waves to her face. He wasn't kissing her because he wanted her. He was kissing her because he wanted to *possess* her. *Just like all the others.*

She sank a palm into his chest and pushed. Caught off guard, he stumbled backward. His gaze flew to hers. "What the—?"

"You are all dogs," she hissed, legs spread wide, feet planted in the sand. "Fighting over what you want. What you think is yours."

He gave her wild-eyed look a wary glance. "You were as into that kiss as I was."

Her elegant blond brows came together. "And now I'm walking away. *Again.* You were wrong, Jared. You aren't any different than the rest of them. You're all the same."

She left him standing there, staring after her, his jaw practically on the ground. Why was she always thinking Jared was different when he so categorically wasn't? Maybe *she* was the one losing her sense of judgment.

CHAPTER FIVE

JARED HAD RUN the path around the rocky beaches of the Cap for fifty minutes before he gave up trying to figure out what had happened last night and pulled up into a walk, sweat dripping from his chin. Given the lack of information coming from Bailey, the only thing that *was* clear was that Alexander Gagnon, Davide's heir apparent and the man who would own the decision as to whether to link Stone Industries and Maison Electronique in a five-year strategic partnership, knew his CMO intimately enough to call out a mole on her behind.

The thought had his already-pumping blood charging through his veins. He scowled and swiped his T-shirt over his face. Bailey had said she'd met Gagnon once, he'd propositioned her, and she'd turned him down. So how would he know about the mole? *And why, in God's name, was that a more pressing question for him than what he was going to do about the changing dynamics of this deal and the impact on his future?*

He let out a colorful curse and raked his T-shirt over his face again. Why wouldn't Bailey tell him the truth? What could be so horrible about her past that she couldn't tell him? That Alexander would call her on? He'd seen that look before, the one on Bailey's face last night. It was the exact same one his father had worn when the hounds had closed in. When his inability to escape had become inevitable—when all of his carefully constructed lies had started to unravel.

His chest tightened. He did not tolerate secrets. What he *should* do was march up there and tell Bailey she either came clean or she was out. There was too much riding on this pitch…this deal, not to have complete transparency. But the fact was, she was his ace in the hole. Davide loved her and her ideas. So eliminating her from the pitch was a nonstarter.

A massive bird of prey flew in from the sea, its wingspan at least eight or nine feet across. His gaze followed it as it arced and headed inland. A vulture? It reminded him of Alexander the way he'd tracked Bailey with his eyes last night. It had been beyond the look men had when they coveted something. It had been something else entirely…

He turned toward the house, his mouth twisting in a grimace. He'd been right from the beginning. The mystery that was Bailey had a history. A history that could blow the lid off this deal if he didn't find out what it was and defuse it. *Now.*

He made his way up the stairs toward their rooms, refusing to let himself address the other lethal ingredient flavoring the situation: the heat that had exploded between them last night. It was one thing to acknowledge an attraction. Another thing entirely to act on it. Because when the cat was out of the bag, it was all too easy to do it again.

Out of the question.

He let himself into his room, picked up his cell phone and dialed the PI he used to track his father, just to make sure he was alive, every now and again.

Danny Garrison picked up after almost seven rings with a sleepy, "'Lo?"

"I need you to dig up everything you can on my CMO, Bailey St. John."

There was a rustling sound in the background. "You do realize at some point I do go off the clock?"

He looked at his watch on the bedside table. Eight a.m. He hadn't even thought about the time difference. "Sorry. But I need this yesterday."

"Considering it *is* yesterday for me,, no problem." Sarcasm dripped from his PI's voice.

"Focus on her time in Vegas. She went to school there."

"Am I looking for anything in particular?"

Jared stared out at the cerulean-blue sky. At the vulture that had looped back over the seashore looking for breakfast.

"Something she'd want to hide."

Bailey shrugged out of an orchid-pink silk shirt, her third choice thus far, and tossed it on the bed. Nothing, *nothing* felt right about this presentation happening in thirty minutes. Nothing had since she'd laid eyes on Alexander Gagnon and realized it was *him*.

She snatched the pewter-gray version of the same shirt off a hanger and tugged it on. She needed to walk into that room today and nail the presentation. Forget the past and focus on the future. But her churning stomach wasn't cooperating.

Her hands fumbled as she pulled the shirt closed and did up the tiny pearl buttons. Would Alexander play nice? And if he didn't was she now playing Russian roulette with Jared's future? With this deal? Could she afford to do that? Should she just pull herself out now and accept the fact that her past had caught up with her? Do the right thing?

Her fingers tripped over the buttons, making her curse and focus her concentration. Surely Alexander had better things to do than focus on a bruised ego. He had a major directional partnership to consider for Maison. A company to take the helm of. He would be all business.

The knot in her stomach said differently.

Maybe Jared would fire her first for the inexcusable things she'd said and get it over with.

She shoved the last button through the slippery material with a vicious movement. How could she have kissed him? How could she have done that of all things? She didn't *feel* lust like that for men. Didn't let them close enough to even inspire it because her father had taught her that men were dangerous, unpredictable. Better avoided.

The arrival of their once-a-month welfare check had sent her father on his infamous benders like clockwork, typically ending with him trashing their house and whichever one of them had particularly annoyed him that day. Her mother had shielded them from him when she could, taking the punishment and sending her girls to the neighbors, but that had only made them feel worse when they'd arrived home the next day to a fresh set of bruises on their mother's face.

Add to that her experience as a dancer, and complete abstinence had been her solution.

A sharp knock on the connecting door brought her head around. She tucked a stray hair back in her chignon, turned and walked over to open it. Storm cloud Jared was in attendance today, his blue eyes crackling with electricity. *All business.*

"You ready?"

She nodded. "Let me get my notes."

Her prep stuff was in a pile on the desk. She'd left the notes on top, ready to grab, but last night in her agitation she'd thrown another pile on there and they didn't seem to be anywhere as she riffled through them, flicking pages upside down.

"Bailey." She hadn't realized he'd moved until he was beside her, his hand closing over hers. She looked up at him, teeth tugging at her bottom lip.

"They're right here, I just can't—"

"*Bailey.*" He took the papers out of her hands and put them down on the desk. "Tell me what's bothering you. Who is Alexander Gagnon to you? We are *partners* in this. I need to know what's wrong so we can handle it together."

She brought her back teeth together before she blew this entirely and pulled her hand free to continue searching for the notes. "He is nothing to me. I told you that."

"Then why are you a total disaster?"

"I am *not* a disaster." She rounded on him fiercely, eyes flashing. "This is personal, Jared, and I won't have it brought into this."

His mouth twisted. "Were you there last night? Because I was. Alexander is now the deciding voice in this deal. He did not take his eyes off you all night and then he followed you to the washroom where he was extremely confrontational. So don't tell me it's *nothing*, Bailey. He is an issue. And I won't have it affecting this deal."

She sank her hands into her hips. "Then pull me out."

"*I can't pull you out.* Davide adores you. He loves your thinking."

She pressed her lips together mutinously. She would rather *die* than tell Jared she'd been a stripper. A man who thought so little of women he'd written a manifesto about their place being in the bedroom. She could only *imagine* how derogatory he'd be. It made her stomach curl. As did the thought that he wouldn't want her anywhere near this deal.

He let out a muttered oath, his gaze on her face. "Tell me it wasn't something illegal. Whatever it is you're hiding."

Illegal? She stared at him in disbelief. *What the?* The flare of anxiety in his eyes, the frown furrowing his brow, made it hit home. His father. Of course he would be afraid of scandal.... Her stomach lurched dangerously.

She wanted to tell him, to reassure him it had everything to do with her, but she could not.

She put her hand on his arm, her gaze imploring him. "It's nothing like that. It's a personal matter Jared, that's all. You need to trust me on this."

He stared at her long and hard. As if he wasn't sure what to do with her. Then he let out a long breath. "Okay, this is how we're going to play it. We are going to walk into that room, blow them away with our ideas and win this contract. You are not going to be distracted. You are not going to address Alexander in any way, shape or form unless he asks you a question. Play to Davide, play to the other two. But do not let Alexander shake you."

Relief flooded through her. He wasn't going to push her. She could have kissed him except that had been a bad idea. "Got it," she said firmly. "You can trust me."

His gaze singed hers. "Too bad that doesn't go both ways."

She shook her head. "It does, I swear it. This is just... different."

The furrow in his brow deepened. "Someone's done a number on you, Bailey."

How about her life? Did that count?

He made a rough sound in his throat. "We have ten minutes. We should go set up."

She nodded and found her notes.

If Jared had expected Bailey to be shaky and off her game in the presentation, he was proven wrong. Something switched on in her brain when she walked into that room. Her survival instincts, he figured. She plowed through her slides with a steely determination and enthusiasm that made everyone at the table catch the spirit and engage. He watched that sharp brain of hers ignite, gather momentum as she fed off the feedback she was getting from the table and push her ideas to an even higher creative level. Not once did she look at Alexander, except to answer his pointed and often challenging questions.

His own strategies had been solid, but they had been lacking the marketing savvy Bailey possessed. Together they made a formidable team.

Don't fight the exodus from retail, she was counseling now, pointing at the screen. Touch consumers where they work and play, *show* them what they are missing in a lifestyle setting like a yoga studio that drives it home for them, then *sell* to them on the spot with the kiosks.

"Intriguing," Alexander conceded, "if a bit sacrilegious to a retailer like me. You're asking us to focus our marketing budget *outside* of the stores?"

"Some of it, yes," Bailey said, nodding. "It's a reality that people are moving away from brick-and-mortar retail to the online space. You need to get ahead of the trend now."

Alexander got to his feet and started pacing the room, a technique Jared figured he used to intimidate. "Yoga is niche, however. How is this really going to impact our bottom line?"

"You replicate it." Bailey flipped to her next slide. "You train demo staff, send them not just to yoga studios, but to running centers, health and wellness clinics, gyms... You seed the instructors first, make them fall in love with the product, and then you capture their students."

Alexander didn't look convinced. Bailey plunged on, undeterred. When she'd finished the last of the slides and Jared had closed with a "why Stone Industries" recap, they wrapped the presentation.

Davide looked at his son. "What do you think?"

"I like it," Alexander said, nodding. "I think the direct-to-consumer ideas are the strongest, they fit with our strategy, our target markets, but I am skeptical they can be rolled out on a large scale. And," he added, dropping a file folder on the table in front of Jared, "I *am* worried from this latest consumer research that you've alienated the target female consumer with your manifesto. You've dropped ten points in intent to buy with females since it happened."

Jared eyed the file in disbelief. "They'll be back up by next week. This is a flash in the pan." *And you know it.*

"Perhaps." Gagnon lifted a brow. "But the fact remains, the female demographic is our most important to capture right now. We can't afford to partner with a company that's alienated the market segment."

"It won't last," Jared repeated on a low growl.

"Likely not," Alexander agreed. "Your ideas are creative and sound. But I'm afraid I'm going to need market research to buy into them. So we're not all having a little enthusiasm party here that isn't based on reality."

Jared folded his hands in front of him, struggling to control his anger. "That will take time." He had a board meeting in two weeks he needed this deal signed, sealed and delivered for if he wanted to maintain control of his company.

Alexander shrugged. "We'd like you to repitch next week in Paris." He lifted a brow. "You're a busy man. If you have other engagements, send Bailey back to Paris with me. I can weigh in with what I know works and we can chew away at it."

Bailey turned gray. Jared's blood heated to a dangerous level. So *this* was Alexander's game? Taking care of unfinished business with Bailey? *Whatever that was...*

He looked at Davide but the Frenchman's expression was one of deference to his son. And Jared had nothing to work with but a botched attempt at humor instigated by a slightly wounded heart and a massive complication between his CMO and Maison's soon-to-be CEO.

He gathered the papers in front of him together with

a viciously efficient movement, refusing to let the fury simmering in his veins find an outlet. "That's very kind of you. But I have a friend with a villa on the outskirts of Nice. Bailey and I will regroup there, flesh the ideas out, and we'll present in Paris."

"I should add," Davide interjected, "that Alexander has indicated he'd like to hear from Gehrig Electronics as well."

Jared felt the earth tilt beneath his feet. "You're adding another company to the mix?"

Davide nodded. "We feel we need to do due diligence given some product launches we've been made aware of."

Due diligence. Jared felt the fumes rise off him. Gehrig hadn't been a factor until Alexander Gagnon arrived on the scene. His gaze flickered to Davide's son, sitting with his elbow on the table, jaw resting in his palm as he watched Jared with the intense interest of a hawk studying its prey. Davide had been right. His son liked to win. Except this had nothing to do with business and everything to do with Bailey.

Frustration clawed at him like a knife. He needed to be back in the States massaging an antsy board. But unless he wanted to muddy the waters with everything he *didn't* know, make accusations he wasn't sure of, he had no choice but to play along.

He forced what he was sure was a poor representation of a smile to his lips and stood up. "We totally understand. No problem, gentlemen. Let the best candidate win."

They answered a few more questions from the marketing team and made arrangements to pitch in Paris the week after. Then he and Bailey left to pack.

She stopped him outside their rooms, her hand on his arm, her face devoid of color. "I'm so sorry, Jared. This is my fault. I should have taken myself out of the deal."

He lifted his head. "You heard his reasons. He thinks I've alienated the female demographic."

"Yes, but—" She hesitated, worrying her lip between her teeth.

"He's playing games, yes," he growled. "We will talk more in Nice. *Much more,* Bailey. But if he wants to make this personal? Let him. I don't intend to lose."

CHAPTER SIX

BY DAY THREE in Nice, Jared was feeling good about the progress they'd made on the presentation. They were holed up in a villa in the hills overlooking the sea owned by one of his friends, where the outside world was a distant distraction and pretty much everything else could wait.

Bailey had been in charge of scaling the creative ideas and adding in the market research data Alexander had requested. Which had, thankfully, proved them extremely viable. Jared concentrated on countering the intent to purchase consumer data Alexander had magically come up with, while also carrying out a full analysis of their competition, Gehrig Electronics, to uncover weak spots they could exploit. Unfortunately, Gehrig was a strong prospect with a rich technological heritage, a company going through a hot streak. And consumers loved buzz.

He tossed his pen down on Hans's desk. They would beat Gehrig, because although the other manufacturer had good products coming, he had better ones. Inspired ones that would set the world on fire. And although he'd had a whole strategic plan in place to unveil those products to the world, maybe it was time to let the cat out of the bag.

He got up and walked over to the window that overlooked the terrace. Bailey was sitting in a lounge chair in the sunshine, bent over her computer, hard at work as she had been for the past three fifteen-hour days. Invaluable to him. *And his ticking time bomb all in one beautiful package.*

She wasn't talking. She refused to address Alexander when he brought him up. It was a problem.

His mobile pealed from the corner of the desk. He walked over and retrieved it. Sam Walters. *Great.*

"Sam." He cradled the phone to his ear as he sat down and swung his feet up onto the desk.

"You didn't call. What's going on with Maison? I'm getting all sorts of questions I can't answer."

Join the crowd. His jaw came together with a resounding crunch. "Davide's passed the decision to his son, Alexander, who will become CEO next year. Alexander has decided he needs to do due diligence and give Gehrig Electronics a shot at the partnership. We're revamping the presentation to pitch against them next week."

"*Gehrig?* I thought this was a one-horse race?"

"Not anymore. Apparently my manifesto has dropped our brand rating with female consumers."

There was a long pause. Jared sighed. "Don't say it, Sam."

"You know I have to…the next time you get inspired to philosophize, Jared…*don't*."

His lips twisted. "I would heartily agree with you, but that horse is out of the gate. Now we have to win."

"Yes, you do. You know I'm doing everything I can to shore things up for you until you get those products to market. But this will make a statement."

The muscles in his head clenched like a vise, a deep throb radiating through his skull. "I'm ultra-clear on this, Sam. Mea culpa, my mess. We will win. Meanwhile, let me know if you've got anything on Gehrig. I have a week to pull them apart."

"I'll make some calls."

"Thanks. Appreciate it."

"Jared?"

"Mmm?"

"You created Stone Industries. You're the only man who should be leading it. That's all the focus you need."

A smile curved his lips. "Thanks for having my back, Sam."

He put the phone down. Wondered what he would have done if he hadn't bumped into Sam at a start-up conference in the Valley and begun a lifelong friendship with the mentor who'd taken him under his wing when his father had gone AWOL. Who'd taught him that sometimes you *could* trust a person, that sometimes they *were* always there for you. And for a young, hotheaded Jared with an astronomically successful start-up on his hands, it had meant the difference between being a dot-com failure and the solid, profitable company Stone Industries was today.

An email brought his attention back to his computer screen. It was from his PI, Danny.

Bingo. Can I say, this one was my pleasure?

Why that made his insides twist, he didn't know. He opened the report, printed it and threw it in a folder. He also didn't know why he did that. Maybe he wanted to give Bailey a chance to tell him herself first. Maybe as he'd said from the beginning, trust was paramount to him. And maybe he knew what it was like to avoid the past because it only brought pain with it. And you couldn't change it no matter how much you wanted to.

Maybe he liked Bailey St. John far more than he was willing to admit.

Bailey was bleary-eyed by the time she dragged herself away from her computer to join Jared for dinner on the intimate little seaside terrace of the villa that overlooked the Mediterranean Sea. Smaller and cozier than Davide

Gagnon's showpiece of a home, it was luxurious but under-
stated. The kind of place you could hide away forever in.

If only she could.

She pushed her hair away from her face and took a long
sip of the full-bodied red Jared had unearthed from the
cellar. You didn't actually relax when your boss looked as
if he wanted to toss you off the cliff you were sitting on
into the glorious azure water below. When decisions you'd
made in the past suddenly seemed questionable when at
the time, they'd seemed like the only way out.

Jared topped up her glass and stood up. "We're taking a break from work tonight. Both our brains are fried."

True. She stifled a surge of relief as she surveyed him
in jeans and a navy T-shirt. Then thought maybe it was a
bad idea because work had meant there was no space in
her brain to remember *that kiss*.

"I think I might try to get some sleep," she demurred.
"I haven't been doing so much of that."

He stared her down. "I built a fire in the pit. Sky's perfect for star spotting."

"And here I did not figure you for a Boy Scout."

"The wood was there," he said drily. "I piled it up.
Come."

He picked up his glass and a blue folder he'd left on the
chair and started walking down the hill. Hadn't he said
no business? Maybe there was a detail he wanted to chew
over, and that was good because then they wouldn't be di-
verging into the personal and Jared wouldn't be prying for
information on Alexander Gagnon.

She stood up and followed him down to the fire pit with
her wine. A series of big boulders with flat surfaces had
been positioned around the pit to sit on. She lowered herself
on one and watched as Jared lit the paper and coaxed the
fire into a steady flame. "My father loved fires," he said.
"Used to see how big he could make them go."

"How old were you when your father embezzled the money?"

He glanced at her, his profile hard and unyielding in the firelight. "More questions while you remain a mystery?"

She lifted a shoulder. "You brought him up."

"I was in my second year of university."

"That's why you dropped out?"

"Yes." He walked around and agitated the logs with a stick. "My parents had been helping me. I couldn't afford it after we lost everything."

"What happened to your father when it was discovered he took the money?"

He put the stick down and came to sit beside her on a neighboring rock. "He went to jail for three years."

Oh. She'd wondered if the more lenient laws on white-collar crime had kept him out of jail. "What does he do now?"

He stretched his long legs out in front of him and looked into the fire. "While he was in jail, my mother divorced him and married the head of the European Central Bank. When my father got out, he disappeared. I had him traced to the Caribbean, where he's been living in a hut on the beach ever since."

Wow. She tried to digest it all. "Do you have any idea why he did it?"

His lip curled, emphasizing the rather dangerous-looking, twisting white scar that ran across it. "Why he stole money from his employer and his closest friends? I'd have to be a psychologist to diagnose, but it might have something to do with my mother. She bled him dry every day of his life. And it was still never enough."

She pulled in a breath. Well, there you go. When you had attitudes like his, they came from somewhere. "What do you mean, bled him dry?"

He looked back at the fire. "She didn't know when to

stop. My father made a fortune in investment banking, but you could tell in the later years, he was done. He needed a break. But she never let him back off. Their wealth defined her. When she couldn't flash the latest hundred-thousand-dollar Maserati in front of her friends, when my father failed to provide, she left." His jaw hardened as he turned to her. "And if you're going to ask what happened then, my father lost the plot completely. As in his mind."

She looked over at him in the silence that followed, as big as any she'd encountered. "Still? Is he still like that?"

He kept his gaze trained on the leaping flames. "I haven't talked to him in a long time. I don't know. I send him money every month and he takes it."

She stared at him. How hard that must have been. How much it must have hurt. His manifesto made so much sense to her all of a sudden.

"Not all women are like your mother, Jared. I'm not."

"See, here's where I'm having a problem with that, Bailey." His low, tight tone sent a frisson of warning dancing across her skin. "I don't even know who you are. I have a multimillion-dollar deal tangled up in a woman with a past that could bring it crashing down around us. And you won't talk."

She flinched. "I've told you all that's relevant."

"Now you're going to tell me the real story." He picked up the folder sitting beside him and waved it at her. "This is where it ends."

She stared at the folder, her heart speeding up. "What is that?"

"It's your past, Bailey. In one convenient little package."

He was holding it with his far hand, far enough out of her reach that she never could have gotten to it. But she realized that wasn't the exercise.

"Who did it?" she demanded quietly.

"My PI. And trust me when I say he didn't miss anything."

Her blood pounded in her veins. Suddenly she felt very, very light-headed. "Jared. I can't—"

"You can. I've just told you the whole sordid story of my family. Now it's your turn. I haven't read it, Bailey. This is your chance."

She watched with big eyes as he stood up, walked to the fire and threw the folder into the flames. It sparked and licked up the paper until it turned gray and curled in on itself. Just like her stomach.

He turned back to her and stuck his hands in his pockets.

"Who is Alexander Gagnon to you, Bailey? What does he have on you?"

The flames licking the folder engulfed the remainder in a fiery glow. His gesture wasn't lost on her. He was giving her a chance to tell her side of the story. To trust him as he'd trusted her from the beginning.

A clamminess invaded her palms, a by-product of her racing heart and the adrenaline surging through her. A million thoughts filled her head. But in the end it came down to the truth.

"I met Alexander Gagnon when he came to my show at the Red Room in Las Vegas."

"The *Red Room*? Isn't that a strip joint?"

"That's right." She met his gaze. "I was a high-class stripper, Jared. I made oodles of money taking off my clothes for men."

His Adam's apple bobbed as if he was going to say something. His lips pursed as words formed, then he stopped, stared at her and waved a hand. "Go on."

She let her lashes drift down over her eyes. "When I was seventeen, I snuck into Tampa with a girlfriend of mine. We were hanging out in the big city, loitering on the street with pretty much nothing in our pockets, when a girl came up to me, a dancer from the hottest nightclub in the city. She told me I should apply for a job there. That I could make good money."

She twisted her hands in her lap and stared down at them. "You have to understand we were dirt-poor, my family. My father was an alcoholic, was off the job more than he was on. My mother was doing all she could to make ends meet, but her hair salon wasn't bringing in much. So when that girl—when she told me how much money I could make dancing, I was flabbergasted. I had dance training. It was one of the few things I was able to do because the local teacher let me study without paying because she thought I had potential."

He blinked. "So you started stripping?"

She nodded. "I made more money in a week dancing than my mother made in a month cutting hair. I took it home, paid for things. But when my father found out what I was doing, he hit the roof." Her mouth turned down. "They weren't making ends meet. My sister had no clothes but my money was *dirty* money. So he kicked me out."

A frown creased his forehead. "How old were you?"

"Seventeen. And believe me," she said bitterly, "nothing was ever so good. My father was not a nice drunk."

His gaze darkened. "God, Bailey, you were a baby. How were you even allowed to be in a bar?

"I lied. Got a fake ID."

He sat down beside her, rested his elbows on his knees and pressed his hands to his temples. "So you move from Tampa to Vegas where you go to school? And you keep stripping?"

"I moved there *to* dance. To pay my way through school. The money is fantastic in Vegas if you know what you're doing. I danced at a couple of different clubs, learned the industry, then I landed a slot at the Red Room. Every girl wanted to work there. It was very burlesque in the way we did the shows, they had the most beautiful women, and it was where all the high rollers hung out. I made a ton of money, easily paid for school every year."

He scrunched his face up. "Didn't it bother you the way men looked at you?"

"Like I belonged in the *bedroom?*" She threw his words back at him with a lift of her chin. "It was a job, Jared. Like any other occupation. I went to work, made a lot of money and got out when I could."

"You took your clothes off in front of strangers. That is not a normal job."

Heat rose up inside of her, headed for the surface. "My body was all I *had.* That was it. My sister, Annabelle, is *still* in Lakeland, working a ten-dollar-an-hour job and dealing with an alcoholic husband of her own." She stared at him, her frustration bubbling over. "I had dreams, Jared. Just like you had. Except you had a brain and I had my body so I used it."

His gaze darkened. "You also have an incredibly sharp brain. Why didn't you use *it?*"

"I didn't know that." Frustration grabbed at her, tore at her composure. "As far as I was concerned, I was low-income trash from the swamp. And no one ever tried to convince me differently. Not my teachers, classmates, not the girls who wouldn't let me into their cliques... I was the poor Williams girl who was never going to amount to anything. Well, dammit, I *did.*"

He rubbed his hands over his eyes. "St. John is not your real name?"

She shook her head. "I changed it when I left Vegas for California."

"Is Bailey your real name?"

"Yes. My mother named me after her favorite drink."

His eyes widened at that. He was silent for a long time,

head in his hands. When he finally looked up at her, his expression was bleak. "When you say high-end stripper, what does that mean?"

Did she do favors for her clients on the side? Something inside her retracted. Curled up before it could be killed off. Before she showed him exactly how much that hurt.

"You want to know if I slept with the men I danced for?"

"Yes," he answered harshly.

"Would it make any difference if I said yes?" *Would it make the stigma of what she'd been worse?*

"*Goddammit*, Bailey, answer the question."

"I danced," she said stonily, "and then I went home and studied. Nothing more. *Ever*."

He let out a long breath. "Where does Alexander Gagnon fit in all this?"

She laced her hands together and stared into the hissing, sparking fire. "Every week at the Red Room, the owner would have his favorite dancer do a special number at the end of the night. You were the star attraction, wore fancy red lingerie, got tons of tips for it. That week, he chose me." She registered the speculative look on Jared's face and chose to ignore it. "Alexander came to the Red Room for the first time on a Tuesday night. He gave me a huge tip and asked me to have a drink with him. For some reason, I refused. He was well-dressed, had this aura about him you couldn't ignore, but there was something I didn't trust. And in that business it was all about instinct.

"He didn't want any of the other girls. He came back two other nights after that, always tipping heavily and asking me to have a drink with him. On the third night, I said no, went to my dressing room and started taking off my makeup. I was the last girl to leave. The others were all in a rush to go out that night and I was just going home to study so I took my time. At one point, I had this feeling I wasn't alone and I turned around and there he was—Alexander," she qualified. "Just standing there."

His gaze narrowed. "How did he get past the bouncers?"

She grimaced. "I found out later he'd bribed Bruno, my manager, to make them look the other way. I don't know what Alexander had on Bruno to make him do that— Bruno was a big gambler, he owed people a lot of money so maybe that was it. Anyway," she said, waving a hand, "I was shocked, totally thrown. I told him to get out. He completely ignored me."

"Then what?" Jared growled.

"He propositioned me."

"What do you mean propositioned you?"

"He offered me fifty thousand dollars to sleep with him." A dangerous glimmer entered his eyes. "For one night?"

"Yes."

"What happened when you turned him down?"

Her fingers tightened around her glass. "He told me everyone has a price. To name mine. I told him to get the hell out again and this time he did."

"And that was it?"

"He came back two more nights to see if I'd changed my mind. I never saw him after that."

"Jesus—Bailey—" He stood up and paced to the fire. Raked his hands through his hair. "Why didn't you tell me?"

"Tell *you?*" She gave him a disbelieving look. "You, the man who just wrote a manifesto about how women belong in the bedroom, not the boardroom? You have to be joking."

"Oh for God's sake, you know that doesn't apply to you." He gave his head a shake. "What did he say to you on the yacht? You looked shaken."

"He realized that nobody knows. That I've hidden my past."

"And?"

She shook her head. "You interrupted us then."

His gaze sharpened on her face. "You can't run away from the past forever. It always catches up with you."

Her mouth twisted. "So I should just tell everyone I was a *stripper*? Get it out of the way? I have worked my *entire life* to put my past behind me, Jared. I'm not ashamed of what I did. But others will judge me. 'Jared Stone's chief marketing officer—former stripper.' How do you think that will go over?"

He was silent. Because she was right.

"He still wants you," he muttered after a long moment. "He wants to win. That much is clear."

Bailey felt her past close like a noose around her neck. Finally it had caught up with her. She'd always thought it might. But did it have to be *now*? Right at the moment she'd thought she just might rise above it?

Tears of frustration singed the back of her eyes. She drained the rest of her wine and set the glass on the ground. "I am now a liability," she said quietly. "You need to take me out of this presentation, Jared. Eliminate me from the equation. You know it and I know it."

Blue eyes tangled with darker blue. The flicker in his was almost indiscernible, but she didn't miss it. The acknowledgment that she was right.

"Pull me out," she repeated dully, getting to her feet. "It's the right thing to do."

And then she walked away before she bawled her eyes out.

Jared watched Bailey go, so dumbstruck by what she'd just told him he was actually incapable of pursuing. *She'd been a high-end stripper in Vegas. She had taken her clothes off for total strangers every night, pocketed scads of money and put herself through school with it.*

The idea of *Bailey* putting herself on display like that, letting men drool over her like that, was so far-fetched it was almost laughable. He would have laughed if he wasn't so appalled. Here he'd been picturing her *selling shoes* at the local mall to put herself through school. *Making cappuccinos at the local café*…instead she'd been balling up the cash men shoved in her G-string to survive and sacrificing her innocence along with it.

Dear God. And then there was the image of Bailey dancing in expensive lingerie on a stage that wouldn't leave his head…how many men had gotten off seeing her like that? And why did that idea *torture* him?

He went for the whiskey then, because quite honestly, he didn't know what else to do. A sixteen-year-old Lagavulin he found in the lounge would do the trick. Might help wipe from his head the look on Bailey's face when he'd tossed that file into the fire and forced her hand.

She'd never wanted anyone to know about that part of her life. And he'd made her reveal it.

He carried the tumbler out onto the terrace and rested his palms on the railing. The sea glistened at the base of the cliffs in the moonlight. The whiskey slid down his throat, smoky and salty, a welcome heat to counter the disquiet plaguing him. He'd needed to know. *Had* to know. The ends justified the means. But now what?

He should take Bailey off the pitch. He should handle it alone for both their sakes. It was clear Alexander Gagnon had a fixation with her. He'd offered her an insane amount of money to sleep with him. And a man like that just didn't give up…he pursued until he won. To hell with his deal.

But there was also Davide to consider. Bailey was his ace in the hole when it came to the elder Gagnon, and he was still very much in the picture. He needed her thinking to win.

The whiskey slid down his throat, smooth and fiery. Bailey's words echoed in his head.

I had dreams, Jared. Just like you had. Except you had a brain and I had my body so I used it.

The look on her face when she'd given up…when she'd told him to take her off the deal.

His guts twisted. Bailey had fought her way out of a life most people would have accepted as their fate and never tried to rise above. But she had. She hadn't let it define her. She was the smartest, most composed, drop-dead beautiful woman he'd ever met. Her brilliant ideas had *made* their presentation.

He stared out at the brightly lit boats bobbing on the sea, their smooth roll telegraphing a calm night to come. And a strange kind of certainty settled over him. Bailey needed someone to believe in her. He was pretty sure she'd never had that. And he wasn't giving up on her.

It wasn't even a question.

It was then that Jared Stone realized his manifesto was the biggest piece of crap he'd ever written.

Bailey had just slipped her nightie on when a knock came at the door. Her emotions far too close to the surface, she stayed where she was.

"I'm fine, Jared. I'm good with all of it. I just need some sleep."

"I'm not leaving until I talk to you. Open the door."

His tone was hard; implacable, like Jared was. She cursed, grabbed her robe and tugged it on. Attempted to compose herself as she pulled the door open and found him standing there like a fierce warrior, filling the doorway with his broad-shouldered frame.

"I am not dropping you," he announced. "We are partners and we are doing this together."

"Jared—" She bit her lip, furiously blinking back tears.

Even after what she'd just told him, he was still backing her?

"We are a team," he said quietly, blue gaze softening. "I've told you that from the beginning. You trusted me enough to tell me about your past tonight and I know that wasn't easy. I *need* you in that room with me, Bailey. You've proven that."

A tear slid down her cheek. She couldn't help it. No one had ever shown such faith in her. She'd been going it alone since she was seventeen and suddenly, she felt so tired of it. Tired of fighting every battle by herself.

"Christ, Bailey." He took a step forward and brushed the tear away with the pad of his thumb. "Did you think I was just going to abandon you? After everything you've put into this? Those are *your* ideas Davide loves."

She looked down, anywhere but at him, but the tears kept rolling. "I thought you wouldn't respect me, that you wouldn't want me anywhere near this deal if you knew what I'd been…"

He slid his fingers under her chin and brought her gaze back up to his. "I am not going in there without you. And as for respecting you? I've never respected a woman more in my life. For who you are. For what you've done…"

Something melted inside of Bailey. Something that had been frozen for so long she'd forgotten it existed. She thought it might be her heart.

"But what about Alexander? Lord knows what he's capable of and I would never forgive myself if you lose this deal because of me."

"I'm not going to lose," he said softly. "Alexander Gagnon likes to win. I like to win more."

"But—"

He pressed his fingers against her lips. She fell silent in a sea of confusion that had only one focal point: the electricity that was so strong between them that it held her completely still as his eyes darkened with an emotion she couldn't read. He put his mouth to the hot, wet tears dampening her cheeks and kissed each one away with a slow drag of his lips that started out comforting and ended up something else entirely.

Hot. Scorching hot.

She didn't know who kissed who first. It was unspoken communication, her hands cupping his jaw, devouring him, while his found the belt to her robe, untied it and pushed it off her shoulders. She moved into him until her bare skin was molded against the hard muscles of his chest, tasting him, knowing him, until she wasn't sure where she started and he ended.

"You are so beautiful," he rasped, his mouth leaving hers to trail a path of fire down her throat. When he hit the ultrasensitive spot between her neck and shoulder, she gasped and arched to give him better access. He took full advantage, nuzzling and exploring until she dug her hands into his shoulders and demanded more.

He drew back and took her in. Color swept every centimeter of her skin. "We can't do this. You are my boss."

He shook his head. "It's never been that simple with us and you know it."

"Jared…"

He slid a finger underneath the spaghetti strap of her nightie and slipped it off her shoulder. Her heart pounded in her chest as he weighed her breast in his palm and learned the shape of her. She could have pulled away then, *should* have pulled away, but the want in her shocked her, the fact she'd never let a man touch her like this becoming inconsequential somewhere around the time he took her inside the heat of his mouth and her knees went weak.

The rush, the sweet, all-encompassing rush knocked her brain sideways. She buried her fingers in his hair and closed her eyes. And for once in her life just let herself feel. *Want.* He slid his jean-clad leg between her thighs and brought her closer. He was hard and rough against her sensitive skin and it excited her beyond belief.

She moved against him and whimpered. "Jared…"

He slid the strap off her other shoulder and flicked his tongue over her engorged nipple. Gave her what her husky entreaty hadn't been able to verbalize. And the unfamiliar throb inside her reached a fever pitch.

Somehow she was in his arms and he was striding across the room to the sofa in the lounge. He sat down, wrapped her legs around him and brought his mouth back to hers in a red-hot kiss that pulled her under again.

She should have been alarmed at how fast things were moving, *that they were moving at all* given her lack of experience, but somehow with Jared, it felt so right. She buried her mouth in the hollow of his neck and explored his musky, salty, utterly male scent.

He found the hem of her nightie and pushed it up. Her gaze tracked his movements as he trailed his fingers over the concave dip where her hip met thigh.

"You are all woman," he murmured huskily.

"Too much, I'd say."

He shook his head. "You are perfection. You know what I was thinking that night you asked me to choose the shoes?"

"What?"

He trailed his fingers along the edge of her panties, down to where she was on fire for him. "This."

His whispered answer sent a shiver down her spine. Her stomach curled into a hard, tight ball as he brought his thumb to her center and rotated it so achingly slowly she thought she might go up in flames.

"I thought that if we'd been on a date," he continued huskily, "I would have kept you there until I'd made you come…at least twice."

She lost her composure then. "Jared—"

He put his fingers to her mouth. "Better late than never, don't you think?"

Having never had an orgasm in her life, Bailey couldn't answer that question. And good thing she didn't have to, because Jared flipped their positions then, went down on his knees in front of the sofa and lifted his gaze to hers.

"Spread your legs for me, sweetheart."

Her pulse went into overdrive, tattooing itself against her veins so hard she thought she might pass out. She didn't know it was possible to feel so turned on and so excruciatingly self-conscious at the same time, but the blazing heat of his deep blue gaze spurred her on. *Lustful. Full of want. Nothing she wasn't ready to give.*

Her thighs fell apart. He worked his palms up the inside of them, arranging her to his satisfaction until she couldn't look anymore and closed her eyes. And then his hands were under her hips, urging her forward; his mouth was hot against her center, burning a trail against her damp panties, and Bailey forgot her name.

He tugged off her underwear with an impatient movement, setting his mouth to her heated flesh, where she was wet and wanting him. Hot, sweet pleasure coursed through her, curled her toes.

"Beautiful, you are so beautiful," he murmured against her skin. "Twice might not be enough."

She closed her eyes. The hot slide of his tongue against her made her whimper. And he did it again and again, varying the pressure and rhythm, asking her how she liked it. She gave him rational, honest responses at first. And then she started shaking and needing something more and she begged him to shut up.

His soft laughter flickered across the sensitive skin of her thighs. The smooth slide of his finger as he eased it inside her tore a moan from her throat. Then he brought his tongue back into play and the world went a hazy gray. This, she realized instinctively, was what she needed.

"Bailey," he murmured, "baby. Give it up."

She arched her hips and clutched the fabric of the sofa as he increased his rhythm. She begged and he gave no quarter, adding another finger, increasing the intensity until she went over the edge, her palm against her mouth the only thing preventing her scream from tearing into the night.

When her body had stopped shaking like a leaf, her brain started to function again.

So that was what all the fuss was about.

Jared leaned forward and smoothed her hair back from her face. "What did you say?"

"Nothing." OMG had she just said that out loud?

He gave her a curious look, then a slow smile curved his lips as he rose to his feet, worked his palms beneath her and swung her up in his arms. "That was *one*."

Bailey's heart pounded with every step he took toward the gorgeous turquoise-blue bedroom. She had to tell him. *Now.*

"Jared." She poked a finger into his shoulder. "Stop for a second. I need to tell you something."

He halted midstride, his gaze flicking to her face. "What?"

Color rushed to her cheeks, rendering them a red-hot mess. "I've never—I mean you should know that I am a—"

The words died in her throat as he went as gray as she was red.

"You are goddamn joking."

CHAPTER SEVEN

THE LOOK ON Bailey's face sent a cold rush through Jared, like the mistral gone awry right up the center of him. He dropped her to the floor so fast she didn't have time to brace herself, and his hands at her waist were the only thing that held her up.

"Tell me you're joking," he repeated harshly.

She pushed a hand against his chest and stood back, her chin lifting to a defiant angle. "What's the big deal?"

His eyes rounded. "You're a twenty-nine-year-old, former stripper, *virgin?*"

Her face went even hotter. "Are you going to tag that description on every time you talk about me now? Because I'm afraid that doesn't work for me."

He closed his eyes and raked his hair back from his face. "I don't understand how this could happen."

Her mouth flattened. "Simple. I haven't gotten into bed with a man. Not that you'd understand anything about that. Half the women in the Valley are walking around with your cute little diamond charm bracelets on as if they were the Medal of Honor."

He let out a harsh breath and opened his eyes. "It was the combination of your age and background, Bailey. You haven't exactly been living in a nunnery."

She put her hands on her hips and stared at him. "What

were you hoping? That I'd have all sorts of tricks up my sleeve, *living the life?*"

His gaze narrowed. "I wasn't actually thinking, Bailey. As you can imagine after what just happened."

Taking her to bed and having her until sunrise had been the only thing in his head...no thinking involved there.

His mouth twisted in a scowl. Not happening now, that was for sure. Virgins wanted rings on their fingers. Assurances of undying love. That part of his manifesto hadn't been wrong.

"Why?" His frustrated, sexually aroused body wanted to know. "Why would you be twenty-nine and a virgin?"

She wrapped her arms around herself. "I dunno, Jared. I'd have to be a psychologist to say." His scowl grew as she tossed his words back at him. "I didn't date in Vegas. The men who asked me out were only after one thing, given my profession. They didn't exactly want to court me. Then when I came to the Valley I was just too busy working."

"And your father," he pointed out. "He can't have given you a very good picture of men to work with."

No. He'd broken her heart. Her mother's heart. *All of their hearts* again and again to match his own broken one. Twenty years of wanting to be the hero you once were.

She brushed her hair out of her face. "I'm sure that had something to do with it."

He frowned. "I don't buy that you were too busy to date in the Valley. I've seen the men pursue you."

"Because I'm a challenge," she pointed out. "You think I don't know what they say about me? The wagers they make? The minute I go to bed with one of them it's going to be all over the airwaves faster than your manifesto." She wrinkled her nose. "I'd rather not bother."

"So what was that?" He jerked his head toward the sofa. "You were all in there, Bailey."

"Stupid me." She rolled her eyes. "We do have this

chemistry, you and I. And for one second, *five minutes*," she amended sarcastically, "I was doing what I wanted. I wasn't holding back."

His heart stuttered. The urge to pick her up, walk into that bedroom and finish what they'd started made him shove his hands in his pockets. Because while he liked Bailey, might even be *fond* of her, despite the fact that he wanted to take her to bed more than he'd ever wanted a woman in his life, he didn't do the big *V*. Wasn't capable of it. It would be like asking him to vote Republican. To suggest he leave a big messy pile in the middle of his impeccably clean desk.

Clean desk, clean mind, his Zen master had told him on that thirty-day search to find his soul. If he slept with Bailey, there might never be enough meditation for that.

He lifted his gaze to her rather glazed one, resolute despite his screaming body. "I just have one question for you."

She gave him a wary look. "What?"

"Don't you ever get...*frustrated*?"

Her eyes darkened. "Get out of my room, Jared."

How were you supposed to greet the day when you'd just spent the night before getting down and dirty with your boss? It wasn't a particular skill Bailey had arrived in France with, and the thought of facing him across a plate of croissants while she remembered him on his knees between her thighs, *devouring* her, wasn't going to fly.

She yanked a pillow over her face and lay back in the big king-size bed. Her only saving grace was she hadn't screamed out loud. But even that was tempered by the fact that her moans of approval *had* been loud and clear. And *if* he'd taken her to bed, she would have let him take her virginity. She would have let *Jared Stone* take her virginity. Because for a moment there, she'd thought she'd seen the real Jared. The man behind the manifesto. The man who thought enough of her that he was backing her when he shouldn't be...

Who had called her the smartest marketing person he'd ever worked with.

I've never respected a woman more in my life. For who you are. For what you've done.

Ugh. She pressed the pillow harder against her face. Had he just been trying to get her into bed? Had he been intrigued by her past and wondering how hot she was? How skilled? But even as she thought it, she knew it wasn't right. Jared was risking too much standing behind her to just be out for sex. His Achilles' heel was his utter and complete inability to commit. This was right within character. A virgin must be an intensely scary, disconcerting phenomenon to him. *What had she expected him to do?*

She threw the pillow off, fury at herself coursing through her. He might respect her even after all she'd told him, but he was still Jared—a man no female should get anywhere near unless she was as shallow as he was when it came to the art of the casual hookup.

It made her wonder about the rest of the manifesto she hadn't read...

She swung her legs over the side of the bed, padded into the lounge and woke up her computer. Gave the scattered sofa pillows a grimace. His manifesto now had five million views. She typed in the word *virgin* and pressed Find. And there it was. Bolded.

Never, ever take a virgin home with you unless you're prepared to open up the homestead to her. Lock, stock and barrel. There is no "see how it goes" with a virgin. I've seen better men than me crash and burn. Hard.

Her vision misted over. What was wrong with her? When had she forgotten exactly who Jared was? *About the same time he had kissed her brain into some sort of ancient and useless artifact.* Because let's face it. Some women would trade their self-respect for that skill in the bedroom.

If she'd kept her mouth shut last night, she would have.

She got to her feet with a jerky movement, strode into the bathroom and pushed her obviously cloudy head under the hot spray of the shower. She was going to pretend last night had never happened. Appreciate what Jared was doing for her because he *was* risking a great deal by keeping her in this pitch, she knew that. And she was going to win it for him. Then she was going to get far away from Jared Stone while she still had her wits about her.

Jared was eating breakfast on the terrace when she arrived downstairs, newspaper spread out in front of him, undoubtedly having already inhaled a couple of the croissants from the basket as he did every morning. He had the highest metabolism of anyone she'd ever encountered, which she had to admit was likely stoked by all the *muscle* on display for her this morning. Athletic shorts and a gray T-shirt left little of it to the imagination.

Not helping.

Heat rushed to her face as he glanced up at her, and the night before slammed into her brain like an unavoidable fact. But this was cool and controlled Bailey in charge now. She could do this.

She sat down opposite him at the little table. His gaze traveled over her face. "Good morning."

She tried to ignore how sexy and rusty his voice sounded before he'd put it to use for the day and muttered a greeting back. Refused to imagine how superhot it would be if she was *still* in his bed at this time of the morning, which of course she was not, because he'd walked out on her as though she was a communicable disease.

Not that she was bitter about it or anything.

She reached for the croissants, still warm from the oven, her fingers closing over one with chocolate oozing out of it. "Georgina outdid herself this morning."

He gave the croissant a hard look. "I've been trying to figure out how they get the chocolate in the center."

"You roll them this way." She spread her napkin on the table and demonstrated.

He lifted a brow. "You're handy in the kitchen, too. That's a big turn-on."

Apparently not when combined with her virgin status. She picked up a knife and sliced through the croissant with a vicious movement. "But then I would want to commandeer all your baking supplies at the homestead. How horrific…"

A smile edged his lips. "I knew you were going to look that up. And actually, Bailey, I love nothing more than when a woman cooks for me. As long as she shuts the door after her when she leaves."

She closed her eyes against the oh-so-tempting vision of him with the chocolate pastry smeared all over his face.

"I don't know if I can do this."

"What? Live with me for another week?" His tone was overtly amused. "Feel free to speak openly."

She shook her head. *No. No thanks.* She was not letting him draw her in again. He was a professional instigator—head and shoulders more skilled than her in that department. She picked up the coffeepot, poured herself a cup of the steaming brew and set the tall silver canister back on the table so it effectively blocked him from view. He reached out and slid it aside, laughter dancing in his eyes. "You think you can block me out with a coffeepot?"

"Not really." She gave him an even look as she stirred milk into her coffee. "But what's the alternative? We talk about last night?"

He shrugged. "At least you had some sort of relief. Me? It took a five-mile run this morning to work it out."

Her already-hot face incinerated. "I am so not talking to you about this. In fact, I suggest we never reference it again."

A wide smile curved his lips. "Fine. I'm just saying you aren't the only cranky one this morning."

Her eyes widened. "I'm not cranky." Angry, more like it. "Reading the rest of your manifesto was a good wake-up call. Stupid me for thinking my virginity wouldn't make a difference to a Lothario like you."

His smile faded. "First, I think that's an exaggeration. And second, there's only one reason I walked away from you last night, Bailey. I don't make promises I can't keep. I don't like taking women for a ride like some guys do. And if that makes me a jerk then so be it."

"Who was asking you for a promise?" She shook her head in amazement. "You're so caught up in yourself, in what you *think* you know about people, you haven't got a clue, do you?"

He leaned forward and rested his elbows on the table, his gaze spearing hers. "Tell me you don't want the full deal. A man who loves you. A diamond ring…everything that goes with it."

She sank her teeth into her bottom lip, knowing he was sucking her in again but too stung to care. "You want the truth, Jared? I don't know what love is. I've never had it so how would I? My parents kicked me out when I was seventeen…dancing pretty much ruined my trust in men…" She lifted her shoulders. "I've been fighting my own battles for so long, I'd settle for a man who respects me. A man who tells me the truth." She angled her chin at him. "One who wants me for who I am."

His lips tightened. "This is about *my rules*, Bailey. Not you. If you hadn't been the last virgin on the face of the planet last night we'd be acting out my deepest, darkest fantasies about you—and believe me, I have many."

Her breath caught in her throat, heat searing through her in a potent combination of lust and humiliation. "You are such a jerk, you know that?" She pulled in a breath and stared at the hard, uncompromising lines of his face. "You know what I think? I think your rules are a cop-out. Your parents' marriage was a disaster so you think all relationships are like that. You avoid ties to anyone so you don't have to face the reality of being in one yourself." She lifted a brow. "I think you're scared."

His face took on a gray tinge. "Look who's talking."

"You're right." She abandoned her croissant and pushed away from the table. "But at least I admit it."

"Where are you going?" he barked. "We aren't finished here."

"I need a walk. All of this denial is making me lose my appetite."

Jared had been trying to avoid the truth the entire two hours he'd been up and Bailey had been in bed. Kissing her, touching her like that last night, had almost been an inevitability. He got that. *Bailey's being a virgin had not.* How did *anyone* reach the age of twenty-nine and be a virgin? Honestly?

He watched her walk down the path toward the beach, back ramrod straight, her shoulders up around her ears.

For once I wasn't holding back. For once I was doing what I wanted.

He scowled and tossed his napkin on the table. How was he supposed to interpret that? What was he supposed to *do* with that? He needed to stay away from Bailey. She was like a flashing neon danger sign for him. A weakness he couldn't afford to indulge at a time when winning this deal was all that mattered. So why was he now striding down the path after her like a raging bull intent on having his way?

She looked warily at him as he fell into step beside her. "Go away, Jared."

"When you said dancing destroyed your trust in men, what did you mean?"

She gave him a long look. "You wouldn't ask that if you'd spent any amount of time in a strip club."

He shrugged. "It's not my thing."

"I don't imagine. Not when the women are beating down your door for a night with the *lion*."

"Bailey..."

"Why are you asking this?"

"I want to know."

She looked as though she was going to tell him to mind his own business. He wasn't sure what was going on in those cool blue eyes. Embarrassment? The need to protect herself? But then she lifted her shoulders. "There are four types of men who come to a strip club. The jokers, the guys who come in with a bachelor party or to party with their friends, they drink too much, leave you nice tips and go on their way. Then there's the regulars. Some of them become friends, they pay you to dance for them, sit with them, listen to the things their wives won't because their marriage is so far gone, they don't listen to them at all anymore."

His mouth twisted. "You realize you're proving my point."

She ignored him. "Those are the good regulars. Who can become bad regulars if they fall for you. Then they decide you need to be rescued. That you shouldn't be living this life and they want to marry you. If you're unlucky, they become stalkers and then they're a real problem."

"Did that happen to you?"

"Once. The club saw him follow me to my car and called the police."

He looked horrified. "And the final kind?"

"The men who want to degrade you. The ones who are unsuccessful in life, feel they aren't appreciated enough at home—the ones who don't feel *manly* enough. They come in to put themselves on a power trip. They'll call you names, call you stupid, whatever makes them feel better about themselves by making *you* feel like you're about an inch tall."

"So how did you deal with that?" A wry smile curved his mouth. "I can't imagine you took it well."

"I didn't. One night when a guy grabbed my butt, I slapped him across the face." Her mouth pursed. "He hit me back, only, much harder."

Jared's heart lurched. "What happened after that?"

"The bouncers threw him out. He came back the next night."

"They let him back *in*?"

"He was spending. That's all they care about."

"Did that happen often?"

"No. It was more verbal abuse. You got used to it, you developed a thick skin, but it still wears away at your self-confidence."

She looked so vulnerable, so tiny beside him when some of those guys must have been twice her size, it made his skin burn just thinking about it.

"What were the rules on personal contact?"

Her gaze skipped away from his. "To make the really good money, you had to do private dances."

"Lap dances?"

"Yes."

He'd never had a lap dance. He'd watched his groom-to-be buddy have one and hadn't felt any desire to do that with a stranger. Hadn't seen the sexiness in it. His buddy had, though. He'd loved having the beautiful girl intimately plastered across his lap.

"Was this," he asked Bailey, his voice a little on the rough side, "all done with or without clothes?"

Rosy color stained her delicate cheekbones. "We had to wear bottoms. We wore two, in fact. I'm not even sure why. It might have been more of a fashion statement."

The thought of Bailey dressed like that, dancing on a guy's lap, had him asking, "Didn't it bother you, doing that?"

"Of course it bothered me," she snapped. "It wasn't Sunday school, Jared. It was a job—a very lucrative job where men paid me a lot of money to take off my clothes. And maybe if I hadn't had to worry about money my entire life, hadn't had to wear hand-me-downs every day to school, I would have chosen differently. But I didn't have that luxury and I wanted to make a better life for myself."

Point taken.

She looked out at the sea, the sun slanting over her alabaster skin. "Most of the men were fine. Most of them respected the line and didn't cross it."

"Except for the ones like Alexander."

She looked back at him, the remnants of a memory in her eyes. "Do you know what he said to me that night in my dressing room?"

He was pretty sure he didn't, but he nodded anyway.

"He said he would respect my hard limits."

Jared's hands clenched into fists by his sides. "You stay away from him in Paris," he said harshly. "I don't want you interacting with him."

She nodded. "I will."

He didn't want Gagnon anywhere near her. He was also sure he never wanted a man to raise a hand to her again. *Put* a hand on her. *Ever.*

He raked a hand through his hair and blinked against the sunshine breaking through the clouds as they stepped down onto the beach. Absorbed the uneasy feeling in his gut as he worried he was seriously losing his edge. Protecting Bailey against Alexander Gagnon was a given. The rest of it—the urge to keep her for himself—that was something he could never, ever do. He wasn't even sure where such a crazy thought had come from.

CHAPTER EIGHT

AN UTTERLY BRILLIANT, rock-solid presentation under their belt, Jared and Bailey landed in Paris on Sunday night after a quick hour-and-a-half flight north from Nice in the Stone Industries jet. A car picked them up from the terminal and whisked them into the city, lights sparkling from every vantage point as dusk fell.

Jared studied the play of color across the Seine as they neared their hotel in the Left Bank, thinking the City of Light was so much more appropriate a descriptor than the City of Love. For one thing, he thought, mouth twisting, love was a myth perpetuated by all the romantics of the world. Secondly, there was no city as gorgeous as Paris at night.

He watched Bailey once again play twenty questions with their driver, asking him about the city landmarks.

I don't know what love is, she'd said. *I've never had it so how would I? I'd settle for a man who respects me. A man who tells me the truth. One who wants me for who I am.*

He pursed his lips and stared out at the elegant facades of the historic buildings that lined the river. Bailey was everything a man in his right mind would want in a woman. Intelligent, stunningly beautiful, interesting and desirable... How had one not snapped her up, pushed his way past that impenetrable facade? Tapped into that wistfulness she kept hidden so well? Had the life she'd led made her bury it that deep?

He put it out of his head as the car whipped around a corner and pulled to a halt in front of their elegant old hotel. It was exactly that vulnerability, the fact that she was untouched, that was going to keep him a hundred paces from her at all times if he knew what was good for him.

Their takeoff spot had been delayed in Nice, which meant they had less than an hour before they were due at the dinner that had been organized for them and their Gehrig counterparts. Enough time to check in to their hotel, change and go. Jared left Bailey to shower and dress in the suite that adjoined his and did the same.

He had showered and was pulling on his shirt when a knock came at the connecting door. He strode over and pulled it open, finding a fully dressed, toe-tapping Bailey on the other side. Her gaze moved over his chest, down over the muscles of his abdomen in a caught-off-guard perusal that couldn't be mistaken for anything but total appreciation.

It made his vow to avoid anything that constituted lust between them snag in his throat.

"I just need a tie," he muttered, turning around and putting distance between them.

Bailey walked in and strolled to the Juliet balcony to look out at the lights. "It's so beautiful at night."

Jared did the buttons of his shirt up. "One of my favorite cities in the world."

"Which you will never enjoy on your honeymoon because you're never getting married. How sad for you."

"How forward-thinking of me," he retorted. "I can bring my girlfriend here instead of paying for divorce proceedings."

Her throaty laugh did strange things to his stomach. "You think you're so tough, Jared Stone," she murmured as she turned around. "But you're really not. You know that?"

He elected not to respond. She was in white tonight, a simple classy knee-length dress that made the most of her curvaceous figure, hair up in a sleek chignon that left her beautiful neck bare. His strict no-virgin policy should have shielded him from the desire to bury his mouth in the exposed hollow between neck and shoulder. Unfortunately, his body wasn't following his strategic plan.

Biting out a curse, he whipped the tie around his neck and tied it with the quick efficiency of a man who hated that particular accessory. *He was not having her.*

Bailey surveyed him with a critical eye. Walked toward him with a purposeful movement that sent his pulse into overdrive. He yanked in a breath as she came to a halt in front of him and pushed his hands aside.

"Your tie is crooked."

As disheveled as his mind.

He kept his hands by his sides while she undid the tie, set it back around his neck and retied it, her technique smooth and flawless. Her perfume drifted into his nostrils, the curves he was almost going crazy not touching so close he would only have had to take a step to feel her against him.

"How did you," he murmured roughly, "learn to tie a tie so well with no lovers in your life?"

She pursed her lips as she finished it off. "Etiquette training."

"*Etiquette* training?" He stared at her as if he hadn't heard right. "As in Pygmalion?"

She smiled. "If you want to put it like that."

"*Why?*"

Rosy color stained her cheeks. "I grew up dirt-poor with no idea of how to function in society, Jared. I was a stripper. Where was I going to learn what to say over a business dinner? What fork to use? I might have gotten an MBA, but it in no way prepared me for any of that. So I had someone teach me."

"Right." His heart contracted. Just a bit.

Every time he built a wall against her, she disarmed him. She said something like that and reminded him just how vulnerable she was under that tough exterior. It made him want to hold her and never let go.

"Jared—" She bit her lip and stared up at him and God help him, he almost snared that luscious mouth under his and did what he wanted to do. But that was absolutely, definitely not happening. Not tonight when he needed his wits about him. When he needed to *win this deal*.

"We need to go," he announced abruptly, stepping back. "We're already late."

The hurt he seemed to be a professional at putting in her eyes gleamed bright. He ignored it and shoved his wallet into his pocket.

"The car's waiting. Let's go."

The seafood restaurant on the Rue de Rivoli was packed with people on the warm, steamy Paris night. The maître d' led them to the chef's table at the back of the restaurant with its much-in-demand view of the bustling, sparkling kitchen in which white-coated chefs worked in symphonic precision.

They were the last in the group of seven to arrive. Their competition, John Gehrig, the CEO of Gehrig Electronics, rose to introduce himself, his wife, Barbara, and his vice president of marketing. Gehrig was a warm, friendly Midwesterner in his early fifties whom Bailey couldn't help but instantly like. As was Barbara, who was utterly charming as his feminine counterpart, and apparently whip-smart as Gehrig's legal counsel.

She moved to greet Davide, then Alexander, who was superbly dressed in a gray suit and navy shirt and drawing more than one set of female eyes as he stood. He bent to press a kiss to each of her cheeks, the touch of his lips sending an involuntary shiver through her. "You look outrageously beautiful," he murmured in her ear as he brushed the other cheek. "Unfortunate Stone had the pleasure of escorting you."

Bailey stepped back, firmly disengaging his hands. "So lovely to see you again."

Jared made a point of sitting in the seat beside Alexander at the round table designed for conversation, which left Bailey to his left and Barbara beside her. A potent predinner cocktail Barbara suggested was a fine method of relaxation, and before long, the two of them had hit it off.

"So," Barbara murmured as the fish course was being removed, "are you and the delectable Jared together?"

She shook her head. "What made you think that?"

"The way he looks at you. Like he'd like to have you for the main course…you might want to address that."

Or not.

"And then there's the dark and dangerous Alexander…" Barbara mused. "Uncatchable, say the tabloids."

Bailey wondered, for the millionth time, why he was fixated on *her*. Surely the man could have any woman with his looks and fortune?

Jared asked her a question, claiming her attention with a touch of his hand on her arm. It was a gesture that did not escape Alexander's attention because he had been watching her like a hawk all night. Bailey leaned into Jared and contributed her thoughts on the changing retail climate. Alexander tracked the movement. That she heartily enjoyed the constant touching when she was supposed to be hating Jared was a matter she didn't care too examine too closely. It was all an act for Alexander's benefit, of course.

Dinner stretched on, Parisian-style, with course after course of delectable French food. More bottles of twenty-year-old wine were consumed than Bailey could count accompanied by enough business talk to make the night worthwhile, but not so much it impinged on the very civilized French way of taking the time to truly savor a meal. Talk turned to port when a cheese plate was placed on the table to finish. Davide and Jared, both huge fans of the intensely flavored wine, were invited down to the cellar by the owner to choose their selection. While the Gehrigs went out for a smoke, and their VP left to make a call, Bailey excused herself to use the ladies' room rather than be alone with Alexander.

She took her time, but when she returned to the table, Alexander was still its only occupant. Jerking her head around, she found the Gehrigs chatting to a couple at another table.

Alexander stood. "Sit down, Bailey. I don't bite."

Yes, you do, she wanted to say. But rather than cause a scene, she did. Alexander picked up his wine, lowered himself into his chair, and took a sip. "How did your strategy session go? Ready for Tuesday?"

She nodded. "I think you'll be very happy with the final plan."

"Good." He set the glass down. "Jared may be a maverick but his vision is right."

Her gaze met his warily. "I'm glad you realize that."

His slate-gray eyes glittered. "Why didn't you take me up on that offer in Vegas, Bailey?"

She swallowed. "It wasn't personal. I never fraternized with customers."

"Yet you fraternize with your boss."

Warmth flooded her cheeks. "Jared and I don't have a relationship."

"Oh, come on, Bailey. You're infatuated with him. If you're not sleeping with him now, you will be."

Her blood pressure skyrocketed. "Pick a more appropriate topic or I will leave the table."

"It's fine, you know," he continued. "I only want one night. Think of it like this, my Vegas proposal, except this time, you don't get fifty thousand dollars, you get to save your boyfriend's deal."

Her jaw dropped open. "*Why?* Why me, Alexander? You could have any woman you wanted."

He nodded his head toward Jared's chair. "I want what *he* has. I want what I've wanted from the beginning."

She shook her head at the direct, unhesitating stare he leveled at her. The man was a sociopath.

His gaze narrowed. "For a woman who stripped for a living you are very naive, Bailey. I want the fantasy. I want what you were selling on that stage—but I want it for me. To know when I sink myself into you, I have what none of them had."

Bailey stood up on shaking legs. "You are insane."

"No," he said underlining the word, "I know what I want." He nodded his head toward the back of the restaurant. "Sit down. They're coming back."

She turned and saw Jared and Davide winding their way through the tables, Jared's gaze pinned on her. She sank back into her chair.

"Don't make a mess of this for Jared," Alexander murmured as the din of the restaurant buzzed on around them. "Think about it."

She wasn't actually sure what happened the last hour she sat there in a frozen state. The port was consumed, the cheese eaten by connoisseurs other than herself, and somehow the evening ended.

Alexander offered to drive them back to their hotel and rather than be rude, Jared accepted. When the Frenchman had dropped them off and they were in the elevator riding up to their rooms, Jared crossed his arms over his chest the hot and bothered look to him suggesting he wasn't so under control.

"What happened with Alexander at the table?"

She leaned back against the wall of the lift, her head

spinning. "He told me if I took him up on his offer from Vegas, I could save your deal."

His head jerked back. "*What?*"

She swallowed hard. "He said your vision was the future and we were the right choice. But that I could seal the deal by sleeping with him. That he only wanted one night."

His nostrils flared, his fingers flexing around the metal bar that surrounded the lift. She was half terrified he would stop the car and go after Alexander from the coldly furious look on his face. Instead, as the lift stopped at their floor, he stepped out, held the door for her and stalked toward their rooms.

"Your card," he barked, taking it and opening the door. It was a good two or three moments before he spoke.

"What else did he say?"

She lifted a trembling hand to her cheek. "I asked him why. He said he wanted the fantasy. That when he was *deep inside me* he would have what none of the others had." She stared at him. "God, Jared. He's sick."

He was so still, so absolutely still, she could feel her heart pounding in her chest. It throbbed once, twice, three times before he took a deep breath and started toward her, his hands cupping her jaw. "He's a megalomaniac who thinks he can have anything he wants, Bailey. But he will never put his hands on you. I promise you that."

She was shaking. He folded her against his chest and held her there, his hands in her hair. "He's bluffing."

She shook her head. "He brought in Gehrig."

"Gehrig was a natural choice. They're an extremely hot brand. I'm surprised they didn't include them from the beginning. It was a smart move on Alexander's part."

She pushed away. "You need to send me home, Jared. This is crazy."

"Not happening. We have Project X. It's going to win this for us. We stay the course, Bailey."

But he'd never wanted to use his secret launch. They had a whole strategic plan built around the products that involved an array of global partners. And now he was messing with that because of *her* past.

She stalked past him to the closet, pulled her suitcase out and started throwing clothes in.

"What the *hell* are you doing?"

She spun around. "I have to go. It's the only way. If I'm gone, Alexander might lose interest and play fairly."

Hot color stained his cheekbones. "Have you been listening to anything I've said? *He doesn't care*, Bailey. You are not a deciding factor. You are a pawn in his game. So forget anything but us going in there and winning the entire committee over. *Making* him make the right decision."

But what if Alexander didn't do the right thing? She shook her head. "I can't take that chance. I will not lose this deal for you." She turned and started dumping her shoes into the bag, tears stinging the back of her eyes. Jared's hands sank into her waist and spun her around.

"How many times do I have to tell you I'm not doing this alone? We're pitching this together and we're winning."

Her gaze dropped to his perfectly knotted tie. A Windsor knot. Her favorite. And she wondered why, why was he doing this? Why was he backing her to his own detriment?

Her mouth twisted. "He told me he wanted to have what you have. Ironic, isn't it, when you don't even want what I'm offering?"

His gaze darkened to a deep, stormy blue. "You know that isn't true."

"How?" She practically yelled the word at him. "I put myself out there for the first time in my life, we share what we shared and then you shut it down as if I'm totally expendable. A dime a dozen…because of your stupid rules."

His face tightened. "They aren't stupid rules. They're designed to ensure you don't get hurt."

"They're designed to ensure *you* don't get hurt."

He lifted a shoulder. "They are what they are."

"Coward." She hurled the word at him with all the hurt and confusion surging through her. "You talk about trust. You want me to trust you on this, to walk into this pitch with you when you won't even be honest with yourself?"

His cheeks stained deeper. "You want the *truth*, Bailey? You want to know what's been eating at me? I've spent the entire evening, the entire *week* telling myself I can't have you. Telling myself I will hurt you. When all I can think of is *having* you. Teaching you what it's like to be with a man and pleasuring you so much you'll never want another." His blue eyes blazed into hers. *"How messed up is that?"*

Her stomach contracted. Dammit, she wanted that. Jared had *seen* her, the real her, in Nice, and he still wanted her. She'd never felt so stripped down, so vulnerable, so needy of what another person had to offer in her life. And she wasn't questioning it. Not anymore.

"Then do it," she murmured. "Forget about your rules."

"Bailey—"

She silenced him with a finger to his lips. "I don't *want anything* from you, Jared. I don't want promises. I don't want the homestead. But I do want to know what it's like between us. It's burning me up…"

He went so still she wondered if he was still breathing. She stepped into him before he regained the control he always found and cupped his jaw with her palm. "Not one more word. I swear if you say one more word about your rules I'll scream."

Those long lashes settled down over his eyes. Then he opened them and rested his gaze on her. "You sure you can handle this?"

She stood up on tiptoe, balancing her palm against his chest. "You sure you can?"

"No," he muttered. "I am not."

He backed her up against the wardrobe, his suit-clad thigh sliding between hers, his hard gaze full of intent. Thought ceased as he rocked his mouth over hers and took it in a kiss that made her knees go weak. Over and over again, he tasted her, commanded her response until he was the only thing in her head. Until she moved against him and surrendered more of herself. As if he knew exactly what she needed in the way her body softened against his. In the way she accepted his tongue into her mouth and met the erotic slide of it against hers with a low, soft moan that told him she was fully his.

When she was there, fully in step with him, he tangled his hand in her hair, arched her head back and took the kiss deeper, his insistent, bold strokes as he explored her mouth sending a hot, honeyed warmth through her. If he'd lifted his head and told her in that raspy voice of his how he would take her, he couldn't have demonstrated more clearly. She moved against him again, needing more, and this time he dropped his hands down her back, cupped her bottom through the filmy material of her dress and brought her firmly against the hard length of him outlined against the fine material of his pants.

Her half gasp, half sigh reverberated against his lips. His mouth left hers to trail a line of fire across her cheek to her ear. "Be careful what you wish for, sweetheart... you just might get it."

His fingers splayed across her bottom and moved her against him in a delicious slide against the hard, thick length of him, and intimidation faded on a wave of pure, unadulterated lust. She'd heard the other girls in the club going on about their sexual escapades as they'd dressed before a shift, but the way Jared made her feel was...*insane*.

He trailed kisses down the length of her neck to the spot at the base that made her crazy. Made her squirm. Jared lifted his head with a curse, sank his hands into her waist and turned her around so her palms were flat against the wardrobe.

"Enough of that if we're making it anywhere near where we're supposed to."

The rough tone of his voice sent a tremor through her. Being pressed up against the wardrobe made it tunnel deep inside. He lifted her hair away from her neck and resumed his kisses with a slide of his lips against her nape. The soft rasp of her zipper as he multitasked filled the air.

The warm breeze from the French doors slid across her skin as he pushed the dress off her shoulders and let it fall in a swish of fabric to the floor. But it was Jared's hands and lips as they worked their way down her back that had her full attention, making her arch into them and plead for more.

She drew in a breath as he sank to his knees and pressed kisses against the rounded curve of her bottom. His hands were reverent, sure on her skin, as if he wanted to memorize every inch of her. Fire lit her belly, licked at her nerve endings. She was sure she wanted him to. And then he turned her around...

His gaze swept up the length of her, from her legs still clad in high heels, over the curves of her hips and breasts encased in the barest hint of lace, and finally to her face. By the time he got there, she was flushed with self-consciousness and excitement so intense, her breath came in short pulls. Which deteriorated into no breath at all when he slid his fingers underneath the thin strips of silk that held her barely there panties in place and stripped them off.

Her legs went another step toward jelly. If she'd hoped he'd lavish the same attention on her that he had on his knees in Nice, it wasn't to be found as he stood, anchored her against the door and brought his mouth back to hers.

"You are so gorgeous," he murmured against her lips. "My words aren't working."

She melted. Figuratively, of course, because she was still standing when he slid his palm up the inside of her thighs and pushed them apart. Still standing when he cupped the heat of her in his palm in an overt claim of ownership that had her pressing her hands against the wood to keep upright. Her mouth stilled against his, her gasp filling the air as he stroked her. She was hot and wet for him, so turned on she thought she might come apart with the lightest touch. But he claimed her with the slide of his finger instead.

"You'll come with me inside of you this time," he muttered. "And not before."

Bailey tried to keep her head but there was no fighting the mind-numbing pleasure he gave her with the firm strokes of his hand. He urged her thighs wider and slid another finger inside her, stretching her, preparing her. It was so good she could have screamed with the pleasure of it. But he stopped before she could.

"There will be a bed this time." He slid his palm to the small of her back and gave her a gentle push toward it. "Maybe not the next."

She sat on the queen-size bed as he stripped off his clothes and revealed the incredible body she'd seen in swim trunks, but never in tight black boxers that emphasized how very well-endowed he was. Apparently the jokes had been true, she acknowledged with a hellishly dry mouth. Maybe she wasn't so wise to choose him as her first....

If there was any way Jared could have gotten his clothes off faster, he would have. Bailey's unabashedly intent look as he undressed, as if he was putting on a show for her pleasure, did something serious to his insides...left his composure hanging by a thread. And if he'd ever needed composure, now was the time. He'd never taken a virgin. Had no idea what made it a better experience for a woman. Add that to the fact that he'd never wanted anyone as much in his life as he wanted Bailey right now and there were all sorts of ways this could go.

Blocking his mind to anything but her, he moved to the bed and took in how outrageously, spectacularly beautiful she was clad only in a lace bra, curled up with those never-ending legs beneath her. But it was her face that held him. Utterly vulnerable, yet tough at the same time. It was a combination he found irresistible.

He sat down on the bed and pulled her into his lap. Turned her so her knees were on either side of him and they were face-to-face. "I have no idea how some man hasn't persuaded you into bed with him before now, but at this moment, I'm glad of it."

She blinked. "That's quite an admission, Mr. Manifesto."

His lips curved in a wry smile. "I think my rule book's been gone for a while."

He watched her process that. Lifted her hair away from her shoulder and took a mouthful of smooth, silky skin, scoring the surface of the elegant curve with his teeth. He was so hard, so hot for her it took all his willpower to go slow. But that was what she needed and that was what he was going to give her. Even if it killed him.

He slid his lips lower to the swell of her breasts above the lace. She moved her shoulders to help him as he slid the straps of her bra down and stripped it off. His hands moved over the weight of her silky, creamy flesh and cupped her breasts in his palms. She was so perfect, so exquisite, her shaky sigh as he brushed the pads of his thumbs over her rose-tipped nipples almost undid him.

"You ready for me?" he murmured against her mouth. "Because I need to have you *now*."

The way she blindly sought his mouth, wound her fingers in the hair at the nape of his neck, was all the impetus he needed to turn and push her back on the bed. Her gaze was steady, trusting him completely as he ran his palm down her stomach and reclaimed the heat between her thighs.

"I need a condom," he rasped, a last sane thought entering his head. "I'll be right back."

Her delicate fingers grasped his arm. "I've been on the Pill for years for cramps."

That was all the incentive he needed to slide his fingers inside her again, his smooth, rhythmical movements increasing in tempo as he brought her to a feverish, desperate state that would make his possession better for her. When she was twisting, writhing under him and begging for more, he stripped off his boxers and moved between her thighs.

He captured her hands in his and pressed them back against the bed above her head so their fingers were entwined and their eyes locked. "I'm right here," he murmured. "Every step of the way. Guide me."

She nodded. Her gaze clung to his as he brought the hard length of himself against her and teased her with it, back and forth until she closed her eyes and gave a soft moan. "Jared—"

He eased inside her, just the tip to allow her to get used to his possession. She was tight, incredibly tight, and he shook with the control it took to stay there and not move. "Breathe," he instructed huskily. Her chest rose as she did, depressed and rose as she took in another puff of air. And he felt her relax around him. He eased deeper, her flesh clenching him; accepting him and rejecting him all at the same time.

"Bailey—" he demanded roughly, "you okay?"

She nodded. "You feel…amazing."

His soft curse split the air. "Wrap your legs around me, sweetheart. I need more."

She did and he pushed deeper, a fraction at a time, stopping to let her adjust as he went. Finally, he reached the

barrier he'd been waiting for, felt her flinch beneath him.
He brought his mouth to hers. "I've got to hurt you for just
a second and it'll be over."

She nodded and closed her eyes. He claimed her fully,
pushing through the barrier with a smooth, sure stroke
that made her gasp and twist beneath him. He kissed her
through it, holding himself completely, agonizingly still
until her body relaxed around his and she sighed into his
mouth.

"That's it," he encouraged huskily, "stay with me.
You're good now."

He started to move, excruciatingly slowly although his
rock-hard body was begging him to go faster. Their hands
were still laced together, her eyes glued to his as he caressed her with his pulsing flesh, her muscles clenching
him as he withdrew and entered her again and again until
she was arching against him and taking him deep.

"You feel so good," he told her, her incredibly tight body
fitting him like a glove, making him swell even bigger.
"Tell me how you like it. How it feels…"

Her eyes were glazed; she was just this side of incoher-
ent. "So good," she muttered. "So good. God, Jared, don't
stop—*please*…"

He released a hand to cup the sexy curve of her hip. To
anchor her to him so he could put more power behind his
thrusts, hit her in that place that gave a woman the deepest, most powerful orgasm.

"Talk to me," he urged, dangerously close to the edge.
"Tell me, Bailey."

"*Amazing*. It feels amazing. Jared—I don't think I
can—"

He released her hands and reached between them,
setting his thumb against the hard nub of her just above
where their bodies were joined. Slowly, deliberately rotated it against her until her hips were writhing against

his thumb. She threw her head back and came for him, her body clenching around his so fiercely, it took him only a few strokes to push himself into oblivion. His body exploded inside her, a hoarse cry tearing itself from his lungs as a shattering release swept over him.

It was minutes, long minutes later before his body stopped shaking. Before the chill in the air stole over him. Bailey shivered, her legs still wrapped around him, his flesh buried in hers. And he wondered how he could still be semi-hard after *that*.

He left the warmth of her body to push back the comforter and tuck her beneath it. Bailey protested, a tiny whimper that made him smile. "One second," he murmured, pressing a kiss to her lips. "I am not nearly done with you yet."

He found a bottle of water on the dresser and drank half of it down while he quite frankly tried to compose himself. Because that hadn't been just sex. He felt open, raw, as if someone had stripped off his layers and left him exposed. And the instinct to roll over, to reclaim his power, pulsed through every cell.

Bailey lay there sultry and replete, platinum hair spread across the pillow, gaze tracking him as he drank. Oblivious to the storm in his head. Watching her there, strong, sexy, *unforgettable*, the thought crossed his mind that he could have her a million times and it would never be enough.

His hand tightened around the bottle. *That was truly crazy talk.* No matter how much he'd wanted a woman in the past, it had always faded. Soured. Relationships ended. People got bored. It was just the way it was.

He set the bottle down. Reached for her. Bailey studied his face as he took her in his arms. "You're regretting this?"

He shook his head. *Lied.* "I want more. And I'm not sure you're ready."

She pulled his head down to hers and gave him a long, lingering kiss as her answer. It was all the encouragement he needed to stir to life. He curved his hand around her shoulder, slid it down to press against her shoulder blade and turned her over.

"Jared—" she murmured, a question in her voice.

"I want you this way," he told her softly, pushing her hands apart and moving over her. It was testament to the trust they'd built that she stayed there, her breath picking up in rhythm as he nudged her knees apart, moved between them and pressed openmouthed kisses from the top of her spine to her waist. When she was fully relaxed and supple beneath him, he slid his hand between her legs and stroked her damp flesh.

"Okay?"

"Yes," she moaned, shifting her legs farther apart, pushing up against his touch. It was all the invitation he needed to slide an arm beneath her, lift her and push inside her hot, welcoming flesh with a smooth thrust.

This time he could move slower, build it up, enjoy every centimeter of her undeniably sweet body. When she dug her fingers into the comforter and came with a guttural moan, as if the control he was exerting over her turned her on as much as it turned him on, it destroyed him completely. She was more than a match for him in every way.

He set a palm to the small of her back, held her where he wanted her and chased his own blindingly good release. When it came, tightening his limbs, sweeping through him like the lazy aftershock of a powerful tremor, he knew he'd never experienced such pleasure.

Bailey tucked into his side, curved against his warm body as the filtered Paris moonlight carried them off to sleep, his denial grew weaker. It was useless to pretend even for a second that nothing had changed. Because everything had.

CHAPTER NINE

THE PEAL OF his cell phone in the adjoining room woke Jared at six the next morning. Blinking against the light filtering through the windows, he slid out of bed, grabbed his boxers from the floor and hightailed it into his room in the hopes of catching it before it woke Bailey.

A glance at the call display told him it was Danny, his PI. Kicking the connecting door closed, he took the call.

"Stone."

"You sound half-asleep. Thought you'd be halfway down the Champs-Elysées by now, running your little heart out."

"Eventful night last night." Jared crossed to the French doors and squinted out at the empty Paris streets. "You have something for me or did you just call to pay me back?"

"It's your father. I had my contact do the usual check-in this week. He said he wants to talk to you."

His father wanted to talk to him? He pressed his palm against the elegantly carved mahogany casing of the door. It had been, what, a year and a half, two years, since he'd talked to Graham Stone in a short, curt conversation to sort out some legalities.

"What does he want? Is he okay?"

"He wouldn't say. Says you need to come to him."

His shoulders stiffened. Why should *he* go running when his father had shut him out for almost a decade?

Danny read the pause. "He doesn't look great, Jared. Pretty haggard from what my guy says."

His chest tightened. This was *not* what he needed right now. "I can't go for a couple of weeks."

"I'm just relaying the message. Oh and Jared?" His PI's voice deepened to a satisfied purr. "That dirt you wanted on Michael Craig's proclivity to abuse his expense accounts? I have it. It's bigger and better than you could have imagined."

A twist of satisfaction curled through him. "Send it through. All of it."

He ended the call and tossed his cell phone on the desk. Michael Craig deserved what he had coming to him. What caused an ache to sit low in his chest, ever-present but more pronounced now, was how much he loved his father. Graham Stone had never been too busy, even with his insane hours as a banker, to spend time with his son. Whether it had been building a car or throwing a football around, he'd always been there, even if it wasn't as much as Jared would have liked. Then slowly, in the later years, his father had begun to sink. The massive amounts of stress had finally gotten to him, sending him to a place his youthful son couldn't understand or help him out of.

A fist squeezed his chest, growing larger with every breath. When his father had made his biggest mistake, had stolen that money, it had been too late, far too late to do anything to save his soul. There likely would never be a day on this earth when Jared wouldn't wonder what else he could have done to prevent it. He'd just learned to live with the guilt.

Or had he? The slow burn consuming him didn't make him think so. He'd always thought that walking away, distancing himself from the shame that had enveloped his family, was the right thing to do for his own survival. For his business, where reputation was everything. His father hadn't wanted his help, so what choice had he had?

Light slanted across his face as the sun rose higher in the sky. He had a decision to make. Did he stop running and see what the man who had once been his hero wanted? Or did he wait until it was too late?

Rather than contemplate a question he wasn't prepared to answer, he headed for the shower. It was too late to go back to bed and really, it was the last place he should be. Why he'd thought he could take Bailey to bed in a no-strings arrangement as she'd offered was the joke of the century.

He turned the shower on and stepped under a steaming hot spray. *No strings.* He might as well have handed Bailey the rope and asked her to tie him up in knots. Because if his Zen master had cornered him now and ordered self-awareness, he would have had to admit the only word for last night was…*emotional.* He struggled to get his mouth around the word because it was so foreign to his vocabulary. Emotion didn't figure into his work or relationships. It was an unwise word that made people do stupid things. But he could not deny the truth. He had never felt so connected to another person in his life. And not just because Bailey had been a virgin. It'd been as if he was in her head and she'd been in his.

God. He tipped his head back and sluiced the water out of his face. He'd told himself not to do it. Had warned himself it was a mistake. Why did he continue to let himself want what he couldn't have? How could he be tangling himself up in a woman who was not only the obsession of Alexander Gagnon, she was rapidly becoming *his?*

He tipped shampoo over his head and attempted to scrub some sense back into his brain. He needed to focus on this presentation and win. Take Bailey at her word. It had been one night of ridiculously good sex agreed upon by two consenting adults.

The fact that Bailey had stolen a piece of his heart last night, had been stealing pieces of it for the past week, was inconsequential. He would never be the kind of man who connected on a permanent basis. He didn't have it in him.

It was time he started acting like it.

Bailey leaned back against the bathroom door, nail in her mouth in an absentminded chew as she contemplated an in-the-shower Jared from the perspective of a woman he'd just taken to heaven and back. She was sure no other man would equal his outrageously good body and technique, and had a newfound appreciation for the tennis bracelet club in the Valley.

She replaced the thoroughly chewed nail with another. Last night had been exactly what she'd needed to take her mind off Alexander Gagnon. Except she wasn't sure it'd just been sex. She could have stayed in Jared's arms forever. And *that* was the problem. Not that he'd sneaked out of her bed.

She swallowed hard. Last night had been unforgettable. The heartbreakingly beautiful way Jared taken her virginity, so in tune with her every emotion…how treasured he'd made her feel…how desired.

Oh, Lord. She snaked a hand through her tangled hair. She'd told herself she wasn't getting emotional about this. *Enough.*

She cleared her throat. "Could you tell me where that research is? I want to read it before our meeting."

The click of the shower shutting off should have been her first clue he was getting out. Why she stood there frozen as he shoved the curtain aside and reached for a towel, water dripping off his utterly delicious masculinity, she wasn't sure.

"Sorry, I—" She took a step backward. "I'll wait for you in the bedroom."

"For God's sake, Bailey." He ran the towel over his hair. "You had your legs wrapped around me last night. It's a little late to be embarrassed."

Yes, well, that was last night and this was now. She bit her lip. "Was that your phone I heard earlier?"

He nodded, relieving her immensely by wrapping the towel around his hips. The hard set of his angular face didn't do a great job of reinforcing that comfort, however. His blue gaze was laser-focused and impersonal as he waved his hand toward the bedroom. "It's on the table by the window. Help yourself."

She shifted her weight to the other foot, studied him. *Regret. Definitely regret.* Fine.

"I ordered us coffee and croissants. I'll go read it."

"Thanks."

She waited, a fraction of a second, just to see if he'd have anything to say about last night. Anything that might make today a little less awkward.

The silence was deafening.

She dug her toe into the tile and looked up at him. "It's clear you regret what happened last night."

He gave her an even look. "I don't regret it."

"Then why do you look li—"

"*Bailey.*" His gaze narrowed. "It was great. It was hot. *You* were hot. Absolutely worth it. What else can I say?"

She squinted at him. Had he *actually* just said that?

A sharp pain gouged her insides. "Right," she said, clenching her stomach and pushing past it. "Good to know. And in case you're running a little scared which is wholly possible, you're absolutely right. I meant what I said. It was one night. We're good."

She turned on her heel and left before she became certified dangerous.

* * *

They spent the morning hearing presentations from the marketing and sales groups at Maison headquarters in the Montparnasse district of Paris. Jared thought it interesting that Bailey sat on the other side of the room from him beside an attractive, very young French marketing executive who flirted with her at every possible opportunity. He told himself it was a smart, strategic move on her part, positioning herself as part of the Maison team.

That was before, however, she walked away from him midsentence during a break. Before she blew off his request to get her a coffee.

"Bailey." He kept his voice low as he cornered her on the way back from the machine, coffee in hand. "You know this can't happen between us. It's a bad idea."

She looked up at him, the only sign there was anything going on behind that ice-cold expression of hers the quivering of her bottom lip. "I told you this morning, I *get* it. Hang on to that impressive set of rules, Jared. It's all good."

He stood there, speechless, as she ducked around him and set the coffee down. *Really? She was going to be like that about it?*

The deep freeze continued throughout the afternoon as they toured three of Maison's stores in Paris. Through the cocktails that preceded the French company's annual summer party they'd been invited to attend along with the Gehrig team. He held it together through it all, until they were speaking to the CEO of a Parisian cosmetics company Maison had a partnership with, Jared laying on the charm because the CEO was a great contact to have. Then Bailey rolled her eyes at him. *Rolled her eyes at him* and muttered something about needing to use the ladies' room.

He stared after her, a dangerous heat filling his head. What was wrong with her? *They had the biggest deal of his life to win tomorrow, he had backed her without fail this entire time, and she was acting like a girl over one night together?*

He made it through the rest of his conversation with the CEO, scouted out the washrooms and found them in a hallway off the restaurant. They were one-person affairs, and there were multiples of them. He eyed the one marked women with the door closed, stuck his hand against the wall and waited.

When the door swung open and Bailey stepped out, he pounced.

"Give me a minute, will you?" He bit the words out as he shoved her back into the washroom and shut the door.

"Jared—" She looked up at him with wide eyes. "This is not the place."

"You're *making* it the place." He jammed his hands in his pockets and stared at her. "You told me last night there were no strings. So for God's sake what is *wrong* with you?"

"Nothing." She bit her lip and made a study of the intricate pattern of the floor tiles.

His curse split the air. He slid his fingers under her chin and brought her gaze up to his. The brightness in her eyes made his stomach clench. "Don't you do this to me, Bailey. You promised me you'd be okay with this."

"I am." She pulled out of his grasp and backed up against the vanity. "I guess I'm just not made of stone like you are. Funny," she derided, forcing out a harsh bark of laughter, "women like to use that to refer to a certain body part of yours, but I think it better describes your heart. You can just turn it off and on at will, can't you?"

He looked at her nonplussed. "Apparently not with you, because here I am when I should be schmoozing executives."

"Oh," she choked out. "I think you were doing an excellent job of that."

"Jealous, Bailey?"

She stared him down for a moment, then leaned back against the vanity and ran her hands through her hair. "I just—I don't…I'm just finding it hard to put last night aside. To pretend it wasn't special when to *me*, it was."

He felt his carefully engineered defenses dissolve into dust. Bailey was like a flaw in his perfectly designed ability not to care. A weakness that would surely dismantle him completely if he let it.

"It was…*special* to me too," he admitted, choosing his words carefully. 'I just don't want us to get too carried away here."

"Why?" She poked him in the chest, and *God*, didn't she know by now how much that antagonized him? "What do you think might happen if you let yourself feel? The earth might open up and swallow you whole?"

"No, Bailey…"

"Then *what*? What do you think's going to happen?"

He reached for her then, his hands purposeful as he sank them into her waist and deposited her on the marble counter. "I might do this."

He brought his mouth down on hers in a hot, hungry kiss that was equal parts punishment and absolution. She pushed her hands against his shoulders as if to reject him, but if he was jumping into the fire, then so was she. He cupped her jaw, gentled the kiss and called himself a complete and absolute fool. A sigh racked her as she buried her fingers in his hair and kissed him back, heated and without reserve.

When he finally lifted his head, it was to nudge her thighs apart, step between them and draw her closer. "You are pulling me apart, piece by piece," he admitted huskily. "And I don't like it."

"I don't, either." She reached up and cradled his jaw in

her palms. "But you hurt me this morning, Jared. Be honest with me, yes, but at least explain where it's coming from."

"I'm sorry." He whispered the words against her mouth. Against the velvety softness of her cheek. Against the perfectly shaped earlobe he bit into, sending a shiver through her. It moved through him, made his heart race as his hands went to the hem of her dress and pushed it up, allowing his palms access to the smooth, voluptuous curve of her hip. The scent of her warm, heated flesh filled his head. He slid his hands under her bottom and dragged her to the edge of the vanity. He wouldn't take her here…he just needed to feel her against him.

"Jared—" She moaned his name as if they should stop and start all at the same time. He pulled her hips into his and kissed her. Bailey whimpered and wound her legs around him, and if he'd been inside her it couldn't have felt better than the sweet torture he was inflicting upon himself now.

He lifted his mouth from hers and framed her face with his palms. "As much as I want this, it's not happening here."

She nodded.

He lifted her off the counter and straightened her clothes, then his own.

"I need to fix my lipstick," she murmured, looking a bit shattered. "You go."

He nodded and pulled open the door. Was halfway through it, when he turned back, pulled her into his arms and stole one last kiss. She wound her arms around his neck and kissed him back. He indulged it for a few seconds, then set her away from him.

"We talk when we get back to the hotel, okay?"

"Okay."

He released her and left. He did not see Alexander until

he just about walked into him. Stopping short, his gaze flickered back to the door he'd just exited from.

"Oh, I caught the whole touching kiss." The Frenchman's smile didn't reach his eyes. "Am I allowed to say I'm jealous? Because I am, Stone."

"Why don't we say we're overdue for a drink instead?" Jared resisted the urge to deck him. He was shutting Alexander Gagnon down and he was shutting him down now.

Alexander lifted his shoulders. "If you say so."

Jared led the way to the bar by way of answer, ordered two scotches and took a deep pull of his before he deigned to speak. "Here's how this is going to go, Gagnon. You're going to stay away from Bailey, you're never going to say another sideways word to her, and if you do, I will take you out at the knees."

Alexander smiled, a lazy, loose twist of the lips that wasn't at all concerned. "You have it bad, you know that, Stone?"

He did. He was only beginning to realize how bad.

Alexander eyed him over the top of his glass. "She said you weren't sleeping together."

"Things change." Jared set his drink down, flattened his palms on the bar and leaned forward until the far-too-smooth soon-to-be CEO filled his field of vision. "You aren't ever having her. Get that through your head."

Alexander took a sip of his scotch. "*No* isn't a word I tend to take very seriously. It only makes me want something more."

His mouth twisted. "You couldn't even *buy* her. What makes you think you could ever have her?"

A warning light flickered in those slate-gray eyes, but his shrug was elegantly dismissive. "This deal will make or break you, Stone. Decide your future at a very rocky point in your company's history. Why not set Bailey free for a night? Donate her to the cause? You can put her in the shower afterward and pretend I never happened."

He froze. Clenched his hands by his sides. A fury like he'd never known blanketed him. "You are a sick bastard, you know that?" he gritted out. "She told me you wanted what I have. Well, you will never have what I have, Gagnon. Ever."

Alexander's face tightened. "You are walking a thin, thin line Stone."

"As are you," he bit out, shoving his drink on the bar and pushing to his feet. "I should have taken her under your nose tonight. That would have given me a deep sense of satisfaction."

He walked away before he lost his mind. Then thought he might already have. Because he shouldn't have said that. He should not have gone there.

Bailey reentered the restaurant just as Jared got up from the bar, a coldly furious look on his face, and walked away from Alexander. The matching look the Maison heir wore sent alarm bells ringing through her. What could possibly have happened in the last ten minutes?

Before she could snare Jared and find out, Davide was flagging him down to introduce him to someone. Then they were being rounded up for dinner with both Gagnons, the Gehrig team and several marketing executives from Maison. Jared sat beside her at the round table of ten, quietly seething, leaving Bailey to carry the conversation from their end.

"So," she offered valiantly, "you must all love living in Paris. It's so gorgeous."

Davide nodded. "Although I intend on retiring to the house in the Cap. To me it's *le paradis sur terre*. Heaven on earth."

"Agreed," Bailey nodded. "I love the climate. Perfectly temperate."

"But you must like the extreme heat," Alexander interjected. "Given that you lived in Las Vegas."

The edge to his tone made Bailey set her wineglass down with a jerky movement. "I do," she agreed evenly. "But I much prefer the more moderate Northern California climate."

"Speaking of Vegas," Alexander waved an elegant long-fingered hand at her, "I remembered last night where I met you. I usually have such an impeccable memory…it was driving me crazy."

Bailey froze. Jared's gaze flickered to Alexander, a warning glint in it. "Gagnon—

"It was the Red Room," Alexander continued. "How I could have forgotten when you were so *memorable* I don't know."

John Gehrig's mouth dropped open. The room began to spin.

"Do you know the Red Room?" Alexander turned to one of his marketing executives. The perfectly put together Frenchman shook his head. His boss sat back in his chair and folded his arms over his chest. "You must go the next time you're there. They have the most drop-dead beautiful women on stage; my clients used to salivate. But there was one dancer," he commented, looking over at Bailey, a dark glitter in his silver eyes, "who called herself Kate Delaney who held us all spellbound. We couldn't take our eyes off her."

A buzzing sound filled Bailey's head. Davide gave his son a confused look. "What does this have to do with Bailey?"

"Kate Delaney was Bailey's stage name."

"*Oh.*" Davide ran a hand over his jaw and looked at Bailey. "So you were one of those…what do they call them? *Burlesque* dancers?"

"No," Bailey corrected quietly, bile climbing her throat at an alarming rate. "The Red Room is a high-end strip club."

Davide's eyes widened. "A strip club?"

The couple of execs who'd had their heads buried in their smartphones the entire meal looked up, eyes fastening on her. Bailey swallowed hard, heat flooding every inch of her skin. "Yes. It was how I paid my way through school."

A frown creased the elder Frenchman's brow. "That must have been…"

"Lucrative." Bailey dropped her gaze to the candle flickering in the center of the table and absorbed the total and complete silence. Wished she could disappear into the red-hot flame.

John Gehrig cleared his throat. "Well, I for one love the Red Room. The ladies are all just beautiful and I'm sure," he said, shooting a red-faced look at Bailey, "you looked just…lovely."

"There wasn't an unaffected man in the room," Alexander agreed. "Isn't it great to see the American dream alive and well? From stripper to CMO…how *inspiring*."

The bile in her throat threatened to make an immediate appearance. She pressed a hand to her mouth and swallowed hard. Jared made a sound and pressed his palms into the table. Bailey covered his hand with hers. "Don't."

He stared at her hand for a long, hard moment, then lowered himself back into his seat. Davide flicked his son a reprimanding look.

"If you were a gentleman you would pick another line of conversation, Alexander, but since your manners often escape you, *I* will."

Davide started a discussion about foreign exchange rates. John Gehrig hurriedly joined in. Bailey drew in a breath, then another. Told herself walking away from the table right now wasn't an option. But it was painful, physically uncomfortable to sit there with the young executives shooting speculative glances across the table at her. One of them was tapping away on his phone, then slid it discreetly toward his coworker. Photos of her as Kate Delaney no doubt. She'd tried to get the club to sell the promotional photos to her, to take them off the website, and they'd agreed, but nothing ever really disappeared from the internet. It just pretended to.

Jared laid his palm on her thigh. "Breathe."

She pushed his hand away and stared sightlessly out the window at the glittering Eiffel Tower. Felt everything go gray around her as she retreated. She knew the routine. Knew this humiliation like a second skin. It was a familiar, hateful feeling she'd never wanted to feel again.

She drained her wineglass. Smiled tightly at the waiter as he appeared to refill it. Growing up in her house, it had been taboo to say the word *alcoholic*, even though her father had clearly been one and his booze-induced rages had been a monthly fixture. As if none of them said it, it didn't exist.

Apparently she'd also decided to live her life in denial. If she didn't acknowledge the past and the choices she'd made, it could never hurt her. She could go on pretending she was something she wasn't.

But that was all over now. With those men looking at her like this, she felt like a Jenga puzzle someone had pulled the last piece out of.

"I need to go," she muttered in a low, harsh voice to Jared as their dessert plates were cleared. "Tell them I have a headache, tell them I'm exhausted…tell them whatever you want."

She stood up, grabbed her wrap and skirted her way

through the tables to the exit. On the street, she flagged a cab. Jared caught up with her as she was about to slide in.

"Get in," he said grimly, climbing in behind her when she did.

Neither of them spoke until they were in Bailey's hotel suite. She tossed her bag on a chair and turned on him. "Why would he do it? Why would he humiliate me like that? What happened between the two of you?"

Jared sat down on the sofa near the windows. The guilty schoolboy look he wore as he raked his hands through his hair made her heart sink into the ground.

"Alexander saw me coming out of the washroom. He made some comments I couldn't let pass. I figured it was time we had a chat."

She felt the color drain from her face. "We weren't going to do that."

"I changed my mind. I said some things I shouldn't have."

"Like *what?*"

His mouth flattened. "When I made it clear you were with me, he said he didn't care. He said I should take one for the deal. Give you to him for a night then put you in the shower afterward and forget it happened." He pressed his fingers to his temples. "I lost my mind. I went too far."

A wave of nausea flashed over her. "What else did you say?"

"I told him I wished I'd taken you right there under his nose so he would know what he could never have."

Her breath left her. "You didn't."

"I did."

Her hands curled by her sides. "You...."

He stood up. "Bailey—"

"*No.*" She hurled the word at him. "You do not get to be excused for this, Jared. You do not get to be excused for egging him on in some testosterone-fueled duel when you *knew* what he was capable of. You *knew* he would not hesitate to throw my past in my face."

His face grayed. "I wasn't thinking."

"No—no, you weren't. You were too busy *bragging* about being the one to get me into bed. Making it impossible for him to not retaliate…" She threw her hands up in the air. "My God, Jared, I'm falling for you. *Falling for you.* How could you do this?"

He covered the ground between them with swift steps. The fire in his eyes set her back on her heels. "I have put this deal, this *must-win deal*, on the line for you this entire time, Bailey, because of my feelings for you. So *do not* question my intentions. Yes, I made a mistake tonight…I let my temper get the best of me, and I'm sorry for that. But it's done. And maybe it's a good thing, because you need to move on, you need to stop letting the past hold you captive."

Her eyes widened. "You're kidding, right? You think it's a good thing that the entire table of men I have to present to tomorrow will now be picturing me naked on a stage rather than listening to what I have to say?"

He lifted a brow. "So what? Who cares what they think? You're brilliant. Your ideas are brilliant. You want to defy the naysayers? Prove my manifesto is crap? Then get tougher, Bailey. Get a whole lot tougher than that."

The fists she had clenched by her sides tightened. She thought she might hit him then, and he eyed her as if he would take it. Instead, she felt big, huge, fat tears burning the backs of her eyes and backed away from him before she gave in to them.

"You said earlier you wanted to talk. Let's talk then. This is proving very illuminating."

He shook his head. "I don't think now is the right time."

His eyes said more than his words, the grim look stretching his face making her chest go tight. He was second-guessing what he'd said earlier. Second-guessing his feelings for her after what had happened tonight. After he'd watched an entire table of men react to what she'd been just as he had the first time she'd told him. Shocked. Appalled. She could *see* it on his face.

Anger built inside her, a white-hot storm that was impossible to control. She clenched her hands by her sides. How was it that every man in her life eventually rejected her? Her father, who'd thrown her out? The man she'd liked in Vegas who'd wanted only one thing? Now Jared.

Shame washed over her, stained her skin like a brand. He had treated her like a power play with Alexander because that's what she was to him—expendable.

"Now that you have me," she lashed out, so hurt she couldn't see straight, "why not enjoy the full benefits?" She reached down and yanked her shoe off and threw it at him, a silver missile he plucked out of the air with cat-like reflexes. "I know you're curious," she continued. "You asked me about it in Nice…why not sit back and let me demonstrate?"

His gaze tracked her as she bent her leg and reached for the other shoe. "Bailey—"

Wham. The shoe smacked his outstretched palm and fell to the floor. He took a step forward and reached for her, but she backed away, flashing him a furious look. "*Sit.*"

He sat. Likely because he didn't know what else to do with a crazy woman on the loose. Bailey's fingers moved to the buttons of her shirt, stumbling as she undid them. "That was hot, right, on the sink in the washroom? I'll make it hotter."

He shook his head. "Stop it."

"Oh, come on, you'll love it." She tore at the last button and yanked the shirt off. "Get in the spirit, Jared."

"Bailey." His eyes flashed a warning. "Put your shirt back on."

"Why? All you want is this. You made that clear this morning." She eased her skirt over her hips in a seductive, admittedly angry twist. "All men ever want is this."

He shook his head. "I care about you. You know I do."

She stalked toward him, sank her hands into his shoulders and straddled him. "You wanted to know how I danced for them? How I touched them?" She settled herself into his hard thighs. "Like this…"

He kept his hands stiffly by his sides, anger darkening his face. It made her furious. Made her push her breasts into his chest and rotate her hips against him in a much more intimate caress than she would ever have given a customer. A harsh breath left his lungs.

"You see," she derided, "you can't deny you like it."

"Of course I like it." He clamped his hands around her hips and held her still. "There isn't a second I don't want you. But you are worth more than this."

She shook her head, tears burning the back of her eyes in a glittering prelude to total breakdown. "I saw your face when I told you what I was. You were horrified."

"I was shocked."

"Shocked, horrified…what's the difference?"

He grimaced. "A big one."

She swallowed hard. Dared herself to ask the question that might break her, because how much worse could she feel about herself?

"Could you ever imagine yourself with me, Jared? With all my flaws?"

His jaw hardened. "I've told you I care about you. Stop pushing me."

The warning in his eyes scared her. The sudden, earth-shattering realization that she was undeniably, unmistakably in love with him was worse.

She reached for old habits, old powers as she pressed a kiss to the corner of his mouth. Slid her palm across his thigh to where he lay stiff and thick beneath his trousers. He jerked against her hand and the triumph rocketed through her like a drug she'd been denied too long.

"No."

He dumped her on the sofa so fast it made her head spin. Stepped back. The rebuke in his face made her heart shrivel. "We have a presentation to do tomorrow. We are going in there as a team, Bailey, and we are winning. We are doing what we came here to do. *This*," he said, glaring at her, "is not happening."

Her lips trembled. "You don't want me."

"You're right," he said harshly. "I want the Bailey I know. The woman who let me look into her soul last night. Not *this*."

He turned on his heel and left, slamming the connecting door behind him. Bailey curled up in a ball on the sofa and cried. Cried for the girl she'd been. For what she wished she hadn't had to do.

At Jared for being so cruel.

At herself for ruining everything.

CHAPTER TEN

BAILEY WOKE WITH the birds. At some point, after Jared had left, she'd stumbled into bed and slept. Given herself over to a seemingly endless series of dreams whose characters and content overlapped without rhyme or reason, which sent her spiraling into the past, then hurtling forward into the present again in a dizzying journey that ended only with the arrival of the first light of day.

And perhaps the appearance of the loud, squeaky garbage truck that parked outside her window. She winced at the piercing, grinding sound, thinking maybe it wasn't as early as she'd thought, and levered herself into a sitting position. Somehow Paris seemed too elegant a city for garbage trucks...but apparently it too had its baggage it needed to get rid of.

She slid her legs over the side of the bed and padded to the window in time to see the very inelegant green garbage truck move on to the next storefront, hogging most of the narrow street with its robust, squat girth. Watching it made her think. Was Jared right? Was her determination to distance herself from her past destroying her instead of saving her?

She opened the French doors, walked out onto the balcony and braced her palms on the railing. She was proud, extremely proud of what she'd accomplished. Of whom she'd become. If she'd hadn't had the past she'd had, she wouldn't be the person she was now. And maybe that was the way she needed to look at herself: accept the parts she didn't like, the parts she was ashamed of, because they were part of the whole package like it or not.

The cold light of day was telling, exposing, and she shivered against the glare of it. Last night as the world had learned the truth of her, she'd felt as if she'd disintegrated into a million pieces. Funny how you could wake up the next morning and still be here. Could still hurt. Could still be angry.

Could discover that even though you thought the past had the power to destroy you, it really didn't. Not unless you let it.

The graffiti-emblazoned garbage truck turned the corner to meander down the next street, leaving only Jared's stark rejection of her in its wake. She'd spent her life being tougher than all the rest. Refusing to give in when the odds were stacked against her. Which explained why his words had hurt so much last night. She couldn't stand to be a quitter. She couldn't stand for *him* to think she was a quitter.

Couldn't stand for him not to love her.

Her heart squeezed hard in her chest. She hadn't even known she wanted to be loved. Hadn't known she craved it, needed it, like some missing piece of the puzzle that was her until now. It was frightening, *terrifying*, and it had made her drive him away last night—perhaps for good.

She pressed her fingers to the pounding pulse at her temples. Jared wanted a woman *she* didn't even know yet. It was a vulnerable, open version of herself he brought out. Not the old or the new Bailey, something else entirely. It occurred to her that maybe that's who she needed to be. A product of her past but in command of her future.

Increased activity on the street told her it was time to go inside and dress. The pitch was today. And the only thing she *was* certain about this morning was that she had to win this for Jared. Support him as he'd supported her this entire time.

She was dressed in a conservative gray pantsuit when she stopped, high heels in hand. No way was she doing this. Downplaying her femininity just because those men now thought she was entertainment for hire.

That would be letting them win.

She shrugged out of the suit and reached for the new chic mauve one she'd purchased on a whim on the Champs-Elysées. The material was gorgeous and the skirt showed a lot of leg.

Jared knocked on the door just as she'd finished dressing. His mouth curved as he looked her over. "That your battle gear?"

"Something like that."

He stepped closer and tucked a chunk of her hair behind her ear. "There isn't another person I'd want by my side today."

The dark glimmer of emotion in his eyes sent a flicker of hope through her. "Nor I."

She led the way out of the room. Today wasn't about emotion. Today was about getting the job done.

Jared spent the short ride from their hotel to the Maison offices finding his center. He'd spent the night sleepless and keyed up, not just because of what had happened with Bailey, but because this was it. One way or another his future would be determined today. He was done romancing the board, done proving himself when that's all he'd done over the past ten years to make money for his shareholders. They had to climb aboard his vision, understand where the future was, or he was out.

He stared out the window, watching the mad drivers dart in and out of traffic with an early-morning fervor that was just this side of frightening. Winning the Maison partnership would be an incredible achievement. He could transform the consumer electronics industry with it. But he could no longer sacrifice his soul for the company he'd built. Maybe it was the summons from his father that had done it, the knowledge that life was finite. But he knew the path and it wasn't this.

He didn't need a trek to the Himalayas to find peace. He needed to trust himself. And he wanted to be back in his labs creating with the engineers.

The car rolled to a halt in front of the skyscraper containing the Maison offices. The Gehrig team had already pitched when they walked into the metal-and-chrome boardroom, filled to the brim with the marketing, PR and sales teams. He read the atmosphere: alive but not buzzing. And knew they just had to set the room on fire and the deal was theirs.

If Alexander Gagnon played fairly. Gagnon was uncharacteristically subdued as he introduced them to the heads of the key departments. They socialized for a few minutes, then began. Adrenaline surged through him as he walked to the front of the room and opened with the history of Stone Industries, the "why us" argument and the successful alliances his company had forged around the world.

By the time he'd laid the groundwork, given an impassioned speech about vision, the room was noticeably energized. He handed the clicker over to Bailey, who looked calm and composed. Gobsmackingly stunning. "We've got this," he murmured. "Bring it home."

She nodded and walked to the front of the room. There wasn't a male eye that wasn't on her behind in the beautifully tailored suit as she stopped and turned around. He was pretty sure the hushed whispers had more to do with the gossip from last night than the subject at hand, and apparently Bailey had figured that out too, a shadow falling across her face. He watched her blink, then visibly check herself. Pull her shoulders back. And begin.

She launched into her slides with an easy, firm command of her ideas. Laid them down as if everyone in the room better be in the game or they were missing something special. Head thrown back, she roamed the room, keeping their interest, soliciting their response. And when the arrogant young marketer who'd passed her photo around last night started a side conversation with a coworker that clearly had nothing to do with the presentation and everything to do with Bailey's assets, she stopped by his chair and asked him if he had a question. Davide's mouth twitched, the marketer shut his and sank back into his chair, and Bailey moved on.

Jared leaned back and simply watched. He didn't sit poised to jump in and help her. Wasn't concerned a fact might be wrong. He knew Bailey now, knew he could trust her. What he was fascinated with, however, was *this* Bailey. He'd seen her confident before, seen her unsure in her own shoes and overcompensating. But he had never seen this version. *Commanding. Fierce. Combative.* And he knew in that moment he'd been wrong the day they'd driven in from the airport into Paris. Bailey was *more* than any man had a right to expect in a woman. She was courageous and vulnerable and stunningly brilliant, everything he'd been convinced didn't exist in a female.

She made him feel things he'd thought he'd never experience for another human being. Realize he was capable of it. And knew she'd been right; he was afraid. Afraid of making the same mistakes his father had made. Afraid of loving a woman who might leave.

Afraid of facing the truth of himself.

He shifted in the chair, his clarity unsettling. Bailey had never had love in her life, never had someone to protect her. Yet she was courageous enough to open herself up in the hopes she might someday have it. He was pretty sure he wanted to be that for her. To be the one to protect her. To believe in her.

He was scared he wanted all of her. Frightened it wasn't within his realm.

He raked a hand through his hair, his guts doing a fine job of rearranging themselves as Bailey sat down beside him, a rosy glow in her cheeks.

He gave her a sideways look. "Where did *that* come from?"

"Garbage trucks."

"Garbage trucks?"

Her mouth curved. "I'll tell you later."

Alexander opened the room to Q&A. There was a spirited debate about their direct-to-consumer ideas, their unorthodox retail strategy. But a seemingly general agreement the ideas were inspired. Alexander spoke last, directing a hard look at Jared. "All very impressive, Stone. We'd no doubt make a great partnership together. But when it comes down to it, it's the products that will win, not the marketing. And to me, you and Gehrig are neck and neck."

Fair point, Jared conceded. If you looked at the here and now. He stood up and walked to the front of the room to advance the slides.

"I'd like," he said, pausing for emphasis, "to introduce you to Project X."

The room buzzed as he unveiled his next generation product line: phones, tablets, computers, home alarms, thermostats all linked by a common platform—the connected home realized. No company, anywhere, had anything like it, and he felt the energy of the room skyrocket as the questions came fast and furious. *How quickly can you bring it to market? Would people really pay that much for a thermostat that controlled their house? Can it really do that?*

Alexander watched it all, a smile playing about his lips. As if he knew Jared had won. As if he wasn't sure he had a choice anymore.

He said nothing until it was just them and Davide in the room. "You didn't deign to enlighten us about Project X before now?"

"No," Jared said deliberately, "I didn't."

Alexander's eyes glittered. "I'll give you a decision within the week, then."

Jared nodded. Said his goodbyes to Davide. The older Frenchman looked heartsick as he kissed Bailey goodbye, and Jared had to smile. She had that effect on men. Now what was he going to do about it?

CHAPTER ELEVEN

For the first hour and a half of their flight back to San Francisco, Jared tore through the wrap-up from their presentation with quick efficiency. He fired a list of to-dos at Bailey, marked items for follow-up and outlined his vision for how he saw their marketing evolving. He wanted to expand her ideas to other partners, make them a cornerstone of their strategy, and although she loved the idea, she was too tired, too emotionally exhausted and too wary of him to really take any of it in.

Were they ever going to have that talk or was he just planning on forgetting they had ever happened?

Her stomach rolled. Had she turned him off that badly?

Jared repeated something in that relentless, authoritative tone that was getting on her nerves.

"What?"

He gave her a long look. "Need a break?"

She threw her notebook on the table in answer, stood and crossed to the tiny windows to stare out at the inky darkness. The snap of his laptop closing cut across the silence.

"Consider our business concluded for the evening, then."

Something, some edge to his voice made her turn around. He was watching her with that strange, contemplative look he'd been giving her all day since they'd walked out of the Maison building, their presentation behind them.

He pressed a button on the console and asked the attendant to serve the champagne.

She lifted a brow. "We haven't won yet."

"You need to be a more positive thinker."

Her chest tightened, lifting her shoulders. "Alexander could still follow through on his threats, Jared. Choose Gehrig."

"He won't. He wants Project X."

"And if he continues to play games for the sake of it?"

He lifted a shoulder. "Then I'll reinvent myself. Frankly, I'm very much in the mood."

He was in *some* kind of mood, that was for sure. Another side of him she couldn't read.

Betty, a young, attractive twenty-something brunette with an eye for Jared, bustled in with the champagne and poured it into two flutes.

"Get some rest," Jared told her. "We won't be needing you anymore."

The brunette put the champagne bottle in the ice bucket, flashed Bailey an "I am so jealous" look and disappeared.

Jared picked up the glasses and crossed over to hand one to her. Warmth seeped into her cheeks as his fingers brushed hers. "You know what she was thinking."

His blue eyes glittered with intent. "Then she'd be right wouldn't she? I don't intend to spend the next thirteen hours studying our stock price."

Her pulse sped into overdrive. "We haven't even talked yet."

"So let's talk." He lifted his glass and tipped it at her. "You were magnificent in that room today, Bailey. Absolutely brilliant. You have earned my trust, earned my respect. You can stand by my side any time and I would be lucky to have you there."

Oh. She rocked back on her heels. His gaze remained on her, purposeful, intent. "You had the room in the palm of your hand. Including me."

Her stomach contracted. "I don't know about that." She rested her glass against her chin, "The garbage trucks woke me up this morning. And there I was standing at the window watching them and I knew you were right. If I don't deal with *my* garbage, with my past, and accept that it's a part of me, I will never truly move forward." She looked up at the man who had never doubted her, not even once, when so many people in her life had. "I wanted to win this for you. That's all I knew."

He captured her free hand in his and tugged her forward. "I didn't walk away from you last night because I didn't want you, Bailey. I walked away because I wanted *that* woman, the woman who blew my mind in that boardroom today."

She pulled her bottom lip between her teeth. "I'm still figuring out who she is."

"I know," he said softly. "Every time I watch you struggle and triumph, it touches something inside of me. I can no more remain immune to you than I can stop the sun from rising in the morning. And that terrifies me."

Her heart slammed against her chest, loud and insistent.

"Last night," he admitted, tracing his thumb over her cheek, "the thought of Alexander getting anywhere near you made me crazy. I had to tell him he would never have you because *I* want you. I don't want anyone else to have you. But I've never been *that* man, Bailey, the man who sticks. I don't even know if I'm capable of it."

She pulled in a breath, but the air in the tiny plane suddenly seemed nonexistent. The joy exploding inside her that she hadn't ruined everything was almost overwhelming. "Maybe we both need to try…" she managed to get out. "Try to move beyond our pasts."

His mouth twisted. "We're quite a pair, no?" He hooked his fingers in the waistband of her skirt and pulled her flush against him.

Her lashes drifted down as heat ignited inside her. "We make a good one, though."

He nodded, his gaze resting on hers. "You said you'd settle for a man who respects you. A man who tells the truth. A man who wants you for who you are. I cannot, will not, make promises I'm not sure I can keep. But I can promise you those things, Bailey. And I'm willing to try with the rest."

Emotion clogged her throat, so big, so huge, she felt as if she might choke on it. She didn't need his promises. It had never been about that with them. It had been about trust. And for the first time in her life, she trusted a man explicitly, without reservation.

"Last night might not have been the last time you need to pick me up," she murmured, offering him an out. "I am definitely a work in progress."

He brought his mouth down to brush against hers. "Consider me on board."

He kissed her then, a long, lingering promise of a kiss that lit her from the inside out. Her arms crept around his neck. He ditched their glasses, swung her up in his arms and carried her into the bedroom at the back of the plane. It was tiny, dominated by a king-size bed and a chest of drawers, and when he set her down on the soft carpet and sat on the bed, her pulse rate skyrocketed.

"Last night," he murmured, leaning back on his palms, "I didn't want sex between us to be about anger. I didn't want you lowering yourself to that. But tonight," he amended huskily, his gaze on hers, "feel free to demonstrate."

She stared at him. "Jared—"

He shook his head. "I don't want that memory between

us. The thought of you doing this for me is a massive turn-on, Bailey. For no other reason than you are you and you do that to me. Not because you did it for hundreds of other men who couldn't have you and I can."

The heat in his gaze got her. The deep, powerful throb of the jet beneath her feet mirrored the one pulsing between them. Her head went there and then her body followed. She *wanted* to do this for him. She wanted to wipe away the memory of last night.

She bent her leg and tugged a shoe off. He held up his hands, eyes glittering. "No missiles, please."

She tossed the shoe on the floor. Reached for the second. Then she moved forward to stand in front of him. His electric-blue eyes darkened into deep metallic as she reached for the top button of her blouse.

"There are rules," she murmured. "No kissing and no touching."

His gaze narrowed. "I think I've changed my mind."

"No, you haven't." She took her time, working her way down the buttons. Watched him as she stripped off the shirt and dropped it to the floor. His gaze fell to her breasts encased in cream-colored lace, her nipples already hard and pressing insistently against the confining material. He swallowed hard.

"Still want to change your mind?"

"No," he rasped. "I'm good."

She straddled him. Waited for the detached feeling that always came with this. But his eyes wouldn't let her; they held hers firm and forced her to connect. With Jared there was only the truth. There only ever had been.

His heavy-lidded stare dropped to her erect, pink-tipped nipples. "I'm not sure why they call this a lap dance. Feels more like torture to me."

"Yes," she agreed, "it could be described that way. Except," she murmured, rotating her hips in a seductive circle against him, "if you're a very good boy you might get more."

He muttered something under his breath she thought she deciphered as, "I sure hope so," and closed his eyes.

He was hard beneath her, thick and long under his suit pants, and this time it was she who swallowed. She remembered how he had filled her. Remembered how her muscles had clenched around him and how powerful her release had been. *Lord.*

She kept up her sinuous rotations. His thighs tensed beneath her, his hands fisting at his sides. "This better be special treatment, Bailey. Because if you did this for another man, I might have to kill him. Kill them all."

She leaned down and gave him a kiss. "Easy, tiger. It is."

He slid his hands over her hips. She removed them. "No hands."

"But you just kissed me…"

"That's because I'm in charge."

Ruddy color dusted his cheekbones. "Go ahead, convince yourself of that."

"No hands," she repeated, swaying closer. "Lips, however, are allowed."

He dipped his head and took her engorged nipple in his mouth. The hot warmth of his lips around her sent a bolt of heat to her core. She arched her back on a low moan and gave herself to him, wholly, sinfully, rocking against him.

He transferred his attention to the other hard peak and took her higher. She felt herself unraveling under his touch, losing the control she'd once so desperately craved. But this was Jared, and she was mad about him.

"Goddammit, Bailey." He lifted his head, eyes glittering. "I'm waving the white flag, whatever you need."

She stood up and slid her skirt off. Her panties. His gaze tracked her every movement, hot, hungry. She came back to him, moved her fingers to the button of his trousers and slid it out of the material. Then she eased his zipper down.

"Please," he was begging now. "Hands are good. I do good things with them."

She freed him from his boxers. Lowered herself to brush against the hard, hot length of him. "No hands."

She was slick and fully aroused, but he was a lot to handle. It took all her concentration to take him inside her, ease herself down on the potent length of him. She hadn't taken half of him when a low groan escaped her lips. "Jared—"

"Oh yes you can," he rasped, reading the look. "But you need to let me use my hands."

She nodded. Closed her eyes as his palms took the weight of her hips and held her over him, sliding farther inside her. He held her there while her body adjusted to him, his superior strength sending a surge of lust through her.

"More," she groaned.

He gave it to her, slowly, inch by inch, whispering in her ear how much he wanted her, how good she felt. His sexy voice excited her, inflamed her, softening her body until she took him all. It was all she could do to breathe with him buried inside her, but his hands supported her hips, controlling the rhythm, easing her into it.

The feeling of intense fullness morphed into a slow, hot burn every time he took her. The angle, the spot he was reaching deep inside her, promised extreme pleasure. Higher and higher he led her until it wasn't enough anymore—until she wanted to scream. She buried her hands in his hair and pleaded in a husky tone she didn't recognize as her own.

He slid his hand between them and pressed his thumb against the throbbing center of her. She looked down, watched him, the erotic sight of the rough passes of his thumb over her throbbing center summoning a wild, shattering release within seconds, her love for him escaping her lips as the white-hot intensity tore her apart.

He heard her, she knew, from the way he froze beneath her. Then the tight convulsions of her body around him pushed him over the edge, an animalistic groan tearing itself from his throat. And then there was no room for thought. Only pleasure.

The fact that he didn't repeat her words as he settled her against his chest and put his lips to her hair, his breathing hard and uneven, didn't completely throw her. This was Jared, after all, who'd just taken a huge step in telling her how he felt. She was going to focus on that and nothing else. Not on the very real possibility he would never get there.

She woke by the light of the moon, by herself in the bed. A glance at the clock told her it was almost eleven, another couple of hours before they would land. She sat up, looking for water, figuring Jared had left her to work. As her eyes adjusted to the darkness, she saw him sitting in a chair by the windows, dressed only in jeans. He looked lost, distant, in his own world.

"Couldn't sleep?"

He lifted his head. Blinked. "No." He didn't invite her over but she went anyway, setting her hand on his shoulder. His stiffness beneath her fingers made her hand still. The utter remoteness on his face made her consider retreating, until he reached up and pulled her down on his lap. Her heart squeezed at the near rejection. He was such a complex, multifaceted man. She was sure she only knew pieces of him.

She stayed there, curled against his chest, until the restlessness emanating from him made her draw back. She traced the hard line of his jaw, the unyielding curve of his mouth, the jagged white scar that bisected his upper lip. "How did you get this?"

He frowned, as if he had to pull the memory from the deep recesses of his mind. "The son of one of our friends my father embezzled the money from went to Stanford with me. After my father was sent to jail, he confronted me in one of the campus bars. He was angry, said some things about my father I couldn't let pass, and we got into a fight." His mouth twisted. "I thought it was a fistfight, but when Taylor started to lose, he added a beer bottle to the mix."

She shivered as she looked at the vicious-looking inch-long scar. "He could have done much worse."

His shoulder lifted. "He was hurting. His family was ruined. I got it."

She ran her fingers across the heavy dark stubble on his cheek. "You were too. Couldn't he see that you weren't to blame for your father's actions?"

"When you're angry and sad, you lash out."

Yes, but it hadn't been his burden to carry. Her heart squeezed. How hard must it have been for a college-aged boy to have to defend his hero.

He pulled her tight against his chest, his hand smoothing her hair. "My father wants to see me. That call you heard yesterday morning was my PI saying he'd done his usual check on him, that he didn't look great and he wants to see me."

The call that had come right before he'd gone ice-cold on her...it made sense now.

"Do you know why?"

"No."

"Are you going to go?"

"I don't know. When he got out of jail, he told me he needed time to get his head together, to figure out what he wanted to do. My mom had already remarried, and many of his friends wanted nothing to do with him. I was it really for him, but he didn't even want to see me. He disappeared, showed up in the islands. I told myself distancing myself from him was the best thing for me. I was hurting so badly, *I* needed space. But we never really reconnected after that, except over legalities. Every time I tried, he pushed me away."

"I'm sure he felt a lot of shame."

His fingers traced the curve of her ear. "I think I was afraid to face what had become of him. He was such a strong, proud man. Afterward…it was like seeing a ghost of him."

Her heart contracted in another long pull. She took his hand in hers and laced her fingers through his. "That could never happen to you. You are self-possessed in a way I have rarely seen, Jared. You know who you are."

His fingers tensed beneath hers as if he might pull them away, then he let out a breath and curled them tightly around hers. "I should have gone to see him. I should have insisted on it instead of just having him watched over. He's my father, for God's sake. He's not well and I've let him become a virtual hermit."

She shook her head. "You were hardly more than a boy when he left. You were sad and angry because he was supposed to take care of you."

"It doesn't excuse my behavior."

"It's never too late to make it right."

There was a long pause. Her fingers tightened around his. "Go, Jared. Talk to him. You won't forgive yourself if you don't."

He was silent then. She curled into his chest and tried to absorb his tension. But this part of Jared, this haunted part, was one only he could deliver himself from. Forgive himself for. She felt it rise up between them like a physical presence as the minutes wore on, creating a distance she couldn't bridge.

She got the message. Dressed and went back into the cabin and asked Betty for a cup of tea. Then sat watching the night as it sped by. Did people ever truly slay their demons? Or was it just easier to accept them as a part of you? She had always done that, but Jared had convinced her to try harder. Now if he could only do that for himself.

CHAPTER TWELVE

THEY NEEDED GLAMMING up.

Bailey came to that decisive conclusion about her slides for the executive committee meeting about the same time she remembered that the steaming Americano her colleague had brought her as reinforcement was sitting untouched on her desk. Tugging the top off the coffee, she brought the steaming brew to her lips. Maybe she needed some graphs. Clip art? Or maybe a joke...those meetings always needed livening up, didn't they?

And where had her concentration gone? She'd been doing so well all morning, ignoring the fact that Jared returned from the Caribbean today. Ignoring the fact that she was dying to see him to the point she really had to wonder about herself. She wanted to know how things had gone with his father. She wanted to know if he'd heard from Alexander. *And shouldn't he be in by now?*

A smile curved her lips. She hadn't needed to convince herself things could be different since she'd returned from France a week ago. They *were* different. She was the CMO of this vibrant, innovative company, she had a gazillion ideas in her head she couldn't wait to execute and yes, there was that little detail that she was in love with her boss.

A zing of anticipation ratcheted through her, sparking a warm glow in her cheeks. She'd spent two nights at Jared's place before he'd left. Two perfect nights in his stunning Pacific Heights mansion cooking together, getting to know each other and finishing off whatever work they'd had. And yes, countless hours in Jared's bed learning each other in different ways. It had been so good, so intimate, she'd laughingly threatened to bake the next time she'd come over. Except the next time hadn't come until the night before Jared had left to visit his father, and he'd been so keyed up about it, it had been a certified disaster.

In the days leading up to the trip, she'd watched him grow increasingly agitated. About everything, she suspected: the board meeting, the deal, the trip. She'd offered to cook for him that night thinking maybe she could distract him. Tempt him with a passionate night in bed. But he hadn't been there, not really. He'd toyed with his dinner, a distant look on his face, and cut the night short after they'd finished, pleading an early flight.

She'd tried not to remember his sarcastic line in Nice about kicking a woman out after they'd cooked for him, but that's exactly what had happened. And she, who wasn't at all sure what being in a relationship entailed, hadn't really known how to analyze it.

Was he pulling back? Did she just need to give him space because of his father? Was she supposed to be unnerved he hadn't returned any of her texts while he was away except to say that, yes, he'd landed fine?

Her heart thumped nervously in her chest. She supposed she was about to find out when he did come in. Which was a good thing because she needed to ground herself. Being with Jared had made it clear her job wasn't enough anymore. That being with someone as she was with him was something she'd been missing her entire adulthood. She *did* want the house and the white picket fence, as long as he was in it. As long as they were equals. And although she knew she needed to take it step-by-step with him, although the idea terrified her as much as it did him, she wanted to know she could have it. That this was real.

The slides stared back at her—clearly lacking. She needed to have them done for Jared so he could review them before they presented at tomorrow's board meeting. With a sigh, she put her coffee down and went searching for clip art.

Tate Davidson waltzed by her desk, leaving a trail of his sleazy cologne. "Big guy's in fine form."

Her gaze whipped to him. "Jared's back?"

"Sure is." He lifted a brow. "Surely he's checked in with his *CMO*?"

She lowered her head and ignored the dig. Tate was insanely jealous she'd been promoted over his head. And more importantly, her brain whirred, Jared was back. How long had he been in? Why hadn't he come to see her?

Her phone rang. She barked a greeting into it. It was Nancy from HR, wanting to schedule a meeting. "Sorry, what is this for?"

"Your sixty-day check-in."

She frowned. "What sixty-day check-in?"

"The one that's in your contract," Nancy said patiently. "Jared wanted to review things at the sixty-day mark."

He did? Wasn't it usually ninety days? Having signed the contract and not read it thoroughly before they'd left for France, she wouldn't know. She whipped it out of her drawer and scanned it. There it was on page eight in the fine detail. *Employee Trial Period: Employee's performance in the role to be reviewed at the sixty-day mark.*

"Isn't it usually ninety days?" she asked Nancy.

"Often, yes, but this is a high-profile role. Jared wanted to make sure he wasn't making any mistakes."

Mistakes? Her blood flashed hot in her veins as she kept reading, scanning through the legalese. *This position can*

*be terminated for any reason determined by the employer,
not limited by underperformance.*

"And *this* termination clause…*can be terminated for
any reason?* Is this normal?"

There was a pause. "That's a little more…stringent than
usual. But again, a high-profile position."

Bailey stared at the words. That clause said Jared could
demote her for any reason after two months regardless of
her performance on the job. Any clause she'd ever had in
a contract had been based on performance.

She pulled in a breath. "You know what, Nancy? I'm
going to schedule this check-in myself. Consider it done."

"Yes, but Bailey we don't do it that wa—"

Slam. She whacked the earpiece on the base. Shot to her
feet. The hallways flashed by in a stream of silver as she
made her way to the elevator and up to the executive floor.
Mary, Jared's PA, gave her a bemused look as she stormed
past her, knocked once on his door and flung it open.

Jared was bent over a pile of papers, a frown on his
face. He looked up in surprise, flicked his gaze over her
and rose to close the door.

"What's wrong?"

"First of all," she bit out, "it's nice that Tate Davidson
knows you're back. It would also have been nice to get
an answer to one of my texts. I know you're a very busy,
important man but I would have enjoyed that courtesy."

His face softened, and now she could see the lines of
fatigue crisscrossing it. "I'm sorry. I was on my way down
after lunch."

"Two." She waved the contract at him. "Did you instruct HR to put that clause in my contract? The one that
allows you to demote me *for any reason*, regardless of my
performance?"

His frown deepened. "Yes. But that was before I knew
what you were capable of."

She crinkled up her face. "You stood here and agreed to my terms. You asked me to come to France, to *save* your reputation and win that contract, when you weren't intending on *honoring* our deal?"

He walked toward her, his hands raised as if she were a child who needed to be calmed. "You were an unknown quantity, Bailey. I could hardly make you CMO without an opt-out. Be reasonable."

"An opt-out?" Her voice lifted a notch. "That clause is way beyond an opt-out. It's an ironclad opportunity to get rid of me whenever you so choose. Even Nancy said it was unusually...what did she say? Oh, *stringent*, that was the word."

"Bailey," he said quietly, holding her gaze, "that clause has nothing to do with the here and now. You have proven yourself to me. The job is yours. If you like, I'll have another contract drawn up."

"What I'd *like* is to know that you believed in me from the beginning. That you are a man of your word and you were going to honor our agreement."

He blanched. "Trust is earned."

"And I gave it to you *every step of the way*." She flung the words at him as she brought herself within inches of his tall, imposing figure. "I opened myself up completely to you, Jared. I let you break me down. And all I required in return was the honesty you promised me."

He shook his head, eyes flashing. "Everything I said to you, promised you over the past couple of weeks, is true, Bailey. Do not let *this*, do not let your insecurities, ruin a good thing."

"*A good thing*." She barked the words out, hands on her hips. "How long should I expect this *good thing* to last, Jared? A couple months? Three? Four? You were already backing off the other night as per usual. Then you go completely incommunicado."

He shook his head. "I've been up to my ears, stressed about my father…"

"So you shut me out?" She pressed her lips together, the insecurity, the hurt she'd felt over the past few days, sitting like the devil on her shoulder. "I'm no expert but I'm pretty sure this is where we're supposed to lean on each other. Be there for each other."

His mouth tightened. "I've been trying. You push too much, Bailey."

The stubborn tilt of his chin, the forbidding line of his mouth, did her in. "I know you heard me say I love you on the plane, Jared. You ignored it completely."

He shook his head, his face losing color. "I told you I don't make promises I can't keep. It isn't in my DNA. You knew that."

He could have said anything, *anything* but that and she might have been okay with it. But a cop-out like that? It made her chest feel so tight she couldn't breathe. Because it wasn't enough anymore. Not when she'd handed him her heart.

She nodded sagely. "Now there's the honesty I need. Because I've decided I can't do this, Jared. You asked me to open up, to trust you. Well here I am. And if you can't do the same, I think we should end it now."

His gaze flashed. "You're using this as an excuse to end things before it's started."

She shook her head. "This is me not wanting to be another casualty of the cult of Jared. I guess it's not in *my* DNA to expect anything less than everything."

"Bailey—" He reached for her, but she shook him off, stalked to the door and left. Enough of this emotional roller coaster.

Jared was debating whether to go after Bailey when Mary stuck her head in his office. "Alexander Gagnon is on the line."

He cursed. If there was a person he did not want to talk to at this moment in time, it was Alexander. However, as the fate of his company lay in the man's hands, he had no choice but to.

He shut the door, walked to his desk, sat down and took a deep breath. Then he hit the blinking line.

"Gagnon."

"Bonjour, Stone." Alexander's smooth, silky voice slid over the phone line. "Good news for you. We have decided we would like to offer Stone Industries the partnership."

The rush of satisfaction that ran through him at Gagnon's words was swift and sharp. But the burn that stung his eyes, the tremor in his hands as he pressed them against his desk, came from a deeper place. A place he'd been loath to acknowledge. He would have walked, he'd been prepared to walk, but *this* was his company. To restore what he'd built with his heart and soul to its former brilliance— he wanted it with every fiber of his being.

"Thank you," he rasped. "I'm very happy to hear that."

"This is dependent, of course," Gagnon said, "on Project X being exclusive to our stores."

"Certain product lines, yes, but not all."

"We can come to some kind of an agreement on that, *oui.* We will need to work very closely together in the beginning. The planning will be key. I want Bailey in Paris for quarterly meetings. How is your beautiful CMO, by the way?"

Jared sat up straight. "Bailey is not part of this deal, Gagnon."

"So vehement," the Frenchman chided. "I merely want her brain. What are you going to do, Stone? Marry her? That would certainly keep the dinner conversation interesting."

His blood bubbled dangerously close to the surface. He

thought he might, actually. Want to marry her. Watching her walk out of his life could do that.

He stared viciously at the phone. "Send the contract over, Gagnon. And forget about Bailey in Paris. You'll have Tate Davidson, my VP."

He ended the call before he said something to trash the deal. Sat back and tried to digest. He was overwhelmingly relieved to be walking into that board meeting tomorrow with Maison in his pocket. Michael Craig's massive abuse of his expenses as CEO had been splashed across the news this morning in a carefully executed plan to discredit him and oust him from the Stone Industries board, thanks to a friendship Jared had with a high-placed reporter at a daily newspaper. Everything was falling into place. But it was Bailey who occupied his head. He'd had to put that clause in her contract. He was running a multibillion-dollar company. He didn't put someone whose ability he'd questioned into a C-suite position without a backup plan.

His chin jutted out, his resolve fierce. Except she was right. He'd promised her the job. The clause should have been about performance. Instead he'd been intent on manipulating the situation to his advantage. That was the real truth. He'd been running as fast as his legs could carry him the last few days.

Bailey was right.

His time in the Caribbean had been mind-altering. Just as terrifying as he'd anticipated. His father was a shadow of his former self; old, suffering from debilitating diabetes and wanting his son to know the truth after reading his manifesto. It had not just been his marriage that had brought him to his knees, his father had told him, but his lack of faith in himself. His inability to follow his dreams. But Jared, he'd counseled, a wisdom in his eyes that seemed out of place in such a weak, frail man, had done just that. He had followed his heart, and that's all a man could do.

You cannot, his father had warned him, *take on my legacy, or you will destroy yourself.*

Achingly honest, frighteningly intense, his conversations with his father had nearly undone him. Had left him shaken and angrier than ever at himself. He should have done more. He should have done something sooner. *He* should have been braver.

The burn in his eyes brought a hot glitter to his vision. He was not his father. He knew that. And Bailey wasn't his mother. He had spent the flight home thinking about the two of them, how very different they were. His mother was brittle, power-hungry, content to live life on the coattails of each successive powerful man she conquered, whereas Bailey was strong in a beautiful, courageous way. Independence personified. You could see how much she cared in her eyes just now. Funnily enough, what he'd thought would never work for him was now the only thing he knew would. To have a woman that strong. His equal.

I know you heard me say I love you on the plane, Jared. Why hadn't he had the courage to tell her? He loved her. Of course he did. He'd been half on his way that night in Nice when he'd learned the truth of her. Fully so after the night she'd given herself to him. And all he'd done since was deny it.

He leaned back and stared at the ceiling. He'd broken Bailey's trust with that clause. The one thing sure to drive her away. And even though he'd had his reasons, they seemed blindingly inappropriate right about now. Not when she was everything he'd never known he wanted.

An idea that might be the product of his jet-lagged brain or pure brilliance, he wasn't sure which, entered his head. He wasn't letting her go. Not a chance.

CHAPTER THIRTEEN

When Bailey had left Las Vegas for California, a freshly minted business degree in her pocket and a lifetime of wisdom garnered from her very real job and her less-than-ideal family background, she'd thought she had it all figured out. Rely on yourself, don't expect too much and keep your eye on the ball, and you'd get where you were going. That mentality, she decided, driving to work the day after that scene with Jared, would have served her well if she'd actually *employed* it with her boss as well as the job. If she hadn't let herself fall in love with a man with a heart of stone. But somewhere along the way, she'd allowed herself to believe, to want far more than her destiny had ever been when it came to him. And suffered the glaring truth of her life-learned rule: wanting more than what you were destined to have was a recipe for heartbreak.

She peeled herself out of her car and walked into her favorite coffee shop in San Jose. Their argument hadn't really been about the clause. It had been about her loving him and being afraid he would never return it.

The lineup of slouchily dressed students, computer nerds and suits was three deep on either side. She chose the typically faster one and tapped her foot impatiently on the faux hardwood floor. Maybe Jared was right, maybe she was running. Maybe it was just easier that way when you wanted what you couldn't have.

The line finally cleared. Christian, the jean-clad, scruffy-looking barista who served her every morning, gave her a curious look as she slid a bill toward him. "Didn't expect to see you here this morning."

"Because this morning is any different from the last five years?" Her attempted humor came out bitter and unattractive. "Sorry," she winced. "Bad morning."

He pushed his funky glasses farther up his nose. "Have you read the paper this morning?"

She shook her head. That was part of her Americano ritual *after* she'd triaged her email. "Why?"

He yelled her order to the barista mixing the drinks. "It's been the talk of the place this morning. You should get on that."

She lifted a brow. "Anything in particular I should be looking for?"

"You'll know it when you see it." He pushed her money back at her. "Drink's on the house, by the way. You look like you need it."

He took the next customer's order. Bailey shook her head, picked up her Americano and drove to work, her re-created resignation burning a hole in her pocket.

Aria called as she was walking through the front doors of the office.

"I gotta admit, even with all his imperfections, *that* would do it for me."

Bailey frowned, using her elbows to negotiate the doors. "What *are* you talking about?"

"Have you read the paper this morning?"

"Why does everyone keep asking me that? What earth-shattering thing has happened? Did Jared make an announcement about Maison?"

"Oh my," Aria sighed. "You really haven't read it. He has certainly made a statement, but it wasn't about Maison."

"Great," Bailey muttered. Another illuminating Jaredism to set the internet ablaze.

"Did you say you have your first executive committee meeting this morning?" Aria asked.

Bailey cradled the phone against her ear and jabbed the call button for the elevator. "I do. If I don't resign first."

"I suggest you read page five of the *Chronicle* before you do that. Then call me. I will kill you if you don't call me."

"Aria." She stepped onto the elevator. "What's going on?"

The iron box swallowed up her call. She hit the button for the twenty-sixth floor, and thought about what Christian had said. *Didn't expect you to be in today…* What did that mean?

She exited the elevator, went straight to the PR department where she collected the *Chronicle* and took it back to her desk. Coffee in hand, she flipped to page five. An open letter from Jared took up the entire page. It was headlined, The Truth about Women—A Rebuttal.

Oh. My. God. He had not. Eyes glued to the page, she started reading.

A few weeks ago, I wrote a manifesto titled "The Truth about Women." Intended as an honest if tongue-in-cheek summary of my views of women both in the boardroom and bedroom, it has provoked a great deal of debate, resonating with some of you and provoking anger in others.

At the time I wrote it I honestly believed everything I said. Experience had taught me that many women do not want the career life we as a society have insisted they do. That cries of a glass ceiling were perpetuated by females caught up in their own self-deception. And if the truth be known, I was not

*overly sold on a woman's place in the boardroom,
nor her ability to stand toe-to-toe with a man.*

*Then I had the chance to work with a woman I
have admired for years, my chief marketing officer,
Bailey St. John. In keeping with my theme of nothing but the truth here, I have to admit I severely un-
derestimated her talent. I did not give credit where
credit was due. She is not only a superior thinker to
any other marketer I have ever had the opportunity
to work with, male or female, she could likely wipe
the floor with most of them.*

*This extraordinary woman also taught me some-
thing else. Something far more important than the
value of a woman in the boardroom. She has proven
me wrong about a woman's place in my life. Hers.
She has taught me that I can connect with another
person on a deeper level, that I do want someone in
my life in a forever sense, not just for the sake of the
nuclear family, but because I love her. For who she
is. For her courage. For what she's taught me. She
has made me a better man.*

*So here is my offer, Bailey, with all my imperfec-
tions as previously noted:*

*I offer you the homestead, and all the baking sup-
plies in it, minus the white picket fence because Pacific Heights does not consider this fashionable.*

I offer you a ring and a lifetime commitment.

*I offer you a lion in the bedroom because that
part is still true and I know you like it. Love it, actually.*

*And most importantly, if I am lucky enough to
have you I am offering you complete honesty—after
a mistake I swear I will never make again. Even
when it's hard. Even when it hurts because that works
for us.*

If you're interested in all I have to offer, you know where to find me.
All my love,
Jared

Her eyes blurred as she read the last sentence. Hot tears spilled down her cheeks in a wet line that dripped into her Americano. She reread the whole thing. Stared at it hard. Vaguely registered the arrival of Tate Davidson and the fact that her executive meeting started in five minutes.

She blew her nose. Fixed her lipstick. Clutched her notebook and letter of resignation to her chest and followed Tate upstairs to the boardroom. It was packed with a full contingent of board members as well as executives at the vice president level and above, presided over by the chairman of the board, Sam Walters.

And Jared. Seated at the head of the table beside Sam, his gaze, which might be described as distinctly hostile, was trained on her. As was every set of eyes in the room, for that matter, and honestly, she could do without that.

Sam waved her and Tate into two chairs at the front. Bailey sat down, glad for the seat given her knocking knees. Tate opened the meeting, and began going through the financials. Jared took off his jacket and loosened his tie. Started drumming his fingers on the table. Tate announced the Maison deal to much applause, the buzz in the room palpable. He waited while the other directors congratulated Jared, then turned to the CEO for a word.

"I'm sorry," Jared said, waving a hand at Tate, his gaze still pinned on Bailey, "but did you read the paper this morning?"

Her lips curved, his disheveled appearance, the agitated air about him, solidifying what she already knew. Jared Stone was irresistible. "Five minutes ago," she said evenly. "I was late this morning."

The scowl on his face grew. "You have anything you'd like to share?"

"Yes," she said softly, because you could hear a pin drop in the room, it was that quiet. "But I'd prefer to do it in private."

He sat back, blue eyes stormy. Julie Walcott, his VP of PR, raised her hand. "Can I make a request? Can we make this the last manifesto? It's such a work of art we should allow it to become infamous."

"Considering this one just about killed me," Jared growled, "that would be a definitive yes."

Sam took control of the meeting after that. Somewhere near the end, she found herself the bewildered owner of a whole new set of responsibilities Jared bestowed on her in a bid to go back to doing what he did best. He relinquished the "first look" privileges he had over Stone Industries' marketing and handed them to her. From now on everyone on the PR, advertising and marketing teams would report to her. He did not, Jared stressed, want to spend his time approving ad campaigns.

She stared shocked at him while Tate Davidson nearly lost his breakfast. It was a controversial call, no doubt, but given the stormy nature of her boss at the moment, no one was saying a word.

Lunchtime arrived. She stood up with everyone else, snatching her resignation off the table. Jared appeared at her elbow. "My office," he growled and propelled her down the hall into his minimalistic haven. Bailey stood, paper clutched in her hands, as he shut the door and leaned against it, his stance turning predatory.

"What *is* that in your hands?"

"My resignation."

His gaze narrowed. "You aren't resigning. I feel a sense of déjà vu here."

She drank him in, the same fierce warrior in evidence

as the one in her bedroom that night in Nice when he'd promised to back her no matter what.

"Did you mean everything you said in that rebuttal?"

He nodded. "Every word. Including the part where I declared my love for you in a national newspaper."

Her heart melted, so full of emotion she didn't know where to start. "Promises aren't in your DNA."

"I didn't think love was in my DNA either," he countered roughly, snagging her sleeve and tugging her closer. "And now look at me."

She was. He was everything she'd never dreamed she could have. And so much more.

"Seeing my father threw me. I needed time to process. To understand my feelings. But never for one minute did I change my mind about you. About what I said on the plane." He ran his thumb across her cheek. "I will always tell you the truth, even when you don't want to hear it."

"I know," she whispered. "I just needed to hear you say it. Write it. Whatever. Actually can you say it?"

He lowered his head to hers. "I love you. I've loved you from that night in Nice."

He kissed her then, slow and deep. She was ready to sink into it completely, into *him* completely, when he set her away from him with a determined movement.

"Hey," she protested. "That wasn't—"

The words died in her throat as he pulled a jeweler's box from his inside pocket. "You weren't supposed to be late this morning. I was going to give you this."

Her heart jumped into her mouth as he flipped the box open. Nestled inside the blue jeweler's box sat a diamond eternity band that sparkled in the light. "You can have another if you like," he said huskily, "you can have ten. But this is my promise to be your constant, Bailey St. John. Marry me."

She shoved her hand at him. He slipped the ring on.

The diamonds, hugging her finger in an unending circle of fire, made her heart take flight.

He brought her hand to his lips. "Is that a yes?"

"Yes."

"Good. After this meeting, I'm taking you home to celebrate."

"After?" she pouted.

"I just gave you direct responsibility for all marketing activity. You'd better take the helm while you can."

"True," she murmured. "I do love you, Jared Stone. I'm not afraid to say it."

His gaze darkened. "You can tell me that again tonight. Over and over."

She did. Many times as he proved his nickname All-Night Jared Stone was aptly earned. The ring sparkling on her finger made that just fine with her. He was hers; he would always be hers, she knew that. And in his arms, Bailey finally found herself. Not the old Bailey, not the new Bailey, just the Bailey she was destined to be.

* * * * *

0517/05